# tattletale

# tattletale

## Sarah J Naughton

*For my husband, Vince.*

First published in Great Britain in 2017
by Orion Books,
an imprint of The Orion Publishing Group Ltd
Carmelite House, 50 Victoria Embankment,
London EC4Y 0DZ

An Hachette UK company

1 3 5 7 9 10 8 6 4 2

A CIP catalogue record for this book
is available from the British Library.

ISBN (Hardback) 978 1 4091 7022 8
ISBN (Export Trade Paperback) 978 1 4091 6694 8

Typeset by Born Group

Printed in Great Britain by Clays Ltd, St Ives plc

MIX
Paper from
responsible sources
FSC
www.fsc.org    FSC® C104740

www.orionbooks.co.uk

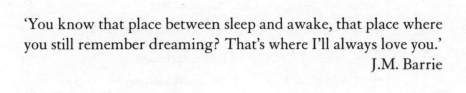

'You know that place between sleep and awake, that place where you still remember dreaming? That's where I'll always love you.'

J.M. Barrie

Before

# Before

On a clear morning the sun shines so strongly through the stained glass it looks as if the concrete floor is awash with blood.

But it's past eight in the evening now and the only light comes from the wall lamps on each floor. Their dim illumination reveals a slowly spreading pool of pitch or tar.

Blood doesn't look like blood in the dark.

Now the adrenaline that powered her scramble down the stairs has drained away, she feels as if all her bones have been pulled out. She can barely stand, has to grasp the metal newel post for support as she stares and stares.

The fourth-floor landing light goes out.

It takes a long time for the brain to process a sudden accident – the nought-to-sixty acceleration from normality to calamity – to ratchet itself up to an appropriate response. She can feel it slowly building in her belly as she takes in the black spatters on the doors and walls of the ground-floor flats, the widening creep of the black pool.

At first she thought he would be OK. A few bruises. A bumped head. There is too much blood for that.

The third-floor landing light goes out.

In the few frozen moments after it happened she was dimly aware of a latch snicking shut, heavy footsteps rattling down the stairs, the creak and slam of the front door, but now everything is silent. The church is holding its breath, waiting to see what she will do.

She takes a wobbling step towards him.

There's a smell, like her purse when it's full of coppers.

He looks so uncomfortable. Why doesn't he move his leg so that his hips aren't so twisted? Why doesn't he turn his head as her shadow falls across him? Why doesn't he call out to her?

She kneels beside him and takes his hand. It's pure white against the blackness that is slowly seeping into his hair and clothes. She tries to say his name but there's a fist around her throat. Her thoughts sputter. There's something she should do. Yes. She should call 999.

The second-floor landing light goes out.

His lips are moving and his eyes are open. As she leans close to him to try and make out what he is saying her hair falls into the pool. Jerking back, the tips of her hair flick against her wrist, drawing scarlet lines on her white skin. Now she can see where the blood is coming from. A small noise escapes her lips. Horror and shock are hurtling towards her like an articulated lorry.

The first-floor landing light goes out.

She must do something for him. Now, here, in this moment, she is all he has. She must take her phone from her pocket, unlock it, and tap in the numbers. But she cannot let go of his hand; she cannot leave him adrift in all this darkness.

Her heart is racing, like the wheeling legs of a cartoon character just before it realises it's run off the cliff edge. Before it falls.

The ground-floor light goes out.

It is the sudden darkness, as much as anything else, that makes her scream. And once she's started she cannot stop.

# After

The lino's slippery with spilled drinks. As he crosses the dance floor a fat girl blunders into his path and he grabs her by the flesh of her waist, making her squirm and shriek. Someone slaps him on the back and he grins, though he didn't hear what was said. The music is so loud the floor vibrates and the disco lights have turned carefully made-up faces lurid colours. All the girls are off their tits, some of the weedier blokes too. Gary and Kieran are draped over one another, bellowing 'Auld Lang Syne', though it's still two hours until midnight. But it takes more than a few double vodkas to affect him. He glances at himself in the dark window that looks over the pitch.

Not bad considering he'll be thirty this year.

In the reflection he sees a woman he doesn't recognise walking across the room behind him. Catching his eye, she pauses and smiles.

He smirks. Still got it.

The toilets stink, as usual.

He pisses for England, then shakes himself off and does up his flies, checking his reflection in the square of buckled stainless steel that passes for a mirror. The shirt is a size too small and pulls tight across his pecs. He washes his hands and runs damp fingers through his hair. He's noticed it thinning at the temples over the past few months and has been considering trying a spray from the chemist.

The new winger comes in and stands at the urinal. He's considerably shorter and weedier than Rob.

'Having a good time, mate?' Rob says.

'Brilliant,' the lad says.

'Just you wait,' Rob says. 'The ladies'll be so pissed you'll be fighting them off with a stick.' He puts ironic emphasis on *ladies*.

The boy laughs.

'See you later.' Rob thumps him so hard on the back he almost overbalances into the urinal. He's laughing as he emerges to a line of grumbling females.

'Sorry I kept you waiting!' he cries, spreading his arms.

'In your dreams,' says Elaine, Marcus's ugly wife. 'The toilet's blocked. Clive's in there trying to fix it.'

'Use the men's, then.'

'The state you lot leave it in? No thanks.'

'Well, don't be surprised if I'm booked up for the rest of the evening by the time you come out.'

'We'll take that risk.'

He bows and pushes open the door to the bar.

The air's heavy with aftershave and cigarette smoke. It's illegal to smoke in here but the lads pay no attention, though Clive keeps threatening to hand the CCTV footage to the police if they don't stop. Through the haze he can make out Sophie muttering to her little coven. Probably about him. He stares at them until she glances up, then gives her a cheery wave. She looks guilty. Bitch can get her own drink.

There's a girl at the bar but he's not in the mood to wait so he raises his twenty and Derek waddles straight up, a craven grin on his puffy face. Either he's scared of Rob or he fancies him. Rob pretends to find the latter idea funny when the boys rib him about it, but if Derek ever so much as touches him, apart from to hand him his change, he'll knock him out.

'What can I get you, mate?'

'Vodka, lime and soda. And you'd better not sweat in it, you fat bastard.'

Derek laughs.

Rob feels the gaze of the girl he queue-barged and his head snaps around, ready for a row. His scowl vanishes. It's the girl from the reflection. She's seriously hot.

'You scored the hat trick, didn't you?' she says, and her voice is smooth like chocolate.

'Guilty,' he says, putting up his hand and lowering his head modestly. Then he wonders if he's used the wrong word. The pre-party friendly had been too much like hard work on last night's hangover and the bloke he'd tackled to get the last try was still in A & E. But when he looks up she's smiling.

'Haven't seen you here before,' he says. 'You with the other team?'

She nods. 'My sister's dating one of the props.'

Good. She wasn't attached. Not that it mattered – *he* was and it wouldn't make any difference.

'You know what, I'm so pissed I can't remember his name!' she giggles.

'They all look the same anyway. Mr Potato Head!'

She laughs uproariously.

He glances over at Sophie, but now she's too busy making a twat of herself on the dance floor to notice.

Thankfully this year Clive and the rest of the old duffers aren't in charge of the music, so there's a lot less Abba and Bee Gees and a lot more hip-hop. Not that he minds a bit of 'Dancing Queen'. Him and the lads like to dress up for that one, demanding an item of clothing from all the women there. This year he'd make Sophie give him her revolting support girdle, embarrass the bitch. With a bit of luck she'll piss off home.

But when he looks back the girl is gone. He swears under his breath, knocks back his vodka, then goes for a dance.

It's coming up to midnight and Derek's so overwhelmed that the lads are just going behind the bar and helping themselves, occasionally pausing to flip the bird at the CCTV camera trained on the till. Boys will be boys.

5

Rob's dancing, his shirt soaked in sweat, his thinning hair plastered to his forehead. Occasionally he'll go up behind a girl and grind his groin into her. Some of them press back and he gets a semi. Most of them aren't attractive enough for the full nine yards. Soph's the best looking of the lot of them, and she's blubbing in the corner, surrounded by clucking mates. *He's such a b-bastard, boo hoo.* Well, she's not going to ruin his night. He grabs the nearest girl to him and gives her a proper snog, thrusting his tongue into her mouth. Her saliva is bitter with alcohol and cigarettes. She pushes him away with a playful slap and he wipes his mouth on his sleeve, swaying slightly in the glare of the lights. His eardrums throb in time to the music. His heart is racing. His muscles hum with tension.

Slim fingers caress his side as someone slips past behind him and he turns to see it's the girl from the bar.

She's even better looking than Sophie. She's – he fumbles for the word – *elegant*. None of the other girls here are elegant. They've all got identical long blonde hair, skirts up to their arses, fake tan, glitter across their tits. This one looks classy. He doesn't try to grind his pelvis into her.

'Hi,' he says. 'How are you doing?'

'Good,' she says. 'It's been fun.'

'You're not going?'

'I'm not sure I'm going to get what I came here for.'

He frowns. 'What's that?'

She speaks so softly he has to lip-read over the music. He blinks rapidly, his lips part. He might have misunderstood. He leans over.

'What did you say?'

As she tilts her head to murmur into his ear her hair brushes his cheek, sleek and cool as satin. He didn't misunderstand.

He doesn't know what to say. He's not used to girls coming on so strong and isn't sure he likes it.

She pulls away. Her eyes hold his. His insides turn to liquid.

'M-me,' he stammers. 'I will. I can.' He sounds like a twat. He rolls his shoulders and runs his tongue across his front teeth. 'You won't be disappointed.' He still sounds like a twat. He regrets the last round of sambucas. 'There's a storage cupboard around by the toilets.' It stinks of bleach but Sophie didn't seem to mind.

'How about something more . . . al fresco?'

This one does, then.

He nods vigorously and glances over at Sophie. She's stopped crying and is doing shots.

'I'll see you outside.'

As she walks away he glances around to see if someone's setting him up and considers for a brief moment whether Sophie's arranged one of those honey-trap things. What does it matter? They're probably finished after tonight anyway.

He crosses the dance floor and passes out into the foyer. The air is cold and clean and he stands in the darkness as the inner door swings shut and the music and screeching laughter becomes muted. The evil red eye of the ancient CCTV camera watches him from the corner.

Is he too pissed to get it up? He's never failed yet, but he's never had a woman like this before.

Only one way to find out. Pushing open the main doors he strides outside into the night.

He spots her by her white top, gleaming in the shadows of the stands.

The pitch is churned and muddy so he walks around the spectator part, breathing slowly and deeply to calm himself down. Stupid, but he feels like he's on the way to an exam. She's something special, this one, and he doesn't even know her name. That makes it more special. That's how he'll phrase it when he tells his mates later. *The mysterious beauty.*

The effect is spoiled when he reaches her and sees that she's covered in mud. It's caked all over her boots, her knees and even in her hair.

'Jeez,' he says. 'What happened to you?'

'Fell over.' She giggles.

It annoys him. She's spoiled the effect. 'You should have walked around the edge.'

'Who cares?' she says. Then she pulls off her top. She must be pissed, because she lets it drop into the muddy puddles on the concrete, then yanks down the vest so roughly the strap snaps.

She isn't wearing a bra. Her breasts are smooth and tanned, glimmering in the lights from the clubhouse. The music is just a throbbing beat now, like a heart. She leans against the bench behind, arching her back.

She's one of those who likes it rough. He puts his hand over her mouth to shut her up and she bites his fingers. She tears a couple of shirt buttons off trying to get to his pecs, kisses him so hard his lips are crushed against his teeth. She even takes a chunk out of his hair, which is not on, considering, and he punishes her for it, thrusting into her so hard she cries out in pain. Normally he's more careful – some girls tear when he does that – but she deserves it. She obviously thinks she's a bit special. The thought of her hobbling about tomorrow, bruised and torn and unable to sit down because of him, gives him a head rush of arousal. He won't last much longer.

The countdown to midnight drifts across the pitch as he's coming, and by the time the fire-cracks of the party poppers have subsided he's done up his trousers and is making his way back to the clubhouse.

The whole thing was over so quickly Soph won't know he's been away. Not that he'll be able to explain the lost buttons or the scratch marks. There's even one down the side of his face. Still, at least he'll have a laugh about it with the boys before World War Three breaks out.

At the clubhouse door he turns back. She's sitting up now, and just for a moment she raises her hand, in greeting or farewell. He doesn't wave back.

As he yanks open the door he's laughing to himself. To think he'd thought she was a notch above the others. Elegant. *Ha*. Not so elegant staggering home covered in mud with her tits hanging out of her top.

Then she starts screaming.

*The sound of the TV is a lullaby, making her drowsy, despite the cold. One of the springs is poking through the musty-smelling mattress and she has to curl up at the very edge so that it doesn't scratch her. They've hung a blanket up at the window to stop the morning sun waking her too early and an orange bar of light from the street lamp outside falls through the gaps, cutting her in half.*

*Her stomach gives a squealing twist and she draws her knees to her chest to ease it. She wishes she had eaten more at school. The after-school club gives you biscuits and she managed to get two before the others grabbed the rest, but she's still hungry.*

*If she can go to sleep she'll forget about being hungry. She will forget about what Stuart Talley will say about her in front of everyone at break time tomorrow. She'll forget about the way the teachers whisper about her during assembly and how everyone knows she steals school uniform from the lost property box. Sometimes she wishes she could stay asleep forever.*

*There are slow footsteps on the stairs and she squeezes her eyes shut and goes very still.*

*The footsteps come into the room and a weight lands on the bed, making the wire mesh under the mattress twang.*

*'I know you're awake.'*

*She opens her eyes.*

*'Want a bedtime story?'*

*For a moment she just stares at him. Then she whispers, 'Yes, please.'*

*She had a bedtime story once before, when one of Nanny's boyfriends came up to her room and started telling her about a brother and sister whose parents left them in the forest. They were trying to find their way home when they came upon a house made of gingerbread and sweeties owned by a kindly old lady. She wanted to hear all about what each part of the house tasted like – especially the windows – but*

Nanny's boyfriend fell asleep, so she had to make the rest of the story up. The people that left them in the forest, she decided, weren't the children's real parents at all. The old lady was actually their grandma and had built the sweetie house all ready to welcome them, while their real mummy and daddy searched the world for them, their hearts breaking with sadness. When they got back they were so happy to see their children they thought their hearts would burst.

'Once upon a time there was a little bunny rabbit,' says the man sitting on her bed. 'She lived with her family in a burrow on a hill.'

The little girl sits up. She likes the sound of this story. There is a bunny on the pyjama top that her nan gave her.

'The mummy and daddy bunny worked very hard all the time, but the little bunny never thought about anyone but herself. She wasn't very clever and she was always disobeying her parents.'

Her eyes widen. Is something bad going to happen to the bunny?

'Whenever they were busy working she would run out of the burrow, laughing, and wander about the countryside, talking to whoever she met, telling horrible stories about her parents that weren't true, to get attention.'

The little girl frowns. This is a bad bunny.

'One day she met a man having a picnic in a field, and because she was greedy and wanted some of his food, she told a lie that she was starving because her parents didn't give her enough to eat.'

The girl pulls the blanket up to her chin and bites her bottom lip.

'The farmer gave her a little bit of bread and while she was chewing he asked her where she lived so that he could bring her round a nice big chocolate cake for her tea. She told him and thought she was very clever for tricking him.'

The man's face is in shadow but the bar of orange light falls across his hand. His skin is rough and purple, and a tattoo of a dragon's claw pokes out from his sleeve.

'But really,' he carries on, more softly, 'she had been very stupid because that night the farmer came with his gun and his dogs, and he shot the little bunny rabbit's mummy and daddy and all her brothers and sisters to make into a pie for his supper.'

11

The little girl starts to cry.

'As the mummy bunny died she said she wished the nasty lying bunny had never been born.'

A car goes past outside the window, its headlights sweeping across the room, casting long curled shadows from the peeling strips of wall-paper. On the other side of the room is another bed, with a motionless shape curled up under its own thin blanket. The headlights pass and the room returns to darkness.

'Do you know what happened to the little bunny who had told the tale?'

The little girl shakes her head. She doesn't want to hear but if she puts her hands over her ears she will be punished.

'The farmer cut all her skin off, while she was still alive, and then dropped her in a pan of boiling water and chopped her into bits to feed to his dogs.'

Her gasp sounds like the page of a book tearing.

The man leans in so close to her that she can smell the sweetness of cider on his breath and the cigarette smoke in his hair.

'If I hear that you've been blabbing your fucking mouth off to anyone at school again about what we do in the privacy of our own home, then that's what'll happen to you, you little bitch. Do you understand me?'

She nods.

He gets up and walks out of the room and down the stairs. The TV gets louder for a moment as the door downstairs opens, and then goes quiet as it shuts behind him.

The little girl lies perfectly still as a blood-warm wetness spreads out underneath her.

# Tuesday 8 November

# 1. Jody

Do you remember the first night we slept together? No, not *that* bit. That's easy. The part afterwards, when the sky had darkened to that greyish orange that is as dark as it ever gets in the city, and we'd gone inside, into the warmth of your flat. Everything was quiet except for the odd distant siren, hurried footsteps down Gordon Terrace as people tried to get home without being mugged, the wind rustling the rubbish blowing around the playground.

I didn't sleep much. How could I? I watched you sleep, watched your eyes moving beneath the lids. Were you dreaming about me? I never asked. Didn't want to seem too keen.

I watched your nostrils flare gently on every inward breath, your chest rise and fall, disturbing the hair that ran in a fine line to your belly button.

Your body was so boyish, the muscles as soft as mine. I liked the way our bodies mirrored each other. You dark and slim, with wide brown eyes and long, black lashes, me fair and skinny, with the lightest of eyes and lashes that are almost invisible. You were a masculine me, and I was a feminine you. Sometimes we would press our palms together and marvel at how similar they were in size and shape.

At least your hands are still the same, resting on the starched white sheet.

You're not in pain. The doctors promised me. In an induced coma you don't even dream. Beneath the lids your eyes are perfectly still. Your lashes rest on your cheek, almost the same colour as the dark flesh. They said the bruises would fade, that the swelling would go down, that your face would become yours again. I can't help thinking (hoping): what if it isn't really you under there? That they made a mistake; that you're sleeping peacefully in another ward somewhere, wondering why I'm not there.

No. It *is* you. I saw you fall.

I twist your ring about my own finger. Press my fingertip onto the engraving so that its mirror image is etched into my flesh.

*True love.*

I know that they're just clichéd words, like the hokey stuff they write in greetings cards, but whoever thought of them could never have known how right they were.

There has never been a truer love. And whatever happens, Abe, whatever you're like when you wake up, my love for you will stay true forever.

I take your hand and whisper the promise into your fingertips.

# 2. Mags

Everyone else is asleep. Wound in their white sheets like mummies, wedged into the tiny open caskets advertised as *fully flat beds*.

God knows what time it is.

I should have changed my watch before the first glass of champagne. It was *personally selected* by some wine guru who must be famous in Britain. They handed it to me when I boarded, presumably by way of apology for the ten hours of cramped, muzzy-headed tedium I was about to endure.

My phone will tell me when we arrive; until then I'm in a timeless limbo.

The remains of the *Cromer crab cake and lime foam* sit, dissected but untouched, on the pull-out table in front of me. Considering how many hosties per pampered fat cat there are in first class, you'd think they'd have figured out that I'm not going to eat it. Even the wine tastes shit, coating my tongue with sourness. I can feel my breath going bad, and though I showered in the club lounge, I feel sticky and smelly.

I tip the vanity bag onto the table, looking for breath freshener. Toothpaste, toothbrush, moisturiser, eye mask, something called 'soothing pillow mist', earplugs and a crappy pair of velour slippers. No breath spray.

I think about putting the eye mask on and *misting* the pillow, but I'm not sure there's any point. My brain is far too wired to sleep and every time I close my eyes the same film runs through my head. I'm falling through darkness, the wind blowing my hair, the circle of light above me getting smaller by the moment.

May as well keep drinking.

The next time a hostie comes past I ask her for a large whisky.

I make another attempt to get into the novel I bought at the airport, a pulp thriller about some woman who thinks her husband has killed their son, but it turns out it was her and she's just forgotten all about it, because he's been spiking her food to protect her. I'm three quarters of the way through and I still don't give a toss about any of them. But it's probably just my state of mind.

The hostie returns and puts the drink down on a little doily.

'This is wine,' I say.

She smiles so hard the foundation at the corners of her mouth crackles. 'Yes, ma'am.'

'I asked for whisky.'

'Whisky?'

'Same first letter, but a sneaky extra syllable.'

Her eyelashes tremble, unsure whether I'm joking. I smile so she knows I'm not. Her gaze becomes glassy. *Another bitch.*

'I'll get your whisky right away.'

'You know what?' I hate it but still can't stop that American uplift at the end of my sentences. 'I'll just go to the bar.'

'As you wish.'

She stands back to let me struggle out of my seat-bed and the smell of perfume is overpowering. Beneath it is something medicinal. Hand soap, perhaps, or those lemon wipes in the economy cutlery pack. It makes her seem entirely synthetic – but what do I expect on a Vegas flight?

I can feel her eyes on my back as I make my way up the aisle to the bar. Stepping through first class into business, the plane gives a little hiccup and I stumble, turning my ankle.

'Careful, now,' she calls after me, and I resist the urge to give her the finger. They can divert a plane these days for that sort of thing.

Jackson paid for the ticket. I said it was kind of him. He said, *No such thing, just another bribe to keep you at the firm*. I resisted the urge to reassure him that I wasn't going anywhere. If you don't keep your boss on his toes, you don't get first-class flights and six-figure bonuses. Not that they do me much good. Now that the apartment's paid for, I find myself throwing money away on expensive crap like the Louboutins I now slip off to massage my ankle.

There's only one other drinker at the self-service bar, a man around my age, whose face has that flaky redness that always gets you on long haul if you don't keep hydrated. Normally I'd have been downing Evian since the wheels left the tarmac, but tonight I don't give a shit. It's not as if Abe's going to notice. I pour myself a large whisky and toss in some ice from the bucket. I think about taking it back to my seat – if I stay there's a definite risk the guy will try to talk to me – but it feels good to stretch my legs, so I lean on the bar stool and flick through the in-flight magazine. There's an article about an actress, the retouched pictures make her appear two-dimensional, and her upper lip is so stretched by collagen it looks simian.

'Going home?'

I sigh inwardly.

'Actually, I live in Vegas. Just going back to . . . see my brother.' I kick myself at the hesitation. It wouldn't have happened in court. I need to get myself together, work out the smooth lie that will stop people trying to talk to me or, worse, sympathise. There hasn't been time yet. I only heard this morning. It's taken me all day to sort out the flights and hotels and hand my cases over to Jackson. Though I've spoken to them all in person and promised I'll be back within a fortnight, my clients aren't happy. No one else in the firm has my track record for helping guilty people get away with it. Jackson is taking over IRS vs Graziano. If the case goes badly, Antonio will spend the rest of his days in a federal correctional institution, trading his ass for cigarettes. Ass. I sound like a true yank. British people say *arse*. Nice arse. It sounds oddly polite with an English accent.

19

'London?' the man across the bar says.

Beneath the ravages of the flight he's good-looking. Square jaw, broad shoulders, blond hair cropped tight to minimise a receding hairline. A man's man. Banker, I think. Or another lawyer. Probably the former if he's travelling in first.

'Yes.'

'Me too. Looking forward to seeing him?'

That hesitation again. The whisky is fugging my reactions. I nod, then spin on the stool until I'm at a forty-five degree angle from him.

'That's not an English accent, is it?'

I spin back, with a polite smile that, if he's smart enough, he'll translate as *get lost*.

'Scottish.'

He isn't smart enough. 'Not strong, though, so I'm guessing you were gone by . . . hm . . . eighteen?'

I raise an eyebrow and, despite myself, say, 'Not bad. Sixteen.'

'Straight to Vegas from Bonnie Scotland? That takes balls.'

'They took a while to drop. I went to London first.'

'College?'

'Yes.'

'You know, you should carry one of those twenty questions gadgets around with you. It could do the talking. Save you the hassle.'

'Yes,' I say. Then a moment later, 'So, what am I?'

I kick myself again. I've let myself be drawn in. I must be drunk.

'Hmm . . .' He pretends to think. 'Are you . . . a hedgehog?'

I laugh loudly enough to draw a disapproving grunt from the fat guy wedged into the casket nearest the bar. 'Yeah. Spiky. Flea-infested.'

'Not a hedgehog. You're travelling in first. Are you an oligarch's wife?'

He waits for me to bite. I shake my head calmly. 'That's nine questions. Twelve left.'

'Jesus, you're counting?'

'Don't take the Lord's name in vain.' I drain my glass and pour myself another.

It takes him a while but eventually he gets there.

'So, how do you get to be a first-class-travelling American lawyer when you left home at sixteen?'

'A levels at night school. Law degree at King's, my juris doctor at Columbia, then straight to Nevada because it looked like fun. Cheers.'

He clinks my glass and we drink. 'You make it sound so easy.'

It wasn't. One term I had five different jobs.

'So, what kind of law?'

'Corporate.'

'Seriously? I had you down for something more exciting.' He gives me an appreciative up and down look, but I don't think he means to be sleazy. I think he's just drunk. Actually, I'm beginning to like him. Maybe I won't rush off just yet.

'I work for gangsters.'

'Defence or prosecution?'

'Defence. I would have got Al Capone off.'

He has a nice smile. My drowsiness is wearing off. I add a Coke to my whisky. A bit of flirtation will be a good distraction from the horror film in my head.

We talk some more. The Coke kicks in and I revive. He asks me how I would have got Capone off and I tell him some of the tricks of the trade: undermining the accused, exploiting technical loopholes, coaching your witnesses. The film is still playing but I'm not watching.

Until he says, 'So, tell me about your family.'

I almost close up on the spot, but perhaps the topic can be deflected.

'What do you want to know?'

'The truth, I guess.'

'I'm a lawyer. I don't do truth.'

'Well, I'm a banker, so I should know there's no such thing as truth. Only what you can make people believe. If I can make

21

you believe shares in that whisky are about to go up five hundred per cent, you go and buy them – and the shares go up. Belief becomes truth.' He waggles his eyebrows devilishly. 'OK, I'll start. My kids live in Islington.'

'You don't have to tell me.'

'I want to. I want you to know. They live there, I live in Vegas.'

'So, you're a bad father. I don't give a shit.'

'Ah, but you should if we're going to date.' He sips his drink, peering over the glass at me archly.

I laugh again. 'I don't date guys with kids.'

'Why not?'

'Too complicated.'

He drinks before he answers, and when he puts his glass down the flippancy has gone. 'Life's complicated. If you think it's simple, you're not really living.'

'Goodnight.' I get up.

'Wait.' He puts his hand on my arm as I pass him. 'I'm sorry. My head always goes when I'm about to see them. I just keep thinking about how bad it'll be when I have to say goodbye.'

I sit down on the stool next to him. He's put on weight since he bought that shirt. It strains across his stomach. I imagine what his skin would feel like beneath the cotton. Warm and slightly tacky, downy blond hair running from his navel to his groin. 'What are their names?'

'Josh and Alfie. And I'm Daniel.'

'I'm Mags.' I shake his hand. 'And my brother's in a coma.'

22

# 3. Jody

They've contacted your next of kin. Your sister, Mary. I wonder why it's not your parents. We never spoke about them. We never spoke about mine either. Didn't want anything to cast a shadow over our happiness. I try to imagine what she will look like. Dark, like you. Slim. Black eyelashes even longer than yours. She'll speak softly like you do. She'll hold my hand and look into my eyes and she'll just *know*. That I'm The One for you, that you're The One for me. That whatever happens I'll stay by your side. I'll be with you while you learn to walk and talk again. Through the tears and the despair, and then the first stirrings of hope. I don't care if you're very changed, or even if you've forgotten me. I'll learn to love the you you become.

My heart clenches when you make a little gurgling noise. As if you've read my mind.

I lean in to kiss your earlobe and my tears fall into the clump of hair they didn't shave off for the operation. They nestle there, like the pearls on the dress I was wearing the day we first met. Do you remember? Is that part of your mind still whole? Maybe you've forgotten. We can remember it together.

I moved in at the end of the summer. The café job they lined up for me had gone badly. The manager was a bully. I used to spend my lunchtimes crying in the toilet, and then I just stopped going in. I lay in the bedsit for hours, unable to eat or sleep.

23

Then Tabby told me about St Jerome's. She sorted it all out for me, came and picked me up on a Sunday afternoon.

She wouldn't tell me much, just that the place was a deconsecrated church, owned by a Christian charity that let out the flats at piecemeal rent to vulnerable people – asylum seekers, people with mental health issues or family problems, former care home kids like me.

As the car pulled up in the little patch of tarmac by the grass I saw you. You must have been on your way out to the high road. You'd paused to watch the kids playing in the playground. It wasn't love at first sight, but it was close.

We were on the same floor. At the time it seemed like a happy coincidence; now I know it was fate. You smiled when we passed on the stairwell.

When you go into a church you don't realise how high it is. All that dusty air, just drifting in the huge empty space above the pews. They fitted four floors in there; we were at the top, looking out across the shops and takeaways to the green parks beyond. Each flat was unique: a mishmash of funny angles and sloping roofs, a gargoyle on the balcony, a column rising through the living room like a huge tree trunk. Some floors cut a stained-glass window in half, so you might have the angel Gabriel's face and the flat downstairs would have his open hands.

I've always had an imagination, and a night in a deconsecrated church should have left me paralysed with terror, especially as it was so quiet compared with the bedsit, where there was always shouting or doors banging. But as midnight came around I could hear music. A smooth woman's voice singing the blues. It was coming from your flat. It lulled me to sleep.

Tabby was good, coming in every day to make sure I was settling in, that my prescriptions were all up to date, that I'd filled in all the benefits forms, that I had enough food.

In the day I pottered around the flat, laying out all my special things, drawing, occasionally popping out to the high road where

24

there were three charity shops, one with just books. I bought a whole set of romance novels and read one every evening. Your music was my lullaby at night.

Then one day you spoke to me.

It was a Monday afternoon. It had been raining heavily and my new book (*The Firefighter's Secret Heartbreak*) had turned pulpy in the carrier bag on the way home. I was wearing a dress from the charity shop, grey silk with little pearl beads around the neckline, and the hem was sopping wet where it hung down below my raincoat. It slapped against my legs as I ran towards St Jerome's. You were going in ahead of me and you stopped and held the security door.

'So much for our Indian Summer,' you said, with a smile that made one of your cheeks dimple.

I told you that my book had been ruined and you showed me how the blue dye of the carrier bag had stained your loaf of bread. You told me your name and I told you mine. Abe and Jody. Jody and Abe.

As we walked up the stairs together I said that I had just moved into Flat Twelve and you said it was nice to have a new neighbour, as the flat had been empty since the last occupant died. That frightened me, and you must have noticed because you laughed and said, 'Oh, don't worry, he didn't die *in* the flat! He was staggering around in the road, drunk, and got hit by a car.'

'Poor man.'

'He was seventy-eight. Not a bad run for a raging alcoholic. Hope I make it that far.'

'You will,' I said, then blushed furiously, because I meant that you looked so young and fit and full of life, with your bright brown eyes and quick smile.

'Lovely dress,' you said as I unbuttoned my coat. 'It looks like the rain.'

And then you said goodbye and went into your flat. I stood outside mine for ages afterwards, thinking *what a beautiful thing to say*.

# Wednesday 9 November

# 4. Mags

I wake at four and can't get back to sleep so I get up and turn on my laptop, sitting in the faux leather club chair by the window that looks out over Hyde Park. Even at this time the traffic on Park Lane is nose to tail, though the double-glazing ensures the room is blanketed in an unnatural hush. The night sky reflects the glow of the city's lights, making it seem neither night nor day.

In Vegas the sun will have gone down over the desert. All the heat and dust will be vanishing straight up into the clear night sky. I'll be opening my first bottle of beer, licking the dribbles of icy perspiration off my fingers.

There are a couple of emails from angry clients. I knock off the usual pat reassurances, ending with a line about my brother to make them feel guilty. As if they're capable of an emotion other than greed.

Then I login to my social media: an invitation to a gallery opening, angry posts about the latest gun rampage, my timeline clogged with endless *Happy Birthday Stu!*s for an ex-boyfriend's thirtieth. I don't know why we're still 'friends': we slept with each other for three months max, and then I finished it. He cried.

I sigh and switch off.

The police are coming here at ten. Six hours to kill. I can't even turn on the news in case it wakes Daniel, who, like me, didn't sleep a wink for the whole ten-hour flight. As I sit, staring down at the brake lights of the cars, I begin to feel irrationally annoyed that he is still here, spreadeagled on my bed, my sheets in a tight twist beneath him.

In the end I run myself a bath.

Catching sight of myself in the steamed mirror, I wonder why he was even interested. My hair's lank and dull, my lips are pinched, my tanned skin has become sallow. The loss of appetite has sucked the flesh from my stomach and my hipbones protrude, making me look rickety and frail, ninety instead of thirty.

The noise of the gushing water must have woken him because a moment after I get in, he enters without knocking.

'Hey. How's your head?'

'Do you mind?' I say.

He blinks at me. 'I've, er, seen it all before. Last night. If you remember.'

'I'm washing,' I say coldly.

'Sorry.' He backs out of the door and closes it softly.

When I come out he is dressed. We gather our things in silence.

'Why are you being like this?' he says finally.

'Like what?'

'I thought we had a good time last night.'

'We did. And now it's not last night any more and I've got to speak to the police about my dying brother.'

'Of course, I'm sorry.'

I stand stiffly as he tries to embrace me.

'This is a bad time for you,' he says, stepping away. 'We probably shouldn't have – but I'm still glad we did.'

'Me too,' I say, more gently. I've been a bitch. Mostly down to dread of what I'm going to have to face today, and the start of a raging hangover.

'Take my number and let me know how it goes with Abe.'

'Sure.' I pocket the scrap of cardboard he gives me. It's the corner of a condom packet he ordered from reception along with the bottle of Jack Daniels. 'Good luck with Jake and . . .'

'Josh and Alfie.'

30

'Yeah. Hope your wife's not too much of a cow.'

He looks at me and raises his eyebrows, and I laugh despite myself. 'Yeah, well, *I've* got a good reason to be.'

He comes over and kisses me. 'You were lovely. *It* was lovely. I'd like to do it again sometime.'

His breath is sour with booze and his skin still looks patchy from the flight.

'When you've sorted things out with your brother.'

'You mean when I've turned him off?'

He has the balls not to look away. Raising his hand to my face he passes his thumb across my cheek as if to brush away a tear that isn't there.

He seems like a decent enough person, for a banker. Although that isn't hard. For a corporate lawyer I'm an angel. Then he slings his jacket over his shoulder and picks up his case.

'Goodbye, Mags.' He turns at the door. 'Is it short for Margaret?'

I shake my head, hesitate, then say, 'Mary Magdalene.'

He looks at me quizzically, waiting for me to explain. When I don't, he opens the door.

'What did your wife leave you for?' I say suddenly.

He turns and smiles. 'Alfie's fencing coach.'


We sit in the breakfast room of the hotel, looking out over a rubbish-strewn side street. The squad car is tucked discreetly behind a four-by-four. There are two of them, a solidly built middle-aged blonde woman, and a thin, lantern-jawed youth, young enough to be her son. Apparently it was her who called me to tell me what had happened. I was at home catching up with work emails before I headed to the office. It felt strange, sitting on my sun-drenched balcony in a playsuit and shades, with a mouth full of blueberry pancake, listening to her talk about *induced comas* and *cranial haemorrhages*.

Now she tells me more, speaking in a soft London accent as the boy takes notes. At first she gives me the logistics, timings, the distance fallen, the hours on the operating table, then slowly

31

spirals back to the night itself, as if it's the only way I will be able to bear it.

'Your brother's fiancée, Jody Currie, was the only witness to the accident.'

'So, you're sure it was an accident?'

At what I considered to be a throwaway comment, I'm surprised to see the boy raise his head and fix his gaze on his boss.

She pauses before answering. 'We've got no reason to suspect otherwise.'

I wait.

She sips her coffee. It's a standoff.

'But?' I say finally.

'There's no evidence to suspect foul play: no CCTV footage and no other witnesses.'

'So, why the question mark?'

I wait for her to fob me off – *What question mark?* – but to her credit she doesn't. 'Relationships are private things. Jody and your brother had both lost contact with their parents and were living quite isolated existences. We have to believe her that the relationship was a happy one.'

'As opposed to a murderous, push-you-down-a-stairwell sort of one?'

She shrugs. *Whatever.*

'So, you won't be investigating further?'

'Like I said, there's no evidence of foul play, so there's no reason not to take her word for what happened.'

'Which was?'

'On the night in question, Miss Currie had booked a meal out. She felt that your brother seemed down and wanted to cheer him up.'

'*That* must be on CCTV, right?'

'It's not police policy to waste resources going through general CCTV footage when we don't think a crime has been committed. Can I go on?'

I give a curt nod.

32

'They returned to St Jerome's, the church where both of them live, at about eight p.m.'

'Isn't that a bit early?'

'Miss Currie thought your brother was tired as he had been quiet all evening and had suggested they leave early. Both her and your brother's flats are on the fourth floor and she told us that they had almost reached this floor when your brother stated that he wanted to go down to check the door was securely closed. There's criminal gang activity in the area and he was concerned that if it wasn't closed properly, someone might get in. Miss Currie went into your brother's flat and, after hearing a noise, came out to find him lying at the bottom of the stairwell. It's her belief that he jumped, due to depression brought about by work pressures.'

She folds her hands in her lap, her face tactfully averted as she waits for me to process the images that have been flowing through my mind.

'Her belief? So there was no note?'

'No.'

'Couldn't these criminal gangs you mentioned have got in and attacked him?'

'If that was the case then either Miss Currie or their neighbours on the top floor would have heard something, and, aside from the injuries sustained in the fall, there were no other wounds. Also, he had no valuables on his person as Miss Currie had taken his jacket inside.'

'Why?' I said.

'Why what?'

'Why did she take his jacket?'

The policewoman smiles. 'You're a lawyer, right?'

'Yes.'

'I can see you must be good at your job. Since they were coming into a warm environment from a cold one he might have taken it off and handed it to her for convenience as he went down to check the door.'

'But he wasn't going to check the door, was he? He was going to jump. So why bother taking off the jacket in the first place?'

'In a police investigation,' she says after a pause, 'there are some questions that are vital to help us judge whether or not a crime has been committed, and some that aren't. I suggest you speak to Miss Currie yourself so that she can give you a clearer picture of what happened that night.'

They get up, leaving two unfinished cups of bland hotel coffee on the glass table.

'If you have any concerns please do get in touch.' As she hands me her card my fingertips brush hers. They feel unpleasantly soft: the nails are bitten halfway down to the cuticle and flesh bulges over the top of the remaining sliver of nail. I glance at the card. Her name is Amanda Derbyshire. A PC. Lowest of the low.

'Thanks,' I say coldly, shaking her hand and the clammy paw of her underling.

'I know you deal with criminals a lot yourself, Miss Mackenzie,' she says, turning to leave, 'but not every tragedy is a crime. Will you be seeing your brother today?'

'Yes. I'm going straightaway.'

'I hope the doctors can give you some good news.'

I give her a dry smile – we both know these are empty words – and she turns away.

Sitting by the window sipping my coffee, I watch them get back into their squad car. They are too stupid to realise that the twists and turns of the hotel lobby have led them out directly beside the window they were, until a moment ago, looking straight out of.

The woman says something and the boy gives an open-mouthed guffaw, displaying rows of silver fillings. In his hand he has one of the Danish pastries from the buffet bar and as he climbs in, eating it, I hear her warn him not to get crumbs in her car.

To clear my head I'd swum for an hour in the hotel pool before our meeting and, thanks to that and my burgeoning hangover, I am finally hungry. I'm glad, as I load up my plate with hash

34

browns, that the policewoman isn't here to see this inappropriate show of gluttony. I should be too grief-stricken to eat, but instead I pour ketchup over my breakfast, head for a table near a TV and scroll through the channels for CNN.

I haven't been in a British hospital for twenty-two years. In Vegas someone would be escorting me through the labyrinth of corridors to the ICU, telling me about my brother's condition as we go, preparing me for what to expect, but here I must find my own way and will have to wait until the doctor does his rounds to hear my brother's prognosis.

He fell twelve metres. It can't be good.

I try to imagine what he must have looked like before the accident. He was always slight. Slim-boned, with narrow shoulders. A child's body even after puberty. I wonder what he does for a living. Did. I wonder how he found me. The picture on the company website would be utterly unrecognisable to anyone who knew me as a child.

I was shocked to get the Christmas card. Sent to the office, to *Mary*, so it took ages to arrive at my desk. *From Abe*, and an address in London. I sent one back – embarrassingly late. *From Mags*. A line of communication, as fine and tight as a wire. I don't know if I thought we would become closer as we got older, that we would forgive one another for the things they made us do. I suppose I did. But now it's too late. There's nothing to miss.

The hospital walls are crowded with bad art. Tasteless collages and insipid watercolours, metal twisted into the shapes of fish and birds. I pass a door marked Room for Reflection and through the half-open blinds make out empty plastic chairs facing a table with a wooden cross.

A bed clatters by. On it an old lady is curled like a chrysalis. Beneath her translucent paper skin dark veins pulse, as if there's something beautiful and new ready to squirm out. She is yellow with liver failure. Perhaps our mother looks like this now. Perhaps she is already dead.

I pass through the door marked ICU. It opens on a small reception area where a nurse frowns at a computer screen. Behind her is a set of double doors, that must lead to the beds. A wave of guilt washes through me. I could easily have afforded to put Abe on my medical insurance policy. Then he would have had his own room.

'I'm Mary Mackenzie. My brother Abraham is here.'

The fat nurse doesn't reply, just holds up her hand: *wait*.

Bristling, I step away from the desk and stare blindly at the huge painting of a peony on the wall. Surely all those blood reds and flesh pinks are inappropriate here. The whole place stinks of piss and disinfectant, that British-hospital smell that screams of underpaid cleaners, harassed nurses, and patients left to stew in their own filth. And then, abruptly, absurdly, tears spring to my eyes. The peony blurs, becoming an open wound.

As unobtrusively as possible I blink them away and breathe deeply. I'm not crying for Abe. I'm crying for myself. Stuck here in this shitty hospital, in this shitty country, away from my friends, my job, the warmth of a Vegas autumn. I will have to wait for him to die. Damn it, I almost feel like ringing Daniel, but a good lay doesn't buy you the right to snivel on someone's shoulder.

'Miss Mackenzie?'

I blink to clear my eyes and turn.

'Your brother's fiancée is with him at the moment. I can ask her to give you some time alone with him?'

For some reason I don't want this nurse knowing that we are such a dysfunctional family I've never even met my brother's fiancée.

'It's OK,' I say. 'Just take me to him, please.'

Despite the bleeps and wheezes of the machinery, the sensation I feel when the doors swing shut behind me is of a heavy, suffocating hush. For a moment I can't take a step. Every nerve in my body is tensed, to stop me bolting, and I stand rigid as the nurse waddles up the room to disappear behind a blue curtain on the left.

There are six beds in all, each separated by a curtain, though most of them are open. The occupants lie on their backs, motionless, pale as wax, everything that makes them human concealed or distorted by pipes and masks and coloured stickers. Most of them are old; sparse white hair slicked across crêpe paper foreheads, gnarled fingers resting on the sheets like the shed husks of spiders.

A wave of nausea reminds me how much I drank last night. I can't be sick here: it would be the ultimate insult.

There are low voices, and a moment later the nurse emerges, gives me a tight smile, and passes back out through the doors.

The fiancée is waiting for me.

My heels click across the lino and the rings clatter loudly when I pull back the curtain.

The girl – and she is just a girl – sits on a plastic chair pulled very close to the bed. She raises her head and attempts a smile. Older than I first thought, in her late twenties perhaps, but her manner is that of a child: shrunken shoulders, nervous eyes that cannot hold my gaze. In appearance she is like my brother in negative: the same birdlike build, an elfin face with a high forehead, large eyes, a small rosebud mouth. But where Abe is dark she is shockingly fair, almost albino, with eyes the colour of dishwater.

For a moment I'm disappointed. I suppose I had hoped for someone like me. Someone I could talk to. I can tell immediately that all conversation with this girl will be punctuated by weeping. I will have to reassure her endlessly that it wasn't her fault, and ply her with cups of tea and tissues.

She gets to her feet unsteadily. 'I'm Jody,' she says, then adds, 'I'm so sorry,' and her face crumples.

Swallowing a sigh, I wait patiently while she composes herself, then extend my hand. 'Mags.' Her handshake is predictably limp and she inhales when I squeeze her knuckles.

Finally I look down at my brother.

At least I assume the swollen, blackened lump of flesh and bone on the pillow is my brother.

37

The top of his head is swathed in bandages that various lines pass into. Another bandage covers his nose and cheeks and a neck brace compresses the lower part of his face. Only his eyes and mouth are visible, the lips purple with swelling. He is naked to the waist and his body bristles with tubes leading to bags and bottles of clear liquid.

I breathe slowly and steadily, feeling Jody's eyes on me.

Finally I'm ready to speak. 'So, can you tell me what happened?'

But before she can answer, a nurse comes over and begins checking the monitors. I take Jody gently but firmly by the elbow. 'Let's talk about it over a cup of tea.'

I buy us drinks from the vending machine and lead her out into a small garden that looks out over the main road. A brass plaque on the wall of the empty fountain announces that this is the Queen Mother Memorial Garden.

Jody takes the lid off her tea and the steam curls up into the damp air. The garden is slightly below ground level and the air is leaden with cold. The sun is too weak to melt the night frost and the blades of grass are stiff and white as icicles. I sip the scalding black water that advertised itself as Americano. It is so far from American I want to weep.

As she stares at the dead fountain I wonder how far her thought process has progressed. Has she yet faced up to the prospect that Abe will die? If not immediately, then at some point in the future when the time comes to turn him off. No one gets up from a fall like that.

'It's my fault,' she says.

I wait for her to continue. Her irises are so pale that, seen from profile, they are no more than water surrounding the pupil, large in the gloom of the garden.

'I should have seen the signs. He was working too hard. Sometimes he wouldn't get in until nine or ten. And it's such a stressful job, being a carer.'

I try not to look disappointed at the revelation that my brother cleared up piss and shit for a living; microwaved ready meals,

38

changed incontinence pants, baby-talked sponge-brained geriatrics. I don't know what I was expecting – advertising? Graphic design? – something like me I suppose. God, what a narcissist.

'There was never enough time to get anything done, to do a good enough job, and you know how much of a perfectionist Abe is.'

I nod, *knowing*.

'And how kind he is. He couldn't bear leaving people when he knew he was the only company they would have for days. He would stay and make sure they were all right, which would make him late for the next appointment. Sometimes he had to miss one entirely. They wouldn't pay him for travelling time, and we were hoping to get married next year, so of course money worries just added to the pressure. It was really getting to him. I could see it. We barely saw each other.' She twists the ring on her engagement finger.

'That must have been difficult.'

'I understood, of course I did. But I hated to see him so stressed.'

'Tell me what happened the night he fell,' I say as gently as possible, laying my hand on hers in a gesture I hope will be reassuring and encouraging. Her skin is rough, chapped from the cold, the nails bitten ragged. I hold it there as long as I can bear, then release it into her lap.

'I wanted to try and cheer him up,' she says, looking away, across the garden to the city beyond. 'One of his patients had been taken into a nursing home, and she was very upset about it. So I booked a table in Cosmo – that's our favourite restaurant. He was quiet during the meal, but I thought he was just tired, so I suggested skipping dessert and having an early night. I should have known. I should have guessed there was something wrong.'

'It's not your fault.'

'We should never have had that second glass of wine. He always gets sad when he's had a drink or two. On the way home he didn't say a word, just held my hand really tightly. We came in and started going up to his flat.'

'You don't live together, then?'

'We've asked the housing association for a bigger place, but we thought we'd keep both flats on in the meantime. When we got to the third floor Abe said he couldn't remember if he had closed the security door properly. Sometimes it sticks and there have been break-ins. He told me to go ahead, so I did. I wanted to get the heating on and light a few candles to try and help him relax.'

The ghost-grey irises swim with tears.

'If I had know how bad he was . . . I'm s-sorry.' Her voice rises tremulously. If she starts to sob I'll never get any more out of her.

'Then what happened?' I say, firmly, as if facing an over-wrought witness.

'I opened the door of the flat and went into the hall and then I heard this . . .'

This time I can't bring myself to make her go on.

'It was such a horrible noise.' Her voice goes up again, on the way to a wail. 'It was so loud. Like there wasn't anything soft about him. Like he was a piece of wood or something.'

I close my eyes.

'I ran out of the flat and . . .'

A lorry trundles by, its tarpaulin billowing in the wind. She waits for the roar of its engine to subside and in those few moments all the life seems to have been sucked out of her.

'I'm so sorry,' she says as the normal traffic noise resumes.

'It wasn't your fault,' I say.


Eventually the doctor graces us with his presence. It's twenty past five and I'm so on edge that every thick, shuddering breath Jody takes is making me want to grab her by the hair and smash her head into the wall. At least the weeping wives who show up in court to plead ignorance of their husband's misdemeanours are faking it. Beneath the act they're hard-nosed businesswomen, doing their utmost to prevent the IRS discovering the little offshore hoards in their names. Jody is something else. She holds my brother's hand the entire time, gazing into his pulped face, occasionally brushing

40

the tube that protrudes from his mouth with her lips. The sight, along with the alcohol tang of disinfection, intensifies my nausea.

I pace to the window and back, trying not to look at the other cadavers, wondering what on earth the point is of spending all this money and effort to keep them in this parody of life. Presumably my brother, if he wakes at all, will be a drooling, infantilised wreck. Jody will lovingly feed him with purees and porridge, wiping the gloop from his slimy chin. At least Alzheimer's or dementia patients have the decency to be old. Abe could go on like that for decades.

Dr Bonville is very young, shorter than me, with the floppy-haired arrogance born out of the British public school system. He takes us to a shabby little room with a blue sofa so small that Jody and I must sit hip to hip.

'Well,' he says, and gives that pressed-lipped smile people use to express empathy. 'The swelling has gone down.'

Jody turns to me and I can almost feel her itching to squeeze my hand. I keep looking at the doctor. I know what's coming.

'So we've been able to assess the damage to Abe's brain.'

He pauses then, rustling the papers on his lap. He doesn't sit behind the table but pulls out the chair to sit opposite us, a more informal, human position that can only mean the worst.

'Abe's cerebral cortex has suffered major trauma. The cortex is responsible for thinking and action. For this reason, when we take him out of the coma, I'm afraid Abe will be in a vegetative state.'

As he waits to let the news sink in I can hear ambulances pulling in and out, their sirens gradually diminishing to be absorbed in the traffic.

The material of the sofa is loosely woven, like slack skin, and the arm is blotched with watermarks. How many tears, I wonder, have been shed here? My fingers are hypersensitive, as if I can feel the microscopic granules of salt beneath their tips.

'Will it heal by itself?' Jody says, her voice clumsy in the silence, making me wince.

'Of course not,' I say.

41

'No,' says Dr Bonville. 'I'm afraid that can't happen. I'm afraid you have to face the possibility that, in the very unlikely event that Abe ever regains consciousness, he will be very different from the man you knew.'

'He blinked,' Jody says. 'I saw his eyelids move.'

'Abe's lower brain stem is intact, so reflexes like breathing, swallowing, reacting to pain, even blinking, can still be present. Abe might even—'

'Stop saying his name.'

He turns his surprised gaze on me.

'Stop saying his name because you think it gives you *the human touch*.'

He looks at me steadily. 'I understand that you must be very upset,' he says quietly. 'Let me give you a minute.'

He goes to get up, but I get up faster. 'Talk to *her*,' I say. 'I've heard enough. Just tell me when it's time to turn him off.'

I walk out of the room and, without a glance at the doors of the ICU, stride down the corridor that leads to the exit. It seems to take years, and when I finally emerge into the grimy London air I gulp it down like water from an Alpine stream.

The traffic roars past and I'm buffeted by blank-faced office workers rushing to get home. It's at times like this that the anonymity of a city is a blessing. Nobody knows I have just walked out on a doctor trying to tell me whether my brother is going to live or die. Nobody cares.

With a glance back at the hospital to confirm Jody isn't coming after me, I join the flow of people heading for the Tube.

It feels like a year has passed when I finally arrive back at the hotel. I go for another swim, try – and fail – to read my book, pick at my room service order: a very poor imitation of a club sandwich. At six I hit the mini bar.

The room darkens.

On the pretext of a work chat, I call Jackson and when he picks up I can hear the hubbub of a restaurant behind him. I want to ask where he is but it might sound like an accusation. I imagine them at Ginelli's down in Paradise, drinking cold beers on the veranda with the smell of the desert on the wind. My heart aches.

'Let me go somewhere quieter,' he says.

'No, it's fine,' I say, desperate for the sounds of home. 'It's just to check in, really. How's Antonio?'

'We made the plea bargain and they're thinking it through. I told him they'll probably go for it.'

'Great. Send him my love.'

Jackson laughs. 'He'll be wanking all night over that one.' He kills the laugh and says, 'How's your brother?'

I exhale. 'Not great. Brain-dead, it looks like. A botched suicide attempt.'

The muted TV at the end of the bed strobes images of a war zone – old women and children crying, grey corpses rotting in the road, an abandoned teddy.

Jackson tells me he's sorry. Then, after a seemly pause, asks me, 'Do you think . . . dying will happen . . . naturally?'

I know what he's really asking. *When will you be back at work?*

'Potentially. But it might come down to turning the machines off and it's a bit early to think about that.'

'Of course, of course.'

'I'd be happy to leave any decision to his girlfriend, but as next of kin I'm supposed to have the final say.'

There's silence on the other end of the line and I can almost hear Jackson trying to frame the words.

'How long will you . . . er . . . wait?'

Suppressing the flash of irritation I keep my tone light. 'It'll depend on the doctors.'

'Take as long as you need, Mags.'

'Thanks. Listen, go and enjoy your lunch. What are you having?'

He clears his throat. 'Lobster thermidor.'

I groan with envy.

'There's one with your name on it, when you get back.'

'Send me a photo. I'll choose him myself. You can put a deposit down.'

'Will do. Take care, Mags. Lots of love.'

I hang up, then open the mini bar. Three gin and tonics later I'm sitting on the bed with the TV blaring to try and numb my head. PC Derbyshire was right, not all tragedies are crimes, but I'm a lawyer, so all I can think of now is questions.

Why haven't they checked the CCTV?

Why did Abe take his coat off?

Did someone get in through the door that he was going down to check?

With such a plainly devoted girlfriend, why on earth would he decide to kill himself?

And if so, didn't she deserve a note?

*She gazes out at the gnarled faces of the trees. They are like people, stretching their arms towards the car to pluck her from the back seat and spirit her away into the darkness. But the car is moving too fast: twigs rattle vainly against the windows as the headlights sweep relentlessly onwards. She twists her head to watch them recede. For a moment each trunk is washed in red, before falling away to blackness.*

*They have made this journey before. She knows that the forest bordering the road will end abruptly, the land flattening out to fields. An occasional house will dot the landscape, its windows butter yellow. But the house they are heading for cannot be seen from the road, and its lights are the cold glare of fluorescent strips.* All the better to see you with, my dear.

*Are there wolves in this forest? The thought does not scare her. An animal has simple desires: to eat and sleep and protect its territory. It mates only to produce children. It loves its children with such fierce passion it would tear your throat out if you harmed one.*

*A wolf would eat her, perhaps, despite her boniness. It would be a quick death. She can imagine her corpse being squabbled over by tumbling cubs, play-snarling at one another, little claws tangling in her hair, needle teeth chewing her finger bones.*

*She slides her eyes across to the child beside her. Like her he stares blankly from the window, the trees throwing moving bars across his face. The air in the car is thick with cigarette smoke and the woman in front of her winds down the window to toss out a butt. A chill wind lifts the hem of her dress and creeps up her thighs. She shivers. She needs a wee but knows better than to ask to stop.*

*In the front they are discussing who will be there tonight. She hears a name she knows and a little bit of wee comes out and wets her knickers. She glances at the boy again. His hands sit limply in his lap, fingers upwards, like dead crabs.*

45

*Now there is a red light up ahead, a vertical sliver of sunset. The trees are coming to an end. They are nearly there.*

*She wishes she could have a drink. The children at her last school said it's illegal to drink wine when you're only seven. They told the teacher and she had to pretend she was joking. A few sips of cider now would smooth the jagged edge of panic that makes sweat prickle her armpits despite the cold.*

*The clear patch of sky widens as they reach the edge of the forest. The man in front exclaims. There is a branch in the road. He slows down.*

*She unclicks her belt and opens the door.*

*The tarmac slams into her, making her bones crunch as she rolls over and over, coming to rest on the edge of the camber, before the road falls away to forest. The car screeches to a halt, then starts reversing. On hands and knees she scrambles down the incline, cutting her shins on needles and pinecones, then she is up and running.*

*The wolves watch her from the shadows as she flies through the darkness, her hair streaming behind her.*

*She is a good runner. Thin and long-legged, like the antelopes on the nature programmes at school. There is just enough light to see her path ahead. She ducks left and right, following the natural instinct of prey animals. The light dims as the trees grown denser, enfolding her. Her footfalls are muffled by the spongy forest floor. She will find a bush to creep into, or else she will shimmy up a tree and conceal herself among its leaves.*

*A huge white shape makes her steps falter. At first she thinks it might be an angel, its wings spread to enfold her, but it is only an owl. A magnificent barn owl, its black eyes glinting. As it sweeps by she feels a whoosh of cold air on her cheek. She keeps running. The darkness deepens and there is a pain in her side. Her shoelace has come undone. She should retie it but she cannot risk the hesitation. She keeps running.*

*There's rustling all around her, like the trees whispering to one another. She is not afraid. The stitch subsides and the air is cold and clean, scouring her out from the inside, taking away all the filth. A snatch of sky. The blood red has been replaced by velvet blue. She can see a star. Moonlight silvers the uppermost leaves.*

*Then her foot comes down on the loose lace, and she is thrown forward, her breath escaping in a grunt as she lands heavily on her stomach.*

*She lies there, catching her breath, the pine needles tickling her thighs. If she lies here long enough a blanket of leaves will cover her. Her fingers will become roots, delving into the dark soil. Insects will make nests in her hair. No one will ever find her.*

*A crack.*

*Her consciousness sharpens, her hearing becoming hypersensitive.*

*There is no more rustling in the undergrowth, no whisper of wings. The creatures of the forest are afraid. Clouds scud across the moon, and the silver light winks out.*

*Another crack. Louder.*

*She would pray, but her lips won't move.*

*The wolf lands on her back.*

*She is wrenched up and spun around. His body is silhouetted against the glare of the car headlights behind him. She had come such a short distance. How foolish to think she had a chance.*

*He hauls her onto his shoulder like a dead stag.*

*'Please,' she whimpers, but her voice is drowned by the crash and crack of the undergrowth as he plunges through the trees back to the road.*

# 5. Jody

My family would have loved you. My dad may have been a forces man, but he was never a bully. He respected gentleness; he knew that strength isn't about muscles and fists, that it comes from inside. He would have seen the strength inside you.

Mum loved him so much she couldn't go on without him. I'm not angry with her for that. I can understand. I feel that way about you – if you die I won't want to go on.

Your sister is so hard. The way she talked about . . . well, about what the doctor said. It was horrible to listen to. Like she doesn't care about you at all and just wants to get it all over and done with. I won't let her, though, don't worry. I won't let them hurt you, Abe. They'd have to get a special court order before they can do anything like that anyway. I read about it once, a case in America where a woman had a stroke and was in a coma. The husband wanted to turn her machines off but her family didn't want to. They went with the husband in the end, which makes me scared because we're not married yet, but also hopeful that they take into account the wishes of the people closest to you. Your sister hasn't seen you in years but she barely looks at you. She doesn't love you. I can't imagine her loving anyone. I'm not surprised she's on her own, even though she's really attractive.

She looks so much like you. The same slim face and wide, dark eyes. The same straight dark hair. You could be twins.

How did your hearts turn out so different?

I came straight back to your flat after the doctor went away, and just being near the things you've touched is making me feel better.

I've lain on your bed for hours, gazing at the photograph of the two of us in that bar in the West End, but now I get up and open the wardrobe. As I run my fingers through your clothes the scent of you drifts out, and I close my eyes and breathe deeply. Then I take out one of your cardigans to put on after my shower, a cashmere one, soft as rabbit fur.

I use your shampoo, to keep my hair smelling like yours, and then I clean my teeth with your toothbrush and dry myself with the towel from the heated rail. A single black pubic hair curls from the weave. Yours. Mine are fair.

I put on your T-shirt and cardigan, and when I close my eyes it's almost like the ghost of you is all around me, embracing me. I wonder if your spirit can move from your body, because of the state you're in, or whether someone has to be dead for that to happen. Even if you die, Abe, it won't be the end – I promise. When two spirits like ours meet and forge such a strong and powerful love it can't just blink out like a light. Something has to remain.

Your flat is so much nicer than mine, and not just because it's filled with you. It's so bright and modern, all greys and whites and the type of wood they call 'blond'. Your window looks down on the grass at the front and the bright colours of the children's playground. Even the kitchen, which is the same in all the flats, looks nicer, somehow. I think it's because of how you've 'accessorised' it. The glass jars of pasta, the silver coffee maker, and the corkscrew that looks like a lady in a dress. It's Alessi, which I know is expensive, because in the charity shop they keep that sort of stuff in a locked cabinet.

It's silly but at dinnertime I lay two places and dish out two bowlfuls of pasta, and then I talk to you as if you're still there.

'How was work?'

*Oh, you know. Tiring.*

'You work too hard.'

*They need me. Mrs Evans was so relieved to see me. I don't think she'd spoken to anyone since my last visit. How was your day?*

'Better now.' I close my eyes and reach across the table and imagine your hand in mine. I can almost feel it, the light touch of your warm fingers against my palm, and then the table starts to vibrate. I jump so hard my fork clatters off my plate and a blob of tomato sauce spatters the sleeve of your cardigan.

It's only my phone vibrating before the ringtone kicks in.

For a moment I think it's going to be you on the other end. But it's not. It's your sister.

'Hello?' I say, warily, wondering if she's going to be nasty.

'Listen, I'm sorry about earlier. I just hate the way these people patronise you.'

'Yes,' I murmur, but I don't really agree. Doctors have always made me feel safe.

'I've been thinking. It looks like I might be hanging around for a bit longer and it's silly to live out of a hotel room, especially when I'm so far from the hospital. I'd much rather have a bit of space and be able to cook for myself, so I'm going to move into Abe's flat. The police haven't returned his belongings yet so I wondered if you had a key I could have.'

My breath catches. She wants to come here?

'I'm not stepping on your toes, am I? I mean, feel free to come around and collect any stuff you've left there.'

'It's . . . not that,' I stammer. 'It's just that . . .' My mind goes blank, but eventually I come up with something. 'I'm not sure the housing association would allow it.'

'Oh, right. Well, can you give me the number and I'll talk to them?'

'Umm . . . wait a minute.'

I put the phone down on the table and stare at it for a moment, my skin creeping. I could say I've lost the number, but she'd be able to find it easily enough. I could give her the wrong one and then stop answering my phone, but she would just come and look for me at the hospital.

50

In the end I get up and head back to my flat, running in my socks so she can't hear my footsteps. As I run past Flat Eleven I can feel the spyhole watching me, black as a shark's eye. Sometimes I think I can sense someone hiding behind the door. Pushing the thought from my mind I go into my flat, find the number on an old letter, and run back.

But the spyhole has given me an idea and, after I read it out to her, I say, 'I don't know if you know, Mags, but this place is run by a charity. So as well as care home kids like me, there are other people, with worse conditions. You know, *mental* issues. I'm used to it, so I know to be careful, but you . . .' I tail off meaningfully.

She hesitates a moment, and I think that she might change her mind.

But then she says she'll call the association and if they say it's OK, she'll come by sometime tomorrow morning to pick up the keys. She adds, conversationally, that the police will be popping round to return Abe's stuff sometime over the next few days, so if I remember anything I haven't mentioned to them already, that would be my chance to tell them.

I put the phone down and stare at your untouched plate of food, my heart thudding.

What does she mean?

# Thursday 10 November

# 6. Mags

I dial the number Jody gave me and a young man with a heavy Arabic accent answers. After I've explained the situation he says he'll put me through to the charity's director, Peter Selby. It rings for a long time before it's finally picked up, by what sounds like a very old man, very posh, and slightly camp.

When I explain what's happened he gasps and his voice trembles when he says how sorry he is. For the first time, the clichéd words sound genuine.

'Did you know Abe?'

'Of course,' he says. 'We interview all our prospective tenants, to make sure they're eligible for our help.'

My interest pricks. 'And Abe was? Eligible?'

He hesitates. 'Well, clearly.' I can hear the surprise in his tone. I'm Abe's sister. How can I not know this about him?

'Abe and I haven't spoken for many years. We had a difficult upbringing. It created a ... distance.' I hate talking about my family.

There's a pause and then the old man says, 'The St Jerome's Foundation offers assistance in the form of subsidised accommodation for minority or vulnerable groups. People who have been let down by society and need a helping hand to raise themselves up again.' I get the feeling he has parroted this line many times before. If they have charitable status, he must have to reapply each year.

I assume by 'vulnerable groups' he's talking about people with mental health issues.

For the first time it occurs to me that perhaps Abe had some kind of a breakdown when he left home. I managed to avoid one by self-medication with alcohol and narcotics, but only just. Perhaps that's when his depression began.

'In that case, you must have seen his medical notes, in order to assess his eligibility, right? Was he clinically depressed back then?'

There's a long pause, during which I hear a creak, as if he's sitting in a leather armchair. Unless it's his bones. Finally he speaks. 'Abe moved into St Jerome's ten years ago, when he was very young. We put him in touch with a support group, and organised vocational training that enabled him to embark on his career – a career which he seems to have been eminently suited for. A charming young man. He will be much missed.'

That's not an answer, but it's clear it's all I'm going to get.

With Jody's words in mind I ask, 'Are they dangerous?'

'To whom are you referring?'

'The people in St Jerome's. What sort of mental health problems are we talking about?'

He hesitates again before replying and I hear the wheeze of his breath through ancient lungs. 'Miss Mackenzie, as I'm sure you can understand, I am unable to share confidential information about our residents; suffice to say that in the twenty-seven years this foundation has been in operation, no resident has ever attacked or otherwise harmed another.'

'There's always a first time.'

He sighs in irritation. 'Whatever you may have read in the tabloid press, those suffering with mental health difficulties are far more likely to be a danger to themselves than others. Now, the foundation would be perfectly amenable to your staying at St Jerome's while your brother recuperates, but it is of course your choice.'

Ignoring his implication that I'm a gullible idiot who believes the mentally ill are all knife-wielding maniacs, I tell him I'd like

56

to move in straightaway. He says the building manager will call to let me know all the various rules and regulations but as I put down the phone I wonder what I'm letting myself in for.

An hour later I check out of the hotel, bumping my wheelie case down the steps, and the doorman hails me a cab. I've dressed down – jeans and Converses and a black rain jacket that looks pretty uninspiring but cost six hundred dollars – but as we travel north, moving closer and closer to the little blue pin on my phone map, I'm glad I did. Edgware Road and Regent's Park are bright and bustling but as we pass through Camden and Chalk Farm the buildings and people become shabbier. Kentish Town is about the last bastion of civilisation before we enter a no man's land of boarded-up shops and run-down council estates.

Even the sky seems dirtier out here. The high-rises stretch away into brown clouds, their walls leprous with rot, plastic bags whirling around their bases.

My phone rings, giving me the chance to excuse myself from the cabbie's monologue about his daughter who has just moved to New Zealand.

It's the building manager, José Ribeiro. He offers to get a spare set of keys cut for me but I tell him I can use Abe's, so he moves on to the building regs. The first lot are simple enough: no pets, no smoking, no subletting the flat, but what with the traffic noise and his heavy South American accent, it takes several painful minutes for me to understand when the bins should be taken out, how to programme the hot water and the account to pay the rent into. He's about to say more but I've had enough: I tell him I'm losing signal and drop the call.

We're close now. According to my blue pin this high street we're crawling down is just around the corner from St Jerome's. There are a few independent shops and cafés, the obligatory charity shop, an Internet café and a place that promises to unlock any phone. Handwritten signs in grubby windows announce *Best Kebab in London!* or *No Groups of Children*. The fruit and vegetables in crates outside are dirtied by traffic but a Greek bakery looks promising, and there's a Food and Wine for basics.

We're stuck behind a bus emblazoned with an advert for the local Baptist church. Shiny faces beam out of the grime, their glow of health and happiness out of place here.

All the passers-by seem bent with age or sickness; they shuffle along, dragging wheelie trolleys overflowing with the blue plastic bags favoured by all down-at-heel shops. There are few white faces, and more full-face veils than I have seen outside news footage.

The cabbie has stopped talking about his daughter and, as we wait for an elderly woman to shuffle across a zebra crossing, he taps the wheel impatiently. He seems as tense as I am. Perhaps I should have stayed at the hotel. I will stand out here like a sore thumb. Or perhaps there's a trendy part – where media types have started to move in and gentrify the place.

We turn into Gordon Terrace, a street of low-rise concrete bunkers with weed-choked front gardens. A teenager lumbers by with a dog so muscular it looks like a screwed fist.

At the end of the terrace is a patch of bumpy waste ground and then I see it. St Jerome's church, its spire silhouetted against the darkening sky.

Goosebumps trickle down my arms. This will be the first time I've been in a church for almost twenty years and, though the original wooden doors have been replaced by a faceless security door, an irrational panic rises in my throat at the thought of passing through it.

The cab stops by the pavement, under a flickering street lamp. 'Twenty-three fifty, love.'

I hand over the unfamiliar notes and, without waiting for change, I get out. A concrete path crosses an expanse of patchy grass, which seems mainly to be used as a dog toilet. It is hemmed in on all sides by a chain-link fence with buildings pressing close on the other side. On the left-hand side of the path, shadowed by a nearby high-rise, is a playground. The sole occupant, a boy of eight or nine, looks up from his swing.

It's colder here, much colder than in the city centre, and a gritty wind snatches at my jacket as I trundle the case down the path. My progress is impeded by annoying ridges in the path, like speed bumps or buried tree roots. Along the top of each ridge the tarmac is cracked like a loaf cake, exposing the black glittering crystals beneath. Soil seeps from the tear.

A moment later I am swallowed by the jagged shadow of the church.

It's constructed of grey brick, in that austere Victorian style designed to intimidate, to make you feel small.

I straighten my back and stare out the two empty arches at the base of the spire, but they gaze impassively out across the shops and tower blocks.

The central section of the building is flanked by a wing either side, with its own small arched windows, the lower of which are covered by security grilles.

From this side, the stained-glass panel above the door is just a sliver of grey, but I feel the eyes of the ghostly figures watch my approach, the case rumbling along behind me, announcing my presence.

And then this sense of being watched grows suddenly more powerful and I stop on the path, my heart thudding.

My head snaps around but I'm too late to catch any more than the flutter of a net curtain.

Someone was watching me from the ground-floor window of the left wing.

I stay where I am for a moment, to see if they will return to the window, but the curtain is still, the unlit room beyond giving nothing away.

The trill of my phone makes me jump. It's PC Derbyshire, asking when she can come and drop off Abe's belongings. I suggest it might be more appropriate for them to go to Jody but evidently, as his next of kin, I must sign for them.

As I hang up it's just starting to rain, that ice-cold drizzle Britain specialises in, creeping down the collar of my raincoat, chilling my hands and soaking through my canvas shoes. I pick up the case and run the rest of the way to the door.

The security panel glows green and next to button ten is a label with Abe's and my surname, written in biro. I buzz Flat Twelve: Currie, and a moment later the door clicks open. It's heavy and gives a loud creak that reverberates across the open ground as I pass through to a dingy foyer with a table piled with post. It all seems to be takeaway menus and flyers.

I go through the inner door, into darkness.

A glowing button at eye level must be the light switch. I press it and a wall lamp stammers into life.

I am standing at the bottom of the stairwell.

Though the light is too weak to reach past the first landing I can feel the weight of the air above my head. It presses on my ears, setting off a high-pitched whine of tinnitus.

I breathe deeply, half expecting to see a spiderweb crack in the polished concrete, some sign of the calamity that occurred here. But there is nothing. Not a single speck of blood on the banisters. The air smells of dust and the ghost of incense.

Leaving the case by the door I walk forward, the rubber soles of my shoes sending out whispering echoes. Now I'm in the centre of the well, staircases rising dimly up on either side of me. In the shadows beneath them there are other doors: presumably Flats One, Two and Three. I was being watched, I am sure, by someone in Flat One and I'm tempted to knock on the door. For what reason, I'm not really sure myself; the occupant is probably just nosy, or lonely, or looking out for a visitor.

My nerves are on edge. I'm standing where my brother fell – to his death. I can face that fact even if Jody can't.

The room turns scarlet.

If it weren't for my black shadow looming before me, I would think something had gone wrong with my vision. Then I remember the stained-glass window.

I turn.

Long time no see, Jesus.

The sun must have come out from behind a cloud because his crimson cloak is casting a strong red wash over everything.

And then the sun goes in again and I'm plunged into gloom. The light has gone off too. It must be on a timer.

I flinch as a door clicks open somewhere above, half expecting a body to come hurtling down through the darkness. Then a wall lamp on an upper floor comes on and the full height of the building is revealed.

I inhale sharply. It is so far. So far to fall. It must have taken long, long seconds.

Soft footsteps on the stairs. At first I think it's Jody come to meet me, but the figure that descends wears a headscarf. A young woman, dressed in a loose, black abaya. A Muslim, but her face is pale, so perhaps she is Eastern European.

I have been too quiet. When she steps out onto the ground floor she starts and I apologise. There is a flicker of a smile, then she dips her head and moves past me towards the foyer.

Jody is waiting for me on the fourth floor. She's still in her nightdress, covered with a pale pink hoodie. As I step out onto the landing, breathless from the climb, I have to grip the banister, dizzied by proximity to the long drop into darkness. Now that the only light is on this floor, it has become bottomless. The rail is about waist height. Could Abe have leaned on it to catch his breath then overbalanced?

'It was here that he fell?' I say.

'Yes. That's where he jumped.'

I walk across to the rail and close my fingers around the slim metal bar. As I lean into it I feel it give a little. Such a fragile barrier between life and death. But I'm leaning too far – my heels are coming off the floor – and I pull myself back.

'Nobody saw him?'

'No.'

'Where were you?'

'In his flat.' She points behind me to a door marked with a metal ten. It's as faceless as all the others I've passed on the way up, painted a dreary grey-blue, presumably designed not to excite the spirits of the fragile inhabitants.

'You came out and . . .' I pause to take a breath, as if the air is thinner up here. 'And you saw him. Lying down there, on the concrete?'

'Yes,' she says, her voice echoing down the column of darkness. 'I saw him and I ran down to him. I held his hand until the ambulance came. He wasn't alone.'

'You said that you screamed. Didn't anyone hear and come out?'

'I don't know. Sorry. I was paying attention to Abe.'

I want her to tell me something different – that someone saw him climb over the banisters, or saw him overbalance – but of course she can't. She can only tell me what she knows.

'Do you want me to show you around the flat?' she says.

'I'm sure I can manage.'

The small sound of the key sliding into the lock echoes through the stairwell: the acoustics of the original church haven't been entirely dampened by the renovations. Unless they've bothered with the expense of soundproofing the flats, you must be able to hear every TV theme tune, sharp word, or intimate murmur of your neighbours. I'm glad I brought the earplugs from the flight bag.

The door swings open and I step into a darkened hallway. Pictures gleam at me from the shadows. My hand tightens on the handle of the case – someone is standing at the end of the corridor.

But flipping on the light I see it's just a navy blue parka dangling from a coat hook. Leaving the case propped against the wall, I go up to it and run my hand across the shiny fabric. With its fur hood and bright orange lining it reminds me of the coats the boys used to wear in our school playground. We were never allowed one – far too common. It looks warm, though, and I've underestimated how cold a British November can be.

At a noise behind me I spin around. Jody is silhouetted against the doorway. I hide my flash of anger. What now?

'S-sorry, shall I bring you a cup of tea?'

'I'm sure Abe has a kettle.'

'Yes, but he only drinks herbal.'

'I'll be fine,' I say, forcing a smile. 'Thanks. If I need one I'll know where to come.'

'OK, well . . . I'll leave you to it. I hope I've left it tidy enough for you. I've been sleeping here a few times to try and . . . you know . . . get closer to . . .'

'OK,' I say. 'Thank you.'

When Jody softly shuts the door I feel guilty. This is her home far more than it can ever be mine. It was good of her even to relinquish the keys. Even so, I walk back and check it's properly closed. I don't want her sneaking up on me again, especially as I'm not sure how I'll feel walking into Abe's domain.

I go up to the inner door.

His whole flat is the size of my master bedroom. At one end is a poky galley kitchen with a worktop separating it from the living area. A shabby leather sofa is positioned in front of a small TV, a grey throw folded on its back. Next to the TV is an electric fire: one of those where pretend flames made of fabric ripple in the glass window when you turn it on. There's a sticker on the side saying when it was last serviced, so it must come with the flat.

At the other end of the room a pine dining table sits by the window. It's part of the stained-glass window I saw in the foyer, bisected by the inner wall of the flat and truncated by the floor. It looks out over the bumpy path and the street where the taxi dropped me.

Even though all the walls are white, the coloured glass gives the room an air of oppression. Through the blue-cloaked upper torso of some bearded apostle I can see the children's playground below. A Staffordshire bull terrier is shitting on the rubber matting surrounding the roundabout, no master in sight. I rap on the window but it pays no attention.

On the back of one of the dining chairs hangs a dark grey pea coat. I check the pockets for a spare set of keys so I can give Jody's back, but there aren't any. However, I do find a wallet, Abe's phone – dead – and some loose change. In the wallet is a measly collection of cards, two five-pound notes, and a receipt for a new pair of Gap jeans. His Oyster is in there too, and slipped into the other pocket of the card wallet is a photo ID card for his job.

I stare at the photograph for several minutes, my brain adjusting to this new, decade-older little brother. His eyes are still puppy-dog large, and dark-brown like mine. They peer out almost seductively from his floppy fringe. I see for the first time that there's something attractive about his slenderness. I used to think it was wimpy, but now I recognise something Bowie-esque about his elegant neck, the sharp shoulders under his leather jacket, the high cheekbones. His lips are shapely and full. I wonder if the stubble is an attempt to add a little masculinity.

I slip the card wallet into my pocket. The taxi driver said it would be hard to get cabs around here and I'd be better off with buses.

A door leads off to a bathroom, musty-smelling, with mildew-spotted grouting and a mirror eaten away at the edges by damp. Male toiletries are lined up neatly on the glass shelf, alongside a single tub of woman's moisturiser. There's no sign of any depression medications.

The only other door leads off from the kitchen area.

I stand on the threshold surveying a tiny bedroom, double bed crammed up against the window on one side, and just enough room to open the cupboards on the other. A patch of damp blooms like an overblown rose in the corner of the room and a few specks of plaster lie like dandruff on the dark blue carpet.

I experience a twist of guilt. The place is a dump. I could have given him the deposit for a flat of his own, or money to rent something better than this. The bed is made, but I'll have to change the sheets – if only to rinse out Jody's tears from the pillow.

There's a full-length mirror in the corner and more toiletries on the shelf beside it. I smile. So, my brother was vain.

Picking my way down the side of the bed I open the cupboard. Slim, tailored trousers and dark cotton shirts, all facing the same way, all perfectly suited to his long, lean frame. A hanger full of tasteful ties in navies and purples, a couple of cashmere-mix cardigans and, in a rack below, brogues, Chelsea boots and a pair of grubby white Converses that are the twin of the pair I'm wearing.

There's just room for a bedside table. On it is a photograph of him and Jody, and a drinking tumbler of fresh flowers: a single stalk with a dense head of white blossom, so I guess handpicked rather than shop-bought. It must be Jody's doing. How far would she have had to travel from this grotty neighbourhood to find wildflowers? I'm touched again by her devotion.

There's also a phone charger and a pulp thriller I'd been intending to read myself. The corner of a page near the end is bent all the way across to the gutter. I do that too.

I'm struck by this and other parallels between us: the taste in books, in clothes, in the colours and textures of our homes. The only mystery is Jody. I just can't see what he saw in such a wet blanket. Was she always like this or has she been broken by grief? I suppose it's my problem to find out. I must try harder with her if I want to get to know Abe. I find that I want to feel . . . yes, I want to feel closer to him. Before the end.

I open the drawer of the bedside table, and step back. Then I laugh.

*Way to go, Jody, you dark horse.*

Handcuffs. And now I can see the rub marks on the rungs of the bedhead.

I really *must* wash the sheets. But first, a herbal tea. Three green teabags might give me a half-hearted kick of caffeine.

At a glance the gleaming white kitchenette had looked promising, but walking into it I see that the counters are laminate and the doors MDF, their edges swollen with damp. But he has done his best with cheap materials and everything is scrupulously clean. The cupboards contain jars of olives and sundried tomatoes; different kinds of oil in slim, elegant bottles; pesto and artichokes and a pack of bake-at-home French bread, still in date. Food I would have chosen myself.

There are the herbal teas Jody warned me about, but there's also a shelf full of hard liquor and – joy of joys – the same brand of knock-your-head-off coffee I drink at home.

In the corner of the worktop is a basic coffee machine and ten minutes later I'm leaning against the countertop, eyes closed, inhaling the scent of home. It makes my eyes prick in a way that seeing his body lying in the hospital couldn't.

I sip my coffee and survey the tiny flat.

Three rooms.

Was he ever happy here? I couldn't be, but whatever the surface similarities, we are very different people. He was a carer. And he loved Jody. At least he *found* love. If it wasn't for her, and the obvious happiness they shared, I couldn't forgive myself for abandoning my baby brother. She's saved me from that guilt, and I should be on my knees in gratitude. So why aren't I? Because I'm a self-centred bitch, probably.

'I promise to try harder, Abe,' I murmur, knocking back the last bitter grinds.

Then I hear a loud buzz. There's an entry panel by the front door, and on the little screen I make out the distorted face of PC Derbyshire. I try the button marked with a speaker and tell her to come up, then press the one marked with a key. A moment later there's the distant creak of the main door opening, followed by the slam as it closes, and then footsteps on the stairs. I hear the scrape of shoes against concrete, the ting of metal against the banister rail – a wedding ring perhaps – the chime of a text message coming through.

How it is possible that *no one* heard Abe fall?

I sit down at the table by the window, with Derbyshire and her pasty underling.

'Did she set your mind at rest?' Derbyshire says, laying out various forms I have to sign before they can release the stuff. 'Miss Currie?'

I repeat what Jody said about them coming home half pissed.

66

'I suppose it might have affected his balance, and the rail is quite low. It could have been accidental rather than suicide.'

'There was no alcohol in his bloodstream,' the policewoman says, gathering the signed forms. 'Though he might have had one glass that was already metabolised before we tested him.'

I frown. Was one glass enough to throw his balance off so fatally? He's pretty slim, so I guess it's possible that he really couldn't handle his drink.

She hands the forms to the underling, who tucks them into his manbag. 'Did Miss Currie mention how they had been getting along? Any relationship problems?'

'No. They sounded very in love. Why do you ask?'

'There was bruising to Miss Currie's mouth on the night of the fall. She told us she slipped. On the blood.'

I stare at her. Then I say, 'If you're implying that Abe might have hit her, I don't think my brother was like that.' As I say it I realise I have no idea what he's like, but it's too late to backtrack because they're getting up to go.

They leave me with a clear carrier bag containing Abe's personal effects. I tip the clothes out onto the carpet, unfolding the parts that are stiff with blood, until I have something vaguely man-shaped.

So, this was my brother.

A pair of brogues, slim black jeans, a dark purple shirt and a cardigan – neat and elegant. Beneath the metallic scent of blood, I can smell aftershave. I dimly recognise the complex and spicy undertones, which means I must have slept with someone who wore it, which means it's probably expensive. I like it that Abe chose to spend the little spare money he had on luxuries.

Then I notice that one of the shirtsleeves is torn at the shoulder seam.

Could the fall have done that? Or did it happen when they stripped him in the hospital?

I pack the clothes back into the bag and stow them away in the wardrobe until I can figure out what to do with them. Then

67

I wash my hands to get rid of the smell of stale blood and set about stripping the sheets, bundling them up with the towel from the bathroom. I stand there at a loss. There is no washing machine. José would probably have told me where the nearest launderette was if I'd given him the chance, but I can't face another conversation peppered with *I'm sorry could you repeat that*s, so I go out of the flat, cross the landing and knock on Jody's door.

It rattles loosely. There's something wrong with the lock. It looks like the wood has splintered behind it and it's just hanging on by one screw.

She opens the door a crack, leaving the chain on, and I glimpse a gloomy hallway the twin of Abe's.

'Just wondering if there's a launderette around here?'

'Oh, sorry. I should have said. It's down in the basement. Wait here and I'll get you some powder.'

She closes the door, and though I am glad she didn't invite me in so I won't have to make small talk with her, it seems uncharacteristically rude.

After a moment my back starts to prickle with the consciousness of that black void behind me. I stood on the edge of the Grand Canyon once and after a minute or two had to step away. The man I was with teased me, but it wasn't vertigo. I just felt this powerful urge to jump. Did Abe feel like that as he trudged up this grim stairwell? Or was it just a moment of existential clarity. *Is this really it?*

Jody returns. She has taken off the pink hoodie and as she hands me the washing powder I notice, in the indentations beneath each of her clavicles, round bruises, the size of pound coins.

'Thanks,' I say.

'Have you got change for the machines?'

'I think so.'

She smiles wanly and closes the door.

I go back to the flat, plug in Abe's phone and collect the washing pile.

*

The laundry room is low-ceilinged and damp, and the walls are covered with the same red lino as the floor, so that I feel as if I am in a horror film as I sit uneasily on the bench, trying to read Abe's thriller while I wait for the wash cycle to end.

A loud beep makes me jump: someone else's load in the drier has finished. A scarlet shirt is pressed against the glass door. I think of Abe's shirt, torn at the shoulder.

I close the book and place it down on the bench beside me.

I think of Jody's cut lip and the finger bruises on her shoulder.

The policewoman asked me if their relationship was stormy. What if she and Abe *did* fight that night? They'd had a bit to drink, after all. I imagine she's the clingy and demanding type. Maybe she was angry about him spending so more much time with his clients than her. What if he told her he wanted to be alone that night? What if he tried to finish the relationship entirely?

What if she pushed him?

# 7. Mira

I stand in the shadows under the stairs, listening as the mad girl tells the sister that nobody saw him fall. That he was alone. That he jumped.

When they have gone away I hurry up the stairs and let myself into the flat, then lean against the door until the pounding of my heart has slowed down. I shouldn't run, the doctor has told me, because of my high blood pressure. I need to be calm, to take lots of rest. But how can I be calm? How can I rest when I know what I know?

Why is she lying for you, Loran?

I go into the living room and sit down on the sofa, slipping off my shoes and lying down with my feet above my heart as the doctor has shown me. I must calm down and I must rest. Or something might happen to the baby. And then I don't know what you would do.

# 8. Jody

The card is still lying open on the floor where I dropped it, like a crocodile's mouth waiting to snap at my ankles. I want to put it in the bin but I can't bring myself to touch it.

It's small, half the size of a normal card, as if it doesn't want to be seen, as if it can hide behind the others. If there were any others.

On the front is a pastel picture of a rose: more a sympathy card than a birthday card. Another year alive. Poor you.

*To dearest Jody*
*Always thinking of you and wishing you the very best on*
*your birthday. I'll drop your present around to the flat.*
*    Helen x*

It's *Helen* now, not *Mum*.

I can't see her. I can't. I can't bear to see the pity and revulsion in her eyes. It's guilt that brings her here, twice a year, on my birthday and at Christmas. The cards are only ever signed by her.

*I know we made a commitment to you but that was on condition that . . .*
*    If we'd known . . .*
*    We're not capable of providing for your needs . . .*

Jeanie and Tom were capable. I stayed with them for two years. Jeanie taught me to knit, Tom took me fishing. They said they would have adopted me if they hadn't been too old. I said I didn't care how old they were. But Tabby cared. She said they might not be there for me during the most important periods of life, like leaving home, getting my first job, having my first relationship. Turns out she was right. Tom had a heart attack a few months after I left and Jeanie's in a home with Alzheimer's now. You would have liked them, Abe. I can still smell the scent of Tom's fingers as he tucked me in: soil and cigars. I used to beg him to stop smoking but he said he was too old to change.

Nobody's too old to change. I changed. I was better, because of you. I didn't need to rely on pills with you in my life. I was so happy I threw them away.

But now I need them. Now . . . this card . . . I can't think straight. My blood is racing. My vision is all blotchy.

If I think about you, about us, it will make me feel better.

For days and days I kept wearing the rain dress, in case I saw you, but eventually it got too smelly under the arms. I realised then that all my clothes were dull and ugly. This is a good sign. In depression questionnaires they always ask if you have lost interest in your appearance, and I had. But now, because of you, I wanted to look pretty.

That Saturday morning I pulled on my jeans and anorak and went down to the charity shop. I had to wait for it to open, stamping my feet in the cold because the sun was still down behind the buildings.

Eventually the fat lady who runs it came waddling up and we went in together and she let me look around while she set everything up. She trusted me, even when she was in the back room, which was nice. I was tempted by a cocktail dress in iridescent navy taffeta. Perhaps if I wore it with a jumper and boots it wouldn't look too over the top.

72

While I was deliberating the old lady from the ground floor came in and she started oohing and aahing over it, so I put it back and went to the blouses section. I was lucky: there was a lacy white top in my size, from a shop I would never have been able to afford normally. I tried it on in the tiny cubicle. The curtain didn't fit properly and the old lady peered in and announced that it really suited me. I tried to smile but she was making me nervous. I wanted to bolt from the shop, but I didn't want to leave without the blouse, so I forced myself to take some deep breaths and calm down.

I could feel her eyes on my body as I slipped the blouse off, and I yanked the curtain across and held it while I got dressed one-handed. I thought about saying something about people deserving some privacy, and had wound myself up so much that my heart was hammering when I came out, the blouse balled in my fist. But she was at the back of the shop now, picking through a basket of cheap-looking beads. Under the heavy panstick make-up she was ancient and her gnarled hand gripped a walking stick, so I changed my mind.

'Ooh, lovely,' said the lady at the till. 'Wish I could get into something like that. You're so lovely and slim!'

I forced myself to say thank you even though my face was burning. Then I pointed to the label and added, 'I like that shop but it's so expensive.'

'We do get stuff from them sometimes – the people in the big houses by the station bring them in,' she said. Her name label read *Marion*. 'If I see anything in your size – an eight, is it? – I'll keep them for you.'

'Thank you,' I said. 'That would be really nice.'

After I left the shop, swinging the bag by my side, I felt sort of electrified. Avoiding contact with people is another sign of depression, and there I was making conversation with a complete stranger. See what you had done for me already?

The sun was shining and the flat was as warm as toast. I put the blouse on and some lipstick and tied up my hair, and then

I got my new book, which I'd dried out on the windowsill, and went outside. I sat on the bench by the playground and waited.

I didn't know what you did for a living then, but I knew you didn't work on Saturdays. I had seen you coming back from the high road, with a newspaper and a bag from the local bakery. Once I had seen you eating a croissant from the bag, so I knew you weren't having breakfast with anyone, which meant you might be single.

The children came out and wanted me to time them as they tried to do the mini assault course, and we were all laughing our heads off because one of the big boys got stuck in the baby swings when a voice said, 'Aren't you cold?'

I was glad you had found me like this, laughing with the children, my cheeks pink from the wind. Out of the sun it was freezing and I wasn't sure how much longer I could have lasted.

You looked terrible, tired and hollow-eyed, with a rash around your mouth. I wanted to put my arms around you and look after you.

'Oh, I don't feel the cold,' I said, trying not to shiver.

'Lucky you! I was going to get a paper, but I don't think I can face it.'

'I'll get it for you,' I said. 'I was heading that way anyway. I need to get milk. The *Guardian*, is it?'

'Is it that obvious?'

'I can push it under the door.'

'No, no, no.' You were shivering under your thin jacket. 'Don't. Borrow some of my milk.'

It was so tempting to share the same carton you had used, but I wanted to do this thing for you.

I smiled. 'It would be a pleasure.'

'You're an angel,' you said, closing your eyes and letting your long dark eyelashes rest on your cheek. 'If you really don't mind, then I think I'll go back to bed.'

I watched you jog back to the door, hunched against the cold, but you didn't turn back.

'Time *me* now!' one of the little boys cried, but I was already halfway to Gordon Terrace.

After I'd pushed the paper under your door, which I had to do in sections because there was so much of it, I waited for a while outside my flat, with my key poised, so that if you came out to thank me it would look as if I was just on my way back in. But you didn't come out. I imagined you curled up in your bed, all warm and musty-smelling from sleep. I imagined myself curled up behind you, my arm around your waist, my face in your hair.

Later on I found a folded piece of paper pushed under my door. It was a biro drawing of an angel with a little heart over its head.

For the rest of the weekend I couldn't stop smiling.

After that day I never took another pill. I never needed to. I woke up with a song in my heart, literally. All the songs I'd learned when I was little came flooding back to me. Songs about love and trust, perfect days and endless nights. Just cheesy pop songs really, but suddenly every word meant something.

I still feel the same Abe. Even now. Even in the hospital, watching you struggle to breathe, watching the machine pump air into your lungs.

It's a perfect day because I'm spending it with you.

# 9. Mags

Flat Eleven is silent. As silent as Flat Twelve, though I know that Jody's in there. What's she doing? Listening, like me?

I breathe as quietly as possible, though my lungs are burning from the long climb carrying the load of folded laundry, still hot from the drier. I thought about dropping it back at the flat, but changed my mind. If I speak to them with it tucked under my arm my questions will seem more casual. *I was just passing and thought I'd introduce myself . . .*

I haven't hit any of the light switches on the way up, and the floor and walls are crazy-paved with colour from the stained-glass window. The brass latches of the doors gleam red from Jesus's cloak. The stairwell is a yawning chasm behind me. Again I feel its pull: a dark pool I can dive into and lose myself forever.

Did Abe feel the same? Was he incapable of resisting? Or did something else happen? I try to imagine his slim fingers digging into Jody's collarbone. It seems so out of character from the boy I knew, who was so self-contained, so restrained. I never knew him express any emotion, barely ever saw him smile. But I suppose he was as fucked up as I was, pushing everything down to stop himself getting hurt. Who knows what his personality was really like under there? Once that lid, so tightly wedged on, was allowed to come off, did he become a monster?

I think of the handwriting on the Christmas card and the security panel downstairs. Small and neat, but pleasantly looping; surely not the handwriting of a bully. But what do I know? I know nothing about him. Only that we have the same taste in shoes and coffee.

The light on the ground floor goes on and I hear one of the flat doors close. Then a rhythmic tapping begins, like bones clacking together. My brain throws up an image of a skeleton shuffling across the concrete and I can't stop myself looking over the banister. A woman with a stick is making her painful way across the foyer to the door.

And then it's as if she feels me looking. She stops, and her head tips back.

When our eyes meet she starts, and her stick clatters to the floor.

Her reaction so unnerves me that I shrink back from the banisters, breathing heavily.

Agonisingly long minutes later the tapping resumes, then the outer door closes and silence falls.

The light ticks off and I stand in the dim puddles of colour, my heart pounding.

The place is playing tricks with my mind, bringing back all those fight or flight impulses from my childhood.

I force myself to calm down, employing the techniques I had to use when I was first called to the bar. Jackson would laugh if he could see me now, sweating and trembling in the dark like a child after a nightmare. My clients would be panic-stricken, my opponents in court would rub their hands with glee: the iron bitch finally brought low.

Eventually my heartbeat is back to its normal rhythm and I tap on the door of Flat Eleven.

Minutes pass, and then I hear a soft rustling behind the door. Someone is there. I tap again and the rustling stops sharply.

'Hello?' I say, as quietly as possible. 'I'm your new neighbour. Just come to say hello.'

I glance at Jody's door with its black spyhole. Is she standing behind it also? A church full of whispering and listening, everyone watching everyone else for signs of sin.

The door opens.

It's the Muslim woman I saw earlier.

'Hi,' I say and stretch out my free hand. 'I'm Mags, Abe's sister. From number ten.'

We shake, stiffly. Her eyes are alert, darting around nervously, seeing if anyone's behind me. It makes the hair at the back of my neck bristle.

'I am sorry for what happened to your brother,' she says. 'He was a good man.'

I don't pick her up on the past tense.

'Could I come in?'

Her face blanks. 'I am sorry but . . .'

'Just for a moment,' and before she can stop me, I step over the threshold.

She holds up her hands. 'But . . .'

I press on and, as if fearful of my touch, she backs up against the wall.

The inner door is open and I walk briskly up the corridor and into the flat, where Jody is less likely to be able to hear us.

A vivid blue line slashes across the carpet. It's caused by the afternoon sun shining through the robe of the woman in the stained-glass window that rises up from the floor. Around her head is a yellow disc and it takes me a moment to realise that the smaller disc, at her shoulder, must belong to the Baby Jesus, separated from his mother by the ceiling of the flat below.

This flat is at the back of the church and directly below the window is a small, empty car park. The place has the damp, heavy smell of boiled vegetables.

A naked light bulb dangling from the centre of the ceiling goes on. The woman stands in the doorway, her eyes wide with alarm. I should not have done this to her. She's clearly new to this country and though she knows what I've done isn't right, she doesn't know how to go about making me leave.

I smile, partly to reassure her that I mean no harm, partly to make her think this is all perfectly normal.

78

The flat is spotlessly clean and tidy, but all that does is emphasise its bleakness. They don't seem to have added anything to the original cheap furniture provided by the housing association, aside from a paisley throw on the back of the burgundy velour sofa, and a couple of mountain scenes on the wall.

A pair of furry slippers and some cement-encrusted workboots are lined up neatly by the door. I wonder why she doesn't put the slippers on since the flat is so cold, but her feet are bare.

'Sorry, what was your name?' I say.

'Mira.'

'Mira. Hi.' I try and think of a compliment, but there is nothing positive to say about her home. Even the view is dreadful. Above the car park the sky is a flat November grey. The wind whines through a cracked windowpane.

She watches me warily, as if afraid I will make some sudden movement. I may as well get to the point.

'I was just wondering,' I begin slowly, 'if you'd heard anything the night my brother fell. Any raised voices? My brother shouting, perhaps?'

Her face closes up at once. I kick myself. If there was anything to reveal she won't tell me now.

'Sorry, but English not good. Do not understand.'

*Like hell you don't.*

I try turning on the waterworks, screwing up my face and looking away. 'It was such a shock. I just want to know what happened. For our parents' sakes.'

This usually works with Europeans, who worship at the altar of *The Family*.

'I very sorry but I not hear anything.'

*So, your English isn't all that bad then.*

'Didn't you go out of the flat to see what was going on?'

She hesitates.

'It's just that someone saw you,' I hazard. 'From downstairs. They thought you might have seen what happened.'

Her eyes flash with something. Could it be fear? Has she come from a country where you are always being watched, and if someone reports you, you might be taken away and never seen again?

'Maybe they were mistaken,' I add.

'There was no one else. Just your brother and the girl.'

'Jody.'

She nods.

'What made you go outside? Did you hear something?'

'The girl screaming.'

'Jody?'

Another nod.

'You didn't hear any shouting before that? Any sounds of an argument?'

As she shakes her head her eyes slide away from mine, but I cannot think of a reason why this woman would lie for Jody. Evidently she doesn't even know her name.

'What about your husband? Could he have seen something?'

'He is at the gym then pub. All night. He sees nothing.'

'What gym?'

'Stone's Boxing Club.'

She seems tired, and as she leans back against the wall her robe settles against her stomach. She's pregnant. No wonder she was scared when I pushed past her. I shouldn't have come.

'I'm sorry,' I say, 'to barge in like this.'

'It's OK. You are upset about your brother.'

'I think he was depressed.'

'Yes. It must be that. He seemed always very sad.'

'I'll leave you to rest.'

I pass back along the darkened hallway and pause at the front door. 'What are you hoping for?' I gesture to the bump.

'A boy, of course,' she says. 'Like everybody.'

'Not me,' I say. 'I'd want a girl. I'm a feminist.'

As she laughs her faces alters, like the sun coming out. 'Not many of these in Albania.'

As Mira closes the door I walk to the banister and try to imagine what she would have seen as she emerged from her flat that night. Jody running down the stairs, screaming for help, my brother splayed out on the concrete far below, in a halo of blood.

An overweight woman is puffing up the stairs, carrying a glittery gift bag that sparkles in the light from the second-floor lamp. I head for Abe's flat and am just turning the latch when the woman puffs out onto the landing. Before I can go inside Jody's door opens.

'Hello, darling,' the woman says warmly. 'I've come to give you your birthday present!' As she waggles the bag the light goes off and we are plunged into the habitual red-stained gloom.

I pause at the door to see if Jody will introduce us before she invites the woman in. She does neither. In fact, she says nothing, and doesn't even reach to take the proffered bag.

'There's a cake that Tyra made. Chocolate and orange. She reckons it's her signature dish!' The woman gives a bubbly laugh, seemingly unfazed by Jody's taciturnity. I retreat into the flat and close the door, though I can still hear the conversation that follows perfectly clearly.

'How is everything?'

'Fine,' Jody says.

I wait to hear if she will elaborate, tell her friend about Abe's prognosis, but either she has already told the woman, or doesn't want to.

'You're eating OK?'

'Yes.' There's a spike of irritation in Jody's voice that I haven't heard before.

'Everything in the flat working?'

Presumably Jody nods.

'Can I come in?'

'It's a bit of a mess,' Jody says. 'Another time.'

There's a silence, then the woman says, 'You've lost weight. Are you taking your pills?'

'I don't need them any more.'

Another silence. I imagine the woman sighing unhappily. She seems very maternal, an aunt by marriage perhaps. What pills was Jody taking? I wonder.

81

'Is there anyone you can spend the evening with, so you're not on your own on your birthday?'

'I'm fine,' Jody says.

'Why don't you come round to ours for supper? Kieran's got a friend over, but the more the merrier. We'll all squeeze in somehow.'

'I'm fine. Honestly. I'll just have an early night.'

'Well, OK. You pamper yourself tonight then, sweetie. You deserve it. And call me if you need anything.'

'OK.'

'Promise?'

'Yes.' She sounds so sad. 'Thanks for the present.'

'It was a pleasure.' There's a whispering rustle, as if the woman has leaned to kiss Jody, and then the door closes and the woman's footsteps descend the stairs, faster on the way down than they were on the way up.

I head for the kitchen and unplug Abe's phone.

Even though I'd expected it, I'm disappointed to find a lock code. I try a few numbers – his birthday, Jody and his flat numbers – but eventually it locks me out completely. Because it's an iPhone it'll probably be encrypted, so I won't even be able to get the dodgy shop on the high road to have a look at it. Texts between him and Jody might have revealed if there were any problems in their relationship.

Tossing the phone in a drawer I make myself a coffee, then sit by the window and watch the children playing outside. The sun is starting to go down and I can feel the cold seeping through the glass. Gradually each child peels away, until one little boy is left alone on the roundabout. He looks Somalian and can be no more than four or five. The roundabout revolves slowly, casting his long shadow onto the scrubby grass. Then some youths climb over the low railing that keeps out the dogs, and go right up to him. Their hoods are pulled up and smoke coils around their heads from the joint they're passing back and forth. I'm too far away to see his expression. Is he scared? Should I go down there?

82

Call the police? I knock back the last dregs of coffee. Perhaps if I just come out of the building it will make them leave him alone.

But I'm too late. One of the youths stretches his arm out. The boy takes it and is pulled to his feet. They move towards the railing, with him trapped between them. But he has left his jacket on the roundabout. Then suddenly he breaks away, running back the way he had come. The youth that pulled him up turns to go after him. It is a Somali girl. The boy retrieves his jacket from the roundabout, then runs back to the group. The girl pulls him up on her hip and he lets his head settle on her shoulder, then they pass out of my sight.

It was just his sister come to collect him. I'm letting my imagination run away with me. It must be stress. I go into the kitchen and look through Abe's booze collection for something to calm me down. As well a four-pack of lager and some hard spirits – I'm not at that stage yet – there are a few bottles of red wine. I open an own-brand Beaujolais and pour myself a glass.

As I drink, the last rays of the sunset throw an amber wash over the grass and the terrace beyond.

It's Jody's birthday, and her fiancé lies in the hospital at the edge of death.

How could I have imagined she had pushed him over the banister? She's so slight even Abe could have fought her off. Abe, who never in our whole childhood laid a finger on – or even raised his voice – to anyone. Mira heard no sounds of an argument, just the screams of my brother's lover as she ran down to try and put the pieces of his head back together.

*Damn.*

I promised myself I'd make more of an effort.

Jody takes so long to come to the door I think she must have gone out or fallen asleep but finally, when I have started down the stairs, she opens it.

'Oh, hey,' I say. 'I was just popping out for groceries and I wondered if you were doing anything tonight.'

Her face is in shadow. I thought I could manage without hitting the light switch, but now I wish I had.

'It's just that I couldn't help hearing that it's your birthday.'

I wait for a response. Eventually she takes a great inhalation of breath, as if she hasn't breathed for hours. 'Yes,' she says. 'Twenty-five. What a granny, eh?'

'Would you like to come round to mine – well, to Abe's – for dinner? I'd love some company.'

'Are you sure?' It's too dark to see her expression.

'Of course. I'm a pretty shit cook but I might be able to rustle up pasta and pesto.'

'That would be lovely.'

'OK, great. What colour do you drink?'

'Sorry?'

'Wine. Red or white. Or pink?'

'Oh, I don't really drink much.'

So, I was wrong about the drunken row.

'Champagne, then. Tonight, we're going to forget our troubles and celebrate, OK?'

She gives a breathy laugh. 'OK, but it'll go right to my head.'

'Excellent. I love a cheap date.'

We arrange for her to come round at eight and I head down the stairs and out of the building. The wind has dropped, but the door still slams shut when I let it go. Experimentally I open it again and this time I hold it as it closes, slowing the momentum right down, until the latch is touching the edge of the door. But when I let go it shunts into place at once. Unless someone's fixed it since the accident there would never be any need to check this door was closed properly. And yet Abe managed to convince Jody that this was exactly what he was going down to do.

I sigh and zip my coat up. Not every tragedy is a crime. And maybe a sudden death always leaves unanswered questions. Abe told her he was going to check the door to get her out of the way. So she didn't think to question him about that. She's not a lawyer, and what the hell does it matter now anyway?

As soon as I step out of the shelter of the building I wish I had worn more layers. It very rarely hits freezing in Vegas, but here it must be a few degrees below. I walk quickly to warm myself up, stumbling over the bumps on the path. Beyond the path of light formed by St Jerome's security light meeting the flickering street lamps of Gordon Terrace, all is darkness.

The wind has dropped, so I hear the rustle quite clearly.

It could be a cat. Or a fox, or a rat.

I think of the gangs Derbyshire mentioned and quicken my steps. I've just reached the relative safety of the terrace that leads on to the high road when my phone rings. An English number, so it can't be the office. Could it be the police? I frown, let it ring, then on the last ring before it goes to voicemail I pick up.

'Mags?'

'Yes.'

'It's Daniel.'

I stop. A man is coming out of one of the nearby houses, so I feel safe enough to pause here. The traffic on the high road will be too noisy to hear him properly. 'How did you get my number?'

'The hotel. But don't blame them; I was pretty sly wheedling it out of them. I just . . . I wanted to say hi, and find out how your brother is.' He continues quickly, 'I figured you might not have a chance to call me, and I thought I'd probably get your voicemail actually and was just going to leave a message. Sorry if it's a bad time.'

This is brave of him, considering how I treated him at the hotel. It deserves some courtesy.

'It's fine. It's good to hear from you. I'm just on my way to the shops. I've moved into my brother's flat.'

'How's he doing?'

'Not great.' I pause as a souped-up turquoise Ford Escort with a spoiler starts up opposite me. The pasty-faced guy at the wheel gives me a leering smirk, then pulls away at ridiculous speed only to come to a jarring halt at the junction.

'There's been a lot of damage to the brain stem. He's basically brain-dead.'

He inhales. 'Mags, I'm so sorry.'

'It's fine. Really. I mean, not for his girlfriend, she's really cut up about it, but I hardly knew him – as an adult – so I can't pretend to be, you know . . .'

'You'd be surprised. It might hit you later. I only started grieving properly for my dad in my twenties and he died when I was twelve.'

'I *would* be surprised. I'm sorry about your dad, but this is different. We were never close. I can't pretend to have feelings just because I'm supposed to.'

There is an awkward silence, which I'm about to break by saying goodbye, when he says, 'If you want to talk about it over a drink sometime, this is my number.'

The guy has serious balls, or else he's too stupid to know when he's on to a bad thing.

'I might do that.'

He laughs, knowing full well that I'm just feeding him a line, which makes me laugh too. 'No, really. I might. Before I head back home.'

'I'll be waiting by the phone.'

'You do that. See you real soon.'

He laughs at my comedy Vegas drawl, then hangs up. I'm still smiling as I go into the Food and Wine.

It's even darker by the time I make my way back and I find myself wishing I'd just brought my cash card, rather than the entire wallet bulging out of my jeans pocket. Several of the street lights on Gordon Terrace are out of order and the weeds in the front gardens are dense enough to conceal an adult male. Most of the windows are dark, and those that aren't radiate a cold glare from eco light bulbs hanging from the ceiling. No luxuries like mood-lighting here. It's almost a relief to reach the end of the street, but then the waste ground opens up before me, the path a bridge of light across a sea of darkness.

I take out my phone and shine the torch app into the gloom. Its pathetically weak beam just manages to pick up the weave of the metal fence, then a pair of yellow eyes flash from the darkness.

I start back, ready to bolt.

But it's just a cat. With impossible agility it claws its way up and over the fence and disappears.

Can it really have been sitting there all that time?

Without pausing to ponder this, I hurry down the path towards St Jerome's, now a jagged black shape cut out of the light-polluted sky.

There are lights in a couple of the windows, including Flat One, and as I approach the main door I'm sure I can make out a face behind the veil of netting. Despite the bitter wind racing around the building, I stop and stare.

A hand reaches forward and pulls the curtain aside.

She must be in her eighties or nineties. Her face is a ruin, folds of sagging, wrinkled flesh clogged with thick make-up, like a horror film clown. I wonder if this is a joke: kids trying to scare the newbie, but then the red slash of a mouth curves into a smile and the clawed fingers bend. She's waving at me.

I can't help it – I run the last few feet to the door.

Thoroughly on edge, I can't even wait for the door to shut by itself and pull it closed with a bang that echoes around the building. The stretch of grass outside the little wire-mesh window is so black I wouldn't see anyone's approach until their face loomed up against the glass. I hammer the light switch and my own scared face jumps into the window.

Forcing myself to turn away (*calm the fuck down, Mags*), I blindly go through the post on the table. The banality of this activity eventually tricks my brain into thinking all is well. My heart settles back to its usual rhythm. I stuff the few bits of direct mail for Abe into the carrier bag and pass through the inner door to the stairwell.

# 10. Jody

Why did I say yes?

I crouch by the door after she's gone downstairs, trying to pluck up the courage to run out and call after her that I've changed my mind, that I'm sick, or tired, but then the front door slams and it's too late.

Maybe it won't be so bad. The card upset me, but thinking about you made me feel better, and it might be nice to have some company on my birthday. I get so lonely without you, Abe.

I remember my last birthday, in the bedsit. The girl next door tried to get me to take drugs with her. It was kind of her, really, because she had to do all sorts of horrible things to get the money for her own habit. That's why I've never taken drugs, even though sometimes I want that oblivion so much. I know what it costs.

I don't drink much either. The smell of alcohol brings back horrible memories. Plus it makes you say things you wouldn't otherwise. It makes you give things away that you shouldn't.

It will be so good to be back in your flat again. I can stand your sister's sharp eyes and loaded words for a while, just to be close to your things again. Perhaps I can bring home another memento.

She might be nicer, now that the shock is subsiding. I want her to like me, Abe, of course I do. She's part of you. I'll bring her something. A present. That's what people do when they go to someone's house for dinner, isn't it? Chocolates or wine. But I don't want to go out again now that it's getting dark.

When the front door gives its characteristic squeak and slam, I get to my feet and creep to the spyhole.

A minute later she comes trudging up the stairs with a clanking carrier bag. She looks pale and drawn. At the top of the stairs she pauses, gazing down the stairwell as the lights on each floor click off one by one. Then suddenly she looks right at me and I am pinned to the spot by your dark eyes.

I know she can't see me through the spyhole. I made Tabby test it out with me when we first got here, but even so I can't move or breathe until the fourth-floor light clicks off and the landing is plunged into darkness.

I hear her letting herself into your flat and the door closing, then she turns on the hall light.

It still lifts my heart to see that line of yellow beneath your door.

I go into my bedroom and put on the rain dress, tying my hair up the way you like it. I even put make-up on, and when I look in the mirror another face looks back at me. A face I can hide behind.

# 11. Mags

The pasta is bland and gritty. I have to add far too much of Abe's rock salt to make it palatable, and then I grate half a packet of parmesan over it and leave it covered with a plate to keep warm while I heat up the garlic bread. I haven't eaten like this since university. At home I mostly get takeouts, or else I'm dining out. Sushi, usually, or Thai. My tongue pricks at the thought of wasabi and Szechwan pepper. I wonder if Jackson's out with a client, or one of the other partners. His favourite restaurant is an Aussie fusion place on the strip. Last time we went I had tuna tartare with yuzu dashi, and a bottle of saki. We laughed so much that the next day I felt like I'd done fifty sit-ups. The sudden longing I feel to be beside him takes me by surprise. Could I be a bit in love with him? Or is it just home-sickness? I should be careful. He's made no secret of his attraction to me, but he's married, with two adult kids from his last marriage, and twin seven-year-old boys from this one. Plus I'm not in the least attracted to him. He's wiry and muscular from his daily sessions with the personal trainer, he works on his tan, and I'm pretty sure he's had a brow lift. I like my men more natural, a little less prissy about their clothes and weight and 'skin regime'. Like Daniel, I suppose. Poor old Daniel. He just caught me at a bad time. I knock back my first glass of wine. Poor old me.

There's a Bose speaker on the kitchen window so I go in search of an MP3 player and eventually find one in a drawer. Some of the bands I don't even recognise – British ones, I assume, who haven't made it over the Atlantic. But there's one female singer who's as big back home as she is here. Her voice is low and smoky, and if you listen too closely to the lyrics when you've had too much to drink they'll make you cry. Abe's got all her albums. I programme them to run on a loop and plug the player into the speaker. The voice washes over me, warm and rich as melted chocolate, and I'm just tipsy enough to sway my hips.

According to the microwave it's 20:00 on the dot when Jody rings the buzzer. The echoes reverberate through the flat, and I imagine all my neighbours' flats.

She is wearing a grey tea dress sprinkled with clear plastic beads. Its ruffled sleeves are starting to fray where the overlocking has unravelled. Her hair is tied up, with curling fronds left to dangle by her ears, and her frosted pink lipstick suits her pallid colouring. For the first time I can see that she is pretty. My sour brain adds, *if you like that 'feminine' look.*

'You look lovely,' I say, feeling, absurdly, as if I'm on a date.

'I brought you this.' She hands me a tiny velvet pouch and stands in the hall, watching me expectantly. I tip it out onto my palm. It is a tiny silver fairy for a charm bracelet.

'Thanks,' I say.

'It's a guardian angel,' she says.

I smile. 'Sweet. Come on through.'

I put the charm in my pocket and forget about it immediately.

As well as a couple of wine boxes, I've splashed out on some Veuve Cliquot – for myself more than Jody. The diminutive Indian shop assistant had to get a set of stepladders to reach it down from on top of the soft drinks fridge, where it must have been gathering dust and grease for years. Jody ducks as I pop the cork and it pings off the metal lampshade over the table.

'Happy birthday.' I clink her glass. 'To absent friends.'

91

Surprisingly enough, it's drinkable. I close my eyes and think of the warm crush of gallery openings and awards ceremonies. Abe would have fitted in perfectly back home; he could have been PA to a producer or, if caring really was his vocation, some ancient celebrity. He might have been left a house down in Malibu. We could have stood by the ocean sharing a bottle of bubbly, toasting our astonishing survival, our success despite the odds.

But only one of us survived.

I moved the flowers from the bedside table to the dining table and now I thank her for them.

'Where on earth did you get them?'

'I . . . Abe did. He picked them from a client's garden.'

'Oh, right. They've survived well, haven't they, since the accident? They look so fresh. Thanks for topping up the water.'

Another beat, then a smile. 'That's OK.'

I pour the remains of the champagne into my glass then go to the kitchen for a box of white. I like to have alcohol close to hand, like a security blanket.

'So, you were talking to Mira earlier,' she says when I come back to the table. Her face is open and guileless; does she know I was checking out her story?

'I just wanted to introduce myself.'

'When that baby arrives it's going to keep the whole place awake.' Jody smiles wistfully. Her baby dreams have been dashed along with the marriage ones.

'They're Albanian, aren't they? How come they got to live here?'

'I think they're Roma. Roma people get persecuted in some of those countries, don't they?'

'I thought Roma didn't like to stay in one place. Aren't there supposed to be special sites set aside for them?'

Jody shrugs. 'I don't really know. They're pretty quiet.'

'What's he like?'

A look of distaste twists her mouth. 'I stay out of his way and he's never around much anyway. He's a builder I think. Never speaks. I don't even know if either of them speak English.'

'She does,' I say. 'Quite well, actually. She understood words like *depressed* and *feminist*.' I don't add that I still can't work out what possible reason she would have to pretend not to speak English.

Jody's staring at the flowers. She doesn't seem interested in her next-door neighbours, or perhaps she's jealous that I'm meeting new people.

Feeling my gaze she gives an almost imperceptible start.

'Sorry. It's the flowers. It's funny, but I remembered them being yellow.'

I shrug. 'Maybe they change the longer they bloom or something.'

I have no idea what I'm talking about. The only living thing to grace my terrace in Vegas is a small and boring-looking cactus that was there when I moved in and has *never* been watered.

Hoping the conversation will become less stilted by a change of subject, I ask whether there's a park nearby for jogging. Any weight I put on here will be trebled when I get back to the land of size-zero gym bunnies and I must be sinking several thousand extra calories a day on booze. But I daren't go to bed sober, for fear of what my brain will throw up for me.

'There's a square at the end of the high road, but it can be dodgy after dark. I think men use it, gay men, for uh . . .'

'I'll be careful not to slip.' I smile.

In the time it takes Jody to finish her champagne, I've sunk two more glasses of white. When I try to refill her glass she puts her hand over the top, but I talk her into a wine and orange juice. It'll be good for her to get drunk. Already I can see her loosening up. Her cheeks are pink and there's a sheen of sweat on her top lip. I've turned the heating up to thirty degrees so that I can walk around in my vest and bare feet like I do at home.

'So, tell me how you met,' I say. 'You and Abe.'

She twists the ring on her finger and smiles coyly. 'Oh, you know, we were neighbours so we used to run into one another.'

'Come *on*,' I say. 'Give me the whole juice. Who made the first move?'

'Well, he actually saved my life.'

It's not as dramatic as it sounds. Apparently Abe came and put out a fire she'd managed to start while cooking sausages.

'Wow,' I say, when she's done, 'I never took Abe for an action hero.'

She doesn't reply to this and I fear I might have offended her by sounding dismissive of her big love scene.

'I left home very young,' I say quickly. 'We didn't really get the chance to get to know one another as adults. He must be different now.'

'That's so sad,' she murmurs. Then she says, 'I grew up in a care home, actually.'

I raise my eyebrows.

'My dad was in the forces. He was killed when I was seven, and then my mum killed herself a year later.'

I am riven with shame at my own self-pity. 'Jody . . . I'm so, so sorry.'

'It's OK. They loved me, and they loved each other.'

'Too much, maybe.'

She frowns again. 'You can't love someone too much.'

'Your mother owed it to you to carry on,' I say, 'after his death. It wasn't fair on you to do what she did.'

Jody shakes her head. 'She was sick.'

I wonder how much of that sickness Jody has inherited. She must be here because of the upbringing in care, but I wouldn't be surprised if there's some mental illness at play too. She seems so fragile, though given what has happened to the man she loves, I suppose it must take formidable strength of character even to get up in the morning. Unbidden, Daniel pops into my head. The way he looked when he said goodbye at the hotel, the expression of bewildered hurt. I wish I had been kinder. I find that I'm glad his number is now on my phone.

'What was it like?' I say. 'Growing up in care?' Looking back, Abe and I would have been better off, but no one would ever have believed us if we'd asked for help. We were on our own and we knew it.

'I was happy enough.'

She sips her wine with the delicacy of a bird dipping its beak into a flower. I reassess my assumptions about her again. To have survived the death of both parents and an upbringing in care, she must be pretty resilient. I wonder if it was his depression that drew her to my brother, the bird with a broken wing. Classic white-knight syndrome. She wanted to save him because she couldn't save her mother.

She lays her glass down. 'My aunt, Helen, was supposed to be my legal guardian. It was in my parents' will. After they died I moved in with her and her husband for a while, but then they changed their minds. Their son was a drug addict and she said it would be too difficult.'

'Shit.' The wine has slowed my thoughts and I can't think of anything else to say.

She smiles. 'But let's not talk about sad things. You wanted to know about Abe and me. Shall I tell you about our first night together?' Her face is flushed. Christ, she really is pissed.

'Well, only if you're . . . umm . . .'

'It was here. On the roof.'

Automatically I glance up at the ceiling. 'You can get up there?'

'There's a door at the end of the landing. Abe took us up to watch the sunset. It was . . . it was beautiful.'

'Enough,' I say, holding up my hand. 'I think you might be about to give me too much information.'

She giggles. 'No, I meant *the sunset* was beautiful. If he . . .' She inhales. 'If he dies I'll go back up there and wait for him.'

I swallow my mouthful too fast and cough. 'You mean his *ghost*?'

She nods guilelessly. 'If you were going to come back, wouldn't you come back to the place you were happiest?'

'I have no idea. I don't know how that sort of thing works. I thought it was all about unfinished business or . . . whatever.'

There's an awkward silence as she gazes down into her wine glass, a half smile on her lips, presumably remembering things I don't want to imagine.

''Scuse me, need a pee.' Getting up from the table I stagger a little and rebound off the sofa on my way to the bathroom.

It's cooler in here and, resting my head against the back wall, I close my eyes to test whether the room's spinning. Not yet. I'm good for another bottle or so. There's an unpleasant crawling sensation at the back of my head as the condensation dribbling down the wall creeps into my hair, so I get up and flush. My neighbours must be getting to know my toilet habits by now, although I'm careful not to flush in the middle of the night, having been woken myself by the nocturnal squeal of ancient plumbing a few times.

As I'm washing my hands my eyes are drawn to the shelf of toiletries – there was something important I needed to ask Jody.

She's staring at the flowers when I emerge, as the smoky-voiced singer croons about lost love.

'Do you know the name of the antidepressants Abe was on? I haven't been able to find any.'

If he ran out that could have been the problem. If so, Jody must take some of the blame herself. She could have spotted the signs.

She shakes her head, blinking.

'Had he been on them long, because some SSRIs have been known to cause suicidal thoughts in young men when they first start taking them.'

Blink. Blink.

'And have you spoken to his doctor since it all happened? I mean, the guy should have been on top of this. Suicide is the biggest killer of young men. We might be able to make a case for medical negligence, and get some compensation. I know it doesn't make up for what happened but these bastards shouldn't be allowed to – oh!'

Jody has spilled her wine all over her dress.

I jump to my feet. 'Quick, take it off and I'll rinse it.'

She gets up too, gathering the sopping hem into a ball around her thighs. 'It's OK, I'll go home and do it.'

'Just get changed and then head back over.'

96

But she's already halfway across the room. 'No, no. It's getting late. I should go to bed.' She stumbles then, like she's walking across the deck of a listing ship, and falls against the bookcase by the inner door. I smile – it's a feeling I know well – but then my smile slips. As her hands jerked up to save herself, the dress rode up and I saw, just for a moment, the unmistakable white scars of a self-harmer.

I look away quickly as she rights herself and weaves off down the hall to the door. 'Thanks for dinner,' she calls back over her shoulder. 'It was lovely.'

'That's OK. Happy birthday!'

She closes the door behind her and her footsteps recede across the landing. Then her door closes, and there's just silence but for the lilting voice of the bereft lover.

Perhaps it's not such a big deal. Self-harming is pretty common among teenagers, especially, I imagine, those who have lost both parents and grown up in a care home. Ah, well, like she says, she's over it all now. Abe saved her.

I sigh and rub my face. See, this is why I don't have relationships. Even if you're lucky enough to meet someone you genuinely care about, someone who feels the same and isn't a complete asshole, as soon as you let your guard down and start to rely on them, then bang! Out of the blue comes some shitty tumour or terrorist attack, or a fall down a stairwell. It's not worth it. You can't miss it if it was never there.

Then I remember I'd meant to ask her for his doctor's name. I've got friends in medico-legal. If someone's fucked up, they will pay. I'll give the money to a charity or something.

I write a note to remind myself in the morning, then set about getting comatose drunk. I know I'll have a shitty hangover, but it's not as if Abe's going to notice, and I stocked up with painkillers at the Food and Wine for just that contingency.

At midnight I decide to call it a day and stagger to the bathroom to clean the black stains off my teeth before bed. There are two faces in the mirror, the second fainter, revolving around the first. I try to hold the gaze of the ghostly pair of brown eyes looking back at me, but it keeps sliding away from me.

'I'm sorry,' I whisper, my voice close in the cramped room. 'I'm sorry that I left you there. I'm sorry that you ended up with another broken person. I'm sorry you're going to die.'

I stumble to bed, relieved I had the foresight to put the sheets back on before Jody arrived, and sink heavily onto the mattress. My limbs are leaden, my brain punch drunk, and sleep hurtles towards me like a freight train.

# Friday 11 November

# 12. Mags

I wake up, completely alert.

Isn't it great the way alcohol kicks you unconscious at midnight only to kick you awake a couple of hours later? A glance at my watch reveals it's barely 3 a.m. Urgh. Turning onto my back I prepare for the tedious slog to dawn. The radio will help numb my brain, but as I reach for my phone to hit the Radio 4 app, my hand stops mid-air.

A noise, close by.

Next-door going to the toilet? Kids messing around outside?

I hear it again. A soft rustle.

Someone's in the flat.

Jody must have a second key. Jesus Christ, she can't keep away. Has she come to dry her tears with his towel or curl up on the sofa they fucked on *just to be close to him*? I'm seriously not in the mood.

I get out of bed and stride to the door. Fortunately it doesn't creak as I yank it open to give her a piece of my mind.

Because standing by the table, his broad shape silhouetted against the window, is a man.

My sharp intake of breath is like paper tearing in the silence.

But he doesn't turn.

I am suddenly aware how short my T-shirt is, how skimpy my knickers. My eyes flick to the hall door. Could I make it before he had the chance to cross the room? But then I would somehow have to get to safety inside one of the other flats, or else run downstairs and out into the night in just my underwear, which doesn't seem any less dangerous.

He turns and my heart jumps into my throat. But he hasn't seen me. He's looking down at something in his hands.

Abe's pea coat.

He must be going through the pockets.

I can hear his stertorous breathing from here – presumably from the stair climb, which means he can't be that fit. I am, or at least was, before I came here and hit the bottle. I might be in with a chance. Without taking my eyes off him, I feel my way along the edge of the kitchen countertop, racking my brain trying to remember which is the knife drawer.

He takes something out of Abe's pocket, his wallet. The guy is big. Not just big – muscular. His torso is a black triangle against the fluorescent sky: broad shoulders, narrow waist, thick neck.

It's not worth the risk. I've seen the youths that hang around this area. They've got nothing to lose. He has the wallet – maybe he'll be happy with that. I should just creep back to bed, call the police once he's gone.

But as I back away my hand brushes the champagne bottle I left on the counter, making it rock.

Clunk, clunk.

His head turns.

I drop to the floor, just in time – I hope – and crouch there on my haunches. The open hall door is blocking my view of the left side of the room, while the kitchen counter blocks the right-hand view. Is he creeping behind the sofa, about to leap out at me from behind the worktop? But now I hear his quiet footsteps moving around the table. If I try and make it to the hall he'll certainly see me. My only option is to hide in the bedroom.

The snick of my bare feet on the kitchen lino makes me wince as I retreat back the way I have come.

I spend fruitless seconds trying to squeeze myself under the bed as all the while the soft footsteps come closer and closer. Then they pause. Has he gone into the kitchen? I have a moment. Should I hide in the wardrobe? No, it's too full. There's nothing for it but to slither under the covers, lie as flat as possible and hope he's already got what he came for. Unless he actually wants to rape or kill someone, there's no reason for him to come in here.

I lie in the darkness, panting.

Where is he?

Standing in the doorway, looking down at my curled body?

My head is at the bottom of the bed and if I lift the duvet slightly I will be able to see the doorway.

I raise it. Through this tiny sliver I can make out the dark oblong of the doorway.

All my senses are on high alert. I can hear the hum of the fridge, a pigeon cooing up on the roof: smell the musty damp blooming on the wall above me.

Little lights are exploding in my strained vision. My heart's pumping so hard my whole body trembles.

Maybe he'll think the noise was just pigeons. Maybe he's already gone.

It's too stifling to breathe and my left leg is buzzing with pins and needles. Can I come out yet? I pull the cover back a little to let in some air.

And then the darkness solidifies and he's there, in the doorway.

Dropping the duvet I press deeper into the mattress, trying to make myself completely flat. But it's no good: he knows I'm here. I can tell by his ragged breaths – not exertion as I had first thought, but arousal.

He's going to rape me.

Should have gone for the knife. *Should have gone for the fucking knife.*

Will he kill me afterwards?

103

As my mind contracts to a single point of terror, I realise that I will do *anything* to stay alive. I will let him do whatever he wants to me. I will beg. I want more life. I'm only half done.

He's coming into the room.

I hold my breath, wide-eyed in the blackness, waiting for the duvet to be flung back.

I hear him walk up the side of the bed then stop.

My heart jumps with hope. Maybe he'll just check the drawers and wardrobe and go. I risk lifting the side of the duvet and see a sliver of pale hand. He's not wearing gloves. Not a professional then. An amateur. In law school they teach you that amateurs are the most dangerous. They're scared and fear makes them irrational, prone to violence.

Should I scream?

But before I can suck in enough air he sits down on the bed.

I freeze, my heart throwing itself against my ribcage.

Is he going to lie down? Is he high and just looking for a place to sleep? Did he think this place was unoccupied?

His back touches my leg.

We both cry out and he springs to his feet.

Throwing back the duvet I scramble off the other side of the bed, snatching up a glass bottle of aftershave from the shelf. But before I can hurl it he shouts something incomprehensible and stumbles from the room. A moment later I hear footsteps retreating down the hallway, followed by the surprisingly quiet snick of the front door, as if, even after all that, he's trying not to be heard.

He's gone.

As I stand there, panting, the glass bottle still raised above my head, I think of everything I could have lost in that moment: my successful life in Vegas, a life of professional and material satisfaction, of clever friends, expensive clothes, fine dining. And suddenly it doesn't seem so much.

Could it be that Jody and Abe, in this shabby little apartment in this grubby city, had something more than me?

104

When I've recovered enough to move, I climb over the bed and wobble to the door. The room beyond is silent, the shadows still. I make my way past the kitchen, turning on the lights as I go, and check the bathroom – empty – then the hallway. Abe's pea coat hangs on the back of the chair. I check the pockets and frown. The wallet has been replaced. I check the front door: closed firmly. No signs of forced entry. Did he have a skeleton key?

Then it occurs to me.

The building manager. José Ribeira.

He offered to get keys cut for me so he must have a master set. I couldn't understand what the guy shouted as he jumped up from the bed – could it have been Portuguese?

I call the police but, even though I'm alone in the house and whoever it was clearly had a key, they won't come over until the morning. When I protest that I may well be in imminent danger they say that it's unlikely that the person will return, but if I'm worried perhaps I could spend the rest of the night with a friend or neighbour.

I'm tempted to tell them where to stick their advice, but it's not a good idea to get on the wrong side of the British police, so I thank them and hang up.

The sofa legs make a horrible screeching noise that must echo through the whole church as I drag it across the floor and force it through the hall door, grunting with effort. It's almost the same width as the corridor and once I've wedged it up against the wall at the end, the door won't open more than a centimetre. Afterwards I sit at the table, huddled under Abe's blanket drinking strong coffee, until the flat light of dawn filters through the stained glass.

But as the tumbler's translucent shadow stretches across the table, I notice something strange.

The white flowers are gone.

# 13. Jody

I can't sleep. Why is she asking all these questions? Is she trying to catch me out? Are the police in on it too? Will she tell them everything I said? They always wanted to punish me for what happened before.

*No no no no no no no no.*

*Nothing* happened before.

Don't think about it.

Think about us.

Our first kiss.

Do you remember?

I've never been much of a cook. At Abbott's Manor all the meals were prepared for you, and in the bedsit I didn't even have a microwave. Besides ready meals, the only things I can really do are Spanish omelettes, which I learned from Jeanie, and lemon drizzle cake, which Helen taught me. But that evening, because my appetite had been so good, I decided to cook myself a treat – sausages and mash. I bought the mash ready-made in a plastic dish to microwave, but when it came to the sausages I decided to grill them. The pack said to prick them to let the fat out but I didn't want it going all over the grill pan, which is hard to clean as the bottom is all black and lumpy, so I put some foil down on the metal rungs, then closed the door and went to read my book for ten minutes, which is how long the packet said to leave them before turning them over.

I'd finished the new book and gone back to one I'd read two or three times before. It was one of those perfect ones you can't put down. The heroine filled with fears and insecurities. Not loads of sex. The path to love strewn with difficulty so that at the end, when they finally get together, you feel like your heart will burst out of your chest and fly up into the sky.

I was so engrossed it took me ages to realise something was wrong. The battery in my smoke alarm's dead, so when the landing one started going off I didn't realise it was anything to do with me. Then I saw the black smoke pouring out of the oven.

I know now what happened. Because the fat couldn't drain away into the bottom of the grill pan, it was too close to the heat and in the end it just caught fire.

The oven door was so hot I burned my hand trying to open it.

You must have heard my scream because a minute later you were banging on my door, asking if I was all right. I was in so much pain I could barely speak. When I didn't reply you started throwing yourself at the door, trying to break it down. That's why the lock's still broken now. I managed to tell you to stop and hobbled over to let you in, still clutching my hand, which had started to blister.

You burst in, wild-eyed. 'What's happened?'

You must have seen the flames licking from the oven, but you seemed more concerned with my hand. Pulling me to the sink, you turned on the cold tap and held my palm under the flow.

'Hold it there,' you said sternly.

Now you went to the oven. The flames were licking almost to the ceiling and in a minute the polystyrene tiles would start to melt. Using the oven glove you managed to pull the grill pan out onto the open door, but the fire didn't go out.

'Tea towel?' you shouted.

'I'll get one.'

'No! Keep your hand under the tap.' Then you started taking off your shirt. 'Wet this for me!' You tossed it to me and I caught the manly scent of fresh perspiration and your flowery deodorant that I liked so much.

I did as I was told.

Grabbing the wet shirt back you threw it over the grill pan and the flames went out at once. You went to the window and opened it, and the air started to clear. Then the smoke alarm stopped, its last ring echoing down through the stairwell.

We looked at each other and then we both laughed.

'Well, that was exciting,' you said.

'I'm so sorry. You've ruined your shirt.'

'Shirts are two a penny. Hands aren't. Let me see.' You came over to the sink, where the water still gushed over my palm. It was the right thing to do. The redness was already going down.

'I've got a burn spray in my flat.'

But you didn't move.

I tried not to look down at your bare chest. There was a tiny speck of soot in one of the narrow shadows made by your ribcage. I couldn't help myself. I licked my finger and wiped it away. I could feel your eyes on mine, your breathing slow and deep. My own heart was beating like a humming bird's wings.

I tried to keep my voice steady, to talk about something mundane.

'Do you think I should tell José?'

'There's been no damage, so only if you want to.'

'I don't want to,' I said.

And then I kissed you.

# 14. Mags

First thing in the morning I call Peter Selby's office and arrange to have the locks changed.

It's gone half past ten when a bored and very young-looking PC arrives to take my statement. She doesn't dust for fingerprints or footprints and doesn't even bother to write down the fact that the flowers are missing.

'So, that's it, then?' I say as she gets up to leave. 'You're not actually going to do anything, are you?'

'As nothing was actually taken . . .'

'Except the flowers.'

'. . . you weren't assaulted, and you've arranged to have the locks changed, we can hope this was an isolated incident. Make sure your door is secure at night, and call us if you experience any more trouble. We'll let you know if we get any leads.'

'Course you will.'

She's too thick or uninterested to pick up on the sarcasm.

Half an hour later there is a knock at my door. A Brazilian guy with neck tattoos introduces himself as José Ribeira. He's wiry and muscular around the shoulders but, I think, shorter than the intruder, plus he smells very pungently of aftershave, which the intruder didn't.

I talk him through what happened and he purses his shapely lips and says I must have been very frightened. When I say not particularly, he gives a gold-incisored grin and says he likes a girl with cahoonas. Despite the weather he is wearing a baggy vest, which shows off his sleek black armpit hair and ripped lats. He reminds me of the pimps that patrol the Strip back home, which makes me like him.

He waits with me until the locksmiths arrive, drinking black coffee and telling me about his cousin who lives in Sacramento, then he gives me his number and makes me promise to call if I ever need anything.

The locksmiths leave me two sets of keys. Apparently this is standard for every flat in the block. It occurs to me that, since I've got Jody's set, and I haven't found any others in the flat, someone else has a set of my brother's keys. I suppose it doesn't matter now that the locks have been changed.

I wonder if Jody's heard the men working. If so, she should have got them to fix her door too. Maybe I should have asked her. I feel guilty enough about it that I don't fancy popping over to ask for Abe's doctor's contact details and so set about calling round the local surgeries.

Abe's not registered with any of them.

A search of the flat unearths a cardboard box full of papers: bank statements and gas bills and salary slips. From these I get the name of the company he worked for – Sunnydale – and a number.

The call handler laughs in my face when I ask if the firm runs a healthcare scheme. I ask to speak to Abe's boss and am put through to a very guarded woman who expresses dry condolences as if she's asking the time of the next bus.

'Was Abe happy in his work?' I say.

'I believe so.'

'Because his fiancée has said that he felt overwhelmed by the workload, to the extent that it brought on depression. Did he mention to you he was struggling?'

There is a long pause, and when she speaks again her tone is even more careful. 'Sunnydale treats staff and patient well-being as its highest priority. Abe made no complaints to us, either verbally or in writing, that he felt stressed or overworked. The caring profession is a challenging one, of course, but whenever he had cause to speak to us, it was with a specific, unexpected problem – turning up to find a client had had a fall, and having to cancel his next client to wait for an ambulance. That sort of thing.'

I stop myself from saying that I thought UK caring company policy for this sort of contingency was to leave them exactly where they landed.

'I must tell you,' I say, 'that if we decide to pursue a court case for, let's say, corporate manslaughter . . .'

She inhales.

'. . . you will be required by law to reveal any correspondence you had with Abe. And there are, of course, ways of retrieving information that has been deleted.'

'I . . .' she stammers. 'We . . . Sunnydale . . .'

'Of course, if you can tell me categorically that Abe never gave you any cause to think he was struggling with his workload, then I'll take you at your word.'

She knows full well that I won't, of course, and I wait for her brain to whirr. Sure enough, she decides to tell the truth – at least, it sounds like the truth and I'm usually a pretty good judge.

'I promise you,' she says, more human now. 'I'm his line manager and he never ever said to me that he was struggling. We would laugh about it sometimes, how crazy it was – I did his job until a couple of years ago – but I really think he liked it. Yes, I really do. Some of his clients were friends.'

I thank her and hang up, then go back to the box in the cupboard and sift through the papers. They don't seem to be in any particular order. His mind was as chaotic as mine when it comes to non-work stuff.

Eventually I find a letter from a 'John Hatfield Clinic' in Camden.

*Dear Mr Mackenzie*
*Your appointment is now booked as per the details below.*

111

*Please arrive ten minutes before the scheduled time. The test will take fifteen to twenty minutes. You do not need to fast beforehand.*

The appointment date was three weeks ago. I sift through the remaining papers looking for the results, but there's nothing.

The letter itself gives little away, just an address, a date, and a cc'd signature from a Dr Indoe.

So, Abe was having tests for something. Was it something serious?

Suddenly I think of the graveyard in our hometown. Full of Mackenzies who'd died young, in their fifties and sixties, some younger. The usual Scottish maladies of heart disease and cancer. At least two aunts died from breast cancer when I was in my teens, and an uncle from bowel cancer. Consequently I've always been paranoid, paying through the nose every year for the west coast's best oncologist to check me over, then ignoring all his advice about cutting down on the booze and upping my fibre. I've been lucky so far, but what if Abe wasn't? What if that was what the Christmas card was all about? Say he got cancer and has been keeping it from Jody to protect her.

Another wave of guilt crashes over me. He had no one to talk to. Could trying to deal with it alone have been enough to push him over the edge?

But this is just guesswork.

I think about calling Jody, but surely she would have told me if she knew. And if not me, then surely the doctors at the hospital.

At a loss, I call the number on the letterhead. There are several options but none of them allows me to speak to a real human being. I won't be able to make an appointment without filling in wads of paperwork, so I end the call, put on my jacket and head out to the bus stop.

The clinic is in a characterless brick building a few minutes from the Tube station. Myriad signs on the way up the stairs tell me to

112

sanitise my hands, to turn off my mobile, to call the Samaritans. I do the first two, then pass through the double doors into the fullest clinic I've ever seen.

The reception desk is manned by a harassed-looking West Indian woman whose neat bun is beginning to unravel, tight black curls pinging out at every angle. When it's my turn I say I'd like to see Dr Indoe. She tells me Dr Indoe's diary is full for the day and I should make an appointment online. I thank her, then while she's distracted with the next person in the queue, slip around the corner to the seats at the end of a corridor of treatment rooms.

When the doctor comes out to call someone through I'll nab her. It's only a quick question after all: what was Abe being tested for and what were the results?

A well-preserved man in his fifties shuffles up to let me sit down. I thank him but he doesn't give me a second glance.

Every twenty minutes or so a doctor emerges to summon someone. They're dressed in normal clothes, with just an ID badge to distinguish them from the patients. After about forty minutes a short, curvy woman of around thirty emerges from a consulting room. She's subtly made-up, her suit trousers and dark green blouse unobtrusively stylish. I wait until I can read her ID badge, then stand to block her path before she can call her patient.

For a moment her eyes are fixed on her paperwork and I wait for her to look up. When she does she gives a little start and tries to get past me. 'Excuse me.'

I block her path. 'My name is Mags Mackenzie. My brother was a patient of yours. Abraham.'

She frowns. Then I remember the photocard in the Oyster wallet. I get it out and show her, and have time to see recognition flash across her face before it's replaced by a guarded blankness.

'He had some tests recently,' I say, slipping the card back into my pocket. 'I'd like to know what they were for.'

'That's confidential, I'm afraid. I would be in breach of our code of ethics. I advise you to speak to your brother—'

'My brother's in a coma.'

113

The hubbub of the reception area dies away as people realise what's happening. Dr Indoe's eyes flick to the desk. The West Indian woman looks back at her.

'He tried to kill himself, Dr Indoe.' I decide to go on the attack, to try and intimidate her into telling me. 'You had a duty of care towards him. Where was the counselling and the support? Where I come from that's called medical negligence.'

Her eyes never leave mine but she makes no attempt to answer me, and now I can hear footsteps echoing up the concrete stairs behind me. *Shit.* She's called security. I'm running out of time.

'Please,' I say urgently as the doors bang open. 'Please tell me what was wrong with him. Was it cancer?'

Her brow furrows for a moment, then she makes up her mind. 'Look around you, Miss Mackenzie. Does this look like a cancer ward?'

I turn. I was so busy watching out for her arrival I didn't pay any attention to my surroundings. Now I see the brightly painted walls are lined with posters. One says *Keep Calm and Carry CONdoms*. Another features a close-up of a woman's knickers printed with the slogan, *I've Got Gonorrhoea*. A third depicts two men kissing and the line *Time You Tested*. The well-preserved man glares up at me from a copy of *Heat*.

I am in a sexual health clinic.

Two burly men stride across the room and position themselves, one on each side of me. 'Time to leave, miss.'

I hold my ground, not taking my eyes from Dr Indoe's face. 'Please tell me. I'm his sister.'

They're about to drag me away when she places a hand on one of their thick forearms. Then she comes very close to me, until I can smell the medicinal freshness of her breath. 'Your brother asked for an HIV test,' she says softly. 'It was negative.'

I am escorted down the stairs and out of the building.

Back in the flat I sit at the table drinking coffee and working my way through a bar of supermarket chocolate I found in a cupboard.

Oh Abe, what have you been up to? Is it as simple and grubby as an affair? Or worse. Have you been visiting prostitutes? Mainlining drugs?

*Fuck.*

I thought he'd be OK. That he'd get out relatively unscathed, like me. If I'd known . . . If I'd known, then what? I'd have given up my shiny new life to come over here and drag him out of whatever shitty mire he'd got stuck into? No. No, I wouldn't. And I wouldn't have expected him to do that for me.

But as I sit there, something niggles me.

When I was as low as I ever got – in the second year of university – my digs were as squalid as a crack house. I had no motivation or energy to keep the place clean. Rubbish stacked up, food rotted in the fridge. The floor was littered with empty booze bottles.

Abe's flat is spotlessly clean and tidy (although that could be Jody's influence) and well stocked with healthy food and the odd luxury. Alcohol, too, but not the strong liquor of a depressive. Reasonable wines and the odd bottle of artisan beer.

And then there are his clothes. The ones in the wardrobe and those the police returned to me.

At my worst I didn't bother with my appearance at all. The clothes I had went unwashed and I certainly didn't buy any new ones. I'd never have thought to apply perfume. Abe was wearing aftershave when he died and, apart from the blood, his clothes looked clean, the combinations of colours and textures put together carefully.

And what about the medical evidence? Where are the sleeping pills, the SSRIs, the doctor's appointments?

I'm sure Jody means well: she's just trying to make sense of what seems like a senseless tragedy, but she never actually *saw* what happened with her own eyes.

I don't know, but it feels to me as if he wasn't depressed. Which leaves me with two options: either he fell by accident or someone pushed him. And if someone did come in after him and attack him when Jody had gone into the flat, then *surely* someone here must have heard something.

There's nothing for it. It's time to introduce myself to the occupants of St Jerome's.

The place is completely silent as I head out onto the landing. I glance at my watch. Midday. I suppose some of them must be at work. But then again, many of them won't be capable of holding down a steady job.

My footsteps are wincingly loud on the steps as I pass down the four flights to the ground floor. I have to steel myself to knock at the door of Flat One – whose occupant has been watching me from the moment I arrived. Standing in the shadows, waiting for an answer, I make out quiet sounds all around me, strands of pop music interwoven with the burble of radios, an odd rhythmic tapping, a flushing toilet, the hum of the washing machines beneath my feet.

When there's no reply after a few minutes I move on to Flat Two, which is opened eventually by a harassed-looking woman with an inch of white at the roots of her hair.

I introduce myself and ask if she saw anything the night of Abe's fall. She says that she was away that evening because her son was on a residential course. I see what has caused the black lines that run all the way down the walls when a disabled boy bumps his wheelchair through the door at the end, and scrapes his way down the too-narrow corridor towards his mother.

'Wait a minute, Dale!' she snaps. 'I'm talking.'

'It's all right. I'm sorry for disturbing you.'

She is closing the door when she sees I am making for Flat Three and calls after me. 'He was sectioned two months ago. I think they're going to relet the flat.'

I thank her and start up the stairs to the first floor.

The occupant of Flat Four takes a long time to answer and when he does it is with an explosion of indignation.

'I work nights! I cannot bear these constant disturbances!'

I can't imagine what night-job vacancies there are for powdered middle-aged queens in silk pyjamas, but when I ask whether he saw anything he practically spits at me.

'Of course I didn't! I was *trying* to get some *sleep*.'

'May I suggest earplugs?' I say, but he slams the door in my face.

There's no answer at Flat Five, though I think that's where the tapping noise is coming from. I move on to Flat Six and, at my knock, am surprised to hear the yap of a dog. A moment later the door is opened by an old man in a shirt and tie. A Yorkshire terrier the size of a kitten scampers around our feet and I lean over to pat its bouncing head.

'Well, hello! And who might you be?'

When I introduce myself as Abe's sister he takes my hand and squeezes it in his warm, dry palms.

'He seemed like a lovely boy. Always had a smile for people. Kept himself nice and smart, not like most of the slobs you get around here.'

I ask if he saw or heard anything.

'I'm afraid not. I was at the care home and by the time I got back the paramedics were here, and that poor girl, crying her heart out.'

'Jody?'

'Sweet thing, isn't she? Brings my post up for me and takes Tessy out when I'm visiting Brenda. That's my wife. Fit as a flea physically, but her poor mind . . .' His voice trembles.

'Ah, well, thanks anyway.'

'You won't get much out of him next door.' He nods towards the door of Flat Five. 'He just plays his organ all day with his headphones on. The queer chap complained when he played out loud, which is a shame really. I liked it. Can you hear his foot tapping?'

He clearly wants to talk, but I thank him and pass on up to the third floor.

The door of Flat Seven is ajar. This is where the pop music was coming from.

'Hello?' I call down the corridor.

'Yeah?' a voice screeches from the depths of the flat.

'Oh hi,' I call. 'I live upstairs. Can I speak to you?'

'Come in then.' The voice is shrill and irritable.

I step across the threshold and recoil from the smell of rubbish and unflushed toilets.

A woman is sitting on the sofa, smoking. She is skeletally thin and her skin is almost as yellow as her hair. She could be anywhere from twenty-five to sixty, and she makes no attempt to hide the track marks on her arms.

I am immediately on my guard. Are we alone in here? If not, will someone attack or rob me? The man who broke in last night? Could he be this woman's pimp? As she bends to stub the cigarette out onto a pockmarked coffee table I dart a glance around the flat. It's filthy but seemingly deserted. On the wall is a single picture: of a smiling baby in a blue Babygro. Embossed into the mount is the name Tyler-James and two dates, separated by an achingly short number of months. No wonder she's a junkie.

A terrible thought occurs to me. Beneath the hollow eyes and sunken cheeks is a ghost of the attractive young woman she must once have been.

Could my brother have been screwing her?

Was that the reason for his HIV test?

'What did you wanna talk about? Not the radio again? If I turn it any lower I won't hear it, will I?'

'I've just moved in upstairs. Did you know my brother, Abe? The man who fell down the stairwell.'

She lights another cigarette and sucks it hard, making the end flare. Her fingertips are brown and cracked. 'Yeah, I knew him.'

As the smoke streams out through her nostrils I try and read some meaning into her words. I know not to push too hard. People like her will clam up unless they think they'll get something by co-operating.

The silence stretches.

'I don't suppose you saw anything,' I say as lightly as possible, 'the night he fell?'

She picks at a scab on her bony knee. Her greasy blonde hair has an inch of black-and-grey roots. 'Weren't even here. Couldn't even get into the building. They thought I was gonna rob stuff. Almost got arrested until that old bag from downstairs come out and spoke up for me.'

'So you didn't hear anything either?'

'What did I just say?' Her head snaps up, then her eyes narrow slyly. 'Is there a reward or something?'

A pause.

'If there was?'

She looks at me for a moment, then she gives a cackle of laughter. 'I still weren't here!'

I get up, resisting the urge to brush the filth from her sofa off my trousers. 'OK. Well, thanks anyway.'

My feet drag on the trudge up to the third floor. I'd prepared myself for disappointment but it's getting me down anyway.

Flat Eight is answered by a swarthy man with a missing arm. Iraqi, perhaps, or Syrian. His eyes are bright and he seems desperate to understand me during our attempts at conversation but in the end I resort to mime.

I roll my arms for the tumble from the floor above, clap my hand to indicate the impact. The sudden splaying of my fingers at the back of my head, to indicate the head injury, makes him flinch.

I place a palm on my heart. *My brother.*

This he understands. His eyes well with tears and he pulls me into an embrace that reeks of stale sweat and nicotine.

Just as quickly he pulls away again.

'Sorry, I sorry . . .' Evidently he has learned that emotional expression is forbidden in the UK.

I point to him, to my eyes, to the stairwell. *Did you see?*

'Blood,' he says. 'I see blood.' That, at least, is a word he knows.

I thank him and move on.

The other two flats are empty so I go back upstairs.

Gazing out of the window at the bleak view I think about the woman in Flat Seven. Like all junkies she is bound to be a liar. *Was* she having a relationship with Abe? Did her pimp have a problem with it and decide he needed to give Abe a warning? A warning that went wrong.

I rub my face and let out a growl of frustration. I'm not getting anywhere. Perhaps there's nowhere to get. Perhaps it's all just as Jody said it was.

But there's one thing I'm sure she's wrong about. Abe wasn't depressed. Not properly, not like I was at uni. He might have been tired, or pissed off, or hating his job, but from what I know of my brother, Abe wasn't the type to do something stupid on impulse just because he was feeling down. Something else happened that night. Something that maybe Jody didn't know anything about. Or some*one*.

Either way it's something Derbyshire should be on to.

# 15. Mira

She is speaking to the police.

I have to put my ear to the bathroom wall to hear properly.

'I don't think Abe had depression,' she says. 'I don't think he jumped.'

There is a silence as she listens. We both listen.

'But he had no symptoms. You're only going by what Jody told you.'

She moves deeper into the flat and I hurry out to the living room and press my ear against the wall behind the television.

'I spoke to his line manager. She said he hadn't complained.'

She listens. I hope the police officer is reassuring her that it was an accident, nothing more.

Then she says, 'What if someone else is involved?'

My bladder loosens.

There is another pause and she says, 'What makes you think they'd say if they *had* seen anything? You can't trust any of them. They're all crazy.' She gives a mirthless laugh. 'You know what? I wouldn't be surprised if it was one of them.'

My legs go so weak I have to lean against the wall to stop me falling. The child starts to kick and I stroke his foot to calm him. *It's all right. It will be all right. I will not let her find out what Daddy did.*

# 16. Mags

When Derbyshire asks me how Abe is, I say, 'Much the same'. The truth is I have no idea. I haven't been back to see him, even though the hospital is barely a mile from St Jerome's. I haven't even bothered to phone to find out if there's been any change in his condition, like a normal sister would do.

Jody, I assume, is there all day, every day. She's never asked me to accompany her. I guess she still considers this intimate time with her fiancé. Or maybe she just doesn't like me. I can't say I'm surprised.

The wind is howling around the building so I put on Abe's parka before I head out.

At the door I pass a woman coming in. I assume she's one of the other tenants, but when I introduce myself she replies, in a strong Polish accent, that she's just a carer, for a Mr Griffin on the third floor.

'Ah,' I say. 'I wanted to speak to him, actually. I wondered if he had seen anything the night my brother fell down the stairwell. Did you hear about that?'

She nods.

'Is Mr Griffin with it enough, you know, in his head, to be able to tell me if he heard or saw something?'

'Is not his head is problem,' she sighs. 'Mr Griffin morbidly obese. Is in bed all time. Cannot get out. If he hears, and this

122

not likely with television – very loud all day, all day – he cannot get up to see what is happen.'

I thank her with a little grimace, and she passes through the foyer into the darkness beyond, a pair of latex gloves waggling at me from her handbag.

There are no cabs out here so I wait at the bus stop, the strip of leg between my trouser cuffs and my Converses getting colder by the second because I haven't worn socks.

By the time the bus arrives there's a crowd of us trying to get on and with no attempt to follow the famous English queue etiquette I only just manage to squeeze in. I'm wedged by an enormous Asian woman in a sari. Her fleshy armpit as she clings to the strap above us is just centimetres from my cheek. It smells of stewing meat.

Eventually I get a seat and stare out of the window, at the filthy shop fronts and broken windows.

On impulse I take out my phone.

'Daniel,' I say, when the voicemail kicks in. 'It's Mags. I don't know if you're still in the UK, but if so I was wondering if you fancied a drink. Or lots of them. I could seriously do with getting shit-faced – and not on my own for once.'

I hang up, then spend the rest of the journey bitterly regretting the message. I sounded completely pathetic – and alcoholic. Hopefully he'll have more sense than to call me back.

Jody is at Abe's bedside, in the middle of a hushed conversation with the fat nurse who doesn't like me. On my approach they immediately stop talking and the nurse waddles off.

I pretend I haven't noticed as I join Jody by the bedside.

Abe's facial swelling has gone down and my brother's features are starting to emerge from the puffed, bruised flesh. At the moment he looks a little like our father, and I want to lift his eyelids to check the irises are brown, not that searing ice blue. I can't of course: I couldn't bear to touch that waxy flesh. Jody has no such qualms. She is stroking his flaccid cheek and murmuring a song into his ear.

I watch her from the corner of my eye. She plays the role of devoted martyr perfectly. Did she know Abe had been busy getting himself an STD behind her back? Or perhaps they enjoyed shooting up together. No, Jody doesn't look like a junkie and there are none of the telltale bruises on her arms. More likely he was having an affair. But surely he could do better than the woman in Flat Seven.

Though if not her, then who?

My phone buzzes. Daniel has replied. I've booked The Ivy for 8. Hope that's OK. Stodgy old British food but fun sleb spotting.

My heart jumps and like a love-struck fourteen-year-old I can't stop myself replying straightaway.

Gr8. See you there, I type, a serious frown on my face, as if it's a professional conversation.

For a seemingly interminable stretch of time we sit there, in a silence broken only by the machines, our breathing, and the rustling of my clothing as I cross and recross my legs.

Jody is staring at my brother's face with such intensity I wonder if she's attempting some kind of telepathic communication.

His eyelashes flutter.

Jody gasps and I admit it's an uncanny sight. I can accept that the lower brainstem being intact means that he can still make reflexive movements, but without any in-depth medical knowledge I can't help wondering why a message would even be sent when all conscious thought is gone.

A sudden and surprising bubble of hope swells in my chest. Perhaps they're wrong, perhaps there will be a miracle. Abe and I will get the chance to know each other again – this is the gift we always needed.

'Abe?' Jody leans across my brother's body, a look of rapture on her face. 'Can you hear me? Give me a sign, my darling. Squeeze my hand if you can.'

He gives no response. Of course he doesn't. He's brain-dead.

But that little futile burst of hope has shifted something in my mind. For the first time, seeing her in the full grip of this self-delusion doesn't inspire contempt in me, but pity.

She has been through so much, been let down by so many people, and now, it seems, even by my saintly brother. I can never tell her my suspicions; she must go on believing this fantasy of the perfect romance. Without thinking, I lay my hand on her arm.

She looks back and smiles at me. 'Did you see?'

I manage to smile back. 'Yes. I saw. I'll go get us a coffee.'

The fat nurse is sitting at her workstation outside the doors. I remember that whispered conversation. Has something happened that they're not telling me? Again that bubble of hope.

'What were you two talking about when I came in?' I say to her.

She opens her mouth and shuts it again.

'I'm his sister. I have a right to know.'

It's clearly distasteful for her to speak to me, and her lips purse so much she can barely squeeze the words through the sphincter of her mouth. 'Jody is very anxious that Abe's life support should carry on for the foreseeable future.'

The bubble deflates. Disappointment brings a rush of anger.

'You can override that, though, even if *I* wanted it too, right? You can go through the courts to get permission if the doctors thought treating him was pointless.'

She looks at me with eyes threaded with burst blood vessels. 'He's your brother, Miss Mackenzie.'

'What's that supposed to mean?'

'Jody loves Abe very much.'

'What, and I don't?'

'Yours is not the typical way of expressing love.'

My hands close into fists at my side. The nurse audibly exhales as I take the side exit out into the memorial garden and stamp up the steps to the pavement that runs alongside the main road. I stand there panting.

*What the hell were you doing making me your next of kin, Abe? Didn't the fact that I left you to Dad's tender mercies tell you that I was a callous bitch?*

I need to go home. I'll book the tickets as soon as I get back to my computer, and Jody can take over with the doctors. Poor,

125

sweet, kind Jody, the saint to my villain, who will at least give Abe a fighting chance at recovery.

I hail a cab and am back at St Jerome's by midday. Letting myself into the main door I glance at the piles of post. There's another sheaf of leaflets for Abe, fastened with an elastic band. But peeping from the garish yellows and reds of the takeaway menus is a corner of white that might be a personal letter. I slide it out.

A blank white envelope. Probably another flyer.

I open it and unfold the single piece of paper.

For a moment I just stare at it. Then somewhere above me a door opens. I screw the paper into my pocket and pass through the inner door, ducking my head as I hurry up the stairs, not pausing until I am inside the flat with the door securely closed behind me.

Written on the paper are just three words.

*She is lying*

# 17. Jody

Our English teacher used to say that cavemen had invented stories to make sense of a brutal and chaotic world. She said that was where God came from. I don't believe that – I have faith – but I do believe stories are important to make sense of things we can't understand. Like dreams.

Dreams can come true.

That was another song from my childhood. I would lie on my bed in Abbot's Manor, eyes closed, dreaming of the future I would make for myself. The past wasn't the truth; it wasn't even a dream. It was nothing, gone, forgotten; only real if I let it be. Like the fairies in *Peter Pan* who die when you stop believing in them.

Today at the hospital I believed so hard that you were going to wake up – and then your eyes opened! Just for a moment, but it showed me that all I have to do is believe harder and I can make it happen. Like us. I believed we would be together and now we are.

You'll open your eyes again, and this time your beautiful brown irises will drift over to my face. It will take a moment for you to recognise me. At first you'll think I'm just part of the strange dream you have been dreaming for weeks. Then you'll remember. Or perhaps you won't. Perhaps you'll just understand in your heart that I love you, that you're safe, that I'll never leave you.

When I get back from the hospital I draw a picture of you, in the hospital bed, but I draw your eyes open, and when I get to your mouth I make your lips parted, as if they are just about to speak my name.

*Jody? Is that you?*

It's not very good, even though I'm copying it from a photograph, but it doesn't have to be. I know your face so well that I can picture it happening. I can hear the crack in your voice because it's been so long since you've spoken, the whisper of your hair against the pillow as you turn your head to look at me.

But just then, as if she's doing it deliberately to ruin my perfect moment, my phone rings. Though I deleted her number long ago, I still recognise it at once. I let it ring and ring until I can't stand it, and press my hands over my ears and scream silently. Then abruptly it stops, leaving echoes like the waves of pain after you stub your toe.

I stare at the phone for what feels like ages, but still jump when it lights up with a message. I can't delete it until I've listened to three seconds of it.

'Hello, Jody. I've got a birthday present for you, but it won't fit through the letterbox so I thought I'd drop—'

*Message deleted.*

Why won't she leave me alone? Why must she force herself back into my life every year, like tearing open the scar of a freshly healed wound? I don't want to think about her, about any of them. I try to push them away by thinking about you, but I can feel the dark waters rising and rising, and then I can't stop them and they break over me.

# 18. Mags

What does it mean?

Is the *she* Jody? Or the junkie? Or could it be Mira?

And what are they supposed to be lying about? Abe's fall?

But then what possible reason would this writer have for sending a note to me rather than going to the police?

I pick up my phone to call PC Derbyshire, then change my mind.

I'm living in a church full of the damaged and mentally ill. Perhaps this is just malice, or delusion, or plain old racism. Someone with a grudge against one of these women. A jealous lover? Before I go to the police and stir up any trouble for them I need to at least make an attempt to get to the bottom of who sent it.

The handwriting is neat – possibly female? – but there's no full stop, which could suggest the writer is poorly educated.

There was no name on the front of the envelope, which suggests that the person who wrote it slipped it inside the rest of his post. This means either they managed to get into St Jerome's to do so, or they were already in. A resident. Letting myself quietly out of the flat I go back downstairs and out of the main door. Huddled against the wind that races around the building I study the entry panel of names. None of the handwriting seems to match the note, but some of the labels are printed, and others might have been written by partners. It occurs to me that I've never seen Mira's husband, only heard their door shutting quietly late at night. She must be very lonely.

Lonely enough to seek comfort with my brother? Surely not right on Jody's doorstep – literally. Plus she's married and, judging by her dress, a devout Muslim. Get a grip, Mags.

As I trudge back upstairs it occurs to me that perhaps the note wasn't intended for me at all, but for Abe. Could there be others?

Back in the flat I forage through the chaotic box of papers but find nothing aside from bank statements, bills and receipts. Then I notice the laptop, tucked on top of a stack of shoeboxes, its charger still plugged into the socket at the back of the cupboard. Green. Fully charged. And when I open the lid the screen springs into life.

A stroke of luck, but also more evidence that he didn't intend to commit suicide? Unless there's a note, or email.

His email account is open and I find an inbox stuffed with junk and mailings from theatres and listings magazines. There are a few messages from Sunnydale reminding him about time sheets and a drug recall, but not much else, certainly no suicide note and, weirdly, nothing at all from Jody. When I'm seeing someone I seem to spend half my time composing clever texts and emails. But it wouldn't surprise me if Jody didn't even have a computer. Abe's is a pretty battered old Dell model. Maybe she can't afford one. The phone would have been more revealing – I know she has one of those – but it's locked and I can't exactly ask to look over her sweet nothings.

Minimising the email I notice that his wallpaper is a picture of a Disney-style castle against a background of misty lilac hills. It seems oddly impersonal. Mine features me and Jackson knocking back tequila shots with a movie star friend of a client.

Then it hits me: the castle is called Eilean Donan. Abe and I went there on a school trip. The whole of the lower school went, seventy-five of us, in two coaches. My best friend was sick and so I agreed to let Abe sit next to me on the bus, mainly because my other girlfriends thought he was *adorable*. This meant that though he was in the year below they still fancied him, but had to pretend they only wanted to mother him.

We travelled north, skirting endless stretches of dark loch, studded by tiny islands that held a single tree or ruined bothy. Abe gazed out of the window. When we went under an avenue of trees his reflection swam up into the glass, dark eyes meeting mine, then looking away. He answered their questions but never offered any of his own thoughts.

We riffled through his packed lunch and took the bits we wanted, leaving him our cheese triangles and pieces of fruit, which he took without complaint.

It must have been autumn or spring because the sun glared through the bus windows, reddening our faces, but when we finally got out in the car park we stamped our feet and swore and wished we hadn't been too vain to bring our coats. My girlfriends carried on complaining as we traipsed out of the carpark and the weary teachers allowed them to go straight to the visitor centre.

But I didn't go with them.

I had never seen anything so beautiful in all my life as that castle shimmering into view out of the loch mist.

I followed the younger kids on the tour, through tartan rooms filled with antlers and thirteenth-century books, and then out to the battlements.

When everyone else had gone off to eat their packed lunches I was still standing there, looking out to the western sky, shot with red as the early sunset crept across the hills.

I became aware of Abe standing beside me. Just the two of us beneath that vast, uncaring sky.

We stood in silence until the sun started going down behind the hills and the cold seeped into my bones.

When I turned to leave I saw he was crying.

The tears had been caught by the setting sun and turned to little droplets of blood on his cheek. Something about the place, its beauty and stillness and silence, loosened my heart just a little bit and I put my arm around him. I had never done it before, and I never did it again, but for a few minutes before the sun disappeared behind the hills and the air grew numbingly cold, we stood together as brother and sister, realising, perhaps for the first time, that the world was beautiful.

How could I have forgotten?

Then we got back on the coach and went home. Thinking about it now, I wonder if that trip was the moment things changed, when we stopped trying to get the other one into trouble, started lying for one another, warning each other when our father was on the warpath.

Perhaps. It all seems so long ago.

When I try to blow it up the image pixelates into meaningless blocks of colour.

Then I spot a folder in the corner of the screen, called *People*. I click on it.

It's divided up into five subfolders and each filename is a surname: Bridger, Khan, Okeke, Perkins, Lyons. I click on the first and a word document comes up entitled *Freddie Bridger*. He's eighty-three, with diabetes and early-stage dementia. There's a photograph of a slack-jawed, bald man in a tank top, alongside an address and a list of dates Abe visited and the medicines he administered. I close it and glance through the other five folders. Aroon Khan: sixty-five, prostate cancer and Parkinson's. Kone Okeke: seventy-nine, diabetes and deafness. Molly Perkins: sixty-eight, arthritis and incontinence. Lula Lyons: ninety, rheumatism, heart disease and high blood pressure. Lula's photo must have been taken in the fifties. She has flame-red hair and scarlet lips and wide green eyes framed by impossibly long lashes. God knows what she must look like now.

Then I see her address.

Flat One, St Jerome's Church, N19.

The creepy old lady from downstairs. And according to the file he visited her twice a week, sometimes spending more than two hours with her. She must have known him very well. Well enough to be able to tell me more about his state of mind?

Then I notice, in the corner of the screen, another folder. This one with a more unusual surname: Redhorse.

I double click.

Instead of word documents, this folder contains a series of jpegs. I click one.

It is an image of two men. They are naked. The man standing is big and muscular, his skin whitish pink and glistening with perspiration, his pubic hair dark blond. On his hip is a tattoo of a red horse.

The man kneeling in front of him, elegant fingers splayed around the other's buttocks, mouth stretched wide to receive his cock, is my brother.

# 19. Jody

The panic attack goes on for an hour. I try to be as quiet as possible, but I can hear the church listening.

Afterwards my stomach aches with the pain of crying so hard, but also with hunger. I haven't eaten all day. I should go out and get something. Tabby always says it's important for me to eat properly because blood sugar affects your mood, but if I went out now I'd have to cross the grass in the dark.

If I still had your keys I could make myself a sandwich with some of the seeded bread you keep in the freezer. It's half finished so I know you've touched it. I think of what I would order if we were going to Cosmo tonight, of what you would have, the wine you would choose, the way we would clink glasses, looking over the rims at one another. How we would come home together, helping each other up the stairs, a little bit tired and giggly from the wine.

Looking out of the spyhole I can almost see us, your arm around me as you let us into your flat.

Then your door opens. For a moment – for the split second until I remember what has happened – I'm paralysed, my breath frozen in my throat as I expect you to walk out onto the landing.

And then you do.

My heart stutters to a halt.

But of course it's not you. It's your sister, in a manly black suit, her hair pulled back into a tight bun. It's a hard look, the sort that would put most men off. Her eyes are so smoky that from the shadows of my doorway they look like deep black holes in her face. Her lips are red like a vampire's.

Where is she going?

She glances over then and I'm pinned down by her dark eyes, the pupils catching a splinter of light from the main entrance far below. Then she starts descending the stairs, her heels clicking.

Where is she going? When will she be back?

She asks so many questions. They're like fingers picking at the edges of my life, trying to peel away the layers to get to the tender part beneath. I daren't go out until she comes back, in case I bump into her.

I wait by the door and eventually fall asleep on the hall chair. I'm woken by laughter and stumbling footsteps on the stairs, and then a white glare slashes under my door as the landing light goes on.

'Shhh,' Mags whispers, giggling, 'they can hear everything here.'

'Not this, they can't,' says a man's voice.

I creep to the spyhole. The man is tall and broad, his blond hair cropped tight. He's grinning as he grabs her around the waist and jerks her into him. My body goes rigid as I wait to see if she will be able to get away. But she doesn't try to. Instead, her arm slides down and disappears between their bodies. He gasps, then gives a breathless laugh.

A trill of repulsion passes through me as she leans into him and their mouths press together.

Wet snuffles and rustles echo through the stairwell. I wonder what time it is, that they can be so brazen, so unafraid that someone will come out of their flat or hear the noise and look through their spyhole. It's long after pub closing time so the man next door will be back soon.

He's kissing her so roughly that she stumbles back, coming up sharply against the banister: a hand slams down to steady herself, making the metal ring. But it doesn't make them stop.

135

She raises her knee high up his thigh and slides her hand under his shirt, exposing a ridge of fat above his waistband.

One hand supporting herself, the other pulling his head down, she arches her back as he buries his face in her chest, like an animal at a feeding trough.

And then, in a flash, it is you bent over the banister like that, gripping the arms that held you, and I open my mouth to scream at him to stop, *STOP!*

But then it's her again.

Just when I think she's going to overbalance and fall backwards, she lunges forward to bite his neck and they lurch away from the banister. Her legs are around his waist now and he's supporting her whole weight. I wait for him to slam her against the wall and force himself into her, but he doesn't. They stay where they are in the middle of the landing, just kissing. I move closer to the door to listen for the words: words that have always sounded more like hate than love – *you want it, you whore, you dirty bitch, you slut* – but there aren't any. They kiss in silence.

My breath steams up the spyhole and I move away to clear it, squatting in the darkness, trying to keep my breath shallow and quiet. Cold air trickles under my door. The scent of perfume mingled with that smell all men have at the end of an evening – sweat and alcohol and harsh medicinal deodorant. It makes the muscles between my legs contract. When I return to the spyhole he has her up against your door and his trousers are around his thighs. His naked buttocks clench as he pushes himself into her. Her black ankle boots, so small around his broad hips, twitch at every thrust and her hands grip his back as if she is in pain.

And then the light flicks off and I can just hear rustling, animal grunts, and a soft knocking, as if someone is trying to get into your flat.

It goes on and on and then suddenly there is a sharp intake of breath, as if he has hurt her properly. The rustling rises in pitch, the knocking gets louder, the man pants like a dog. I should go out and help her, Abe. Like I should have helped you, but I'm

136

scared. Not as scared as I was that night, but so scared that it takes me several seconds to pluck up the courage to reach for the door latch.

But as my fingers close around the cold brass, the rustling and grunting abruptly ceases and there is a beat of absolute silence.

Then Mags speaks.

'Jesus fucking Christ,' she says, in a loud clear voice that echoes through the darkness.

*The classroom is warm. She's trying to concentrate on what Miss Jarvis is saying, but she keeps falling asleep, her chin slipping off her hand to jerk her awake, producing titters from her classmates.*

*'So, somebody tell me one way we can use an apostrophe.'*

*Zoe Hill puts up her hand. 'When we shorten something, like "that's" instead of "that is". The apostrophe goes before the "s".'*

*She frowns, trying to understand, but her head is muzzy and the pain in her back is distracting. She shifts in her seat, making the wood creak, and Miss Jarvis's eyes flick towards the sound. When she realises where it's coming from the teacher gives her a ghost of a smile, then looks away. Sometimes, when the teachers do this – offer her some sign of friendship or sympathy – she feels like a zoo animal, a chimp behind a glass wall. The visitors who walk by feel so sorry for her being trapped in there; they make sad faces at her and shake their heads, then they move on.*

*She shifts again and the pain in her back makes her gasp.*

*Behind her, Emily Bright mimics the sound. She and Emily used to be friends, but then Emily's mum told her they weren't allowed to play together. Emily told everyone that she was dirty and her parents were criminals and that she and her brother did things with each other after bedtime. Emily got into serious trouble for that one, so she keeps quiet now, only tripping the little girl up when no teachers are looking, bumping her tray at lunch so her food falls on the floor, or scribbling over her best drawings, the ones she keeps in her desk to look at when she's feeling sad. Her favourite one was of an angel sitting beside a little girl in a field of pink flowers. She'd done the sky really well, shading in the whole area above the flowers, instead of just putting a blue line at the top like some of the others did. But Emily drew a big brown blob coming out of the angel's mouth that was obviously supposed to be poo, and she drew cuts and purple bruises*

138

all over the little girl. It makes her feel sad to look at it now, sad and scared, and when the teacher isn't watching she will throw it away.

For a while Emily had boasted that her family were moving to a bigger house in a nicer town and the little girl's heart had swelled with hope, but Emily had stopped talking about it now.

Even if Emily does leave, there is still Zoe and Melissa and Stevie Daniels. Stevie Daniels hit her because he said she was laughing when he was talking about his mum's operation. She wasn't. She was just smiling because she wanted to be friends. He got into a little bit of trouble, but not too much, because of the operation. The hit didn't hurt, but now he jumps out at her when she's walking past, slamming his foot down to make her jump and scowling as if he wants to murder her.

Sometimes she wishes he just would.

With a sense of panic she realises she needs the toilet. For the past few days it has been hurting so much to wee and she has noticed the yellow in the bowl has streaks of pink in it. Perhaps she is properly sick and will die.

'Now,' says Miss Jarvis. 'Adjectives. Who can tell me what an adjective is?'

'A describing word,' says Jamie.

'Correct. Now, I'm going to go around the class and we're going to come up with some words to describe a person. Jamie, you begin.'

'Strong,' says Jamie.

'Good. Imran?'

'Clever.'

The list went on: tall, hairy, blond, nice (disallowed), friendly, naughty, noisy, brave.

It came to the little girl's turn. 'Beautiful,' she said. 'Kind.'

'You're supposed to say one, der,' hisses Stevie beside her.

'Good,' says Miss Jarvis. 'Stevie?'

'Stupid.'

'Ugly,' says Emily, and she can feel her former friend's eyes boring into her back.

'Smelly,' Melissa says, and the whole class laughs.

139

Then Jason Hicks cries out, 'The police are here!' and everyone rushes to the window.

'I didn't know we were having a visit today,' Miss Jarvis says, joining them. 'Perhaps it's an Internet safety thing for year six.'

Both police officers are women. One is young and pretty, the other older and grey-haired; neither is smiling at the faces pressed to the windows. They cross the playground with silent purposefulnes, and disappear through the door that leads to the headmistress's office.

'Has Mrs Harrison committed a crime, Miss Jarvis?' says Zoe.

'Is it because her car's too dirty to read the number plate?'

'Has she been murdering children?'

Laughter.

'Quiet!' Miss Jarvis snaps. Her face has gone white. She, like the children, is watching the police officers come back out of the door, accompanied by a grim-faced Mrs Harrison. The headteacher glances up in the direction of Mrs Jarvis's classroom and for a moment a look passes between them.

'Back to your desks,' Mrs Jarvis says quietly, and the children, subdued, do as they are told.

The little girl can barely put one foot in front of the other, she is so scared.

They know what she did last night.

And so many nights before that.

She knows it's illegal. Her parents told her. They said if anyone ever found out the things she had done she would go to prison, forever. She would be in prison with the same men she did the illegal things with, but her parents wouldn't be there to stop them if they tried to really hurt her. They could do anything they wanted to her.

And now the police are here. They will take her to prison and the men will be waiting for her.

Footsteps thud down the corridor. There are no voices. The children around her look at one another. Excitement has turned to trepidation. Is one of them in trouble? Has something bad happened to someone they love?

140

*The footsteps draw closer.*

*She leaps up, making the desk legs screech, and flies for the door.*

*'Where are you going?' exclaims Miss Jarvis, but she is already running down the corridor, in the opposite direction from the three adults who have stopped in surprise.*

*She bursts through the emergency exit and the alarm starts up, an ear-splitting ringing that makes her teeth vibrate. There are shouts behind her, running footsteps.*

*She runs through the playground, dimly aware of faces pressed to windows and hands banging on glass. As she skids around the corner of the building the main gates come into view.*

*She is just tall enough, now, to hit the green button that releases them.*

*Someone is calling her name but she doesn't turn, just squeezes through the widening gap with a moan of pain as the metal bars cause pressure on her bladder and scrape the welts on her back.*

*The belt buckle was square and brass. When she saw him taking it off her heart had sunk, but it lifted again when he didn't undo his trousers. She hadn't understood because she had never met him before. She didn't know it was her pain that gave him his pleasure. He wanted to see her cry and beg him to stop. Her dad stopped it in the end, saying he would break her and then where would he get his fun next time? Heh heh.*

*She is out of the gates and running down the pavement in the direction of the park. If she can get there she will be able to hide in the bushes. Unless they send dogs out for her. Or heat-seeking helicopters like she's seen on the TV.*

*If she jumps into the lake perhaps they will not be able to see her, or smell her. But then she might drown.*

*Footsteps behind her.*

*She manages to speed up a little. She has the body of an athlete, the PE teacher always says. He can't understand why she is so slow, why she tires so easily. He says she is unfit, eating the wrong things, staying up too late.*

*She risks a glance behind and her bladder loosens with a vicious burning sensation. It is the policewomen who are pursuing her – and*

141

*they are fast. The older one, surprisingly, is in the lead, her cap
wedged on her head, her arms and legs pumping.*

*The little girl whimpers and tries to increase her pace as she runs
past the row of houses. But she is so tired, and her back hurts, and
her bladder hurts, and there is no strength left in her legs. She is not
strong, or clever, or brave. She is just tired. She just wants it all to stop.*

*There is a lorry coming. She feels its rumble through her feet
before she hears its roar behind her, drowning out the sounds of her
pursuit. Suddenly she knows what she must do.*

*The lorry is at her back, so huge and loud, shaking the trees and
rattling the windows of the houses.*

*It won't hurt at all; it will be so quick.*

*She stops and turns. The robot face of the cab stares at her impas-
sively, the driver no more than a shadow behind glass that reflects
the trees of the park. They would have found her in the park. They
would find her anywhere. Find her and take her back to the men,
and it would be so much worse than before, though she cannot
imagine how.*

*She bends her knees, ready to leap.*

*The lorry is so close she can smell its dirty, gusty breath.*

*It is a metre away, half a metre; she launches herself upwards,
into the air, closing her eyes, waiting for the huge, shocking impact.*

*Her feet leave the edge of the pavement. The lorry screams, the
whole world shakes.*

*But just in time she is being yanked back. There is an impact, a
painful one, as she lands on her back on the pavement, but the lorry
thunders past and she screams in an agony of despair.*

*The grey-haired policewoman is kneeling beside her, holding her
down as she tries to scramble up and throw herself into the path of
the next vehicle, or the next, or the next.*

*Eventually she gives up, collapses on her torn back on the pave-
ment and sobs.*

*Running footsteps skid to a halt and the other policewoman is beside
her, but they make no attempt to drag her to her feet or handcuff
her. Instead they lift her gently and, like doting parents with a new*

baby, gather her into their arms, not caring that bloody, acid wee is soaking through her threadbare school skirt.

They rock her like that, until she starts to calm down, and can make sense of the words they are repeating over and over, their voices merging together, as if they are singing a round.

'You're all right, now. You're all right. Nothing bad is going to happen to you again. Not ever. I promise. I promise.'

The little girl raises her head and looks from face to face. She is surprised to see that both women are crying.

143

# Saturday 12 November

# 20. Mags

Spending the night with Daniel makes me feel so much better.

Though in fact, as the morning progresses and I'm still floating on a bubble, I wonder if it isn't the sex – which was fairly clumsy and unrewarding due to the fact that we were both drunk – and rather simply waking up with a nice warm human being beside me. I didn't realise how much being alone in this dark flat, in this shitty neighbourhood, in this freezing city, was getting to me. Plus there's no denying I felt safer with a big strong man in the house.

To make up for the last morning we spent together, where I basically told him to fuck off, I leave him sleeping and head out to get breakfast from the local bakery.

I won't go to the hospital today in case I bump into Jody. I still haven't had a chance to gather my thoughts about the stuff I saw on Abe's computer last night. It wasn't just photographs. I opened his history and logged onto a chat room he seemed to have spent a lot of time on. There was a thread from this Redhorse. Predictable enough stuff initially: *Can't stop thinking about the taste of your cock, I want to feel you inside me*, that sort of thing. Porn talk. But the later ones are more intimate. From Abe: *I've been thinking about you all day.* From Redhorse: *Not long before I see you.* Abe: *I'm counting the seconds. x*

My first thought was: did Jody find out he was screwing around on her? He'd set the computer to remember all his passwords so it wouldn't have been hard for her. But that just brings me back to the idea that she pushed him, and I just don't buy it. Say she confronted him about it and there was a struggle, she isn't physically strong enough to overpower him. Plus, would you really confront a cheater on your way home from a night out? Wouldn't you do it in the privacy of your flat?

On my return from the bakery with my bag of croissants Jodie is coming out of St Jerome's. When she sees me she stops dead on the path. I'm wearing Abe's parka – it's far warmer than the rain jacket – and maybe I look a bit intimidating. I pull the hood down and force myself to smile.

'Where are you off to?'

She blinks rapidly, then finds her voice. 'The hospital.'

'Oh.' My smile falters. Guiltily I screw the croissant bag up until it's as unobtrusive as possible. *While you're enjoying a nice slow morning screw she'll be conducting her bedside vigil for your brother.* I'm the bad guy yet again.

I could get rid of Daniel and go with her, but I'm not sure I can sit there beside her and pretend nothing's happened.

'Tell him I'll try and pop by later.'

She nods quickly, tucking her hair behind her ear in that coy way she has. I don't think she even realises it looks flirtatious. The ring on her engagement finger has twisted around and now I can see the whole phrase that has been engraved into the stainless steel (as I now know it must be – not silver).

*True love waits.*

My eyes widen. Seriously, Abe? I know you didn't have much money but was this all you could manage for an engagement ring?

It's a purity ring, given to Abe and me by our parents when the first wisps of pubic hair appeared. I took mine to university with me, determined to be wearing it as I lost my virginity. Friends at King's came up with the nickname when they found it in my stuff. The name on my birth certificate is Mary Martha, but they thought that was inappropriate, so I became Mary Magdalene, the whore with the seven demons inside her.

148

But my friends didn't know their scriptures. The Magdalene may not have been the Virgin Mother, but she was by Jesus's side when he was crucified. Not a whore but a saint. Either way I played along and the name stuck. Magdalene. Mags.

At the end of the first term I laid my ring carefully down on the railway line and the fast train to London obliterated it. I can understand why Abe kept his – to laugh at, or hurl across the room when he thought of our parents – but why give a chastity ring to his lover? Ironically? Somehow Jody doesn't seem the type to get the joke.

As I watch her hurry away to be by his side, my wave of pity is accompanied by anger. How could he do this to her?

Piles of post sit on the table in the foyer. A pile for everyone who lives here. The bountiful friendship of the takeaway. Even the junkie in Flat Seven has a generous handful and she doesn't look as if she's eaten in years.

Abe's is held in an elastic band. A white corner is just visible between the menus of Bengal Kitchen and Pronto Pizza.

Sliding it out I open the blank envelope.

*She was there*

I pass my fingertips over the indentations from the biro, as if they will tell me something my eyes can't. I know for certain now that this note is meant for me.

And I'm pretty sure what they mean by *there*; they mean when he fell.

'*Who* was there?' I call up the stairwell, and the echoes of my voice seem to go on for long moments.

Then my door opens high above.

'Mags? You OK?'

'Fine. Be up in a minute.'

Tucking the paper into my pocket, I start climbing the stairs. On the second floor I pause, wondering whether to knock on the junkie's door. Clearly Abe was bisexual: could she have been one of his lovers too? She's probably capable of anything to get the money for her next hit, but I'm not sure Abe was that desperate, not with Redhorse on the scene. Unless she was before Redhorse, before Jody and now resentful of the love that she had with my brother? Resentful enough to try and set Jody up?

No. She said she was out that night and stuck with her story even when she thought there might be a reward for saying she'd seen something.

I pass the grumpy queen's door. Potentially another jealous lover?

I realise, suddenly, how desperate I am to try and prove that someone is jealous of Jody and is trying to drive a wedge between us, because the alternative – that this letter writer is telling the truth – is unthinkable.

Jody's lying to me.

She was there when Abe fell.

Daniel is standing by the window drinking coffee when I get back in. The flat always gets the morning sun and his blond hair is lit up with all the colours of the apostles' cloaks. He's wearing jeans and a T-shirt of Abe's – I said he could – which is a bit too tight because his muscles are just starting to turn to fat. He turns and smiles at me, and for a moment I feel a rush of emotion, like the release of some narcotic into my bloodstream. I bustle around the kitchen until it has passed, then lay out the croissants and the paper.

'Well, this is nice,' he says, sitting down at the table. 'You'd make someone a lovely wife.'

'Piss off,' I say half-heartedly and pick up the money section, though my eyes skim across the page, unseeing.

I know he's got to go. He's promised to take his sons to the Warner Brothers Studio, but when he glances at his watch and sighs, I feel a sudden stab of desolation, and when I kiss him goodbye he says, 'Careful.'

'What?'

'Almost let some feelings show, there.'

'Yeah, the feeling of wanting you to piss off so I can get on with some work.'

He grins, his teeth Vegas-white.

I hear his footsteps all the way down the stairwell and then the creak of the door opening, and then silence. I'm alone again, and the oppressive atmosphere of the church returns, as if the lead roof is pushing down on me.

# 21. Jody

It was a beautiful evening because of the volcano. On the news they said it was something to do with the layers of ash in the atmosphere. As the afternoon wore on the sky became streaked with a million different shades of red. I tried to think of all the different names as I gazed out of the clear patch of window in my flat. Crimson and scarlet, vermillion, fuschia, cherry, burgundy, ruby, baby-pink, pillarbox, blood.

But it seemed as if this wonderful gift was all for me: the people scurrying down Gordon Terrace kept their heads bent, and the high road was as noisy as ever, with roaring bus engines, horns and sirens and the occasional shouting match. No one else had noticed what was spread out above them.

There was a tap at my door; it sounded hesitant, as if the person had come to ask a favour. I thought of my silent neighbours. Perhaps the woman next door wanted to borrow something. I decided not to answer. To become friends with her would mean having to have contact with her partner, and he frightened me. On the few occasions I'd actually seen him in the flesh he seemed to me, like most men who choose to look that way, more like an animal than a person.

The tap came again.

I sat still and silent by the window. Then I saw Mira walking across the waste ground in the direction of the high road.

If it wasn't her at my door, then who? What if it was her partner? He knew I lived alone. What if he—

'Jody?'

I sprang to my feet with a gasp and raced to the door.

You stood there, your body half turned away, as if you were about to leave, and my heart jumped into my throat – I came so close to missing you.

'Hi, sorry, I didn't hear the door,' I gabbled.

You turned back. You were all dressed up to go out – a big parka with a furry hood. My mind raced with the possible reasons for you coming round – could I take in a parcel for you, could I let you back in because you'd lost your key . . . ?

Then I noticed what you were carrying. A bottle of wine in one hand, and two plastic wine glasses in the other, a grey woollen blanket over your arm.

'I'm going to watch the sunset,' you said.

'I thought I was the only one who'd noticed it.'

Our eyes met. 'You're probably busy. And it's cold, but I was wondering if you wanted to co—'

'Yes!' I almost shouted, then was stricken with terror in case you were going with someone else and wanted me to lend you a corkscrew or something.

But you exhaled with relief. 'Great.'

I stepped out onto the landing and went to close the door.

'Erm, you might want to put something warmer on!'

That was just like you, Abe, to think about me and how I was feeling, before yourself. Your sister was right about one thing at least – you *can* love someone too much. You should have thought about yourself more, my darling. You should have told me how you were feeling. I could have helped you.

'Come in a minute. I won't be a sec.'

You came in behind me, shutting the door softly. I led you through to the living room and you went straight to the window. I watched you for a moment, silhouetted against the red sky. So beautiful.

Then I went to change. It felt strange as I hurried into my bedroom, knowing you were there, in my flat. A raw sort of feeling, as if I'd peeled off a plaster and the newly exposed flesh was throbbing in the air. Not painful, just sensitised.

I pulled off my jogging bottoms, my sweatshirt and T-shirt, sniffed my armpits, and then, on a whim, I changed my knickers, from the boy-shorts I've always worn, to a pink pair with lace at the front that one of the girls in the bedsit gave me. You can just glimpse my pubic hair through the lace and, looking at myself in the mirror, my heart started to pound. What was I doing?

I told myself to calm down, that I just wanted to feel confident and attractive with you.

I put on the rain dress, with a cable-knit Aran jumper over the top and a pair of pink cashmere socks – both Christmas presents from Helen. Then I pulled on my charity shop boots, brushed my hair, and at the last minute, put on some lipstick.

It would have to do, I told myself, as I slipped out of my bedroom to find you still by the window. You started when you saw me, then you smiled.

'My favourite dress.'

I looked away, the blush deepening.

'Well, come on then, rainwoman, this wine won't drink itself.'

When we got out of the flat I started going down the stairs because the best view would be around the back and we could sit on the wall that surrounds the car park.

'Where are you going?' You leaned over the banisters, grinning. The banister rail pressed into your hips and your T-shirt moved in the currents of air rising up through the stairwell.

I'd passed the door at the end of the landing every day since I moved in, but never thought to wonder where it led. Somehow you got it open and as soon as you pushed it wider and the cold air rushed in, I realised – it led to the roof.

Giving me the wine bottle to carry you took my other hand and began leading me up a flight of concrete steps. The door below us swung shut and for a moment we were in total darkness.

My grip on your hand tightened.

'It's all right,' you murmured. 'Don't be scared. I'm here.'

I squeezed your hand. 'I'm not.'

I remember thinking how soft your hands were. Not rough and coarse like a normal man's, but soft as mine.

It was so dark that I couldn't see where I was going and when you got to the door at the top I didn't stop in time and bumped into you. You held me to stop me from falling back and for a moment we were in each other's arms. The fur of your parka was against my cheek. It smelled warm and cosy, like fresh hay.

You held me just a second longer than was necessary and then you pushed open the door.

The lead was slippery with rotting leaves and the soles of my boots had no grip, so I didn't let go of your hand as you led me out into the middle of the roof.

A low crenellated wall surrounded the spire.

'We could sit here,' you said. 'The view's OK. Or,' you grinned and raised your eyebrows, 'we could go higher.'

I followed your gaze towards the little door set into the spire, and then up. Just before it narrowed to a point, there were two arched apertures, open to the elements.

'The view from there will be amazing, but it'll be pretty windy. Will you be OK?'

I held your gaze and said, 'As long as you keep me warm.'

It was shockingly brazen of me. You might even call it *provocative*, but I knew I could trust you, Abe, and I was right.

The little door opened onto a spiral staircase and a moment later we stepped out onto a stone floor covered in twigs and dry leaves, I guess from birds making nests higher up. Opposite the windows that looked towards the high road, there was another pair, looking west, into the sunset. For a moment I couldn't catch my breath.

'Careful,' you said, as I went over. 'We're pretty high now.'

The view was incredible, stretching right across London. I could see Hampstead Heath and the Emirates Stadium, as well as all the office blocks and cranes in the city.

You came to stand beside me, resting your arm on my shoulder. I could feel the stiffness in your muscles, as if you weren't sure you were doing the right thing, and I slid my arm around your waist to let you know that you were, that I was comfortable with you. More than comfortable – I was happy.

'I bet we've got the best view in the whole country right now,' you said softly.

I let my head fall on your shoulder. The fabric of the parka was cold and slippery under my cheek.

'Wait a minute.'

To my disappointment you took your arm away, but then I understood. You were taking your coat off and wrapping it around my shoulders. Now I was nestled into the sweet warmth of your body.

For several minutes we just watched the sky. The wind had blown up again and the bands of different colours were coiling and unravelling under high, gold-bellied clouds.

'What are you thinking about?' you said.

I looked into your eyes and my voice was barely audible when I spoke. 'You.'

I placed my hand on your chest. It was rising and falling so fast. You stayed perfectly still as I rose up onto my tiptoes and kissed you. Your lips were so soft. For a moment you didn't respond and I was terrified I had misunderstood your intentions, as I always do, but just as I was about to pull away you circled me with your other arm and kissed me back. Time seemed to stand still. Even the wind dropped. The sun must have come out from behind a cloud because my eyelids glowed red. I was overcome with such dizziness that if you hadn't been holding me up I think I would have tumbled out of the window.

After a few more minutes you pulled away and smiled at me, but I didn't want it to stop. And more than that, I wanted it to go further. I had waited so long.

I moved my hand across your chest and you caught your breath.

156

I started unbuttoning your shirt.

'Are you sure?'

I nodded and you kissed me again, and now I felt the tip of your tongue against my own, I responded, and you held me tighter, crushing me to your body. Something was rising in me that I had never felt before.

You lowered me gently down onto your coat and, with the dry leaves whispering around us, I lay back and closed my eyes.

Then you were inside me, moving in me. And then we were moving together. We were like one person, our breath, our heart-beats, the slow coming together and moving apart: all synchronised, as if our bodies knew one another already.

Something inside me opened then, like a flower blooming. For the first time I felt like a woman.

You whispered my name breathlessly and I murmured yours, moving my palms up and down your smooth back, feeling the energy that rippled through your body. Your lips were on my neck, on my shoulders, my breasts.

Heat flowed across my skin. All my nerve endings were alive, as if my whole body thrummed with electricity. In the core of my being I felt a bursting warmth, like a wellspring, bubble up and start to flow through my veins.

'Jody,' you said, your voice cracking. 'Jody.'

Afterwards, for those still seconds as you lay on top of me, your breath in my ear, your heart thudding against my ribs, I looked out at the last flare of the dying sun, and I knew that I had left it all behind, all the pain and fear and shame. Down there, where the rubbish whirled around the broken tarmac – that was my past. Up here, in the cold, clean eye of the wind, with the bloody sky stretched over me – this was my future. With you.

You pushed yourself onto your elbows and smiled at me. 'All right?'

I knew I wouldn't be able to tell you just how right I was, so I just smiled back at you, touched your face.

'I know this will sound strange because we hardly know each other,' you said, your hand cupping my cheek. 'But I think I love you.'

I love you too, Abe.

I love you.

I love you.

I love you.

I love you.

I love you.

I love you.

# 22. Mags

I decide to print out the messages from Redhorse and show them to Derbyshire. If this were my case there are several lines I'd follow. One: Jody found out Abe was having an affair and pushed him. Two: Abe tried to end the affair and his lover pushed him. Three: An as yet unidentified third person pushed him for unknown reasons, but someone witnessed this.

If I can't get Derbyshire to take any of these scenarios seriously then I'll either have to call in some favours with private investigator firms in the US – see if they can't trace the IP address where the chat room messages came from – or give up and go home. To be honest, the latter option is by far the most attractive, but I feel like I owe it to Abe to at least try.

I save the messages onto a stick and head to the Internet café on the high street. There's a queue for the printer so I order a latte and sit at a table to wait. The girl behind the counter is Eastern European; her skin has a greenish waterlogged pallor that makes me think of a drowning victim.

Outside a wall of buses inches by, slower than walking pace.

Sipping the latte I flick through one of the coffee-ringed magazines. It's filled with gleeful descriptions of celebrity break-ups. *Friends say Kelly just couldn't take his hostility towards her BFFs. Friends say he didn't like her leaving her dirty underwear around the bedroom.*

I toss the mag down in a pool of coffee. A whole industry based on *schadenfreude*, making their inadequate readers feel smug about their drab little lives and relationships. Celebrities break up because their egos are solid enough not to put up with other people's bullshit. The rest of us don't have the balls, because we're too insecure to be alone. Maybe you have to be as wet as Jody to be really happy.

She'll be at Abe's bedside by now, gazing into his grey face, clutching his flaccid hand, her lips moving in silent prayer.

How could he do it to her?

Was it simple cowardice? Easier just to let her believe that they had the perfect romance than admit that he was not only unfaithful, but also bisexual? That wouldn't really fit into Jody's dreamscape. If she'd found out it would have been such a horrible shock. Enough to make her do something entirely irrational and out of character? Something violent? Jody? It seems so outlandish.

I can see her with a knife, wild-haired and crazy-eyed, slashing with anguished abandon at the murderer of her dream, but pushing someone over a banister? That feels like a man's doing.

I recounted to Daniel Jody's story of her and Abe's first kiss, hamming up the scene of Abe stripped to the waist, beating down the flames with his sodden shirt while Jody swoons by the sink.

He said, 'Then did he sweep her off on his Arab stallion to his yacht in the Caribbean?'

I laughed. 'What do you mean?'

'Well, it's a bit Mills and Boon, isn't it?'

At the time I'd been more interested in teasing him about his knowledge of pulp romance plots, but now . . . I don't know. Is it all a bit *too* perfect? Is Jody making things up to make her relationship look rosier? If so, is she hiding more about herself? Is there actually a violent psychopath hiding behind the mask of pathetic little victim? Am I that bad a judge of character?

Christ. How much longer do I have to wait in this dump?

One guy's hogging a computer while he gabbles on his mobile in some obscure guttural language, Latvian or Ukranian or something. I feel like going up to him and tearing the phone out of his hand. I close my eyes and breathe deeply, while manic Latvian laughter ricochets around the café. I'm in the throes of that post-sex low when all I want to do is ring Daniel and ask him back for more. That's the last thing I should do, of course. I already said he could call me, but I'll just send him straight to voicemail. I certainly don't want to be embroiled in a relationship with a man who has kids and an ex-wife.

Finally the Latvian logs out and I print out the messages and leave.

Returning to the flat is a battle against the relentless wind. It tugs at my clothes, roars in my ears and up my nose, as if it's trying to get inside me. By the time I get to Gordon Terrace I feel like I've run a marathon, but as I turn towards St Jerome's it starts buffeting my back, thrusting me forward, making me stumble over the ridges on the path. They look like tree roots pushing up through the tarmac, but there isn't a single tree as far as the eye can see.

A woman is standing by the main doors. As I approach the building I see she's carrying what looks like a large basket wrapped in paper with a repeating pattern of teddy bears.

'Sorry.' I move past her to open the door.

'Oh, excuse me,' she says. Her middle-class accent is incongruous in these surroundings. From behind she looked younger but her face suggests she must be in her mid to late sixties. 'Do you know Jody Currie, on the fourth floor? It's just I have a parcel for her but she doesn't seem to be in.'

'I can take it.'

Then I catch sight of the label: *To Jody, with all my love, Helen.*

So, this is the aunt who was supposed to be Jody's guardian but kicked her out to grow up in a care home: now trying to buy off her own conscience with what smells like a hamper full of bath bombs.

Without catching her eye I hold out my arms to take the package.

'Actually,' she says, 'perhaps I could pop up? Maybe she hasn't heard the buzzer.'

'I saw her go out,' I say coldly.

When she doesn't hand over the present I look up. Her eyes are hazel and heavily ringed with brown. She's breathing heavily, the silver locket on her bony chest bouncing the light as it rises and falls.

'She's told you, hasn't she?' she says.

I make my expression blank. 'I'll make sure she gets the parcel.'

'Well, it isn't true. None of it. You should know you can't believe a word she says.'

*She is lying.*

I glance down at the label again. It's in slanting block capitals where the notes were in a more looping lower case. But even if she was disguising her handwriting, I can't imagine what motive she would have to leave me them.

'What do you mean?'

'All the fairy tales about her past, her family. My son. The rape.'

I stare at her. The rape?

'No smoke without fire, they say, don't they?' Her eyes are a mass of tiny thread veins. 'He could never get away from it. What she said he'd done, him and his friend. Their mates stuck by them, of course, but there are enough people who insist you always have to believe the victim. They never took into account her background. She was so damaged . . .'

Her junkie son raped Jody and now she's accusing Jody of lying about it. Disgusted, I push past her and open the door.

'Goodbye.'

'We loved her,' she says.

'Clearly not enough.'

Her face twists in anguish. 'But we had a responsibility towards our own flesh and blood, didn't we? If it had been just us, then we would have managed, but when she started lying about our son . . . Her accusations destroyed him.'

'Sounds like he destroyed himself. It was nothing to do with her.'

162

Helen's hands are still clasped around the present, gradually turning blue in the cold. There's a sudden snatch of wind and the label twists and tears itself free to flap across the grass, but her eyes don't leave my face.

'What did she tell you?'

So, Jody never mentioned this rape. Why should she? But still I can't quite bring myself to close the door.

'You promised to look after her, to bring her up as your own, and then because your son became a drug addict you decided you couldn't cope and kicked her out. And these *accusations* . . .' I emphasise the words with contempt. 'If it comes down to Jody's word versus the word of a drug addict, I know who I'd trust. You had a responsibility to look after that girl. However difficult it was, you were her aunt. Her parents entrusted her to you.'

I hold Helen's gaze. I may not have been the best of sisters to Abe but I'm here, aren't I? I'm doing my duty. This woman abandoned hers.

'But I'm not her aunt.' Helen's bloodshot eyes are wide and bewildered. 'I was her foster mother.'

I stare at her for a moment, then I force the door closed.

'Felix turned to drugs because of what she did!' Her voice is muffled by the glass. 'She cried rape against our son and his friend and it destroyed his life!'

I push through the inner door, my chest tight.

'She lies about everything. Everything.' Her voice is drowned by the wind. 'She's dangerous!'

Inside the sanctuary of the stairwell I stop and lean against the wall, breathing heavily. My head is spinning.

Jody lied to me about Helen.

The light through the stained glass is subdued, a dull red wash darkening the concrete.

What else has she lied about?

I run back outside. Helen is hobbling along Gordon Terrace now, hunched against the wind, the basket wobbling in her hands.

163

Dodging the piles of dog shit and ridges of bursting tarmac, I set off after her. I need her to tell me exactly what happened with this alleged rape. Did Jody make it all up, or are Helen's maternal instincts blinding her to the unpalatable truth about her son, the rapist junkie?

I step out onto Gordon Terrace, my Converses slipping on a discarded crisp packet – or maybe they're Abe's Converses: I've started wearing his clothes without a second thought, as if they are my own.

Helen is almost at the high road but to get there she must run the gauntlet of a gang of youths in low-crotch jeans and pulled-up hoodies. They've separated into two lines on the pavement to let her through, but they are clearly saying something to her. Their laughter's like the yapping of dogs. One of them reaches out for the parcel and she yanks it away, breaking into an awkward trot, making them laugh all the harder.

I think about calling out to her, but that will attract their attention.

What's the point anyway? I slump against a lamp post. Who's to say Helen will tell me the truth any more than Jody? What was it Daniel said? There's no such thing as truth, only what you can make someone believe. Helen will want me to believe Jody is guilty so her son can be innocent.

She reaches the end of the terrace and turns onto the high road, the awkward parcel still clutched to her chest. The youths have noticed me, so I turn and head back to the church. But the idea of passing another evening in gloomy, wine-fogged solitude is pretty unappealing, so against my better judgment I take out my phone to call Daniel.

I sit, revolving slowly on the roundabout, as we talk for almost an hour. He had a good time with his boys. So good that when he describes how they cried as he dropped them off, his voice cracks.

'They love you, Dan,' I say softly, cupping my hand over the receiver to protect it from the wind. 'That's why they're upset. Isn't it worth it to know that?'

It's not like me to issue words of comfort, but I'm desperate to keep him on the line.

He sniffs. 'Sage words from the mistress of the heart.'

I guess he feels he has to lighten the tone or risk spooking me.

'How was it with . . . your wife?' The pause is almost imperceptible.

'Donna? She wants me to move back and give it another go.'

To my utter surprise my heart lurches and it's hard to catch my breath.

'Mags?'

'Sorry, I can't hear you very well over the wind.'

'Go inside then, you nutcase.'

'I will.' I glance over at the church, becoming blacker and more forbidding by the moment. If I don't go now I may just chicken out and book into the hotel again. 'In a minute. What did you say to her?' I keep my voice light.

'What, you mean did I say, *Sorry, I'm in love with someone else*?' His tone is mocking.

'Hey, look, I should really go. Good luck with everything. I hope it works out for you.'

'Mags.'

I hang up, feeling inexplicably wounded.

The roundabout makes one more slow revolution and I find myself face to face with the group of youths.

'You got a joint, sexy?' says the tall one at the front.

'No.' I stand.

'Can I have a look?' He fingers the zip of my bag.

'Like hell you can.'

'No need for that, bitch,' says one of the others. I glance back at the church but the windows are all dark. On Gordon Terrace the few functional street lamps are flickering into life. The street is deserted.

'Gimme the bag,' says the tall one conversationally.

'No.' It's hanging across my body. He will have to physically assault me to get it off. Unless he cuts the strap.

165

He produces a knife. It has a shiny blue handle with a spider graphic. The blade has holes down the blunt edge, and is jagged from halfway down the sharp side. I find myself wondering about the holes, then I realise. They're like the ones in a cheese knife – to prevent them from sticking inside the thing you are trying to slice up.

The tall one's eyes are black and pitiless. 'Gimme the bag.'

'Or he'll cut your tits off,' another adds.

I have no choice. No one is coming to help me. I'm about to lift the strap over my head when, from behind me, comes the characteristic creak of the church door opening. The security light blares on

The boys' attention is diverted. This is my chance. I glance back to see whether whoever has come out will retreat rapidly when they see what's going on, or whether they might hold the door open for me to flee into the block.

To my surprise it's the old lady from Flat One. In the harsh light her hair is the colour of Fanta, moulded around her head like a crash helmet. Even from here I can see the splodges of rouge on her cheeks and the ragged slash of shakily applied lipstick. She's holding up a tablet in a fluffy pink case, the camera trained at our little group.

Over the wind her voice is quavering but strong. 'Can you see, Martin? Are you recording? There are five of them.' She describes them in turn. 'Yes, I've already called the police. They're only in the high road.'

'She FaceTimin' us, isn't it,' one of the boys says.

'Should teach that old bag a lesson,' another says. He takes a few steps in the direction of the church. The old woman doesn't move. The pink fluff ripples in the wind, but her hair remains utterly still.

A police siren wails in the distance.

'Feds comin', man.'

The tall one flicks his chin contemptuously in the direction of the church. 'Bitch lives *here*. She ain't got no shit worth havin,' then he turns and starts walking back across the grass to the low fence that stops the Staffies getting in.

166

I have the satisfaction of seeing one of them trip over the fence. As he stumbles his hoodie rides up, revealing an expanse of white underpants and the crack between his pale buttocks.

I resist a jeering laugh – that might be pushing my luck – and set off quickly in the opposite direction.

The old woman holds the door open for me and we hurry into the foyer, making sure it's shut firmly before passing through to the stairwell, where we pause, panting.

She extends a hand. 'Lula Lyons. Pleased to meet you.'

'Mags Mackenzie.' Her hand is paper-dry but the grip is firm. 'I think my brother was your carer.'

She nods, her milky eyes bright. 'Do you know, the first time I saw you coming up that path, bumping your case over the bodies, your hair all tied back, I thought you were him. Gave me quite a turn.' She shakes her head. 'He was such a pretty boy.'

'Thanks,' I say, nodding at the tablet, hanging slackly from her grasp, 'for what you did. And please thank the person you were talking to as well, for recording them.'

'Martin?' She gives a wheezy laugh. 'Martin Scorsese was my cat. Died last year. And this bloody machine,' she waggles it contemptuously, 'hasn't worked for weeks. Your brother always sorted out my technology. Taught me how to FaceTime my friend in Catford. Not that we really want to see one another's faces these days. Come in and I'll give you something to settle your nerves.'

She moves haltingly, as if in pain, but her clothes are that of a woman sixty years her junior: a gold lamé top with sequined sleeves, a fitted black skirt with a thigh slit, royal blue fishnet tights, and a pair of crocodile skin, kitten-heeled ankle boots. I smile as I follow her in, then make my face serious again as she turns and asks me to sit down.

Her flat must have the same dimensions as Abe's, but you'd never know. The place is decked out like a Persian bazaar. Silk throws billow from the ceiling, studded here and there with silver lanterns, and what I took to be net curtains at the window are actually pieces of antique lace. The floor is layered with what look like flying carpets at rest. The sofa's a huge mahogany thing, piled with cushions and a slightly chilling rag doll with green paste jewels for eyes. I sit down in the opposite corner to the doll as Lula hobbles to the kitchen behind me. Again, it's similar in layout to Abe's, but instead of cabinets, there are rows of open shelves heaving with bric-a-brac: old tins and bottles, jars of multicoloured pulses, copper pans, stacks of old pudding basins, flowery jugs of utensils.

'Whisky? Or brandy? I think I've got some schnapps here somewhere.'

'Christ, yes, please. Whisky.'

On a mother-of-pearl inlaid table beside me is a lamp, draped with a fringed shawl. It casts an ethereal glow over the photograph next to it – a large version of the one in Abe's file. It looks like a film studio shot from the forties or fifties. The eyes of the woman in the picture are emerald green, like the doll's.

'Are you an actress?' I say.

'Was,' she snorts. 'Last job I did was a corpse in *Casualty*. But now I'm too old even for that!' She gives a wheezy laugh.

With her gnarled fingers she fills two greasy tumblers to the brim and brings them over, then sits down on the club chair opposite with a grunt of effort. Cataracts have turned her green eyes milkily opaque.

'What did you mean, when you said you saw me bumping my case over the bodies?'

She sips her whisky. I notice her lips pull up at each side, Joker style, perhaps from a primitive attempt at a facelift.

'This is a church,' she says. 'So, where's the graveyard?'

'I assume they moved it.'

'They moved the headstones, but left the bodies. Over the years, they've been gradually coming to the surface. Sometimes the dogs dig up a bone.'

I grimace, thinking of what I have been walking over every day and she laughs again. With the draperies muffling all sound, it seems eerily close to my ear.

168

'Isn't there anyone you want to call? It can really shake you up, that sort of thing.'

There is. I want to speak to Daniel so badly my chest aches, but that's precisely the reason I can't. Relying on someone else as an emotional crutch means I'll just end up like Jody.

'If you don't mind my just sitting here for a bit, I'll be fine.'

'Not at all, lovely. It's nice to have a visitor. Especially one who reminds me so much of my beautiful boy.' She sips her drink, leaving a scarlet semicircle on the glass.

'Did you see Abe often?'

She sighs. 'Every Monday evening he'd come down and have supper with me. Meatballs, or smoked haddock with mash, and liquor, half a bottle of whisky and sherry for afters. Lovely. I miss him.'

I smile at the thought of them getting pissed, then maybe dancing together to some music hall tune.

'He's not going to wake up, is he?'

My smile fades. I shake my head.

'I could tell when I saw him, that night. All that blood. I didn't want to look but you can't help yourself.'

'Did you see what happened?'

'I heard footsteps on the stairs and then that poor girl screaming. By the time I got outside she was kneeling by his side, all covered in blood like the one in that Stephen King film . . . *Carrie*.'

'I'm sorry,' I say. 'If there's anything I can do, then please—'
I bite my tongue immediately. I don't want to be spending my Monday nights down here eating smoked haddock and discussing Lula's past glories.

'He was *your* brother, darling,' she says gently. 'I'm sorry for you.'

'And Jody,' I say. 'She's the one really suffering. Abe and I barely knew one another.'

There's a beat of surprised silence.

'Jody?'

I can't read her expression. My heart pounds faster. Did Abe tell her something about their relationship? Some secret? But she

169

called Jody *that poor girl*, so she can't think Jody had anything to do with his fall.

'He wasn't . . . violent towards her, was he?'

She raises her drawn-on eyebrows. 'Your brother didn't have a violent bone in his body. Though I wouldn't have blamed him.'

I put the tumbler down, half finished. 'Why do you say that?'

'Ah, she just wouldn't leave him alone.' She rolls her eyes and a flake of crusted mascara drifts down onto her blouse. 'Whenever he turned around, there she was, like a bad smell.'

Sounds like the old lady's jealous. Perhaps she was hoping those drunken Monday nights might turn into something else. A friendly fuck now and again, to remind her of the beauty she used to be.

She's watching me and there's something about that heavy-lidded gaze that makes goosebumps spring up on my arms. I'm not sure I like her, or the dismissive way she talks about Jody. I find myself bristling on Jody's behalf.

'She *was* his fiancée. It's not abnormal to want to spend time with the person you're about to marry.'

Lula laughs then, loud and ringing, like the crowing of a cockerel. 'Fiancée? Abe didn't have a fiancée! He didn't have a girlfriend at all, my love.'

The way she's staring at me, with an expression of pitiful disbelief, makes me feel like slapping her.

Abe didn't have a girlfriend, so what was Jody? A casual shag who got the wrong idea? No, no, it's more than that, it has to be. What about the ring? The photograph? He didn't tell Lula because he thought she'd be jealous.

'Don't tell me you didn't know?'

My heart is pounding now, with anger and with something else. I'm beginning to understand. Oh, God.

The sequins on her sleeves shimmer, making me dizzy. Her red lips open, a string of saliva stretching and breaking. 'Abe was queer as a nine-bob note!'

170

'No,' I say stupidly. 'No, he . . . she . . .' But even as my brain struggles to process the information I know it's true.

I'm looking into his eyes on the parapet of Eilean Donan castle and I know he's different. The girls' cooing means nothing to him, but his hidden heart yearns to open up to someone the same way mine does. Was he trying to tell me then? I could have guessed, if I hadn't been so wrapped up in myself. I could have helped him, taken him with me. I could have stopped him having to pretend to be something he's not.

But he's in London now, with a million other men just like him. There's no reason for shame or fear. Our parents are five hundred miles away. What possible reason would he have to pretend?

'Then why . . .' I begin, and my voice is thread-thin. 'Then why was he stringing Jody along? Why didn't he just tell her?'

'He wasn't stringing her along. She knew perfectly well, just pretended it wasn't happening. She's mad, of course. You're not going, are you? You haven't finished your drink.'

But I'm already up, hopping and stumbling over urns and Ali Baba baskets in my rush for the door.

I take the stairs two at a time, thumping the light switches as I go. Bursting out onto the fourth floor I hammer on Jody's door, hard enough for the splintered lock to crunch and give a little more.

'Jody! Jody! Open the damn door, now!'

171

# 23. Mira

I have got what I wanted. I have made the sister think it is Jody that killed Abe.

Bang, bang, bang, on the door.

She is shouting and swearing and threatening. I crouch in the hallway, praying for Jody not to open up. The sister is so angry she will hurt her, I am sure. And it will be my fault. I should have thought. I was trying to protect you, Loran, and now that poor mad girl will suffer for it.

There is a louder bang and the wall I am leaning on shudders. She has broken the door in.

I hear her footsteps pound up the hall and another bang as she kicks open the inner door.

I know I should keep away, look after the baby and you, but how could I live with myself if Jody was hurt because of what I did?

I open the door of the flat, just a crack, to listen.

There are no sounds of an argument. Perhaps Jody is out. Has the sister already gone away, or is she waiting inside the flat for her? Should I call the police and say there has been a break-in? Perhaps the sirens will frighten her off and I will have a chance to warn Jody.

But when I return from getting my phone I hear something that makes my heart squeeze up in fear.

Footsteps on the stairs.

I pray that I will hear them stop and one of the other flat doors open, but they continue on, up and up and up.

And then her face comes into view, behind the bars of the banisters.

She is pale and sad, like always. She has no idea what has happened. What is waiting for her.

She comes out on the landing. And still I am too much of a coward to open the door and stop her. I tell myself I am thinking of the baby, of my blood pressure, but it is just fear. Fear to admit what I have done. Fear of what will happen to you if I do.

Then there is no more time. As she passes in front of my door the breeze from her skirt wafts against my face and then she is gone, into the flat.

There was a time when the difference between right and wrong seemed so simple – before I met you. I was brave, then. I was brave because I was surrounded by people who loved me. Now they are very far away and all I have is you, and you do not love me.

I stand up.

I may have changed much from the girl I used to be. I may have become afraid, shameful, unlovable. But I will not let this happen. I will face whatever harm may come to me – and yes, the baby too – because I cannot live with the woman I have become. A woman who will allow others to suffer because of her own lies and cowardice.

I go out on the landing.

Now I hear voices

They are speaking too fast for me to understand. But I can clearly make out the harsh anger in the sister's voice and Jody's trembling, high-pitched responses, like the fluting of a tiny *kaval*. She is afraid. I have passed my fear onto her because I could not stand the burden of it. I must have the courage to take it back.

Jody's latch lies on the floor, the wood splintered where it was torn out. She must be strong, this woman, though she is as slight as her brother. Perhaps she would not be so easily hurt.

I creep over the threshold, cupping my belly as if a comforting hand will somehow make up for the pounding of my heart and the rushing of my blood. The baby will feel my fear and be afraid too. I am unworthy of him.

As I pass up the landing, the shouting goes on.

I reach the open door.

I have never seen inside this flat before. It is as shabby and poor as ours, but the walls are covered in pictures. They are, I think, supposed to be drawings of Abe. In the middle of the room is a table. A pair of scissors lie open.

The sister stands at the table, her face as white as *sultjash* as she snatches up scraps of paper and hurls them to the floor, shouting all the while. Jody is pressed against the wall, sobbing.

It does not seem that the sister plans to hurt her. I could go. They haven't seen me.

The sudden silence when the shouting ends is almost shocking. My ears ring with it and my pulse pounds in my head. The baby is so still inside me. Have I frightened him to death?

Abe's mild eyes look down at us from the pencil drawings.

She picks up the last piece of paper — or two pieces taped together. I cannot make out the image and I think she is going to toss it to the floor with the rest, but she doesn't. The next words she says are so cold and clear that I understand them perfectly.

'You were never his fiancée. You were his stalker.'

Now, with a curl of her lip, she brings both hands up to the top of the paper and starts to twist her thumbs. She is going to tear it in two.

Jody screams then. 'No, no, no!'

And before I can do anything, she lunges for the scissors.

*She sits quietly, her homework on her lap, pencil poised, head bent as if she is reading it. But she isn't. She can't concentrate. Her brain is throwing off pulses of warmth that fizzle through her blood, making her fingertips and the ends of her toes tingle.*

*Her brother sits beside her. It's a double bed so there's plenty of room, but still they sit close – well, she sits close to him, close enough to feel his chest rise and fall at every sigh and every impatient jerk of his pencil, as if the movements were made by her own body.*

*The duvet is soft under her bare thighs. And so clean! They change the sheets every single week and pour a thick blue liquid into the tray of the machine that makes them smell like flowers. The carpets are a sort of fudgey beige and most of the furniture is white. Their father drinks lots of coffee from an expensive stainless steel machine, and so, from breakfast onwards, the house is filled with its rich musk. Their mother bakes. From scratch. Using free-range organic eggs with bright orange yolks. She has promised to teach her how to make a lemon drizzle cake. Which is easy, apparently.*

*Her brother huffs and drops his head back onto the headboard.*
*'Bollocking hell.'*

*She smiles. She would like to be able to help him, but though they are the same age, he is working at a far higher level. She is dyslexic. Not thick and useless and a waste of space, but dyslexic. Her new parents suspected it and the teachers tested her. That is why she's so creative, they have told her. Dyslexic people are more imaginative than other people. They call it 'having an imagination', not lying, and she doesn't feel the need to lie any more. There is nothing to hide. Nothing to be ashamed of, they have told her. Nothing.*

*'Wanna play* Grand Theft Auto*?'*

*She screws up her nose. She promised their mother that she wouldn't let him distract her. She has been making good progress. She can read*

Harry Potter, *now. She is on a special programme at school called Soundbites, and that has helped her with her spelling.*

'Come on. I can't be arsed with this.'

*He slides off the bed, scratching his lower back, making the T-shirt ride up. The skin on his back is completely smooth and blemish-free. His deodorant has a pleasant minty smell, and sometimes after a match he smells of sweat. But not the stale, fetid reek of poor hygiene: a fresh, young smell, that you could bottle and sell as a perfume. She can feel love creeping up on her, warming her up from deep inside all the way to her fingertips. But she's not afraid. This is not a love born of desperation, but one she can rely on forever. Her brother will always be there for her. They will grow old together. He will be a doting uncle to her children. She will have children. They've told her that she still can, despite everything.*

*He swigs from the litre bottle of Coke on the bedside table, the muscles in his throat rippling as the liquid passes through. When he has finished he hurls the empty bottle at the waste paper basket and misses, then wipes his arm across his mouth.*

'Come on, dopey. What are you staring at?'

'What if Mum comes up?'

*He snorts.* 'Mother wouldn't dare come in here without asking. I might be wanking!'

*He gives a barking laugh and she smiles.*

*They play the game for more than an hour and she is glad when he announces that he is hungry and tosses the controller onto the carpet. He stands and stretches. His stomach is muscley and a line of dark hair runs from his belly button into the low waistband of his sweatpants. Suddenly, for no reason at all, her throat tightens.*

'I'll go and make you a sandwich,' *she says quickly.* 'What would you like?'

'Bacon. Loads of ketchup. Microwave the bread first so the butter melts. Oh, and a cup of tea, please, Sisterella.'

'Coming right up!' *She smiles and tries to haul herself out of the beanbag, but it's too low and she stumbles back. He sniggers and grasps her arm, yanking her up so forcefully she stumbles into his*

176

chest. It is rock-hard from all the exercise he does. She can feel his blue eyes on her face but she doesn't meet his gaze.

'What do you fancy?' he says. His breath is sour from all the Coke.

'I'm not hungry.'

'You should eat more. Look at you. Flat as a pancake.'

'I will.'

'Good girl.' He smacks her bum as she goes out of the room.

# 24. Mags

I sit alone in a squalid little interview room. The table is pocked with cigarette burns, little black scoops I can just fit my finger-tips into. I've been doing this for three quarters of an hour, waiting for PC Derbyshire to come and take my statement, all the time resisting calling Daniel, who is probably on *date night* with Donna.

Jody's attempt to murder me was laughable. The hand holding the scissors shook so much the light bounced off the blades like a disco ball. I leaped at her and snatched them from her hands and I might very well have used them on her if weren't for the sudden entrance of Mira. She thrust herself between the two of us, waving her hands and crying, *'Ndal! Ndal!'*

It was the sheer melodrama of the scene as much as anything else that chastened me, and I sat down at the table while she called the police and Jody wailed like a child and tried to gather up her papers.

There were several letters from Abe, asking her to stop, warning her that he'd speak to Peter Selby, letters she had cut words out of to make new ones that said what she wanted them to. *My Jody . . . I love you . . . I will be yours always . . .*

The walls of her flat were covered in awful pencil drawings of Abe. Abe smiling. Abe sleeping. Abe gazing into the distance, a Pierrot tear on his cheek. Laughable if they weren't so pathetic.

There were a few photographs too, that I assume she stole from his flat after the accident. One had been grainily enlarged on a copier and clumsily spliced together with a picture of her. Full-size it was obvious, but she had managed to shrink it down – perhaps at the Internet café – to create something vaguely convincing, if you didn't look too hard. I'd been convinced. It had been sitting there on the bedside table all that time and I hadn't given it a thought.

My cruel impulse to tear it to pieces in front of her eyes was what triggered her pitiful attack, but I'm glad it stopped me. This was evidence after all. Evidence that she was a psychopath who had stalked my brother and pushed him to his death when he rejected her advances.

How could I have been so stupid to believe all her stories? They might as well have been about fairies and unicorns.

The door finally opens and PC Derbyshire enters. 'Miss Mackenzie.' Her voice is clipped and professional. Hopefully she's feeling rather foolish for all that *not every tragedy is a crime* stuff.

'I've written out my statement,' I say, pushing the paper across to her.

It takes her a long time to read it. Finally she looks up at me. 'You seem convinced Miss Currie attempted to murder your brother.'

'Of course she did. And it won't be *attempted* murder when I have to switch his machine off.'

She shifts in her seat, making the swivel mechanism squeal, then places both hands palm down on the table. I wonder if this is in the police handbook under *placating gestures*.

'Miss Currie denies having anything to do with your brother's accident.'

'Oh, so it's an accident now? You do know she's a notorious liar? You told me she wasn't known to you in a criminal capacity. That's bullshit, though, isn't it? Eight years ago she was done for crying rape.'

'Charges were never brought, and I didn't feel it was relevant to this case.'

'Not relevant that she's a liar? You believed her story without making any attempt to investigate.'

Derbyshire inhales and exhales before she speaks again. 'The unfortunate fact is that there were no witnesses to your brother's fall, and the evidence is circumstantial at best. Aside from the caution over the rape claim, Miss Currie has never been in trouble before, she never threatened your brother with violence, and your brother never complained to us that he felt in danger. Plus I don't think she'd have the physical strength to overpower him.'

I fold my arms. 'Don't they call stalking "murder in slow motion"?'

She blinks her porcine eyes, the lashes clogged with brown mascara. 'Your brother never reported a stalking incident to us. It seems to me that Miss Currie just had a very strong, unrequited attachment to him – and she does have a history of forming these powerful crushes.'

'What sort of history?'

'The boy she accused of rape – the foster brother – she had, by all accounts, developed a bit of a thing for him too.'

'*A bit of a thing?*' I stare at her. 'She accused him of rape when he rejected her. And now my brother rejects her and, lo and behold, he ends up brain-dead. You can't see any sort of connection there?'

'Shall I help you out?'

Her square cheeks are reddening now as she tries to stop herself saying the things she really wants to. She's not silly. She knows I'm a lawyer, can probably guess that I'm recording all this with my phone.

'Crying rape and murder are very different crimes, with very different criminal pathologies.'

'That boy turned to drugs because of her. A good life ruined.' I remember how cold I was to his mother, Helen, and guilt only fuels my anger. 'She should have gone to prison.'

The policewoman sighs. 'Jody Currie has only ever been a danger to herself, Miss Mackenzie. There's not enough evidence for us to charge her with your brother's attempted murder.'

'I want to see your superior officer.'

She breathes deeply, gathering herself. 'Your brother was a strong, fit young man. He'd been a member of Stone's Boxing Club for five years.'

I open my mouth to protest that this is the first I've heard of it, but remember in time that everything Jody told me about my brother is a lie.

'We've spoken to the manager, who said that though he was lean he was a very powerful fighter. Apparently he had been the victim of homophobic attacks as a teenager and had learned to defend himself.'

An angry flush rises to my cheek. 'You knew my brother was gay and you never thought to mention it to me? You just let me believe that crazy bitch all along.'

She looks at me steadily. 'People's private lives are complicated, Miss Mackenzie. It only becomes our business when a crime has been committed.'

'Like pushing someone over a stairwell?'

'As I was saying, it's very unlikely Miss Currie would have the physical strength to overpower your brother.'

'She could have caught him off-balance.'

'If there had been a fight or argument someone in the building would have heard something.'

I snort. 'Those crazies?'

'We've spoken to her social worker who agrees that she is not a violent person. In her statement Miss Currie says that she came out of her flat after hearing a strange noise – sound carries in that place, as I'm sure you've noticed. It was then that she saw your brother lying on the concrete floor at the bottom of the stairwell. She went down to see if she could help him, then called 999 on her mobile. I can play you the recording if you like. She's hysterical.'

'So she's a good actress. She had her mobile with her, so either she'd just been out and was coming in or she was just about to go out, right?'

'Some people keep their mobiles in their pockets all the time. Or she looked over the stairwell, saw what had happened, and ran back inside to get it before she went down to Abe.'

I stare at her. Useless bloody British police. I could pursue a civil case: the circumstantial evidence is pretty strong.

'You are at least going to prosecute her for wasting police time, right? All the lies about him being depressed?'

'We've cautioned her.'

'Another caution? After everything she's done?'

'I accept you must feel that she made a fool of you, but injuring someone's pride is not a crime.'

I hesitate before answering, to make sure my voice is steady. 'So, if you're so convinced this psycho had nothing to do with it, how *do* you think my brother fell?'

There is a long beat of silence.

The policewoman's lipstick is seeping through the wrinkles around her mouth. Why do they do it, these women in positions of power? Why do they cling to these outdated conventions of femininity? She looks like an aging air stewardess.

'I still think he might have been depressed,' she says, and her voice is human again. 'I believe there's a history of mental illness in your family.'

I stiffen.

'We spoke to his GP in Scotland. As you probably know, Abe was treated for depression when he was fifteen.' She's carefully avoiding my gaze. 'He was working extremely hard and his employers admitted he was under a lot of pressure. I think he jumped, Mary,' she says gently.

I breathe slowly, tempted to correct her – *It's Miss Mackenzie to you* – but what's the point?

She gets up from the table, taking my statement, with all its allegations about Jody, and tells me I can stay in the room as long as I need to.

When she's gone I stare at the pale blue wall, with its single claw mark gouged into the plaster.

It's not my fault. I was a child, the same as Abe. We both did what we had to to survive. I'm not surprised he was depressed. He medicated with Prozac while I did so with booze and casual sex. The former cry for help always inspires more sympathy than the latter, of course.

In the silence I hear muffled voices and doors banging, the occasional laugh. Is she here? Have they finished with her already? Sent her home to spin some new tale in which I am the wicked sister who poisoned Abe's mind against her, or killed him to prevent them being together?

I could just go home. Back to my old life. Back to Jackson for some no-strings distraction. Leave Abe's future in the hands of the doctors. Leave Daniel to Donna.

I close my eyes and push my fingertips back into the scorch marks. The room smells of stale smoke. They can't have changed the carpets since the ban came in.

My phone, on silent, buzzes angrily in my bag. I force myself not to look, but can't repress the childish hope that it might be Daniel.

Perhaps Derbyshire is right. Maybe Abe jumped. He was overworked and exhausted. Jody was on his case the whole time, so he must have dreaded coming home. Perhaps the relationship with Redhorse came to a bitter end and left him heartbroken.

And yet the picture Lula painted of my brother was not of a depressive. He might have been as a closeted gay teenager, but now? The novel on his bedside table was half finished; I came to the page he had turned down, just after the plot twist when everything was thrown up in the air. It sounds silly, but wouldn't you find out what happened before you jumped? Unless it was on impulse. On the way back from a lonely night drowning his sorrows? Except that he hadn't drunk anything. And it happened early evening, only an hour or so after he'd got back from work.

I think of the bruises on Jody's clavicles and Abe's torn shirt, both signs of a struggle.

The fact that Abe was not wearing his jacket with his wallet in the pocket, as if someone had knocked on the door of the flat and called him outside for a moment.

I think about the fact that she was prepared to destroy the life of the last man who rejected her.

She did it, I'm sure of it, but with so little evidence what can I do?

Getting up from the table my legs feel like lead. I pick up my bag and walk back through the corridors of the police station, then ask to be buzzed out into the main reception area.

The woman who visited Jody on her birthday is there, speaking quietly to the duty officer. She breaks off when she sees me.

'Excuse me, Miss Mackenzie. My name's Tabitha Obodom. I'm Jody Currie's social worker. Could I—?'

I push past her. I don't want to hear whatever sob story she's going to concoct to make me drop my accusations. I'm done with stories.

It's dark outside and raining just heavily enough to be unpleasant but too lightly to make the pavements glitter. I must confront Jody, but the last place in the world I want to be is back at St Jerome's. I just don't have the energy to sort out a hotel. I'll go back, have an early night, and then tomorrow decide whether to stay and see this thing through or else give up and go home. I'm not usually a quitter but tonight I feel beaten. In fact, when a passing lorry throws up a cascade of filthy puddle water all over my legs, I feel like crying.

Instead I take out my phone to call a cab.

The missed call was from Daniel. He didn't leave a message. I don't call him back.

# 25. Mira

The sister told the police that they must arrest Jody for murder. They didn't, though. They didn't say, *You have the right to remain silent*, as I have seen on British police programmes. They just said they would take her to the station for a little chat. They treated her gently because she was so very upset, and for that I was grateful.

I don't know what she will tell them at the station. Will she carry on protecting you?

You are still not home when I start preparing our dinner. The smell of the onions makes me feel sick. I know that a piece of bread and butter will take away the feeling but I do not have any. You said that women use pregnancy as an excuse to become fat pigs.

Is that why you went with another woman?

You think I didn't guess?

The *kondomat* in your gym bag.

The late nights spent in the pub with the guys from the building site?

The times you crept out in the middle of the night, like you did a few nights ago.

The sudden smiles as you thought about something – about someone – that wasn't me.

It's as if you wanted me to find out, but I stubbornly refused to, didn't I?

Because where will I be without you?

I will have to go home. To the shame of being unable to keep my husband. The dishonour surrounding me like a bad smell, revolting all other men who might once have wanted me. The sullied woman with her bastard child.

They will think it strange, the people who gave us the flat, that I can just trot back to Albania where we were persecuted for being Roma. We are not Roma. Why did you tell them we were? Because it would be easier for us to stay, you said. Why do you not want to go home? My parents do not understand. *I* do not understand. You have cut all ties with our mother country as if you believed the lie you told the English authorities, that we were in danger of our lives, that we could never go back.

Could you bear to leave the baby, Loran? He, at least, you seem to love.

It is a miracle I am pregnant at all. We make love perhaps once or twice in a month when you are drunk. You want a son. Then, you say, you would not be sad to come home every night to a miserable house. You would call him Pjeter, which means rock, because this is how a man must be. A man must be strong because women are weak. It is your burden to look after me.

The burden of my mother and sisters rested lightly on my father's shoulders. Papa often laughed. But all men are different, and all women are different.

The day I left her Mama told me to be a good wife for you. She was crying as she said it. You stood by the car with your face as hard and cold as the ice on the puddles in the ditches. Papa told her to hush because she was upsetting you. He was grateful that you had chosen me because you were from a better family than ours. Mother said it was you who should be grateful, that I was the most beautiful girl in the whole of Tirana and could have any man I chose.

I chose you. Papa would not have forced me into marriage if it wasn't my desire. I did it for love: but not of you, of them. I could not bear to see them disappointed. And I thought I could make you love me. It had been so easy for me before you. I had

186

thought men were simple creatures, that all you had to do was smile and wear pretty clothes, to paint your lips and listen to their woes, to make them supper and open your legs. I thought love would follow.

I could tell you did not desire me, even as you asked for my hand. This had not happened to me before. It excited me, the thought of bringing you round. I imagined the moment you would break: as you made love to me, suddenly love would come upon you like a wave crashing over your head. But you fuck me like my *pidhi* is just a hole in the mattress.

What is *she* like? Is she tighter? Softer? Does she smell better?

Is it Jody? Or the drug-addicted woman downstairs? If so, I shudder to think of what you bring back to our bed.

I swallow the nausea and chop the onions, then I wash and dry up, then I fold the towel and tuck it into the handle of the cooker so that the back and front edges are lined up. You like the house to be tidy.

I don't know what else I can do.

If I were at home I would feed the pigs now, or collect the eggs, or cut off the runners from the pumpkin plants. Or I might treat my hair with olive oil and simply lie by the window, reading Kadare, while the oil sinks into my hair to make it glossy and thick for a man to run his fingers through.

I am glad to hide my hair under a scarf now. Seeing it would only make me sad.

There is nothing else to do but wait, so I watch television – very quietly so that I can hear your footsteps echoing in the stairwell. I watch the programme where English people shout at each other because they have behaved badly towards one another. Sometimes it makes me laugh. Always it lightens my heart because it shows me that all people have troubles, that mine are not so great.

# 26. Mags

Daniel leaves me a message, asking how my brother is. It's a stupid thing to say and probably only born out of guilt over his rekindled domestic bliss, so I don't bother replying.

From the police station I head straight to the hospital.

Jody isn't there. The nurses don't seem aware of what's happened. If I told them she'd be barred from visiting him, but this is the one place I can guarantee to see her, so I don't.

I ask for Dr Bonville and they say he is coming to see another patient so I can catch him then. I'm intending to tell him I want Abe's machines turned off. But as I sit down beside my brother's bed, I find I cannot concentrate on the novel. I read the same page six times without taking it in, then finally close it with a sigh.

Abe's face is almost as pale as the pillowcase. The bruises are greenish yellow now, as if he's been painted with glow-in-the-dark paint.

I cannot fawn over this near-cadaver, like Jody, but I could at least hold his hand.

The rush of blood in my ears drowns out the monitors as I reach forward and take his limp hand in my own.

'Hello, Abe. It's Mags.'

It's the first time I have touched him since Eilean Donan castle.

His fingers are cool and dry. I was afraid they would be clammy with death. Carefully I slide my palm beneath his until we are palm to palm, then I clasp my fingers around his.

All sounds recede as I close my eyes and focus on the connection between us. A channel of electricity, or magnetism, or whatever it is that makes up the human soul.

Good God. I can't breathe, or swallow, or open my eyes. I'm as paralysed as my brother. My beautiful, kind, self-sacrificing brother, who ate fish suppers with a worn-out starlet, who loved a man with a red horse on his hip.

Fingers clasp mine. Just for a moment.

Then the fingers slacken and the hand becomes limp again.

I open my eyes. My brother lies motionless, his eyelashes still against his cheek. The respirator sucks and blows, the heart monitor bleeps. Somewhere far away, in the bowels of the hospital, an alarm sounds.

I don't lean forward and beg him to give me a sign that he can hear me. I'm not under any illusions. It is a reflex, that's all.

But I don't let his hand go.

Dr Bonville arrives on the ward but I'm already pulling on my coat. I've changed my mind. Was I actually going to let my brother die just as a way of getting back at Jody? What's wrong with me? Have I spent so long repressing all human emotion that I've become inhuman?

Bonville is busy with a patient at the end of the room, but as I pass him he looks up and moves towards me.

'Miss Mackenzie. I was intending to phone you but we've been very busy. May I have a word?' He gestures to the door, for me to follow him.

'We can talk here,' I say. 'It's not as if Abe's going to hear.'

He looks torn for a moment, then seems to give up. When he speaks again his voice is very low. 'Your brother developed a chest infection and by the time it was spotted it had become pneumonia.' He adds hastily, 'This wasn't down to anyone's negligence. These things happen with our very sickest patients.'

'So you've put him on antibiotics?'

He hesitates. 'We have.'

189

'Fine. You don't need to ask me about that sort of thing, right?'

'We don't.' He glances up at the door, as if seeking a way out, and I think again how young he is.

He inhales. 'Pneumonia is very dangerous for people in Abe's condition. Especially if the infection spreads to the bloodstream and causes sepsis – blood poisoning. I'm afraid the tests for sepsis have come back positive.'

He waits for me to process this fact – that my brother might die without my having to make any decision at all.

'I wanted to let you know, even though I'm not required by law to do so, that we've added a DNR to his notes.'

'Do not resuscitate?'

He nods, watching me warily.

I'm not sure whether to be angry or relieved. A wave of heat passes over my skin, followed by a wave of ice.

'There are several reasons for this, not just that his quality of life would be—'

'You don't need to explain,' I say. 'I under—' To my surprise, my voice cracks on the last word. However hard I try, I cannot force it out. And then I break down in tears, there, in the middle of the ICU, surrounded by the bleep and whir and gasp of machinery.

He lets me cry for a moment, then he puts his soft young hand on my shoulder. 'I really am so sorry.'

I know it's just what everyone says and means nothing coming from a man who must parrot it every day, but I reach up and clutch his hand as if I'm drowning.

'I can remove the DNR, if that's what you want.'

It takes me a minute to get myself together again, and when I'm finally able to speak my voice is soft and high as a child's. 'No. Leave it. Probably the best thing. And call me Mags.'

I raise my eyes to meet his gaze.

'I knew when I first saw him that he wouldn't last long,' he says. 'I've seen people of Abe's age with lesser head injuries and I've seen them get better enough to go home. But when I look

190

at them slumped in their chairs, dribbling, I think, if it were me, I'd rather be dead.'

I can tell he thinks he's made a mistake to talk to me that way. He fingers his name badge, blinking his long eyelashes. I want to tell him that it's OK. That the fight is seeping out of me by the day, that I can feel Abe's ghost creeping into me, softening me. But I can't speak.

'He sounded like a good man. I wish I'd had the chance to know him. And I promise you, Mags, I won't let him suffer.'

He squeezes my shoulder then and I reach up to clutch his hand, eyes closed, trying to suck enough oxygen into my lungs that I won't cry again.

When I'm sure I'm in control I open my eyes and smile at him. 'Thank you.'

He dips his head, then turns and walks away. A moment later the door swings shut and I am alone among the silently dying.

He has given me a gift. I won't have to make the decision to end my brother's life. I thought I could do it, but am I beginning to understand that I cannot trust myself any more. The person I thought I was, the person I made myself into, was a lie. And the lie is cracking like an eggshell, gradually exposing something new and white and clean.

I take the bus back to St Jerome's, hoping to compose myself during the journey. I can't confront Jody like this.

A work chat will sort me out. It's one-ish back home so Jackson will be back from his Saturday morning run. I take out my phone and hit the contacts, but on my way to his name I overshoot and Daniel's rolls up. I let my thumb hover over the number. Then I swipe up to Jackson's. Back down again. Back up. I am about to make the call to the US when the phone shudders in my hand and starts to ring. I almost drop it with shock. A number I don't recognise.

I answer.

'Miss Mackenzie?' A woman's voice, vaguely familiar.

'Who's calling?'

'It's Tabitha Obodom, Jody's social worker. The police have told me that you believe Jody pushed your brother over the stair-well. They said you're considering bringing a civil case against her.'

'And you want to try and talk me out of it.'

'Yes. Yes, I do.'

I tell her I'm not interested in hearing any bleating about Jody's difficult childhood. I tell her that England is too damn full of bleeding-heart social workers making excuses for criminals. I'm about to say that maybe the US states with the death penalty have got it right, but stop myself just in time.

'Please,' she says. 'Just a few minutes of your time. Just hear me out.'

It's nearly nine o'clock on a Saturday and this woman is prepared to come to St Jerome's for what is bound to be a hostile confrontation and then travel home again in the dark and cold. I think of Abe. I think of his kindness.

I say yes.

# 27. Mira

I am watching at the window when you finally come home, Loran. I see you park the car but you don't get out straightaway. You just sit there in the darkness. I wonder if you are looking at your phone, if you are texting *her*. But if you were on your phone I would see the glow of the screen.

After a while you get out. I watch you walk around the side of the building and then, just as you are about to disappear, you look up. I shrink back from the window in case you accuse me of spying on you, but you are not looking at me. You are looking at the flat of the man who fell, where the sister now lives. It cannot be her that you like – this affair was going on before she came. Before Abe fell.

Poor Abe. He always seemed such a kind, gentle man. The first time he spoke to me it was to offer help.

I was taking out the rubbish. Three big black bin bags, mostly clothes I knew I wouldn't wear again after the birth: tight dresses and short skirts, clothes from my life before. They weren't heavy, just awkward to carry, and it was taking me a very long time to get them down the stairs. Then I heard a door open on our floor.

'Let me help you with that,' he said.

'It's OK,' I said, but he was already taking two of the bags, his fingers brushing my own. I followed him down the stairs, a few paces behind so as not to have to speak to him. The only sounds were the rustling of the plastic and our quiet footsteps on the stairs.

We went out into the sunshine. It is not often sunny in England and when it is it makes me feel strangely sad. It makes me think of long summer evenings at home, lying out in the back field with my sisters, always barefoot, our feet nut brown and dirty as children's.

The sun on my skin was like a lover's caress and I paused for a moment with my eyes closed, letting its warmth spread across my face.

When I opened my eyes he was waiting for me at the corner of the building. I went to join him and we walked together to the bin store around the side. It's a disgusting place; in the summer I could not open the windows because the whole flat would smell of rotten meat and fermenting vegetables. As we threw down the bags there was an explosion of flies that made me jump back. I tripped on the handle of a toy pushchair and almost fell, but he caught my arm just in time and pulled me upright.

He smiled at me as I adjusted my scarf.

'Why do you wear that?'

'For modesty,' I said.

He laughed. 'You can be too modest, you know. Let the world see how beautiful you are. It doesn't last long.'

English people think it is funny to insult you, and I thought it was funny too. I said, 'Actually, I am seventy-two.'

At first he just stared at me – it took him a very long time to realise an Albanian Muslim woman was making a joke. Then he laughed so loudly it echoed around the building. I liked the way he laughed, with his whole body. He was so long and lean it was like a violin bow bending back.

My face warmed up, and my heart beat faster, and I realised I was feeling something I hadn't felt for three years, not since we left Albania. I was feeling attraction for a man. I didn't want him to leave.

'You are my neighbour,' I said.

'Only for the past two years,' he said, and his brown eyes sparkled. 'When's the baby due?'

I told him. 'I hope you have—' I gestured, poking something into my ears.

'Not at all,' he said. 'This place could do with a bit of life. Perhaps your husband will let me babysit.'

'Perhaps,' I said.

For a moment he just looked at me, and my smile faltered a little, because I knew the look was not one of desire, but of pity.

Then he looked over his shoulder. I followed his gaze and my blood turned cold.

You were watching us, Loran. You were standing by the corner of the building, with your work bag slung over your shoulder, and your face was white. Then you stepped to the side and were hidden by the building.

'I have to go,' I said, and hurried away, but when I got to the main entrance you had already gone.

I heard Abe's footsteps behind me, and I was so scared that he would try and talk to me again and you would see that I set off at a run across the waste ground, and the children in the playground laughed to see a Muslim woman running, with her black dress flapping.

You were nowhere to be seen, and when I got to Gordon Terrace and glanced back, I saw Abe going back into the building. I stood there for some minutes, feeling foolish, until the boys in hoods came walking down from the high road and then I hurried back to the building.

You were very late back from the pub that night, and I lay awake, terrified that this time you would actually strike me for behaving like a whore with another man.

But you did not.

You came into the bedroom and undressed and showered, then you made love to me, silently, in the darkness. I was glad because I had made you jealous.

Your key in the lock makes me jump. I did not hear your foot-steps on the stairs.

I wipe my face with a tea towel and run my fingers through my hair. It is short now, because you said it is more becoming for a married woman. I slip on my shoes too, because you say it is slovenly to go about barefoot, and I am smiling when you come into the room.

You do not know that I know.

'*Si je?*' I say.

'Mira.' You smile back at me, but the smile only reaches your lips. Your eyes are so sad and you drop your work bag onto the floor as if it was heavy as a dead body.

'How was your day?' I say.

You shrug. 'We are delivering cement.'

'Oh.' I smile, blinking, wondering how it can be so difficult to talk to a fellow human being. It is as though we are from different species. But the way you look back at me, I think perhaps you feel the same. You take out your phone.

'Look at these. They are cement silos. They store the powdered cement. We have to climb all the way up there.'

You point to a tiny ladder, as narrow as a zipper, running all the way up an enormous cylinder.

'You must be careful,' I say. 'If you fell you would break your neck.'

'Better that than falling into the silo. Then we would drown in cement powder and no one would ever know.'

'Don't say that. It's horrible.'

You are quiet then, frowning, lost in thought. Have I upset you again?

'I have made us *gjelle*,' I say brightly.

After a moment you raise your head. 'I can smell it. It smells good.'

'The baby makes it smell bad!' I say, and try to laugh.

Then, as if he is listening, he starts to kick.

'He is kicking, look.'

I know you would not want to see my bare belly so I press my dress against the bump and a tiny lump appears. The heel of the baby's foot.

I fear you might be disgusted, but now your smile goes to your eyes. You come over and cup your hand around it, and then it pushes out even further.

'He knows his father's touch,' I say.

For some reason tears start to my eyes, and then I see they are in your eyes also.

You stand with your hand on the baby's foot and we both know that you are only touching me to get to him.

'Does he hurt you?' you say.

'A little. Sometimes.' Your smile fades and I am sorry.

That night you do not go to the pub, but go to bed straight after dinner and cry yourself to sleep. When I thought you were happy with another woman it was bad, but this is worse. Loran, what are we to do?

# 28. Mags

Tabitha is short and overweight, but close up she has the face of a supermodel, with smooth, glowing skin and tranquil black eyes.

We sit down at the table, streaked blue by the street light through the stained glass. I've made her tea and myself a strong coffee. Even though the heating is up to maximum I feel cold and stiff, like an old woman, and I hunch over the steaming mug, trying to inhale some of the heat.

She sips her tea and then puts the mug down deliberately. 'Have you spoken to her yet?'

'I've tried, but she's not answering her door or phone.' I don't add that I'd been fully intending to break in if she hadn't had the locks changed. That must have been what she was busy doing when I was at the hospital.

'She'll be scared.'

'With good reason.'

'She didn't push Abe, if that's what you think,' she says. 'She was obsessed with your brother, but it was an infantilised thing. A pre-teen sort of crush. Had he shown the remotest interest in her sexually, she'd have been terrified. That's why she fixated on him. I think she knew underneath that he was gay and that she was perfectly safe from any adult involvement.'

'What makes you so sure she didn't do it?' I say. 'Seems to me British social workers have a habit of giving their clients far too much benefit of the doubt.'

She looks down at her mug, then back up at me.

'Your brother suffered her attentions with very good grace. She was happy with the status quo and his gentle discouragement did her no harm. There was no reason for her to challenge things. Even if she wanted to hurt him – and these letters contain no suggestion of that – she's far too physically and mentally fragile. She could never have managed it.'

I experience a strong sense of déjà vu. 'She could have caught him off guard. There's evidence of a struggle. And who knows what she's capable of when she lies all the time.'

Tabitha sighs unhappily. 'I accept Jody is strongly self-delusional. She constructs these fantasies because the truth of her past is so unbearable. Her father was never in the forces, if that's what she told you. He didn't die in a plane crash and her mother didn't kill herself.'

I hold her gaze. Nothing she can say will surprise me.

'She died of a drugs overdose a year or two after Jody was taken into care.'

So what? Plenty of care home kids go on to lead fully productive lives and don't become pathological liars/stalkers, so if she's trying to make me pity Jody she's going to be disappointed.

'It wasn't because of the drugs,' the woman goes on. 'Why she was taken into care.'

I sigh. 'Go on then.'

'Her father was part of a paedophile ring. Jody and her stepbrother were traded back and forth between men on a farm in Surrey.'

Sickened, I look away. Then I look back and my lip curls. 'Sure this isn't one of her tall tales?'

'Five of them are serving life sentences in Woodhill Prison. Jody has severe internal injuries consistent with sustained abuse as a very young child.'

199

In the silence that follows I can hear the swings creaking in the playground below.

Abe and I used to play in the local playground next to our house. We had to be back in time for tea or my mother would shout across the little park to us: 'Daddy's waiting to say grace!'

It was humiliating when that happened and the kids mercilessly ribbed us for it, so most days we made sure we were back in good time. But one day when Abe called me, I ignored him and carried on playing in the sandpit.

He climbed in and yanked at my sleeve. 'C'mon Mary.'

'Git tae fuck!' I shouted and pushed him so hard he fell back and banged his head on the wooden wall.

The playground fell silent.

Then all around me I heard the little thunks of spades and buckets being dropped into the sand. Abe was crying but no one went to comfort him. I knew why. I could feel the presence behind me, huge and dreadful as a monster from a nightmare.

'MARY MACKENZIE.'

My father's voice was like a sonic boom echoing across the mountains behind the estate. Slowly the other children got up.

'I don't think she heard Mrs Mack calling,' one of them said shrilly. I never did find out who had tried to defend me, but Christ, they were brave.

He ignored them. His shadow turned the yellow sand grey.

'Up.'

I carried on playing, grimly pouring sand from a plastic watering can to make a little hill that never got any higher.

'Up.' His voice was getting quieter and quieter.

The last dregs of sand poured out. The watering can was empty. I stared at it until the bright colours smeared together. It was so quiet you could hear the hairdryers growling in the salon down the road.

'Git tae fuck,' I said quietly.

He yanked me up so forcefully my humerus fractured with an audible crack. I screamed, and carried on screaming as he dragged me by my broken arm across the cold concrete, through our side gate and up the steps to our kitchen. Only when I started vomiting did they call the ambulance.

The doctor at Inverness Hospital had used my father's roofing firm and wasn't inclined to question his account of how my arm 'twisted awkwardly when I pulled her up'. It didn't sound so bad, and it wasn't a lie. The other children told their parents what I'd said and they all thought I deserved it. At church the following Sunday he received understanding pats on the back while I, the cross he had to bear, sat in the back pew with my arm in plaster, fiercely ignoring the shaken heads and pursed lips. For a time after that I thought about cutting his throat when he slept, but later I discovered boys and decided there were plenty of better ways to get my revenge.

The bastard ruined my childhood, but compared to Jody's he was Ned Flanders.

'I understand you're angry, Mags.' I bristle at her use of my first name. 'You feel humiliated and betrayed because you believed her. Don't be. She's very convincing. Of course she is. Even *she* believes everything she says, on some level at least.'

'So, what does she say when you pull her up on it?'

'We don't engage with her on those subjects. We let her tell herself the stories she needs to to keep herself strong.'

'You let her delude herself?'

'It's harmless. The whole thing about reliving your past to come to terms with it has actually started to be discredited. Everyone deals with trauma in a different way. Some people in Jody's position experience a complete fracturing of their personalities as they try to block out what happened to them. They become drug- or drink-dependent. Jody was a self-harmer for a while. But now she manages to keep her head above water with anti-anxiety medicine and a few harmless delusions – like the delusion that your brother was in love with her.'

'But they're not harmless, are they?' I get up and walk to the window. 'What about when she cried rape against those boys

– her foster brother and his friend? That could have seriously affected their futures, and probably did do some real damage. Enough people still think there's no smoke without fire.'

When she says nothing I turn around. Tabitha is looking at me.

'Don't tell me you actually believe her.'

'Yes, I do.'

I laugh. 'Oh, get real. She's a fantasist! I feel sorry for her, I really do, but she's clearly mentally ill.'

Tabitha's expression hardens. 'Abuse often leads to mental illness, but does that mean we should never believe a victim? Of course not – although abusers have used it as a defence for years. You must have read reports of the more high-profile cases in the press, bringing up the troubled lives and suicide attempts of abuse victims. It's done deliberately to trigger doubt in our minds: they're unstable, their story's a fabrication. Poor politician, or TV presenter, or whatever, their lives turned upside down by these twisted liars.'

She pauses to take a breath. 'That's the line those boys' lawyer pulled. It's called discrediting the witness and it should have been made illegal years ago.'

'It's not discrediting if it's true.'

'She was covered in bruises. Her vagina was torn.'

'Self-inflicted.'

Tabitha shrugs. 'That's what the judge said. Anyway.'

She gets up and the dark velvet skirt falls from her wide hips like a theatre curtain. I never thought a fat woman could be so beautiful. She is wearing a wedding band and a diamond solitaire engagement ring. I bet her children adore her.

'You know what I've often thought,' she says softly. Her eyes are nearly black, with just the merest prick of light at their centre. 'If I were a rapist I'd choose someone just like Jody. A self-harmer. A fantasist. Someone no judge in his right mind would believe.' She picks up her tapestry bag and slings it over her shoulder. 'Easy meat.'

After she's gone, I open my first bottle of wine.

# Sunday 13 November

# 29. Mags

I wake at midday with a pounding headache and a churning stomach that only eases after I've made myself sick in the toilet, the sounds of which presumably echo through my neighbours' pipework.

Every half hour throughout the day I knock on Jody's door, but either she's too scared to answer or she's managed to slip out without my noticing. Even though I know it's pointless, that she will just spin me some new line, I have to speak to her. I know she knows more about what happened to Abe than she's letting on, and I can't believe the police are letting her get away with flat-out lying to them.

By three I'm going stir crazy, so I decide to head to the Food and Wine to stock up on booze for later.

Letting myself out of the main door onto the deserted waste ground I'm suddenly convinced that Tabitha has already spirited her out of my clutches and I go around the side of the building and look up at her window. It reflects the darkening sky. I wouldn't even know if she was up there looking down at me.

I realise I'm not alone. The junkie from Flat Seven is standing behind the bins, smoking. She's wearing a short black lace dress and patent leather high heels. Heavy make-up masks the worst ravages of her face and I suspect whoever she's waiting for won't care that the wasted arms protruding from the lace sleeves are track-marked.

Turning to leave I tread on something slippery and, fervently hoping it's not a used condom, glance down. The flowers are incongruous among the fast-food wrappers and nappies. Some are still crisp and pink, the others, now brown and dying, must once have been – I catch my breath – white.

They're the flowers from the tumbler on Abe's bedside table.

The man who broke in must have thrown them down here on his way out of the building. His reasons for doing this are as mysterious as his reasons for taking them in the first place.

I go back the way I have come, then head across the waste ground towards Gordon Terrace.

Passing the playground I experience that familiar, unnerving sensation of being watched and turn, expecting to see the cat, or the junkie gazing balefully from the corner. But the grass is deserted and Lula's curtains are still.

I catch movement from the corner of my eye, but am only in time to catch a flicker of shadow disappearing down the other side of the building. Just someone on the way to the car park, perhaps, but in that case why didn't I hear them come out of the building?

Could it be Jody waiting for me to leave so she can creep back home?

I call her name, and my voice sounds lonely and small in the silence.

A minute passes.

Should I go after her? Assuming it is her. Assuming it's anyone.

No. I turn back and set off quickly for Gordon Terrace, where I'm relieved to see a mother with a double pushchair trundling towards the high road. I fall into step behind her.

Coming back from the Food and Wine half an hour later with two clanking blue carrier bags, I see a man waiting outside the main door. On the concrete beside him sits a large Amazon box.

As I come next to him I see the address label.

*M. Ahmeti, Flat 11, St Jerome's Church*

It must be something for the baby. A flatpacked cot or a baby bath, perhaps. She can't lug it all the way up the stairs on her own. And I can take the opportunity to thank her for preventing me murdering Jody.

'I'll take that up for her,' I say to the delivery man, averting my eyes from the piercings through his cheeks and eyebrow.

'It's OK,' he says. 'She's on her way.'

'In that case I'll wait and help her up with it.'

Opening the front door I see Mira's shadow through the frosted glass, coming down the last flight of stairs. After a glance at the piles of post – no telltale white corners protrude from the pizza menus – I hold the door open for her.

She doesn't catch my eye as she comes out.

'I'll help you,' I say loudly and clearly. 'With the parcel. Up the stairs.'

'No, no,' she mumbles. 'Is OK. I manage.'

She moves past me, wafting the baby-scent of talcum powder, and takes the electronic pen the delivery guy is holding out for her. I didn't plan to – though I don't know why I hadn't thought of it – but something makes me glance over her shoulder as she signs the screen.

The man slides the parcel through the doors and then goes. Mira bends to lift it and I take the other end.

We climb wordlessly. Past the first floor of the cripple and the bitter queen, past the junkie's flat and the fat man's, up to our floor. The alcoholic, the fantasist, the poison-pen writer.

She murmurs words of thanks and insists that she will be fine, but I just smile as she fumbles with her key, and say nothing. Perhaps she knows what's coming.

Once she has the door open she kicks the box through, slides through herself, and tries to close it again.

But I'm too quick for her.

The door twangs against my foot and I force it open, driving her back. We stand in the darkness of the hallway, both breathing heavily.

She says nothing. She knows why I'm here.

'You saw something, didn't you? The night my brother died. That's why you wrote the notes.'

I wait for her to deny it, but she doesn't. There is a rustle as she leans against the wall and takes a shuddering breath.

'I am a bad person,' she whispers. 'I think Loran is having affair with her.'

I sigh, disappointed. I thought she was going to tell me something real. Thought perhaps she might have seen what happened after all. Though Jody has managed to pull the wool over my eyes quite spectacularly, of one thing I am certain: she only had eyes for my brother. Is it possible that Mira, living right next door, could not have known that?

'I don't think so. Jody was in love with my brother.'

'I know, I know. I just stupid, imagining things.'

'Like what?'

'What?'

'What were you imagining you saw between Loran and Jody?'

And then, without warning, the door behind us opens and a man walks in. For a moment he is just a shape in the darkness, but at once the whole atmosphere in the room changes.

As the light flicks on Mira starts, her shadow jumping on the wall.

A big, Eastern European man, dressed in heavy work clothes, his black boots crusted with cement, a rucksack slung over his shoulder. He's in his early thirties, at a guess, with a broad, flat face and fair hair cropped so short he is almost bald.

How can he have come up without us hearing? Unless he was trying to be quiet, to catch us doing something wrong.

I glance at Mira. All colour has drained from her face.

But when I turn back to the man, I see that he too is as white as a ghost and he's staring at me with an intensity that makes my heart pound, his eyes passing down my body, then up to the parka's fur trim around my neck. Is he going to hit me?

He's blocking my exit and there's nowhere to go but back into the flat. I finger my phone in my pocket.

'What do you want?' His voice is low. The thick accent, so familiar these days, is suddenly threatening.

How much has he heard?

'I was just helping your wife with this heavy box.' My voice is steady and I force myself to meet his cold gaze. Surprisingly, he doesn't seem able to hold mine, and his grey eyes flick away. 'Can't be long now until the baby comes. You must be very excited.'

He glances at his wife and she stares back at him with wide dark eyes. She's afraid of him. Does the bastard beat her up?

'Thank you, thank you, it was very kind of you,' she gabbles, trying to herd me to the door but he doesn't move to let me past. The hands hanging by his side are large and rough.

I straighten my back to let him know that he isn't scaring me and the parka rustles softly.

Then something in him gives. His shoulders sink, his head drops, and we both press ourselves into the wall as, without another word, he stalks up the hall, wafting the smell of sweat and dust.

Kicking open the inner door, he crosses the room, dumps his bag on the sofa and kicks off his boots, sending chunks of cement skittering across the floor. Then, as if I'm not there, he starts undressing, dropping his bomber jacket where he stands, then pulling off his T-shirt before disappearing from sight. A moment later I hear the characteristic drone of the shower pump kicking in.

'Thank you,' Mira murmurs. 'He would be very angry if he knew what I had told you.'

'That's OK,' I manage, but I'm barely listening. I don't even glance at Jody's door as I make my way back across the landing and into the flat, where I close the door and lean against the wood, breathing heavily in the darkness.

I don't know what it means yet, but I know what I saw.

As Loran undressed I caught a glimpse of a tattoo just peeping from the waistband of his tracksuit bottoms. A tattoo of rearing hoof and the feathery tips of a mane, inked in red.

Loran is Redhorse.

*The stereo is on too loud for her to hear what they're saying, so she just gazes out of the window at the terraced houses flashing past. Felix's friend is driving too fast, occasionally slugging from a can of lager. So is Felix, and he already seems drunk, though the other one doesn't seem to be affected by it. Occasionally he glances at her in the mirror and waggles his eyebrows. She thinks he's trying to be funny so she smiles, but when his eyes go back to the road she shuffles along the back seat, out of his line of vision. The car's in a disgusting state: fast-food cartons litter the footwells, the upholstery is stained and clotted with mud, and CDs and magazines are scattered on the seat and the parcel shelf. The front covers of the magazines either feature bare-chested muscular men or almost-naked young women. The lower half of one of these front pages has torn away to reveal an article entitled: "Potting the Brown – honest, love, me knob slipped!" The picture is of a woman's buttocks in a G-string. It makes her feel sick.*

*This boy is Felix's oldest friend. They'd been at nursery school together and only separated when Felix got into the grammar school. The other boy's parents had sent him to a private boys' school specialising in sport, but the two of them play rugby every Sunday morning for the local club. He is much bigger than Felix, as if a cursor has been put in the corner of a normal nineteen-year-old and then dragged out a bit.*

*Today is Monday and Felix's parents won't be back from their long weekend in Whitstable until the following morning, so both boys have bunked off school for a bit of fun. They persuaded her to join them and for a while she was flattered, but now she just wishes she was at school. Back at the house they made no attempt to include her in the conversation; in fact, they positively excluded her, whispering and giggling in corners like seven-year-olds.*

*She gets out her phone to check the time.*

'No phones!' the big one barks and thrusts his arm between the seats, beckoning with his fingers for her to hand it over.

She does so automatically and regrets it immediately. She has always been too biddable. To her horror he throws it straight into Felix's lap.

'Any dirty selfies?'

'Felix, please.'

She watches helplessly as he scrolls through the shots of the roof-tops she took from her bedroom, the dead Red Admiral butterfly, and the unsuccessful attempts to capture the full moon. She squeezes her eyes shut and waits, but when it comes, the explosive jeer makes her start from her seat and the inertia-reel snaps tight across her chest.

'What are you, a fucking stalker or something?' Felix shouts over the music.

'She's probably got a pair of your skiddy pants under her pillow!' the other one bellows.

She makes a dive for the phone but Felix whisks it out of her grasp. On screen is the close-up of his face that she took when he fell asleep on the sofa.

'Ahh, bless,' the big one coos. 'Ook at iddy biddy Fewix!'

'Piss off!'

Her breath is speeding up. In a minute she will cry, which will either antagonise or encourage them.

But then a worse thing happens. Felix has carried on scrolling through the pictures and now he comes to one she has forgotten she even took.

'Shit,' says Felix, holding the phone out for his friend, who snatches it and stares at it even though he should be concentrating on the road.

'Gross,' he says, tossing the phone back again. 'You got some disease or something?'

She had been trying to get a picture of the scars on her buttocks and thighs, to see if they would be visible if she wore boy-leg bikini bottoms instead of the Bermuda shorts she habitually wears on their family trips to the pool on Saturday mornings. They were. They fanned out from the inadequate strip of fabric, still livid purple, despite the doctors' promises that they would fade to white.

'Self-harmer,' Felix says, dismissively.

She is about to correct him – he knows at least some of the things that have happened to her – but changes her mind. Self-harming is something this other boy can get his head around. The other stuff isn't.

'Wow, you really are fucked-up, aren't you?' he says, craning his bull-neck to try and catch her eye in the mirror.

'Drop me off here,' she says suddenly.

She waits, with her fingers poised on the door handle, for the car to slow, but it does not.

'Let me out,' she says, her voice rising. 'Please!'

'Ah, come on,' Felix says softly. 'Let's just forget it, mate. Let her out.'

'Keep your hair on,' the friend says, but his tone is gentler. 'I'm only messing with you. Look, we're there now.'

And now it's too late – they're driving through the gates of the rugby club.

# 30. Mags

He was screwing my brother while his wife was pregnant.

And now she's trying to protect him.

At least, I assume that's what the notes were for, to deflect attention away from him and onto Jody. And there's only one reason I can think of that he needs to be protected.

If he pushed Abe.

Mira knew he was having an affair but she thought it was with Jody. Maybe Abe threatened Loran that he would tell her the truth. A heterosexual affair she might be able forgive, but a gay one? Especially as she's a devout Muslim. She would leave him. He would lose his child.

So he pushed Abe over the stairwell to keep him quiet, and Mira saw him do it.

She said he was at the boxing club the night Abe fell and I rack my brains to think of the name Derbyshire told me.

*Stone's.*

I look it up on my phone and find an address. North from here, in the no man's land between Crouch Hill and Hornsey, places I never knew existed before. I check my phone app and find a bus that runs from the high road.

*Stop. Think.*

Do I really want to get into this?

Jody's one thing – a mentally unstable, rather pathetic young woman, physically weak and easily intimidated. But Loran is something else. If he did push Abe then he's capable of anything, and clearly his wife is scared of him. He could simply kill me and then head back to Albania. Am I prepared to risk that just to find out the truth?

But have I ever risked anything for Abe? Isn't it about time I did right by him and ensure that whoever hurt him is caught and punished?

I scroll through my phone contacts for Derbyshire's direct line, but then I hesitate. With only a few porn photos and some sexy texts to go on, who's to say she'll do anything?

I need more.

I'll just have to be careful.

Checking the address one more time I let myself quietly out of the flat and head downstairs.

There's no sign of the gang and for once Gordon Terrace is busy with people returning from work. Under the dull orange street lights the faces look sallow and ill. No one gives me a second glance. A woman in the baggy, chequered trousers of a chef lets herself out of a front door and I hear a snatch of the boisterous family life going on within. She closes the door and walks down the path, looking tired.

I follow her to the high road.

The bus stop is crowded and I ease myself into a gap beside a pushchair with a listless toddler staring at a tablet.

It's getting colder. Under the canvas of the Converses my feet are numb. I wiggle my toes and stamp my feet, smiling at the toddler who glances up at me with blank eyes. The eyes of her mother, who is arguing with someone on the phone, telling them that *it's not fucking acceptable*.

The rush hour traffic is heavy. Nose to impatient tail. Checking the bus app to see if it's close I see a text has come through from Daniel.

I've told Donna I can't try again because I've met someone I care about. I know it's tough with your brother but if we take it slow . . . ?

I'm seriously not in the mood.

214

*I told you I didn't want a relationship.*

The bus arrives and I get on. Instantly too hot in the parka, but feeling somehow protected by its bulk, I find a seat at the back. Heat is pumping from vents by my calves and the shudders of the engine pass straight through my spine, but at least no one can sit behind me.

I realise that I am scared. It's an unfamiliar feeling. An unpleasant one.

The buildings thin out as we turn off the main road and we speed up, past rundown housing estates and warehouses with all their windows broken. The few cars parked by the kerb are scratched and dented. Some have crude signs offering them for sale at a paltry few hundred pounds. The pavements start emptying out, leaving only the drunks and the elderly and a few hurrying schoolboys. The street lights cast their faces in a gritty orange glow.

As we draw nearer to the gym the bus and a car behind us are the only vehicles on the road. If I thought the area around St Jerome's was bleak, this place is infinitely worse.

Perhaps all this fuss I am making is for nothing and Derbyshire was right all along. Perhaps Abe did kill himself. If I lived here, I would.

I hear the rumble of trains before I see the bridge.

Stone's Boxing Club is set into the arches beneath. Surrounded by a concrete forecourt, the door is a slab of metal, its windows protected by metal shutters. The effect is almost comically macho. I presume Mira has never been here, because surely even *she* couldn't miss the fact that this is a gay gym. To my relief, just above the main door is a CCTV camera.

I get out and the bus roars away. The burgundy hatchback that was following us turns into a side street and I am left completely alone under a street lamp.

I take out my phone to photograph the place and see another text from Daniel.

*Message received. Over and out.*

I stare at it for a moment, wondering whether to reply. It's so quiet that the sudden thunder of a train passing overhead makes me start. The silence resumes, but for some reason the hairs on my back are prickling. I turn again, but the street is deserted in both directions. Then I notice a man smoking outside a pub a little way up the road. A squat, drab building with an ugly case of concrete fatigue, its incongruously pretty name is the Blue Mermaid. As I watch he tosses the butt into the road and goes back inside.

The sooner I'm out of here the better.

I take the photos and pocket the phone, then, pulling the coat tighter around me, stride up to the metal door and hammer on it with my fist.

An ugly teenager opens it. His vest and boxing shorts reveal a physique far too bulky for his years. Steroids probably. Perhaps he's hoping to distract attention from his underbite and acne, but the effect is just orcish.

He looks me up and down with an expression of distaste.

'I want to speak to the manager.'

'Stanley!' he shouts, then waddles away, his thighs so big his legs don't scissor properly. As he opens a door at the end of the corridor there's a sudden cacophony of animal noises – grunts and squeals and roars, added to the slaps and thuds of impact.

Did my brother come here? I wouldn't have thought it was his scene, but then a beautiful black man emerges from the same door and pads down the corridor to the water fountain. I avert my eyes from his buttocks, clad in shorts so tight they look painted on. *Fair enough, Abe.*

A wiry man who must be in his seventies at least emerges from a door to my right. His tracksuit is halfway between street style and PE teacher. He's even got a whistle.

'Can I help you?'

'I need to talk to you about my brother, Abe Mackenzie.'

We enter a little office that looks out over the rings. Beyond the glass men are sparring, pummelling punch bags, running at

216

each other with giant plastic pillows, and dancing around like ballerinas, all the while looking intensely, aggressively serious. I stifle a laugh.

'Sit down, please.'

I lower myself into a rickety wooden chair with a cracked red plastic cushion, oozing foam. He sits behind the metal desk, his back to the glass.

'How can I help you?' His voice is expressionless. I'm already the enemy and I don't think feminine charm is going to cut it here.

'I need to see your CCTV footage from the night of my brother's accident.'

He looks at me steadily. 'Why?'

'I want to know if Loran Ahmeti was here at the time, as he claimed to be. I have reason to believe that he might have been involved in the accident.'

'You speak like the police – only you're not.'

'No.'

'So why should I hand over the footage?'

'Firstly, because I'm asking you nicely, and unless you're trying to protect him for a reason, I don't see why you'd be reluctant. Secondly, I'm a lawyer, and if I decide to bring a private prosecution against Mr Ahmeti you will be called as a witness. If you can't then produce the CCTV footage of the night in question, the judge will want to know why you've deleted it. I imagine they will want to look more carefully at your business.'

We stare at one another. It was just a punt but I'm pretty sure this place is not completely above board. There's the illegal steroids, for starters.

'What if I say it's not working?'

'Then I'd be inclined to call the police right now.'

He sighs and pushes his chair back, gazing across at the men slogging it out in the ring.

'Loran and Abe were close,' he says. 'I don't see why he would hurt Abe.'

'Lovers have rows. Don't tell me he's not capable of it.'

'Controlled aggression,' he turns back to me, 'is not the same as violence.'

'Do you have the footage or not?'

He hesitates, then gets up.

I follow him down the main corridor and he unlocks a door that leads into a storeroom. A black-and-white screen displays the front entrance of the gym, so still it might as well be a photograph.

The scene vanishes as he flicks out the disc from the machine on a shelf beneath.

'You're lucky.' He holds it out to me. 'There's fifty-four days on there, and it only goes up to sixty before we overwrite.'

'You're going to let me take it away?'

He holds my gaze. I guess his faded eyes must once have been a quite startling blue.

'Abe was one of ours. I don't believe anyone here would ever have harmed him, but if they did, I want them caught. Whoever they are. Tell me what you find.'

'I will. Thank you.' I slip the disc into my pocket and reach for his hand. His grip is crushingly firm.

It's only as I step back onto the cracked concrete and the metal door clangs shut behind me that I realise I should have stayed inside and waited until the bus was near. Pressing my back against one of the metal grilles I check the app. Twelve minutes. *Shit*.

There are no new messages from Daniel. That's that, then. It's what I wanted, I suppose. His fault if he's screwed up his chance with Donna.

Nervously I glance across at the Blue Mermaid. The strains of 'Babooshka' drift across the pavement. No one is outside, but now I notice that although the place is a complete dive, someone cares about it enough to decorate it with hanging baskets. The pink, yellow and white flowers draw my eye: they're the first flowers I've seen outside the hospital.

There's something familiar about the white ones, the single stems branching out into a knot of blossom.

No one's outside so I cross the road and approach the pub. The street lamp shining on the window means that while I can't see in, those inside will be able to see this lone woman approach. I must be quick.

It only takes a moment for my suspicions to be confirmed.

The white flowers are the same as the ones in the jar on my bedside table.

Growing beside them are some yellow pansies and the same kind of cerise blossom I found around by the bins.

Is this the pub Mira mentioned? The one Loran went to after the gym?

Could it have been him who had my brother's keys?

Him who came in that first night and took away the dying white flowers?

Was he also planning to leave some fresh pink ones? The ones that ended up by the bins so that Mira wouldn't find them?

Were they a token of love? Or guilt? Or just flowers for the dead?

There's a burst of laughter from inside. If this is Loran's pub he could arrive at any time. I turn and start walking quickly, back the way I came.

But coming level with the gym I see there isn't a bus stop on this side of the road. The closest one is behind me, just past the Mermaid, but now three men are standing outside, lighting up. I will walk further up.

As I cross the side road I notice the burgundy hatchback that was following the bus, parked just down from the corner. The driver is still sitting in the driving seat.

It's Loran Ahmeti.

Our eyes meet.

I'm halfway across the road now, so I keep walking – perhaps he hasn't recognised me in my hood – but once I've passed out of sight around the corner I quicken my pace.

The hood against my ears muffles the sound, so I pull it down. I'll be easier to spot but at least I'll hear any footsteps following me.

But why should he be following me? How can he know what I have discovered? He might just have been heading for gym and stayed in the car to make a phone call, or wrap his hands, or whatever boxers do.

Unless someone at the gym has warned him I was there asking questions.

The sound of a car engine starts up.

I quicken my pace. Glancing behind I see the burgundy nose of the hatchback nudging out of the turning. From the angle I know that it's not going in the direction of the gym.

He's coming for me.

But I'm in luck. A van is coming down the main road and he must wait for it to pass before he can pull out.

I run.

Up ahead the road divides into two, but they're both dead straight. Whichever one I take he will see me. The bus stop is a few hundred metres down the left fork, but there's no one waiting and the houses that surround it are in darkness. Then I notice a little way down the right-hand fork there is a block of shadow. It must be the entrance to an alleyway. A place to hide.

There's no time to think of another plan.

With the brief shield of the passing van I sprint across the road and dive down the alley.

Broken bottles crunch under my feet and, as my eyes get used to the gloom, I make out high breeze-block walls that have been liberally graffittied. There's a faint glow coming from the other end of the tunnel. It must be a short cut linking the left and right forks of the main road. That's my escape route if he comes this way.

But I can't hear the engine any more.

I ease along the wall and peer out. There's no sign of the car. Maybe he wasn't coming for me at all. Maybe he just went home.

Deciding to wait a bit longer before emerging I retreat into the safety of the darkness, my ears pricked for any sound. A couple of cars go by, none, I think, the hatchback, and I back up further to escape the sweep of their headlights.

I have no idea where I am, or what time it is. I just know I don't want to be here when the pubs chuck out. I'll check when the bus is due and then dive out at the very last minute. I take out my phone and tap it into life, casting this small section of the alley in a cold pool of light.

Loran Ahmeti is standing a few feet away from me.

I try to run but he grabs the hood of the parka and yanks me back, throwing me against the wall. His grip on my shoulders is iron, thumbs driving into my clavicles. I scream, but the sound is swallowed by the high walls. No one is coming to help me.

# 31. Mira

You are back.

I hear the car engine and look out of the window. As you head towards the building you glance up again at Abe's window.

Is it the sister that you like? She is a fine, handsome woman. Handsome in a European way, like a man almost. She does not wear feminine clothes, or sparkly make-up, or curl her hair into the full waves of the women in magazines, but perhaps this is what you like. Perhaps England has spoiled you for farm girls like me.

When I hear the door go I check my appearance in the black mirror of the oven and am smiling when you walk in.

You do not look at me.

You go straight over to the sofa and open one of your fitness magazines. The knuckles on your right hand are bleeding and there is a cut on your forehead, just below your hairline. I thought you always wore gloves to box. I wonder whether to ask about it, or just to bring you a bowl of warm water and cotton wool. But your jaw is set and your brow is low, so I leave you alone and start slicing tomatoes for supper.

The flat is so silent that I hear when your breathing catches. I wait for you to cough. I will bring you a drink. But you don't cough. Your breathing shudders, and then you are sobbing.

The pages of the magazine flutter in your shaking hands, making the glossy brown flesh smear.

Drying my hands I go over to you and kneel down. It is difficult now that the bump is so big.

I take your injured hand and am glad when you squeeze it back. Your grip is so tight it hurts, and you look at me with red, hollow eyes. How long have you been crying?

I wonder if she has ended things with you. Or perhaps you ended it. For the baby. For us. I know what it feels like to lose someone you love, and though I should feel jealous, I just feel pity for you.

'It's all right,' I murmur in our language. 'When the baby comes it will be all right. I promise. We will love him. That is all the love we will need.'

You grip my hand so tightly the bones crunch together and the eyes you turn on mine are beseeching as a child's.

'I'm sorry,' you say. 'Mira, I'm so sorry.'

When you say my name I start to cry.

# 32. Mags

If I'd worn my stilettos I might have been in with a chance, but the Converses are too soft to hurt him as I kick out wildly.

The phone light went out when I dropped it and the darkness is filled with my snarling cries and his grunts as he tries to restrain me. I give up on the kicking and start trying to knee him in the groin, my brain spinning through all the ways he might kill me. A slash of broken bottle across my throat, those big hands strangling the life out of me. Or simply kicked and beaten and left to bleed in the darkness.

Then, a miracle. My knee makes contact and he grunts and loosens his grip.

I twist free and bolt for the light of the road, slipping on the remains of old takeaways, the blood rushing so loudly in my ears I can't even hear if he's coming after me.

The alley elongates impossibly, the road becoming more distant the faster I run. My thighs burn, my lungs ache, my veins are electric wires of adrenaline.

I've almost made it. I can see the bus stop.

Someone there! A stocky skinhead in a bomber jacket. If I scream loud enough he will surely hear me. I open my mouth.

A hand slaps over it and I am wrenched back into the darkness.

As I slam into his body I can feel the slabs of muscle moving against my back. He must be twice my weight, strong enough to lift me off the ground with one arm, until I'm thrashing through air, trying to bite the fingers clamped around my mouth.

In desperation I jerk back my head. There's an explosion of pain in my sinuses and a sickening crack. And then I am falling, free. Landing heavily I roll onto my back. Oblivious to the glass and food slime I kick out at him, aiming for any target that might come within range as I scramble crablike towards the road.

But this time he doesn't try to stop me. He stands back, holding his palms up. In the light from the street lamps I can make out his face more clearly. His lips are moving; he's saying something I can't make out over my screams.

Eventually my voice grows hoarse and still he has made no attempt to silence me or murder me. My adrenaline is subsiding, taking with it my last ounce of strength. Dragging myself to the wall I lean there, panting. For a brief moment of silence we just stare at each other.

His face is white. A black line of blood runs from his hairline to the bridge of his nose, but he makes no move to wipe it away. His big, pale hands hang by his side.

Then he speaks.

It takes me a beat to make out the heavily accented words.

'Will he be OK?'

Slowly, my eyes never leaving his face, I get to my feet, clinging to the wall for support.

'Abe. Will he live? Please tell me.'

I manage to get my breath under enough control to be able to speak. 'Didn't you see what happened?'

He tips his head back and closes his eyes. A single star is visible in the strip of night sky above us.

'I wait for him here, at Stone's. He never comes. I get back to the church and all I see is blood. Only . . . blood.'

His voice breaks.

I wait. After a few moments he lowers his head and crosses his arms over his chest, as if he's cold. 'Will he be OK?'

'No, Loran. He's going to die.'

225

He stares at me, his face a wax mask.

'Hey! What the fuck's going on?' The skinhead is standing at the entrance to the alley.

'It's all right,' I manage. 'I'm fine.'

I want to talk to Loran, to find out more about his relationship with my brother, but before I can stop him he has spun away from me and stumbles into the darkness.

The skinhead runs over and helps me up. He is about to race after Loran, but I manage to stop him, gabbling that I fell, that there was a misunderstanding, that it's complicated. He doesn't believe me, but clearly decides it's safer not to get involved in a domestic and contents himself with walking me to the bus stop.

When the bus finally arrives I barely have the strength to raise my foot to the step. My shoulders hurt where Loran gripped me and I slump into the first seat I come to, letting my head loll against the shuddering window and wondering if I'm going to be sick.

I thought he was going to kill me.

I thought he had tried to kill Abe.

It turns out he just loved him.

# 33. Mira

You lie with your back to me and I am curled behind you, holding you. You have stopped crying and we lie on the sofa in peaceful silence.

I think about touching you. Perhaps making love will ease your pain. But your body is not my possession: I must wait until you want it.

But our moment of intimacy is passing. I know you sense it too, because your body is gradually stiffening and your breathing becomes lighter.

'You must be hungry,' I murmur. 'I will finish dinner.'

You sit up to allow me to pass, but I can tell you are still heartsick. I sit beside you and take your hand. You look up at me and I know you want to speak. You are ready to confide in me. I am glad. This terrible thing has brought us so much closer.

I squeeze your rough hand and whisper to you in our language, 'You are a good man and I know you are suffering for what you did. But it's OK. I am glad. It shows you love me.'

A shadow passes across your face. 'What?'

'I know you pushed him.'

'Who?'

'Our neighbour. You pushed him down the stairwell.'

You stare at me a moment, then snatch your hand back and shrink away from me. 'What?'

'You pushed him because you thought he wanted me.'

You shake your head, your eyes wide with shock.

'I saw you. It's all right. I understand. It was the only way you knew how to express your love.'

You jump to your feet. 'What are you saying?'

'Don't worry. I will never tell. It will be our secret. It will bring us closer to—'

He lunges at me, grasping me by the shoulders and shaking me. 'Shut up!'

'It's all right. It's all right.'

'Can't you understand? I could *never* have hurt him!'

He is shaking me so hard my head waggles. 'Stop. You will hurt the baby!'

'Fuck the baby!' he screams in English, loud enough for all the flats to hear. 'The baby is a lie. It was not made with love! We are nothing to one another, Mira, don't you see! I married you because it would make it easier to get to the west, where people like me can live without fear. The baby will be nothing too. Hollow. An empty shell.'

'Don't say that!'

'I cannot do this any more. I cannot do it to you, or to me.'

'Stop. Where are you going?'

'Goodbye. I am sorry.'

'No! No! Come back!'

He is making for the door but I fly after him, screaming. 'You cannot leave me! I will not let you!'

You have taken my looks and my spirit and now you will abandon me. My child will be a bastard.

I fling myself onto your back, my arms around your throat. If you want to leave you will have to kill me first.

# 34. Mags

After I've I watched the footage I save it onto the iCloud and eject the disc.

Then I just stare at the black screen. I can't make sense of anything any more.

Abe was happy; he didn't want to kill himself.

Loran loved him, he couldn't have hurt him.

And yet Jody is lying.

And Mira is lying.

Why?

*Why?*

Once more I stalk out of the flat and cross the landing to Jody's.

'Answer the door!' I hammer it with my fist. 'You need to tell me what happened, Jody. Because I know you know a whole lot more about this than you're letting on.'

The flat is silent. The insolent spyhole stares me out. I kick the door, making a sound like a gunshot, and I think I hear a whimper on the other side.

'I know you're there,' I hiss into the gap between the door and the frame. 'You really don't want to go up against me in court, Jody. You don't stand a fucking chance.'

After a few more growled threats I head back to the flat and pour myself a drink, staring moodily down at the playground as I knock it back with grim determination, swiftly followed by two more.

I'm dozing on the sofa when the buzzer sounds. It's Jody's social worker, Tabitha. I ignore it, but she won't go away and eventually I buzz her in. Maybe she's trying to get through to Jody too. Maybe with her social worker for backup Jody will open up and speak to me.

For a woman of her size she's very fit because within a minute there's a sharp rap on my door.

'Can I come in?' she says curtly when I open it. Her lips are tight and her black eyes flash.

I move to let her pass and she marches up the hall, swinging her bag, and then turns on me.

'You need to stop harassing my client.'

'What?' I splutter.

'Jody. You need to leave her alone. You're making her ill.'

'You are kidding me, right? The only person doing any harassing around here was *her*. I just want her to tell the truth about how Abe fell. To go to the police.'

I walk past her to the kitchen and grab a beer from the fridge, smacking it open on the worktop, taking a chunk of MDF with me.

'The truth?' Tabitha laughs grimly. 'When no one believes you then it stops being truth and becomes slander. Last time, when she was raped—'

'She wasn't raped!' I cry, slamming the bottle down so that the froth surges up and over the counter. 'That was made up, the same as everything else!'

'When she was *raped*,' Tabitha goes on, 'they threatened her with jail. And with all the things that would happen to her there. This is a girl who has been abused as far back as she can remember. What would you do under those circumstances, Miss Mackenzie? Would you agree that you had lied, or just been confused, and go back to trying to live a quiet life where no one bothers you? Or would you put yourself through the horrors of a trial and all that that would rake up? Would you face those boys, with their upstanding families and admiring teachers, across the courtroom and hear yourself branded a liar and a fantasist and worse? The truth costs, Miss Mackenzie. And that cost is too much for people like Jody.'

Her chest heaves.

I am about to say that I don't give a shit what happened before: this is about *my brother*, but she has turned away and is riffling through her bag. Hopefully she's getting her phone to call a cab. There's no chance of her helping me winkle Jody out of her hiding place now.

She straightens up and slams a blue document file on the table.

'What's that?'

'Proof. People like you need that sort of thing, right? Have a look, and then please tell me how you can live with yourself, bullying that poor girl.'

'She's a woman,' I say. 'Not a *girl*. She's responsible for her actions.'

But Tabitha isn't listening. Swinging her bag over her shoulder she turns and stalks out of the flat, and a moment later I see her squat black shape hurrying across the waste ground.

I stare at the file, swigging my beer, then I flip it open.

Ten minutes later I'm vomiting in the toilet. The mixture of beer and wine, alongside the medical reports and photographs contained in Tabitha's file, were too much for my now daily hangover.

Eventually, when the last of the bitter yellow bile is flushed away, I straighten up and wash my face, then I go back to the living room and tuck the papers back into the file.

Jody's haunted, seven-year-old eyes gaze at me from the last page I tuck back inside.

It was harrowing and pitiful reading, but it's not the proof Tabitha claimed it to be. I can believe Jody experienced all that, and I'm sorry for it. But that doesn't mean she's not capable of crying rape. In fact, I'd say the opposite is true. That kind of trauma could fracture a personality completely. She might have believed she was raped, like she believed Abe loved her. I'd been coming round to agree with Derbyshire that Jody wasn't

231

physically capable of pushing Abe, but now I'm not so sure. Can psychosis give you unnatural strength?

Flashes of the demon child from *The Exorcist* pass through my mind and another wave of nausea washes over me.

All I want is another drink but instead I put two slices of freezer bread in the toaster and sit down at the table to plough through them, dry. I haven't bothered to put the light on and I'm glad I didn't when I see that the gang's back in the playground, their shadows darkening the bench, the roundabout. One is on a swing, the tip of his cigarette drawing a red line through the darkness. I suppose it would only have been four or five years ago since he was asking his mum for a push. What happened to him? To all of them?

I think of another darkened window. Above the front door of our semi in Scotland. I'm standing in the hall. My brother is close beside me. My mother's head is silhouetted against the window. I'm looking up at her from a long way down, so I must be very young. I'm wearing my favourite orange coat with the blue stitching and am too hot. I wish my mother would let us go outside but she won't. We are waiting. Waiting for my father who is sitting in front of the TV in the living room. Cold white TV ghosts loom and shrink across the threshold.

It wasn't dark when we put our coats on to go for a walk in the park, but me and my brother had been rolling a penny along the floorboards and had taken too long getting our shoes on, so my father decreed that if he had to wait for us, then we would wait for him.

I don't own a watch or know how to read a clock but it feels as if we have been waiting hours. My brother is crying: silently, because otherwise my father will punish him, but I can hear his thick, wet breathing.

I'm not crying. My five-year-old mind seethes with loathing.

When the theme tune of his programme comes on and he's finally ready for what must now be a short stroll around the block, I refuse to move, and am carried upstairs, thrashing and scratching, and hurled onto my bed hard enough for the centre slats to splinter. My brother is taken out by my father to collect a fish-and-chip supper for the three of them. I'm given nothing to eat that night, and in an act of defiance I refuse to eat for the whole of the next day. By evening my mother is in tears but my father asserts that I will eat when I'm hungry, and of course he is right. As I tuck gratefully into my mother's macaroni cheese I despise him more than ever.

This was some years before the Great Conversion, while my father was just your average domestic tyrant, rather than one with God's stamp of approval. The Conversion (or *breakdown* as it was referred to in a doctor's letter I steamed open) happened halfway up a mountain on a volunteer's training exercise for the mountain rescue.

He came down from that exercise convinced that Jesus had spoken to him from the sky.

It's not fashionable to be a Christian fundamentalist any more. There's something a bit twee about arguing over the consistency, fleshly or otherwise, of the communion wafer when compared with the beheadings and immolations indulged in by other brands of religious lunacy. It's almost comforting. But growing up tiptoeing around the hair trigger of my father's rage was exhausting and terrifying.

He had always been a bully and now he had God to back him up. Our home was run like a prison camp. If we showed any form of dissent we were locked in our rooms and starved until we begged forgiveness for dishonouring the Lord. Sometimes I think my father got mixed up who was God and who was the self-employed roofer, but, deluded as he was, he was clever enough to understand the concept of divide and conquer when it came to his children. When one of us was in disgrace the other was treated like a prince or princess, so we learned to view one another as the enemy.

Looking back, I was far worse than Abe. In fact, I was a monster. Like my father.

There's *my* proof, Tabitha. There's my excuse.

A scream shatters the silence.

I jump up from the table and run to the door, bursting out onto the landing.

'Jody!'

But the screaming isn't coming from Jody's flat. Mira's door is open. I run inside. The door at the end of the corridor is open and I see on the floor, lit by that single harsh light bulb, a wide smear of blood, as if a body has been dragged across the room.

Has Loran lost his mind and killed his wife?

A woman sobs.

Mira.

Was it her all along? Were the notes to deflect attention from her own guilt rather than Jody's? Did she kill Abe because he was having an affair with her husband? And has she just killed her husband?

The sob becomes a moan of pain.

My thoughts fracture. I am losing their thread. Has Loran attacked *her* and then fled?

I burst through the inner door. Mira is bending over the back of the sofa. For the first time I am seeing her in normal clothes, without the abaya: a pair of cheap supermarket jeans and a flowery shirt I have seen for sale in the market in the high road. At first I think the jeans are black but then I notice that the cuffs are pale blue.

They're not black – they're drenched in blood.

She looks up at me, her face the colour of marble.

'The baby,' she says. 'Help me.'

*The clubhouse smells of stale beer and the floor is sticky with spillages. It takes a moment for her eyes to adjust to the gloom because the two boys didn't want to open the curtains and risk being seen. They had left the fire exit open the previous day for the express purpose of coming here to get lashed for free and nobody had noticed.*

*Felix's friend is already behind the bar.*

*'What's your poison, Jody?'*

*'Coke, please.'*

*He gives a bark of laughter. 'Vodka and Coke it is.'*

*The boys play pool and drink steadily, pints of lager with Jack Daniel chasers. Every time the big one knocks one of these back he gives a violent shudder accompanied by a loud grunt. He's like an animal, she thinks, and as the afternoon wears away he starts to smell.*

*Felix does too. Sweat beads his forehead and upper lip despite the fact that the clubhouse is getting cooler as the sun goes down.*

*The next round of drinks takes two of them to prepare, and for a moment they stand with their backs to her, whispering.*

*Felix brings hers over, another vodka and Coke, and something makes her glance into the glass. There's just the slightly flat brown liquid and a slice of lemon from a glass jar behind the bar. She does what she did to the previous four drinks and pours sips of it into the pot of the ailing yucca plant when their attention has turned back to the pool table.*

*'Let's have a look at those scars, then,' the friend says when they've finished their game.*

*She stares at him. 'I . . .'*

*'Come on, I'll show you mine.'*

*His hands go to his belt and before she can say anything he has dropped his trousers. He's wearing tight white underpants that cling to the outline of his large penis, flopped over to one side. He hesitates a moment, his eyes on her face, then the corner of his mouth twists into a smile.*

*'Nah, not there, darling,' he says. 'My knee. Tore my cruciate ligament.'*

*There's a long scar running down from his lower left thigh, across the kneecap and down to his shin.*

*'Oh,' she says vaguely. 'That looks painful.'*

*'Felix has got one too.'*

*'I know.'*

*'Oooooooooooooh!' he jeers, falsetto, and Felix pretends to smile.*

*As the next game progresses she catches them glancing up at her frequently, then the friend says, 'How are you feeling?' His voice is thick with drink.*

*'Fine, thanks.'*

*'Fuck's sake,' he slurs. 'You some kind of bionic girl or what?'*

*She doesn't know what he's talking about.*

*Felix puts the cue down and straightens up. 'It's getting late. We should go back.'*

*The big one rounds on him. 'Don't bail on me now, you pussy.'*

*'I'm ready to go too, Felix,' she says.*

*'I'm ready to go too, Fewix,' the other one mimics.*

*She goes to the door and stands there.*

*The big one bangs the cue down on the table, making both her and Felix start. Then he grins. 'You love him, don't you, eh?'*

*She hesitates. 'He's my brother.'*

*'It's more than that, though, isn't it?'*

*She stares at him. She doesn't understand what he wants her to say. What can she say that will make him let her go?*

*'We know what happened to you, and that's really shit. Seriously.'*

*She blinks at Felix. He has told?*

*'But it's not like that normally. You should try it again. You'll like it. And I bet you've learnt stuff, haven't you? I bet guys would pay you for the shit you know now.'*

*He's coming towards her.*

*'Felix.'*

*Felix moves closer to her.*

*'Go on, mate. Show her. Show her how nice it can be. For both people. For all of us.'*

*Felix's Adam's apple bobs, then he turns to face her. His skin is waxy. 'It's all right,' he says. 'You love me, don't you?'*

*She blinks and nods. She does love him. And he loves her. He would never hurt her.*

*'Go on, mate,' the big one murmurs. 'My cock hurts.'*

*Felix pulls off his T-shirt and stands bare-chested in front of her, like one of the men from the magazines. Then he raises her hand and lays it against his chest. His skin is clammy with sweat and she can feel his heart throbbing beneath her palm.*

*'See, Felix here has never done it before. Not properly. He needs a girl with a bit of experience to show him how.'*

*Felix's eyes are closed. She wills him to open them and look at her. They can both leave. Go home. Eat bacon sandwiches in front of the TV.*

*'Jesus Christ, mate, just get out of the way!' Felix stumbles aside and it's the other one looming over her, his alcohol breath hot on her face.*

*She doesn't say anything when he squeezes her breast, sniggering like there's something comical about it, rubber fruit from a comedy sketch. She doesn't ask him to stop. She knows there isn't any point. He won't stop, whatever she says. She has seen that look in men's eyes before. The cold, glazed stare of a shark. He is drunk and aroused and Felix has told him everything about her. He knows a hundred men have fucked her. He probably thinks: what's one more?*

*'Come on, Jode,' says Felix. 'Don't cry.'*

*'Shut up and have another drink, you queer. It might give you some balls.'*

*Felix watches from the pool table, slugging from a bottle of Jack Daniels, as his friend pushes his slimy tongue into her mouth, right to the back, as if it wants to slither down her throat. Automatically she makes her throat go flaccid. She learned a long time ago how to deal with the gag reflex.*

Her mouth is stretched as wide as it can go without the corners of her mouth cracking. Then she feels a familiar burn in her nipple as he grips it between finger and thumb and twists.

'Enough,' says Felix. Tossing the bottle onto the table he staggers over, pushing his friend out of the way.

Her heart lifts. They will go home now. Felix will never see this monster again.

But he doesn't take her hand. There's a hard glitter to his eye, and as he leans into her she can feel the lump in his trousers.

'Way to go, Felix!' the other one crows.

She loves him, so she kisses him back, even as tears trickle down her cheeks. The sweetness of the Coke has turned bitter on his furred tongue. She wraps her arms around him, her palms on his warm back, pressing him into her as if to protect him from what is going to happen.

Then his body moves away from hers and she thinks he is going to stop. She will run out of the clubhouse, then, and along the residential streets until she finds a bus stop.

But he's only giving himself room to allow his fingers to slide inside the cups of her bra. They're cold and wet from holding glasses with ice.

She tries to push him away then, but he holds her tight, his fingers digging into her clavicles. There is a grim look on his face now. His friend watches hungrily.

She closes her eyes. The hands squirm inside her bra, and now she feels others at her back, slipping the hooks of her bra in one deft move.

The bra loosens and these hands, bigger and rougher than Felix's, move to the button of her jeans. One boy is behind her and one is in front.

Fingers worm into her knickers then push their way inside her.

'Shit, man, she's loose as an old granny!'

Felix stops then. The hands cupping her breasts go still, his tongue freezes in her mouth.

Then the other one is pushing him aside. 'My turn!'

Felix staggers away, dazed, his mouth glistening with spit. He stares, stupefied, as his friend propels her forward until she comes up *against the pool table. The impact makes her fold at the waist, and with the hand at her back, she is forced face-down onto the table.*

*Her jeans are yanked down.*

*'No!' she shouts, but it becomes a grunt as air is forced from her lungs when he slams inside her.*

*He is big. It hurts. That dull ache in the cervix, the tearing caused by the friction of dry skin against dry skin. He should have used lubrication. If she had known this was going to happen she would have got some liquid soap from the toilet.*

*The rough baize scrapes up and down her cheek.*

*Let it be over, just let it be over.*

*But he is drunk. It will take ages.*

*She raises her eyes up above the ledge of the table, to the soft gold light filtering through the thin curtains. Through a gap she sees an expanse of grass and she thinks of horses running, the wind in their manes, their tails flipping.*

*Then, to her surprise, he grunts and withdraws. The hand is lifted from her back and she tries to straighten but it comes down again with a slap. And then he is back inside her again, but now he's only semi hard. This is even worse. He'll never come like this. He will blame her.*

*It flops out. He has lost his erection.*

*'Out of the way, you gay. Let the real man finish off.'*

*Felix?*

*She stares, green suffusing her vision.*

*It was Felix?*

*The thrust is so hard her hips slam into the wooden table edge and she cries out with pain.*

*'That's it, bitch,' the friend pants, through gritted teeth. 'That's what you want, isn't it?'*

*The big hands slide underneath her chest and start twisting her nipples. Is he one of those who gets off on inflicting pain? Will he twist until he draws blood? He's growling like a dog.*

*Hurry up and come.*

*Hurry up and come.*

*Hurry up and come.*

*Someone is being sick. The warm splatter hits her foot. She manages to raise her head enough to turn it, her chin scraping the baize. Felix squats beside the pool table, his face ghost-grey, his eyes hollow as they stare back at her, unseeing.*

*A thrust so hard she screams: from the pain in her hips, and a deeper pain inside. The sensation of something breaking open.*

*They said she might be able to have children.*

*Felix is sick again.*

*And then the heavy body slumps over her, squeezing the air from her lungs. She can't breathe. She will suffocate. She struggles and he moves away, his still-hard cock twanging out of her with a wet sucking sound.*

*As soon as she is able she straightens up and stumbles around the table, making it a barrier between them as she pulls her jeans up, refastens her bra and yanks her T-shirt down. She's panting like a dog. She must control her breathing or she will start hyperventilating. She needs to stay in control. She needs to get out of here in case they decide to do it again, or something worse.*

*Felix's friend is at the bar drinking his JD and Coke.*

*Felix is still crouched on the floor, like a trapped animal. His eyes are wide with pure, cold terror.*

*She runs to the fire door and they don't try to stop her.*

# Monday 14 November

# 35. Mags

By some miracle they save the baby.

A little girl. With no name because Mira was so sure she would be a boy.

Mira has lost several pints of blood, and for a while it looked liked she might not pull through, but she has. I sit quietly by the bed as she slumbers in the peaceful depths of the anaesthetic. Somewhere in the hospital my brother slumbers too. I will go and see him when I have the strength to get up. At the moment all I can do is drink my warm sweet tea and stare at the light from the traffic outside strobing across the bed sheet.

At first I thought it was Loran – that he had kicked her or pushed her across the room, thought her insistence that he had done nothing was just to protect him. Again. But the nurses said that the bleeding was caused by something called *placental abruption*, and was due to Mira's high blood pressure.

The door opens quietly and a nurse comes in carrying the baby swaddled in a white waffle blanket.

'Would you like to hold her?' the nurse whispers. 'I'm sure she'd like some human contact until Mummy's feeling better.'

And then, without warning, this tiny scrap of flesh and bone is placed into my arms.

She is as light as a paper kite.

'Are you sure?' I stammer. 'What if . . . ?'

'What if you break her?' The nurse chuckles. 'You won't. She's a fighter, this one. You can lay her in the cot afterwards.' She gestures to the Perspex box by Mira's bed.

'What if she starts to cry?'

'She won't be hungry yet awhile. You're safe for a bit.'

And then she's gone, and it feels to me as if there's only me and this tiny girl in the whole world.

I pull back the blanket from the downy cheek. Her eyes are open a sliver so I hold my hand up to shield them from the light above the bed. They open a little wider, then a little wider, until I'm looking into a pair of huge eyes, as dark and glistening as pools of tar.

'Well, hello,' I murmur. 'I guess this is a first for both of us.'

She starts to wriggle and whicker like a pony. Afraid she's about to cry, I loosen the swaddling to give her a little more freedom of movement. A tiny arm shoots out, pink and skinny, the fingers splayed. I raise my forefinger and touch it to the little palm and the fingers close around it.

The grasp is so tight. *Never let me go.*

When she falls asleep in my arms it feels – and though I want to, I cannot find a better phrase than one of my father's – like a blessing.

I raise her up until she's resting on my chest so that I can hear the high breaths. Damp strands of black hair are plastered to her forehead, as if she has exerted herself forcing her way out into the world.

When I feel myself slipping into drowsiness, I lay her in the cot, tucking the waffle blanket underneath her. We all sleep.

The entrance of the nurse wakes me.

Mira is awake now too. She lies there staring at the ceiling, as the nurse quietly checks her blood pressure.

'Can you manage a little breakfast?' the nurse says to her.

There are slivers of morning light through the blinds. I glance at my watch: 10.15.

'A cup of tea, please,' she says meekly.

244

The nurse turns to me. 'And one for you?'

I thank her. My mouth is furry from yesterday's drinking.

The baby starts to squawk. An impressively assertive noise for such a tiny creature, and the nurse lifts her from the cot and places her in Mira's arms. As she looks down at her daughter, tears roll down Mira's cheeks.

The nurse tugs back her gown and pushes the baby to her breast. The little hand appears, batting at the air, and then it settles, comfortable against her neck, and the breaths become muffled. I feel a pang of envy.

The nurse beams. 'There. You're a natural.'

'Did he come?' Mira asks me when the nurse has left the room.

I shake my head and wait for her to crumple, but she doesn't. 'He wanted a boy. He will not like her.'

'More fool him. She's perfect. What will you do?'

'I will take her back to Tirana. We will be feminists together and all the men will fear us.'

They must hear my laugh halfway down the corridor. Mira laughs too, and with her ruffled crop, her flushed cheeks and bright eyes, I no longer see the faded, downtrodden, oppressed Muslim wife, but a strong and beautiful young woman.

Then her face becomes serious.

'I lied to you.'

'I know.'

'Then you must know why. It was weakness and cowardice. I hope you can forgive it.'

I think of Daniel. 'We're all cowards sometimes.'

'Let me tell you the truth. And this time I will swear it on Flori's life.' She looks down at the baby. 'That is my mother's name.' Then she looks up at me. 'Before the scream, before that terrible sound of your brother striking the concrete, before Jody crying, I heard voices.'

I breathe slowly, in and out, trying to calm myself.

'One of them is Jody. She sounds afraid. The other is a man's voice. Not Abe's. I cannot hear the words because of your brother's music. There are bumps and rustling sounds and I begin to think that Jody is struggling with someone. I go into the hall then, and pick up the baseball bat Loran keeps by the door in case of trouble.'

I try and picture her, eight months pregnant, armed and ready to fight off Jody's attacker. She is certainly brave.

'There is a big bang and Jody screams your brother's name, and then he comes out. The music is louder now and I cannot hear what they are saying. There is a little light from Abe's flat, so I look out of the spyhole.'

As she looks down at Flori's head I hold my breath. This is it. This is the moment I will find out the truth. The rumbling traffic outside makes the windowpane rattle, like the chatter of teeth.

'What did you see, Mira?'

She looks up at me. 'I see Loran.'

I blink at her, trying to make sense of her words. 'This was at the time of the accident? Eight in the evening?'

She nods miserably. 'I watch them struggling, just black shapes in the dark. I see your brother bent backwards over the banisters – I can tell him by his build – and I hear Loran grunt as he pushes him, and then there is only one of them. There is a sound. A thud. Jody screams.'

She squeezes her eyes shut. 'Loran pushed Abe. And then he ran away.'

She turns her head away from me. The baby stops nursing and moves its head away from her breast, gazing up at her mother with those impenetrable dark eyes.

I take my phone out of my bag. 'He can't have done. Look.'

Logging in to my iCloud account I bring up the fuzzy black-and-white video of the railway arches, and fast-forward. Men go in and out of the metal door at high speed. The scene darkens as the clock in the corner of the screen ticks by, and then brightens again as the street lights come on. When a bald man cycles up and dismounts I stop fast-forwarding. He is folding his bike up when the door opens and Loran steps out onto the concrete. The two men pause to talk.

'Look at the clock.'

I close up on it. Mira reads out the date and time and then she frowns up at me. 'They must have changed it.'

'The guy gave it to me as soon as I asked for it. He had no time to doctor it.'

Back in full-screen mode the man on the bike walks into the gym and Loran moves away, out of picture, in the direction of the pub. I fast-forward to eight thirty, nine, ten o'clock when Loran finally emerges from the pub. Then I stop the video.

She raises a hand to her face and the tube from the catheter coming out of it starts to tremble.

'Did you see his face, Mira? Could it have been someone else?'

'He had his back to me but I knew him by his build.'

'Lots of men are built like that. Why assume it was Loran?'

'Because otherwise Jody would have had to let him into the building, and why would she if it was a stranger? And I did not hear the buzzer, which is very loud.'

I don't know the answer to this. 'What was he wearing?' I hazard.

Her eyes drift away from mine. 'It is true I do not recognise the writing on the back of his sweatshirt. It is *something something RFC*. I thought he had borrowed it.'

We sit in silence but for the rattling of the window and small rustles from the baby. I'm not sure how to put what I'm about to say.

'Mira, what motive did you think Loran had to hurt Abe?'

She shakes her head. 'I don't know. I wonder if he is jealous because your brother liked me.'

Even as she speaks I know she doesn't believe it. That she doesn't expect *me* to believe it. I don't think that what I am about to tell her will come as a shock.

'Mira. Loran and my brother were in love. Loran's gay.'

She stares at me.

'You understand? Gay. Homosexual. He loves other men.'

The swaddling blanket rustles as Mira's chest rises and falls. The baby watches her face.

Then she nods.

She looks down at the baby and then up at the ceiling, and then starts to cry, quietly first, then building and finally breaking into a sob.

I reach forward and take her fragile hand. 'I'm sorry.'

But when she looks up at me she's smiling through her tears. 'No, no, no. I'm happy. There is a *reason* why he cannot love me.'

'You need to tell the police what you saw.'

She nods, wiping her eyes. 'And Jody. You must get her to speak to them. She must know this man. This man who killed Abe.'

My lip twists automatically. 'Who's going to pay any attention to what Jody says?'

But before she can answer me the nurse comes back in. I turn around to smile at her. Only she and I know that, aside from the medical staff, I was the first person in the world to hold Flori. I am amazed to find it means something to me.

But she doesn't return my smile. 'Miss Mackenzie?'

'Yes.'

'They need you down at ICU. You need to get there quickly if you want to—'

But I'm already out of the door.


Jody is hunched, foetal position, on the chair beside the bed. Wrenching sobs shake her whole body, as if an invisible giant is punching her again and again.

I feel no anger towards her. I feel nothing. It is if I am watching action unfold on a screen: action which I have walked in on halfway through, before I've had the chance to care about the characters.

The nurses move around the bed. Above the rustling of the clothes and sheets I can hear Abe's breathing. They have taken the ventilator away. It sounds as if he is choking.

'Shouldn't you be doing something?'

'It's too late for that, I'm afraid.' Dr Bonville is standing next to me by the bed. 'Abe is dying. Sit down, Mags. It can take a while for a person to pass.'

'So, do something! Is it because I agreed to the DNR? I take it back. I want you to save him!'

'His system is shutting down. There's nothing we can do – and it was nothing to do with the DNR. Don't blame yourself.'

I sit and the foam seat cushion gives a heavy sigh.

'His system was irreversibly compromised by the accident. He was never one of those patients that would linger for years. Better this way, I think. Don't you?'

The nurses move away and I see that all the monitors have been switched off. One by one they slip away through the blue curtains, but Bonville stays.

Minutes pass. Abe's rattling breaths become more and more spaced out and Jody is now crying quietly.

And then his breathing stops.

My eyes are fixed on his face, watching for the moment of death, to see if something tangible will leave his body. I realise then, in the cocoon of those blue curtains, that however far and fast I ran from our father's creed, I never quite left it behind.

I am watching for Abe's soul.

The sudden choked gurgle makes me cry out and Dr Bonville lays a hand on my shoulder. 'Not yet.'

I don't know how long it takes, but it's exhausting listening to those last agonised breaths. The light strengthens and shadows pass across the bed. The morning rush-hour traffic begins. Engines are revved bad-temperedly, horns are sounded.

My mind drifts back to Eilean Donan. I wonder if we were both thinking the same thing as we stood on that parapet. *Is it worth struggling on?*

It was, Abe. For you at least. You, of the two of us, made something worthwhile of your life. You were loved, and you gave love. Whatever I used to think, I am sure now that this is all that matters.

I realise that several minutes have passed since Abe last breathed. I glance up at Dr Bonville, who has stood sentinel behind me all this time.

He steps forward and takes Abe's wrist. A minute passes, then he raises his head. 'He's gone.'

When I was nine I borrowed *Peter Pan* from the school library and would read it, hidden under the covers, listening for my father's footsteps on the stairs. I remember so much of that forbidden book, with all its blasphemous magic.

As I gaze at the body on the bed I think of Peter, flown off into the night, leaving just his shadow, tethered with lines and tubes. I stand up and begin to pull them out, one by one – pushing back the bandages, peeling off the tape – and Bonville does not try to stop me.

Finally I can see my brother clearly. He looks like a boy asleep.

*I taught you to fight and to fly,* Peter says to Wendy. *What more could there be?*

And yet without me you learned so much more, Abe. You learned to care for people. That, I have never learned. And now you are not here to teach me.

I don't want to see death take hold of him. I don't want to see his lips go slack or his skin turn grey, the eyelids peel back to reveal eyes as dull as pond water. And yet I cannot tear my gaze from my brother's face.

A flash of memory . . . Abe asleep on the sofa when he should be reading his Bible. Me leaning over him, a delicious sense of anticipation blooming in my chest as I realise I have something I can tell on him for. I will be rewarded. Daddy will be happy with me. So happy he will let me beat Abe myself. I have come to enjoy my brother's tears and pleas for me to stop because they mean that my star is in the ascendant. My fingers itch to feel the slippery length of leather, the chill of the buckle that will leave such precise half-moon bruises.

I lean over and kiss Abe's lips. They are warm and soft, but no breath tickles my cheek.

I've lived in America too long to place any store by *I love you*s, but I wish I'd had time to say that I'm sorry. For all that I did to him. For leaving him alone there. To tell him that it wasn't fear of our father that made me leave, but fear of myself, of what I had become.

I think of the last, meagre words we shared. Words on flimsy Christmas cards, hastily inscribed, destined to arrive late and unlooked for.

*From Abe. From Mags.*

But perhaps, after all, they said all we needed to.

*I know. I understand. I forgive.*

Ah . . . I have to go.

When I've moved away Jody falls on his body and howls. I watch her for a moment, transfixed. This liar. This fantasist. God, how she loved him.

I travel back to St Jerome's in a daze, and as I let myself into the flat I can barely remember how I got there.

Somewhere in the depths of my subconscious I must have always believed we would be reconciled one day. Now I am gripped with a wild panic. He is gone and I must imprint all that remains of him onto my mind before the darkness takes him away from me forever.

I pull open drawers, looking for photographs, mementoes, anything that will let me glimpse the real him, even just for a moment.

In the bedroom I become Jody, riffling through his wardrobe, trying to catch a fleeting scent of him.

I upend the box in search of letters or email print-outs, something that will let me hear his voice again in my mind.

A Christmas card falls out.

On the front is a picture of the Eiffel Tower wearing a Father Christmas hat. It takes me a moment to realise that it is not the real thing, only the mini one from the Las Vegas Strip, and another to realise it was I who sent the card.

I sit down on the bed and open it.

*Seasons Greetings from Sin City!*

I can barely remember scrawling my name at the bottom, but it is clear that it was done with little care, knocked out from duty, a year late because his had only reached my desk that February.

*From Mags.*

I close it and run my fingers across the embossed image. Then suddenly I remember Abe's card. A snow-covered castle on an iced-over lake, a trail of ducks padding across the ice towards the distant horizon.

You and I stood on that parapet, wondering whether to drown ourselves. Whether life would ever be bearable.

But we didn't need to go under. We could walk across the water to freedom. I suppose you never meant it as a metaphor, just a reminder of that time, that single time, when we were truly brother and sister. And contained within that, the hope that we could be again.

The cards we sent were more than the flimsy paper they were printed on and the trite sentiment within.

They were a covenant. A promise we made to one another to forget the past, to do right by one another in future.

I know then what I have to do. I start packing my case.

*The lady's expression is so hostile the girl wishes she didn't have to sit next to her. Her eyes flash with the light from the fluorescent strips above the table, as if there are torches shining out from behind the black irises.*

*'Let's just get this over with, shall we?' Her voice is dangerous.*

*The policeman stacks his papers on the table, as if he's not really interested. He's wearing a short-sleeved shirt and his arms are thick and shapeless as sausages. Gingery hairs sprout from the freckles. Ignoring the lady he looks up at the girl. His orangey brown eyes match his hair.*

*'Before we begin, I need to confirm with you that you understand the significance of an official caution and you have given informed consent to receive it.'*

*'The Goddards gave consent on her behalf and they're hardly disinterested parties. I should have been called way before this.'*

*The policeman turns on her. 'Firstly, they were her legal guardians up to today.'*

*Were? The girl stares at him.*

*'And secondly . . .' Just for a moment he is the hissing, spitting bully who terrified her into saying she was lying – into thinking it too. 'You're lucky we decided to offer it at all. She could have gone to prison, you do know that?'*

*'Oh shut up, Kellan. You know as well as I do that a jury would never have convicted her. The case would have been thrown out and you'd have been wiping egg off your face until next year. I've named you personally in my complaint to the IPCC.'*

*He smiles drily. 'And your complaint will be fully investigated. Now, if we could get back to the job in hand?' His amber eyes click back to her. 'Do you understand the proceedings up to this point?'*

*She's supposed to agree with this so she nods.*

253

'Good. I'm cautioning you for wasting police time and making false allegations. These are very serious crimes. You do understand that?'

She nods.

'This caution will appear on any CRB certificate applied for, for a period of two years, and will then remain on your criminal record and may be used as evidence in a court of law should you commit another offence.'

'Another *offence*?' the lady explodes. The girl wishes she would just be quiet. She just wants it over and done with so that she can go home.

'If you continue to be disruptive I'll ask you to leave.'

'No you won't,' the lady replies. 'I'm her legal chaperone.' But she settles nevertheless, literally shaking herself down like a fat pigeon after a rainstorm.

The girl glances behind her at the door. Why didn't Mum come in with her?

'A condition of the caution is that you will issue an apology to the boys involved.'

'Oh fuck off.'

'Watch your language, Mrs Obodom.'

'She's not apologising.'

The policeman turns to the girl, smiling. 'You ever been to a prison, young lady?'

She shakes her head.

'Some of the women there, well . . .' He looks her up and down and shakes his head.

'You aren't seriously doing this? You do know her history?'

His smile slips. 'I've read the file.'

'So don't threaten her, or it won't be just the IPCC I'll be going to. It'll be the press. They *won't* have forgotten her.'

The policeman pushes his tongue into his bottom lip. Finally he says, 'Because of what you've been through in the past we'll waive the apology, but if anything at all happens like this in the future—'

'Come on, sweetheart.' The lady gets up. 'We're done.'

Mum and Dad are waiting for her outside. Mum is crying. Dad's face is as grey as his suit. He steps forward as she emerges.

'Mr Goddard.' The lady shakes his hand. 'Mrs Goddard.' But her mum won't take the proffered hand. She presses her tissue to her eyes as if she can't bear to look at it.

'There's her stuff,' Dad says.

The girl looks in the direction he's pointing. She recognises the red suitcase they took to Majorca in the Easter holiday.

'If there's anything we've left out we'll send it on. Email us, please. No phone calls. I won't have my wife being upset.'

'You're doing a good job there, then.'

Multicoloured ribbons flutter from the handle of the case. She and Mum tied them on to make it easier to spot on the baggage conveyor belt.

'Let's not draw this out any longer than necessary. You got the papers I sent last week?'

He's asking the lady, but she's just staring at the girl.

'You did tell her, didn't you?'

Last week was when Felix was staying with his Auntie Carol and she was in the house alone with her parents. Up in her room mostly, listening to the creaks and ticks of the silent house, trying to breathe air that seemed to have less oxygen, as if it had all been used up by the shouting and crying.

'I'm . . . sorry . . .' It seems like it's difficult for him to say the word, like his tongue has suddenly stiffened. '. . . it had to end like this. Goodbye, Mrs Obodom, and we really do wish her the very best of luck in the future.'

She wonders who he's talking about, because he isn't looking at her.

He turns then and clasps his wife's arm, but she shakes him off.

'Let me talk to her, David, please.'

He makes an angry noise as she moves past him. Her face looks so weird, all red and swollen, and her eyes are crusty and half closed. She takes the girl's hands and the trembling passes into her own arm.

'We had to choose.'

'Mrs Goddard, please be mindful of—'

'We had to choose and he was our son.'

'I'm your daughter,' she says, her voice rusty from disuse. 'Aren't I? That's what you said.'

'Helen, let's—'

'GET OFF ME, DAVID!'

It's the first time she's ever heard Mum raise her voice. The foyer of the police station falls silent. Even the drunk on the bench stops humming to himself.

Her dad's face goes tight and pinched up. 'Tell her whatever you need to. I'll be waiting in the car.' And without a backwards glance, he stalks out through the police station door.

The lady waits until Mum has finished talking, and then she takes the girl's hand and helps her over to the bench. The girl watches her mum's blurry figure, haloed by sunlight, as she opens the door and follows her husband out into the warm afternoon. A moment later the car engine starts. The girl remembers the way the car always smelled of boiled sweets and Felix's trainers.

The lady hands her a tissue but her hands are so numb she can barely hold it.

# Thursday 17 – Saturday 19 November

# 36. Jody

It's three days since you passed on. I can't bring myself to call it anything else. I have to believe that you are somewhere. That one day, perhaps, I might reach you.

Every minute takes forever to crawl by. I watch the shadows in the flat creep across the floor and then up the walls where they spread out like ink in water. I sit in the darkness. I'm still sitting there at dawn.

I haven't washed or brushed my hair or cleaned my teeth since I got back from the hospital. I suppose I must smell.

It's so quiet.

Nobody hammers on the door any more. Nobody orders me to open up and explain myself. Even the baby has stopped crying. They've gone, she and her mother, back to Albania. The husband never came home.

Your sister pushed a note under my door.

*I'm returning to the US. Have the decency to go to the police and tell them what you know, for Abe's sake. Mags Mackenzie*

I watched her through the spyhole as she let herself out of your flat for the last time, in her masculine suit and tight ponytail. Her high heels clip-clopped down the stairs and then the front door banged closed and a moment later there was the sound of a car engine. Her taxi? Or the man I had seen her with that night?

Now I'm alone up here at the top of the church. Tucked away in the space near the roof. If St Jerome's was still a working church the congregation would be sitting in their neat rows far, far below, heedless of my existence. Just the way I like it. You were the only one who ever made me want to be noticed. Now I will fade into the background again. A grey girl in a grey dress in a grey city, living a grey life until it's my turn to pass. Will I see you then?

Yes.

You loved me.

You gave your life for me, Abe, and if that's not love I don't know what is.

I didn't need the pills when I had my love for you to keep me grounded. Now I do. I took the ones I had left but they ran out and the next morning I felt like going up onto the roof and throwing myself off. I could see myself lying spreadeagled on the tarmac of the car park, utterly still and peaceful. The image brought such a sense of release. But what if it went wrong? I'd end up like you did, or worse. And with no one there to hold my hand.

Oh God, I can't keep thinking like this.

In desperation I call Tabby and she organises for a prescription to be left for me at the chemist on the high road.

It's so cold now. The sky a dense white with no sign of the sun. We must be nearly in December. Christmas is coming. The mere thought of that is enough to make me want to step out in front of the bus passing the corner of Gordon Terrace. Helen will send a card, maybe even a pair of slippers or a set of bath oils that I will give to the charity shop. Tabby will buy me chocolates and her daughter will bake me another cake that will only make me feel more alone.

I cross the road and go into the chemist.

The pharmacist starts to smile when I go up to the counter, but then she looks me up and down and her face falls. She asks for my name then hurries into the partitioned section where they dish out the pills.

I wait by the window, looking out over the high road.

Cosmo is busy with lunchtime office workers. I close my eyes and picture the two of us there, sitting at our favourite table at the back, where we can hold hands and kiss without anyone noticing. I picture us chinking glasses as we talk about the wedding. You want a big one – you are proud of me, you want to show me off – I want to keep it small. Just one or two special people, because really I can only think of inviting Tabby and her daughter and maybe the lady from the charity shop.

I am smiling when I open my eyes.

The smile freezes.

*You are there.*

You are inside Cosmo.

Standing in the shadows at the back, the customers and staff milling around you heedlessly. If I didn't know you by your build, by your clothes and hair, I would know from the intensity of your gaze. I'm pinned to the spot, unable to breathe.

'Miss Currie?' says the pharmacist. 'Are you OK?' I tear my eyes away from you. She's holding out a paper bag. Hurrying to the counter I snatch it from her and go out.

The road is as busy as usual and I'm stuck on the pavement, dancing from foot to foot as I wait for a break in the traffic.

Eventually I dive out between a bus and a minicab, ignoring the angry beeping.

The window of Cosmo is a flat reflection of the street scene in front of it. To see inside I have go right up to the glass, ignoring the strange looks of the customers on the other side as I peer in.

You've gone.

If I'd just mistaken you for someone else and that person had left the restaurant I would have seen them walking up the high road, but no one has left, I'm sure of it. Ours is the only empty table in the whole place.

I know what Tabby would say – that I imagined seeing you because you're on my mind so much.

Perhaps she's right.

I try to put it out of my head as I turn for home.

I wake up in the middle of the night.

This is wrong. The pills are supposed to help with insomnia. But I realise that something specific has woken me when I hear it again. A woman's cry, like a wail of grief.

It's coming from close by. One of the other flats on this floor, surely.

I sit up in bed, staring into the darkness.

Is it Mira? Has she come back from Albania? Has her husband found her?

But it's not a cry of distress. It's a woman singing the blues. Now I can hear the words.

I get up and go into the living room. Street light spills through the window to form orange puddles on my bare feet. I breathe shallowly, listening to the words I know so well.

It's one of your favourites. You would play it late at night, when you came back drunk. I'd watch you through the spyhole weaving unsteadily to your door, blundering your key against the lock. And then you'd go inside and the music would come on, lullabying me to sleep when the pills couldn't.

And now it's playing again. How?

I creep down the hall and, as quietly as possible, turn the latch and step out onto the landing. The woman's voice streams out of your flat, echoing down the stairwell.

I grip the banister rail and look over the edge. Unless another listener is standing down there in the darkness, I'm alone. Can no one else hear this? Is it all in my mind?

The lino is cold beneath my feet. My breathing is quick and shallow with fear, and something else. Excitement? Then it catches in my throat.

I can smell your aftershave.

The black spyhole on your door glitters as I pad across the landing.

I press my ear to the wood and listen.

262

But the music is too loud to hear if there is any movement inside.

Then it hits me. All the flats come with two sets of keys, but I only found one of yours: the one I gave to your sister, that she must have sent back to the housing association.

Who has the other?

Are they in there now? Playing your music? Wearing your aftershave?

'Hello?' I say clearly and loudly.

The music shuts off and the darkness throbs with the sudden silence.

For a moment I'm paralysed with fear. Was it all a trick? Is some stranger going to wrench open the door and drag me inside?

Is it *him*?

Somehow I get my feet moving. I run back to the flat, slamming the door behind me and curling up into a ball on the floor. I stay there until the sun begins to come up, but your flat remains utterly silent. Finally I creep back to bed.

Nothing's working any more.

My vision is blurry.

I keep tripping over and dropping things. I scalded myself with a cup of tea and a large blister, tight and red and fragile, has come up on my right thigh, making me too scared to wear jeans in case it pops.

My stomach churns and I have to dash to the toilet three or four times a day.

I go into a room and forget why I went there.

My hair is falling out.

I went to the charity shop to buy some books to try and distract myself, but when the woman behind the counter tried to talk to me I felt the first stirrings of a panic attack and had to run out.

I know that some of these are side effects of the pills, but I'm scared that something else is happening to my brain.

I'm seeing things.

Ghosts.

*Your* ghost.

I try to tell myself that it's all in my mind, keep my head down, stay indoors, don't talk to anyone, don't look out of any windows. But sometimes I have to leave the flat for groceries, and it's then that you come.

Checking the instruction leaflet in the pills I see that in the side effects section under *Rare: fewer than one person per ten thousand* it says *hallucinations*.

But the thing is, unless I'm imagining this part as well, other people can see you too. I watch them adjust their course to let you by. I see them standing on a full bus when you are seated in front of them. I see them serving you in cafés – but when I go in you're gone.

You're always moving away from me. On a bus or walking just too fast and too far for me to catch you up.

Tabby phones. She says the pharmacist has been in touch with my doctor, saying they're worried about my state of mind. Am I all right?

'I'm fine.'

A pause.

'You must miss him a great deal.'

I cannot stop my breathing from thickening.

'Just remember, that though they're gone from our sight, the dead are always with us, Jody,' she says gently. 'In our hearts and our memories.'

How can that ever be enough?

'I think you should start going back to the group, and stick with the pills – they'll take a couple of weeks to work after a break. I think that will help any negative thinking or . . . delusions.'

I want to tell her that you aren't a delusion. If it was all in my head would people be moving aside to let you pass them? My whole life I've been told that what I'm feeling or thinking isn't real, that I can't trust myself. Tabby was the only one who ever believed me, and now she's doubting me too.

264

I get her off the phone, saying I've got an upset stomach. It's not a lie. Though I don't want to have to see the woman who's been reporting me to my social worker, I need to go back to the chemist for something to settle it. I walk quickly, head bent so low all I can see are people's feet, and even then my heart lurches every time a pair of Converses or brogues steps into my line of vision.

The pharmacist doesn't try to talk to me this time, or slip any more leaflets into the bag when she hands me the medicine. I'm trying so hard not to look in Cosmo that I open the door without looking and almost walk straight into a young woman. At her gasp I turn and apologise, and it's then that I see you. Standing on the corner of Gordon Terrace. From this far away it's hard to see properly but I think you're looking back at me. Waiting.

I've spent such a long time trying to convince myself that these visions are wrong, something to be ashamed of, something to fear, that for a moment I don't move.

Then a wave of love and happiness so powerful washes over me that I think I might collapse. A woman looks you up and down as she passes and then I know for sure. I'm not imagining you, Abe. You're here. You've come back to me to show me that, whatever anyone else says, our love was real.

I run.

But by the time I've crossed the road you're nowhere to be seen. I stand on the corner, panting, waiting for the dizziness to pass, my eyes pricking with tears.

As I trudge back to St Jerome's the youths peel out from the shadows, but do you know? I'm not scared at all any more. The worst thing has happened to me – I've lost you – and now I don't care about anything else.

They ask me the time but I keep walking. One of them steps out in front of me and says that his friend asked me a question so I should have enough respect to reply.

I stare at him, dull-eyed. *Do what you want.*

He looks me up and down and wrinkles his nose in disgust. Then he lunges for my bag. There's nothing in it of value: the few pounds change from my shopping, my keys, a couple of tampons, but I cling to it like it's bursting with fifties. I squeeze my eyes shut. I know why you've come back, Abe – to tell me that you're waiting for me. Well, I'm ready.

'Give me the bag.'

I hold on tight.

'Let. Go. Of. The. Bag. Bitch.'

I hear the rasp of a knife being taken from a pocket, and the flash of light, reddened by my eyelids.

It's time. I'm ready.

'Hey!'

I open my eyes. A middle-aged man with a Staffie stands at the corner of the high road, his legs spread as wide as his dog's. He might have been muscly once but it has all turned to fat. Under the football shirt his stomach is broad and squarish, like the shell of a tortoise.

The youths smirk as they look him up and down, but when he sets off at a fast stride towards us, the dog loping along by his side, they disperse, catcalling and gesticulating as they go. The man stops at the edge of the grass, panting, perhaps with the adrenaline rush of a narrow escape, or maybe just because he's fat.

I set off across the waste ground to the church.

'Don't fucking thank me, then!' he calls after me.

I turn, suddenly angry. *Thank you for what? I was* ready! But he's already stomping back to the high road.

I watch from the window of the flat as the light drains away and the remaining street lights on Gordon Terrace buzz on. I've microwaved a plastic tub of lasagne, but find I have no appetite. Instead of the usual aroma of cooked meat and cheese, the food smells sour, like bad breath. I guess that's the pills again.

José the building manager arrives, lugging a new mattress, and disappears through the front door, so I guess someone new is going to move into the empty flat on the third floor.

A lonely night stretches ahead of me. At least I should sleep properly. I've forced myself to stay awake for the past three nights, in case you play your music again, but all has been quiet.

After throwing away the lasagne and rinsing the fork under the tap, I get into bed and put the radio on. My bedroom window glows pink. The man on the radio says there's been a sandstorm in the Sahara and for the next few days the sunsets will be beautiful.

I turn my face to the wall and try to sleep.

On Saturday morning I go out looking for you. I try Cosmo and the baker's and even the Food and Wine where you would sometimes get a newspaper, but it's as if I was imagining you all along.

I wander up and down the high road until my hands are numb with cold and I can't feel my feet.

The pharmacist comes out and asks if I'm all right so I have to stay on the other side of the road after that.

The sun starts going down and I get scared then because it's Saturday. Match day. Buses are backing up along the high road, their windows reflecting the sky. I hurry back to Gordon Terrace and across the waste ground, pausing for a moment at the children's playground to gaze at the church spire silhouetted against the sky.

The radio was right. It's going to be the most amazing sunset. The sky is streaked with a million different shades of red. The clouds curl like petals. The wind has dropped. From up there you could look out on the whole city, all pink and glowing like it's fresh out of a hot bath.

I realise that this is the night I described to Mags. The night you and I spent together on the roof. And then, for a moment, I think I see a figure standing in one of the windows of the spire.

It resolves itself into a block of shadow and I sigh and make my way to the door.

There's no post for me, as usual, and I'm relieved, having half expected a letter with an American postmark, threatening to sue me. Passing through the inner door all the rich colours

267

of the evening are dulled. The sunset is behind the building so the stained glass is flat and grey.

I stand for a moment, gazing at the tranquil lake of concrete that shows no sign of what it did to you. I can remember the chill hardness of it under my knees as I crouched beside you, whispering that everything would be all right as your blood seeped into my jeans.

You were looking at something far away that I couldn't see, but then you must have felt my presence because your eyes moved, locking onto mine. We held each other's gaze for a moment – a minute? An hour? – and then your eyelids fluttered closed and I never saw them open again.

He must have come down behind me, have passed by while I was kneeling beside you, but I never heard his heavy footsteps, or the crash of the door closing. He might have been just a bad dream.

Turning on the light I start climbing the stairs. On the first floor I pass the grumpy man's flat, and Brenda's husband's, and the man who plays the silent organ. When I get to the second floor I walk quickly. Here lives the junkie, who terrifies me because of what I might have been, and the man who is eating himself to death because his mother died. I have just stepped out onto the third floor when the light clicks off and I'm left in darkness.

But not total darkness.

A red light spills down the stairs from above, as if from an emergency generator.

I listen. I can hear a whispering moan. Like the sound you made as you lay dying. But this time it's just the wind. I feel it on my face, lifting my hair, pushing my skirt between my thighs.

I grip the banister and continue climbing.

When I step out onto the fourth floor – our floor – my heart catches.

The door to the roof is open.

Blood-red sunset spills across the landing. I stand at the edge of the puddle of light, afraid of what will happen if I step inside. Am I finally going mad?

The air smells of your aftershave.

Movement by the door catches my eye. A strand of wool is caught on the latch and blows in the wind.

I have to force myself to cross the landing and unhitch the strand. I run it through my fingers. Cashmere. No one else in this place wears cashmere. Only you. This thread is from the diamond pattern on your cardigan with the big collar.

There's a footprint in the dust at the bottom of the staircase. The Xs and diamonds of a Converse sole.

The dull grey concrete steps turn shimmering gold as they rise up before me, like a stairway to heaven.

They were *wrong*. They were all wrong. You *did* love me, and now you've come for me. You're waiting for me up there in the sunset.

I put my foot on the first step.

# 37. Mags

I admit I enjoyed it.

From my table at the back of Cosmo I could watch the street. So many times she missed me as she hurried past with her head down, but I only needed one moment. It was busy that day. I'd just sat down at the one remaining table and was glancing over the menu I knew quite well by then when I saw her. A drab figure merging with the dullness of the street, I only noticed her as she moved across the brash window of the bookie's on the other side of the road.

When she went into the pharmacy I stood up, willing her to see me. And then she did. I held her gaze, wondering how good my disguise was, whether this close she would see that my hair was straighter, my shoulders narrower. But I guessed from her expression that she was taken in and I experienced a shiver of delight as the colour drained from her face.

When she turned to the woman behind the counter I retreated to the toilets at the back of the restaurant to wait until she'd gone. I knew she wouldn't have the courage to come in.

I'd told Peter Selby that I had to stay on for a week or so to arrange the cremation. But when I explained that being around Abe's stuff was proving too painful, the sentimental old queen readily agreed to my moving into one of the unoccupied flats.

270

José met me at the Moon and Sixpence at the far end of the high road to give me the key and we got semi drunk. The new flat smelled of stale alcohol and urine. The alcoholic's mattress had been destroyed so he went for a new one straightaway, hoping, I suspect, he would have the chance to christen it. I pretended to be busy when he came back, tapping away on my computer, ostentatiously oblivious to his shirt-stripping and sweat-from-brow-wiping as he manoeuvred the mattress into position.

He was halfway out of the door when I called him back. He returned, grinning.

'Can I borrow the roof key?'

His face fell. 'Ah, is not safe up there. What you want it for?'

'There's been a huge sand storm in the Sahara and apparently it's going to be a beautiful sunset for the next few days. I thought there'd be a good view from up there.'

'Sounds fun,' he said, leaning on the door frame. His after-shave was so strong it gave me the same head rush as alcohol. 'Like some company?'

I smiled. 'If I do, I'll give you a call.'

He slid his hand into the pocket of his low jeans and drew out a key ring.

'Don't lose it or I will spank you.'

'Sod off, José,' I said good-naturedly, and he swaggered across the foyer and out into the dusk.

After that I just had to lay low and wait for the right moment.

This morning I had my first attack of conscience as I watched Jody cross and recross the end of Gordon Terrace, searching for her phantom lover, and decided that, for better of worse, it would have to be tonight.

As the afternoon wore away I dressed up in Abe's trousers, shirt and cardigan, gelling my hair into his careful waves in front of the mildewed mirror in the bathroom.

And now I stand here, by a windowsill strewn with dead flies, swigging from a quarter bottle of whisky to calm my nerves while I wait for Jody to come back.

I had wondered, as the barber on the high road cut my new style, whether Daniel would still fancy me with short hair, but it's an academic point, since I won't be seeing him again. He and Donna probably have a cosy night planned, with a Netflix boxset, a nice bottle of chardonnay and a takeaway curry, the kids slumbering peacefully upstairs, happy in the knowledge that Mummy and Daddy are back together.

I throw the remains of the bottle down my throat and grimace. Is my contempt just sour grapes? Christ, who knows? I *thought* I was jealous of Abe and Jody.

The glass stops halfway to the sill.

She's coming.

Her steps drag down Gordon Terrace, her shadow yawning behind her. I would have spotted her before but her colouring merges with the grey pavement.

She reaches the end of the street and steps onto the grass. At any moment she could look up and see me. A part of me wants her to, wants her to guess what's going on so I don't have to go through with any of it. But she doesn't.

Grabbing Abe's aftershave and the key from the stained Formica dining table, I let myself out of the flat. I take the stairs two at a time and have made it to the third floor when I hear the creak of the main door opening. Swearing under my breath – I should have moved earlier – I drop to my haunches and crawl up the final flight of steps. But my luck's in – for some reason she's lingering downstairs.

I crawl past Abe's door, then Mira's and Jody's, to the other end of the landing. A sliver of grimy wind creeps under the threshold where a semi circle of dust and grit has formed. A stroke of luck.

Awkwardly lifting my knee while trying to keep my head down, I press the sole of Abe's shoe into the dust, then I slide the key into the Yale lock and turn it with the utmost care. There is the tiniest scrape of metal and then the door unfastens, swinging out towards me. I catch it, and let it out slowly, wincing as it creaks a little. I can hear her coming up the stairs. She must be on the first floor.

Careful not to disturb the footprint, I climb into the stairwell, spritz the aftershave a couple of times, then run lightly up the cement steps to the door at the top.

Opening it I am assaulted by the wind. Fortunately José has thought to leave a chunk of breeze block up here and once I've secured it I straighten up to look for a place to conceal myself.

For a split second I forget why I came and simply stare.

The sky is on fire.

Ribbons of gold and scarlet light stream west to east, studded here and there with fireballs of slowly revolving cloud. The buildings are charred black stumps, with an occasional window dazzlingly aflame.

My hands are red, and so are Abe's Converses, as if I have been paddling in blood.

Behind me faltering footsteps scrape the gritty surface of the cement steps.

She has fallen for it.

Where can I hide?

The church spire lances up into the roiling sky. There are louvred windows on both sides, one set looking out over the high road, the other looking back over endless council estates. A small door in the wall must lead to a staircase. Is this the place from her imagination? Where she and my brother had their first earth-shattering night of passion?

It's pitiful, laughable. But I don't feel like laughing any more. I dive across the lead roof and conceal myself behind the spire.

Dead leaves crackle under my feet as I peer around the edge of the wall.

I squint, unable to distinguish her shape from the pink shadows on the wall of the stairwell, until she steps out onto the roof.

Close up she is so frail I fear that the wind will buffet her straight over the edge. Beneath the scarlet wash of the sunset, her face is drained, her eye sockets dark-ringed.

273

I assume she is blinking because the sun is in her eyes but then the tears spill out, the sun catching them and turning them to livid scratches down her cheeks. Like some kind of martyred saint.

No. I mustn't allow myself to think she is the victim. I must go through with this. Or I will never know.

She takes a step forward, then another, catching her toe on the edge of the leadwork and stumbling, then righting herself.

'Abe?' Her voice trembles.

I step back as her eyes scan the rooftop.

'Abe, I'm here.'

She walks hesitantly towards the door in the spire; presumably she intends to climb up to the windows. I hear a rattling. The door is locked. Poor Jody. No ghostly lover waiting to enclose her in his cold embrace after all.

I ease myself around the spire to approach her from behind.

Her body is angled away from me so it takes a moment for her to register my presence.

Jerking around she cries out, her hands flying to her face, and I realise, with incredulity, that even now she thinks I'm Abe. It must be the tears clouding her vision – or the pills clouding her mind.

Either way she stands rigid with shock, which gives me enough time to get between her and the steps that lead back down to the fourth floor.

'Hello, Jody.'

The hands fall from her face. Her eyebrows contract, tilting upwards as her face crumples with disappointment. No, more than disappointment. Anguish. She gives a moaning exhalation, as if she has been kicked in the stomach, and actually bends a little at the waist.

'You've been avoiding me. What was I supposed to do?'

I sound like a Bond villain. If I were watching this tableau on a film, I'd be willing her to snatch up the brick door prop and hurl it into my face before making her escape. I set my jaw. It has to be done.

'I need to know what happened – and you're going to tell me.'

Her eyes are dull. Her face has slackened, as if a little bit of her soul has drained away. Even the wariness seems blunted because when I step towards her she makes no attempt to evade me.

'You're not getting off this roof until you do.'

Her eyes slide away from mine. It's the only signal that she is alive or conscious.

I am ready to hurt her. It is the natural progression of my behaviour over the past week – watching her, following her, deliberately setting out to unnerve her. I've been stalking her. Murder in slow motion.

'You're going to tell me what happened that night. Who pushed my brother over that stairwell?'

She is silent.

Striding up to her I slap her hard enough to make my palm sting.

Her head stays where the blow put it, angled away from me, her wide eyes staring down at the lead.

'Say something, Jody, or I'm warning you . . .'

But I'm losing hope already.

She is a broken doll, propped awkwardly on spindle-legs, unstable, liable to collapse like pick-up sticks. I grasp her bony shoulders, my thumbs digging into her clavicles, and give them a sharp shake as if I'm trying to dislodge something that's sticking. Her head waggles stupidly, the hair falling in front of her face, hiding her eyes from me. I yank it back, hoping to see fear, but they are blank and glassy.

'You owe me this, Jody. You owe it to Abe.' I force this attempt at emotional blackmail out through gritted teeth. In a minute I'll stop trying to keep a lid on my fury. It's getting dark. Our figures will no longer be silhouetted against a treacherously bright sky. I can do what I like to her and no one will ever know.

No one would care.

No one would believe her.

'Answer me!'

275

I count down the seconds: three, two, one.

Time's up.

And now a part of me doesn't even want to hear her story, it just wants to hurt her, to punish her for everything that has happened. For Abe, for our shitty childhoods, for the wreck of my emotions, for her own weakness, which has allowed people to hurt and abuse her for her whole pathetic life. She is a rag doll upon whom others can take out their misery and pain. And now it's my turn.

I drag her to the edge of the roof, where the lead falls away sharply, then kick her legs out from under her. She lands on her back with a grunt and before she can roll to safety I drop down to straddle her, my hands around her throat, forcing her head back over the edge. Her hair streams out in the wind.

'This is what it was like for Abe!' I snarl. 'Hanging over that banister, wondering if the person that held him would let him go. Was it you, Jody?'

Thrusting my hips I nudge her forward, and now her shoulders are off the edge. I only manage to stop the inexorable slide of the rest of her by grasping the head of a nearby gargoyle. Its pointed tongue stretches down between its legs and I want to snatch my hand back, but if I do she will fall. Even holding onto it I feel unstable. Perhaps we will both go over.

Somewhere a police siren wails. The vertical wind pummels my chin, all scent of aftershave long gone, replaced by the gritty, musty perfume of the city.

The siren recedes and an eerie quiet descends.

She isn't screaming or crying or begging me not to hurt her. She doesn't make a sound. Her eyes simply gaze skywards, like a long-suffering saint seeking deliverance from heaven. Her chest brushes my thighs as it gently rises and falls. She is totally calm.

I ask myself again: who is she protecting?

Whoever it is it seems she'd rather die than betray them.

How far will I have to go to make her tell me?

276

A gull swoops down in front of us, red-backed. We must be above the bins. Jody's view, in all these years of living here, has been of people's rubbish being fought over by gulls and rats and foxes, and the occasional whore turning tricks. The gull swoops up again, a chicken bone between its beak. Eating it's own kind in its greed or desperation.

And then it hits me.

I have been so stupid.

What was it Daniel said? There's no such thing as truth. Only the story we choose to tell, to others, and ourselves. Jody is sticking to her story to the bitter end. Sticking to that fantasy in which her life is bearable, in which she is loved and needed, even though it might kill her. Because what on earth is the truth worth to Jody? Nothing. Nothing but pain and despair. But in her parallel universe she is about to follow her darling into eternity.

Who is Jody protecting? Herself, of course.

Look at my knuckles, white with the strain of gripping her. I thought I'd left that girl behind, the one who took pleasure in inflicting pain, but she's been here all along, hiding under my skin, waiting for the next victim. The next piece of easy meat.

I loosen my grip. Suddenly released, she starts to slip and I have to grab her by the arm and yank her back. For a few agonising seconds I wonder if we will both fall, but then she seems to wake up from whatever stupor she has been in, and with my help, hauls herself back onto the safety of the leadwork.

We crawl away from the precipice on hands and knees, and don't stop until we have reached the spire. Suddenly exhausted, I lean against the cold stone and let my head drop to my knees.

I have become a coward and a bully again, like my father. Was the truth worth that?

I hear a rustle and raise my head.

Jody has crawled over and slumps against the wall beside me.

The wind rises, catching the gelled wave of Abe's hair and tugging at it, as if to tear it away from my skull. The last sliver of sunset bleeds across the horizon.

'I'm sorry,' I say. 'It doesn't matter any more. He's dead. I don't care who—'

'Wait.' Jody's voice is strong and steady.

I blink my eyes clear.

'Listen.'

*It's getting dark. Normally she's home before dusk. She doesn't like walking down Gordon Terrace after six, when all the residents are home from their cleaning or catering jobs and are safely tucked away in their concrete boxes, curtains closed like a charm against the packs of feral youth prowling outside.*

*It was the psych assessment. They were running late.* Saturdays are our busiest time, *the receptionist said accusingly.* You should have booked for another day.

Sorry, *she said. She didn't even know she could; she just came when she was told to. Her appointment was for four but they didn't call her in until half past five and now it's almost seven.*

*The bus sits in traffic for so long that when a more ballsy passenger punches the emergency door-opening button she slips out after him and crosses the high road. It's about a mile to Gordon Terrace, but there's no point hurrying – it's already dark. When she gets to the corner she will just have to pick her moment – a late commuter returning, a car pulling up – and sprint for St Jerome's.*

*Lights glare from the fast-food outlets. Someone is having an argument in the kebab shop. The manager of the Greek bakery is pulling down the shutters. They are covered with graffitied names: Toxo, Barb, Stika. Like alien planets instead of human beings. The man in the Food and Wine is shouting down the phone in a foreign language.*

*The traffic is solid all down the other side of the road and as she walks past a stationary bus she senses a face turn in her direction. Ducking her head she quickens her steps and is passing Cosmo restaurant when a voice calls out behind her.*

*'Hey.'*

*She turns around.*

279

Her legs become matchsticks and she almost falls to her knees on the pavement.

'Hey,' he says again, holding up his hands, palm first. 'Hey, don't look so freaked out. I just wanted to say hello.'

If she could move she would run now, as he comes towards her. She would run in front of the traffic and be hit by the now moving bus rather than have him come close to her.

But her legs won't work and now he is so close she can smell the beer on his breath and that oh-so-familiar deodorant, with the reek of stale sweat beneath.

'Hey, Jody.' His voice is soft. 'How are you doing?'

He looks the same, only bigger, and with less hair. His eyelids are heavy. He is drunk. 'Cat got your tongue?'

'Sorry,' she says. 'I'm fine, thank you. How are you?'

'Yeah yeah, not bad. Just had a fixture against Hackney. Nailed them. On my way home to get ready for the club later – couldn't believe it when I saw you. What you up to?'

'I'm on my way home.'

His head rocks backwards and forward. He doesn't know what to say to her. If she stays quiet he will get bored and go.

'You hear about Felix?'

She presses her lip together and shakes her head.

'Mainlining heroin now, apparently. Completely fucked.'

The high-pitched sound in the back of her throat is lost in the traffic. Her beautiful Felix. Still beautiful in her mind, whatever he did to her.

'Lost half his teeth.'

'Stop,' she says. 'Please.'

'Oh yeah, I forgot you had a thing for him. Don't reckon he'd twist your lemon these days, sweetheart. He stinks.'

He's looking at her, waiting for a response. She tenses up, trying to think of something that won't agitate him.

'I'm sorry to hear that.'

And then suddenly all his affability is gone. 'You should be, though, right? I mean, all that shit with the police. That's what really sent him over the edge.'

*It's like being punched in the stomach. He's saying that it was her fault, what happened to Felix. She can't catch her breath as his cold eyes drill into her.*

*And then he smiles.*

*'Hey, listen, no hard feelings, though, OK? I mean, all that shit you said could've really fucked my prospects, but it's water under the bridge now, right? I've got a nice accounting job. Good money. I'm not bitter. In fact . . .' He grins. 'To prove it, why don't I walk you home? Make sure you get back safe.'*

*'Thanks, but it's not far.' Her smile is skull-like.*

*'Nah, it doesn't bother me.' His huge hand closes around her upper arm. 'Lead on!'*

*He walks very fast and sometimes she stumbles. Now she remembers how his normal breathing sounded like panting. Like a dog. Her arm is in the grip of its jaws.*

*They reach the corner of Gordon Terrace. The boys are there, sitting on one of the garden walls, smoking.*

*Hearing footsteps their heads turn as one.*

*They know her, know that her bag is unlikely to contain anything but a few coins and a second-hand paperback, but surely this middle-class white boy, with his bulging kit bag and expensive-looking watch, is more promising. If they accost him he'll have to let go of her to deal with them.*

*But his steps do not falter as they come level with the group.*

*'Evening, fellas,' he says and one of them actually grunts a response.*

*A moment later they have passed by. She turns her head and the youths gaze back at her with flat, dead eyes. Where is the shark's bite when you need it?*

*Up ahead, St Jerome's is a black spike against the dark sky. Perhaps he will simply leave her at the door. He's a grown man now, not a reckless teenager. Back then it was Tabby who insisted it was rape, but the judge said it was no more than raging hormones, that she had willingly taken part, until the sober light of day had brought with it a sense of shame at her own promiscuity. That she had made the accusation to assuage her own guilt. Did she give them some sign that she wanted them to do what they did to her? Over the years she has decided that she must have done, that if she had been clearer they would have stopped. It wasn't rape, just a failure of communication. Her* fault.

*They reach the door.*

*'Thank you,' she says.*

*'My pleasure.'*

*He makes no move to go. Hopelessly she slips her key from her bag and pushes it into the latch. The foyer door opens.*

*'Thanks,' she says again. 'Bye.'*

*She walks in. He follows. The door shunts closed.*

*They stand in the gloom of the foyer.*

*'I'll be all right from here.'*

*'A gentleman always sees a lady to her door.'*

*He holds open the inner door and she steps through. A sliver of light spills from Mrs Lyons' flat, illuminating a semi circle of concrete. Should she scream for Mrs Lyons to help her? To call the police?*

*But what would they say at being called out because someone had the temerity to try and see her safely home? She was warned before about wasting police time.*

*'What floor you on?' His voice is loud and intrusive. No one speaks loudly in St Jerome's. From upstairs she can hear the lilting murmur of Abe's music.*

*'The fourth.'*

*His heavy steps echo through the stairwell as he follows her up the stairs.*

*'This must keep you fit, eh?' he says. 'No wonder you're so skinny. I always liked that about you. If you just had some tits . . .'*

*'Thank you,' she murmurs.*

*'Wanna know the other thing I've always liked about you?'*

*They're on the third floor now.*

*She gives a wan smile. 'What?'*

*He gestures for her to go on and she starts the final ascent to the fourth.*

*'That you're so completely full of shit.'*

She hesitates. Has she misheard him over the music?

'Seriously, you're fuckin famous for it. Who were your parents again? Not a pair of kiddy fiddlers who pimped you out to dirty old farmers? Course not.' He laughs.

She stares at him.

'Remind me how they died again? Wasn't your dad castrated by his cellmate? Oh no, my mistake. He was shot down over Iraq, wasn't he? A war hero. You must be so proud.'

Her chest cavity fills with ice.

'And your mum found God, didn't she? Said the devil had made her let men stick farming implements up her six-year-old daughter? Hell, Jody. What a life, eh?'

Her trembling hand makes the carrier bag rustle.

'Now.' He steps up onto the fourth floor. 'You owe me, for what you did to me back then. What you did to poor old Felix.'

'Sorry. I'm sorry. I'm—'

'And this is payback time. A good match always makes me horny, and what's one more cock for a slag like you? Now be a good girl and don't make a fuss, because you know what happens if you try to stop me, right? I fuck you anyway and then it's my word against yours. And what do you think your word's worth, Jody?' His bottom lip pokes out and he shrugs. 'You tell me, honey. I might just sue you this time, for defamation. I could have done before, but I let you off cos I like you.'

She backs towards her door, fumbling for her keys.

'Did you get that stitch Felix was on about? Hope so, cos seriously, it was like driving a minibus through the Grand Canyon.'

His laugh is a rifle shot ricocheting around the stairwell. Her fingers close around the keys. She won't have time to open the door, dash through and close it again, but if he attacks her out here, surely someone will come out.

On impulse she hurls the keys over the banister.

He grins. 'Nice try.' Then he lunges at her, shoving her up against the door so hard the wood splinters. His thumbs gouge her shoulders.

She should have screamed before, when she first saw him. She should have screamed and run and not stopped until she reached the

283

*sanctuary of the church. This is her chance. Her last chance to save herself. To be saved.*

*'ABE!'*

*He punches her. Her lip splits and warm blood flows into her mouth.*

*'WHAT DID I SAY?'*

*The lock is loose now. One more blow and they will be through, into the flat, and he will be able to do whatever he wants to her. He yanks her body into his then throws it back to ram the door. Her head rebounds off the wood but though the lock rattles it still holds.*

*'Hey!'*

*Two heads turn in the direction of Flat Ten.*

*Abe is silhouetted against warm light. The music is louder and the lemon scent of washing-up liquid drifts across the landing.*

*'Piss off, mate,' her attacker sneers.*

*'The hell are you doing?'*

*'None of your business. Piss off back inside.'*

*'Jody?' Abe takes a single step out onto the landing. 'You all right?'*

*'Seriously. Get lost.'*

*She watches him, holding her breath. If she has truly been imagining his love for her all this time, Abe will do as he's told and go back inside.*

*Another step. 'Jody? Answer me. Are you all right?'*

*Their eyes lock. She is dumb with fear, but she doesn't need to speak. They have such a powerful connection he can read the truth in her eyes.*

*His brown eyes harden. 'Let go of her. Now.'*

*Miraculously the other man does so. Then, in one fluid, muscular movement, he crosses the landing and throws a punch that sends Abe crashing back against the door frame.*

*For a moment he sways, unsteadily, but though he is slight, she knows that Abe goes to the gym under the arches every day. As the other man draws back his fist, Abe bends at the waist and powers forward, butting her attacker in the abdomen, driving him backwards until, with a hollow ring of metal, the bigger man's meaty back comes up against the banister rail.*

*He has to grip the rail with both hands to stop himself tipping backwards and is helpless to protect himself as Abe draws back an elbow and punches him once, twice. The bigger man's nose explodes with blood and he gives a gargle of surprise, then brings his hands to his face, swearing.*

*Abe turns to Jody. His face is flushed. The mop of fringe falls damply across his forehead. She can hear the whisper of his shirt against his skin as his chest rises and falls. 'You OK?' He reaches out for her with those long, elegant fingers.*

*She is so filled with emotion she cannot speak. He loves her. He loves her.*

*She reaches for him. Their fingers are almost touching.*

*Then the monster raises its head. Over Abe's shoulder she sees black eyes glaring from a blood-streaked face.*

*'No!'*

*Abe turns too late. The creature clamps its thick arm around his neck and drags him to the banister. There is a sickening crunch as his spine makes contact with the metal handrail.*

*It all happens so quickly.*

*Abe's feet scuffle against the lino, and then the scuffling stops and he is kicking through air.*

*'No!'*

*He bends like a high jumper.*

*He is balanced on the small of his back, a human seesaw. Then the seesaw tips.*

*Her feet carry her to the banister and the rail crushes the air from her lungs as she strains forward, reaching for his flailing arm. She manages to grasp the fabric of his shirt sleeve, but the stitches give and it slips from her fingers.*

*For a split second he is frozen in time, arms outstretched like wings, an angel flying out of the darkness. Then he is gone.*

# 38. Mags

We sit side by side against the wall of the tower. Through Abe's shirt I can feel the rough stone against my back. It is as cold as the lead beneath me, as cold as her hand resting on mine.

She has stopped speaking.

Blown by the wind her hair is a silver curtain across her face. I push it behind her ears so that I can look into her eyes. They are watery grey, red-rimmed with the loss of my brother and perhaps the loss of everything she has ever dared to value.

'Abe didn't love me in the way I wanted him to,' she says softly. 'But if he didn't care about me at least a bit, why would he have given his life to save mine?' Her eyes search my face. 'It's true. Please believe—'

I smile at her. 'I believe you.'

Then I tell her a story of my own.

My father had found my stash of the pill that I'd persuaded the doctor to give me without their consent. When I got home from school he dragged me to the bathroom and held me, fully clothed and bellowing, under the hot shower, as punishment. I was fighting him so much that he'd actually had to get in the bath with me and was suffering under the scalding flow as much as I was.

I suppose it must have been shortly after Eilean Donan. Something had changed in mine and Abe's relationship. If not

286

actual affection, then something like a mutual respect had grown up between us. We were partners in misery after all.

Without warning, my silent, self-contained brother burst into the bathroom and started trying to pull our father off me. As he pulled and I pushed, the old bastard slipped, cracking his head on the tiles. It wasn't much of an injury, but Abe knew what he would get for it.

The beating he received for protecting me was the impetus for my leaving home. In case he tried to stand up for me again. Because as he stood there, back straight, stony-faced, while my father clambered out of the bath with blood dribbling down his scalp, I knew that he would. He may have been skinny and young and scared, but he was brave.

I don't have much faith in Jody, but I have faith in Abe. I think he would have come out of his flat to help her when she called his name. He would have taken on a bully who was bigger than him, stronger, crueller. For love. Not the love Jody's talking about, but because he cared about people. Funny. She believed in guardian angels, and in the end one came to her aid.

When I've finished speaking she is smiling. But then the smile falters and she starts to cry. 'I'm sorry. He did this for me. He saved me, but I was too scared to do something for him. I should have told the police. I just knew they'd never believe me.'

The wind buffets her narrow frame, snatching at her hair and the grey dress, with its cheap plastic beads. The things that I sneered at her for when we met – the frailty, that yearning to please, to be loved – now twist my heart.

I'm not a good person; I know this. I'm impatient, selfish, contemptuous of people more vulnerable than me. I can be cruel. But how could anyone get pleasure from hurting someone like Jody? Like a child torturing a kitten.

What kind of a man would do that? Someone who must dominate the weak to make him feel less inadequate? A calculating psychopath? Or just a mundane bully satisfying his most basic urges?

He thought it would be easy. Easy meat. He knew he would get away with it, just like he did before, because who would believe someone like Jody? They didn't the last time he raped her; they considered themselves lenient in letting her off with a caution, free to return to the wreckage of her life. But if she dared to cry rape a second time, to throw their clemency back in their faces, she would have to be taught a lesson. No wonder she was afraid.

I take her by the shoulders and look into her eyes.

'They might not believe you, Jody. But they'll believe me.'

Then I smile.

He won't know what hit him.

# New Year's Eve

# 39. Mags

Jody and I have Christmas together. I intend for us to spend it quietly, in memory of my brother, but then I think screw it, and book us into Claridges for Christmas dinner and a room for the night. It costs more than my flights, but we agree that Abe would love the idea of us being here. He would appreciate the spa-brand toiletries, the Egyptian-cotton bedding and deep-pile dressing gowns Jody swans around in. I tell her that they, and the contents of the mini bar, come with the room and she should help herself.

Over breakfast on Boxing Day I explain my plans for New Year's Eve. She blanches, but I reassure her that everything will be all right and, trusting soul that she is, she believes me. Later she returns to St Jerome's in a cab with both our cases, while I head off to the Boxing Day rugby fixture.

My father loved rugby, my brother too. Just being at the ground takes me back to my childhood. A bit of sentimental nostalgia to ease my homesickness, which is always worse around Christmastime, especially since I've just lost my brother. I couldn't resist popping in on my way past, during one of the longs walks that I've taken to making, to clear my head and process the last month's sad events.

This is what I tell the old duffers propping up the bar at half-time. Clive and his merry band compete to impress me, with their stats knowledge and witty banter. They buy me drinks and I'm careful to explain that I'm off alcohol since my brother's accident (*we think drinking may have exacerbated his depression*). Not that it stops me enjoying myself, I insist. New Year's Eve is my favourite night of the year, although this year it will be a lonely affair . . .

Right on cue they bring up the party I've known about ever since I started researching the team.

Would I like to come, as their special guest, in memory of my brother?

'I wouldn't know anyone.'

'You'd know us!' They link arms, all rivalry for my attention forgotten.

'That's very kind of you. I might just take you up on it.'

My day's task successfully fulfilled, I can concentrate on the rest of the match. I spot him at once, from Jody's description and the name printed on the back of his shirt, and am relieved to discover how easy it is to dislike him: the way he stalks the pitch as if he owns it, the casual violence against players that oppose him, the unsportsmanlike crowing over points scored, and petulant protests when they don't go his way.

He comes within touching distance of me as he clumps past on his way to the dressing room, his flesh red with the blood pumping around his muscles, nostrils flared, smelling of sweat and victory. So big, so powerful. He must think he's invincible.

I smile and wave at the old duffers making their way back to the bar, and then I head for the bus stop.

He's clearly not expecting the call. I sense wariness in the careful neutrality of his tone but he's still in London and agrees to meet me in a coffee bar in the city, near to the bank where he works. They're in the middle of a corruption scandal, he says – that's why he hasn't yet returned to the US – so he won't be able to stay long. A get-out clause if he needs one.

I arrive early and scroll through all the possible ways I can frame the request I plan to put to him, all my possible bargaining tools. Free legal advice with his divorce, sex, money. I know gangsters; I can feel that greasy aura that tells you a person has a price, and usually how much it is. Daniel never had it.

He arrives before I've come up with anything.

He looks better than last time. His skin is smooth and his hair has grown and started to curl. He wears a grey suit with an open shirt and a pink tie flops like a dog's tongue from his pocket.

Clearly married life is doing him good. I resist the urge to say so as I rise from the low-slung armchair. It will sound like sour grapes.

He hugs me, without a word, and for a moment I let myself sink into him. His neck smells of soap. Lucky Donna.

Then I take a deep breath and pull away. He's not mine to enjoy.

'Another coffee?' he says.

'Latte, please. No sugar.'

He brings the drinks on a tray with two pieces of cake.

My lip twitches. 'No sugar, but I want a super-healthy chocolate brownie?'

'You could do with putting on a few pounds. You don't look great.'

'Gee, thanks. You do.'

Shit, *shit*. We both studiously look in opposite directions.

'I meant,' *oh, here I go*, 'you look well. You must be happy. I'm glad it's all working out. With Donna.'

He cuts his brownie in half and clears up the crumbs with a licked fingertip.

'So, what can I do for you? After some investment advice?'

I look away. I deserve the insult.

'Sorry,' he says quietly.

'Don't be. I asked for it.'

His face is as expressionless as it has been since he arrived, then, heart-breakingly, he smiles. 'You did.'

I sigh. Too late now.

'I wanted to ask you something. To *do* something for me. A small thing.'

He watches me steadily, sipping his coffee. He knows it isn't a small thing.

I feel myself redden. It's an odd sensation. I haven't blushed since I was a child. The truth is, I have no idea how to approach this. I could pretend it was all true. *Truth is what you can make people believe*. I could make him believe the lie.

Or I could tell him the real truth.

I close my eyes and step out into the abyss. 'Someone might ask you . . . about the nights we spent together.'

His mug pauses halfway to his lips.

I take a deep breath. 'There's a court case. I've made a rape claim against someone and they will want to imply that I enjoy casual sex.'

He pales. 'Bastard.'

I hold up my hand. 'It's not as simple as that, Daniel.'

He leans towards me, head bent, waiting for me to continue.

I sip my coffee and put it down on the table. It's too milky, half cold. My hand is trembling and the liquid sloshes over the untouched brownie. Sweat is breaking out around my hairline.

'I want you to say we didn't sleep together.'

He frowns. 'But I asked the concierge for condoms.'

'Say we changed our mind, decided to wait. You're the only potential weakness in the case.'

He swallows. 'What did he do to you? The rapist.'

Around us the noise of the café becomes muffled, as if we are enclosed in a bubble, a quivering wall of tension surrounding us.

'He killed my brother.'

I tell him everything. When I've finished there is a horribly long silence during which I want to stab myself with the brownie knife. What a stupid thing to do. I came here to patch up a potential weakness in my case, and now I've blown a hole in it so big it might not even get to court. Daniel might march straight to the police and tell them everything. They'll assume I've been taken in by Jody's lies and may be lenient with me, given my recent bereavement, or they may just charge me with wasting police time. Otherwise it's perverting the course of justice. If Jody's called in, it might very well be prison for her this time – for both of us.

I blunder to my feet, knocking over the cardboard cup, spilling beige milk all over the table.

'I shouldn't have come. Please, please forget everything I told you. Please don't go to the police.'

'Mags—'

'He's a bad person, Dan. Don't feel the need to protect him. He *did* rape her, the first time. Her social worker is a hundred per cent sure. She had injuries and—'

'Mags! Calm down.'

My heart is pounding and I can barely catch my breath. I sink back into the chair. He reaches across the table, his sleeve dragging through the puddle of coffee.

I grip his hand like a terrified child, but after a moment he lets go, slipping his fingers from mine and getting up.

'Let me think, OK?'

And then he's gone. A dark shape in the huge mirror on the wall opposite me, as he passes the window and is lost in the crowd.

What have I done?

# March

# 40. Mags

The Crown Prosecution Service team's junior lawyer, Rauf Chaudhry, is a young Pakistani who took his degree at some crappy college in the Midlands, but I suspect he's going to be seriously good one day. He's clearly rabidly ambitious and when he finds out I'm a lawyer myself, pumps me for information about the US legal system.

His official role is to keep me informed about how the trial's progressing, but I tell him that after I've given my witness statement I intend to sit in on proceedings. He does his best to persuade me to present my evidence via video-link, as is the right of all rape victims, but I tell him that I want to face my attacker. I add, with a meaningful smile, that I also want to make sure the CPS doesn't balls up the case.

I wear a navy suit to court, no make-up, tie back my hair, put on my reading glasses. My rapist will struggle even to recognise me. No one in the court will remember me after the trial ends.

I'm the first witness and the court falls silent as the heels of my low pumps tap up to the stand. I can feel eyes upon me, trying to penetrate my drab disguise, to see the trembling victim – or the drunken slut beneath.

The jury's an even split, male and female, many of them under forty, which is good. Old prejudices about women who ask for it – with their clothes or their alcohol consumption – die hard.

That's why I stuck to Coke on the night of the rape. *He said he'd tell you I was drunk*, I told the police, *that you wouldn't believe a word I said*. The blood and urine test proved I was stone-cold sober, giving credence to my assertion that I'd just gone outside for a wee because the toilets were blocked. You're not allowed CCTV in a toilet so there was no evidence of me stuffing the bowl with hand towels until the water rose to the rim. It wouldn't even occur to them to suspect.

I face the court, unsmiling, and when the judge tells me to begin I give my version of the events of New Year's Eve with quiet determination, studiously avoiding the accused's eye – no tears. I'll let the photographs and the DNA do the work for me.

His girlfriend sits, stony-faced, listening intently. Sophie, I think. A standard-issue blonde with orange make-up and heavy eyeliner. After a few minutes she gets up and walks out of the court without a backwards glance. It wasn't hard to convince her that her boyfriend was a rapist. This makes me feel better.

I talk for half an hour or so and by the end the jury are sipping their water and fanning their faces.

It's all gone very well, I think, and it's hard to stop myself smiling as the judge calls for a break in proceedings before my cross-examination by the defence barrister.

Rauf is waiting for me outside and escorts me to a witness room with a coffee machine and a sagging sofa pocked with cigarette burns.

'I think that went pretty well, don't you?' I say, flopping onto the sofa and kicking off the frumpy shoes. But my smugness falters when he turns back from the coffee machine and hands me my drink.

'What?'

He shrugs. 'It sounded like you were reading a script. The jury didn't warm to you.'

'Frankly, it doesn't matter whether they warmed to me or not. It's an open-and-shut case. Wait till they see the photos.'

He gives me a penetrating glance then, which makes me wonder if he's guessed I'm hiding something. I can't tell him the truth, or he'd have to drop the case, but I want him to understand.

'He a violent rapist, Rauf. He deserves to go down. And he will.'

Rauf runs toffee-coloured fingers through his hair and leans against door. 'You've been living in the US too long. The white British male is an endangered species. Look at him, standing there in his too-tight suit, big hands hanging by his side because he doesn't know where else to put them. It's pathetic. The older women will want to mother him, the white men will see themselves. It only needs one or two prepared to give him the benefit of the doubt – that he's too thick or too unreconstructed to know when a woman means no.'

Before I can say anything the tannoy system announces that the court is about to go back into session. Rauf opens the door for me and as I move past him he murmurs, 'I want us to win this case as much as you do so just try and be a bit more . . . victim-y, OK?'

I smile indulgently, but as I follow him out into the corridor I'm feeling rattled. And now I must face cross-examination. I know how brutal that can be. I've done it myself.

This time I study the jury more carefully. A young overweight woman squeezed into a wrap-dress casts fluttering glances at the defence bench as the accused whispers with his brief. Is she one of those insecure, desperate types who writes to serial killers in prison, and occasionally marries them? Perhaps she will resent me for being slim and successful. Beside her is an elderly Asian man. He's beardless and in Western dress, but may still frown upon women who go out to parties without a chaperone.

Then there's the token middle-aged white guy: bald, overweight, tattoos peeping from his shirt cuffs, he looks like an older, poorer version of the man in the dock. Shit. Maybe Rauf was right. I need to get them onside. Show some vulnerability.

Except that's the one thing I'm no good at. I can shut down but I can't open up.

I should take some tips from Jody, who trembled so much when I said goodbye to her this morning that she resembled an out-of-focus photograph. I told her she didn't have to attend if she didn't want to, but as I take the stand again I spot her, shrinking behind a pillar on the back bench. She keeps her head down and worries at the buttons of her cardigan as the judge speaks. By contrast Mira, beside her, is straight-backed, her eyes alive with intelligence as she follows the proceedings as best she can. She came back from Albania ostensibly to give Jody and me some moral support. But I think it's more than that. I think she knows what's going on, though neither of us has told her. I think she's here for Loran. To bear witness as the murderer of the man he loved is brought to justice.

Or not.

Not if I can't play my part.

*Come on, Mags*, I tell myself as the defence barrister gets up. Make it up. Put on a show. Pretend you're trying to convince your dad how sorry you are for smoking at the bus stop so that he'll stop cutting up your *little tart's* clothes.

She's tall and rangy, with thin dark hair that looks painted to her head and a hooked nose like a bird of prey. As our eyes meet I think I see a flash of recognition, one lawyer to another, both of us determined to play the trial like a game of chess. I look away quickly, dipping my head, the picture of demure trepidation.

But she's not stupid.

'It takes guts to face your supposed rapist in court, Miss Mackenzie, especially since you could have given your evidence behind a screen.'

I straighten my back and swallow hard. Here we go.

'And only a very self-assured young woman would walk alone into a party full of strangers. Just as it takes a certain devil-may-care confidence to urinate outside when other women are waiting patiently for the toilet to be unblocked. And yet,' she glances at the jury, 'we are being asked to believe that you are a shrinking violet, unable to defend yourself against my client,

302

too frozen with terror to be able to utter an audible peep to alert the partygoers to your plight.'

'The countdown to midnight was happening,' I say. 'It was too noisy.'

She ignores this. 'You are a lawyer, Miss Mackenzie. Last year you defended a man charged with evading forty million dollars' worth of US tax, a man who, in his twenties, was convicted of the murder of three business rivals.'

I scowl at the CPS barrister. *Come on: object.*

'I put it to you, Miss Mackenzie,' she says, 'that you are a strong, clever, calculating young woman who is, for reasons best known to yourself, trying to manipulate the court.'

'What possible reason would I have to put myself through this?' I say, but I know at once I have made a mistake. She has caught the flash of anger in my voice, even if the jury hasn't. She knows this line is worth pursuing.

'You left home at sixteen, am I right?'

'Yes.'

'Why was this?'

'My relationship with my parents broke down.'

'Your parents? Or just your father?'

'My parents.'

'Is it the case that you reported your father to the police for false imprisonment?'

I hesitate. 'Yes.'

'And that you claimed he had beaten you, but no charges were pursued because he said you had attacked him and fallen when he pushed you away.'

I nod. She has spoken to my teachers.

'So, there has been a history of making false claims in your past?'

'They weren't false claims.'

'Your father was retired from his role in the Mountain Rescue for health reasons. What were these?'

'He had a nervous breakdown.'

'And your brother recently committed suicide.'

'Yes.'

'Do you believe mental health problems run in your family?' My lip curls. 'No.'

She gives a small smile, flagging up to the jury my reluctance to co-operate. The glances they shoot in my direction are closed and hostile. Rauf was right. They don't like me.

'I put it to you, Miss Mackenzie, that as a young girl with a bullying father, you developed a hatred for men that has continued to this day and has rendered you unable or unwilling to form meaningful relationships. This fact, and your strongly religious upbringing, has resulted in a very conflicted sexual identity. After sexual relations you are so disgusted with yourself you have to lay the blame on someone else – in this case, my client. I suggest that the mental health problems that dogged your father and brother also affect you; that they drove you to make false accusations in the past, and that the cry of rape against my client is just another of these.'

She gives a sad smile and I want to claw out her eyes with my fingernails.

'You are a traumatised young woman who deserves our sympathy, but whatever your problems, you must not be allowed to bring down an innocent man.'

The jury's faces turn to the accused, slumped in his chair, the patch of fluff between the two glossy stretches of his receding hairline stirring in the breeze from the air con. He looks up at them with wide, bewildered eyes. *What did I do?*

'No further questions.'

Rauf is honourable enough not to say *I told you so*.

'Surely,' I rant, 'the jury isn't gullible enough to believe such convoluted nonsense?' But it's a rhetorical question. Of course they are. Juries will believe any old shit – look at O.J. – and I've made my living out of this fact.

I should have swallowed my pride and squeezed out some tears. I'll make sure I put on a better performance in the public gallery, in case the jury looks over at me to gauge my reaction to any other evidence or witnesses, but Rauf doesn't need to tell me I've missed my chance.

And there's worse. Before we say goodbye I ask him why the defence barrister didn't grill me about my sex life. Rauf says they've made it much tougher to go down that route. I should have known this. I should have found it out before I went shooting my mouth off to Daniel. They wouldn't have been able to call him as a witness to my loose ways so there was no need to tell him anything.

Let alone everything.

Back at Abe's flat that evening I experience my first unpleasant stirrings of doubt. I sluice them away with a bottle of wine.

The next morning I tell Jody and Mira I'm having breakfast with Rauf so as not to have to travel to the court with them, trying to keep the mask of unshakable confidence in place. I've lost track of the days, but a free paper I pick up on the bus tells me it's a Thursday. Always my favourite day in Vegas. The weekend just starting to get going and the air throbbing with anticipation. Jackson has given me a six-month sabbatical. Others have taken over my cases and are, according to him, doing *awesomely*. That'll teach me to think so much of myself. A little humility might have saved me yesterday's car crash.

Over a lonely coffee in a greasy spoon around the back of the courthouse I resolve to try and let go a little, let the CPS do its job. I've done all I can, for better or worse: it's up to them now to make the case. When I spot Rauf as we file back into court I don't even ask for the sheet of the day's proceedings.

There are the sounds of people settling, the clunks of knee against pew back, coughs and rustles, the slosh of the jury's water bottles. Mira and Jody are already here, two pews behind me. I give them a quick smile, then sit down with my back to them.

The next prosecution witness is called, the policewoman who found me sobbing in the rugby club toilets, being comforted by a couple of the older wives.

After her it's Elaine, one of the wives, who makes perfectly plain her distaste for Rob. Then the medical examiner and his sheaf of photographs.

I hope Jody doesn't catch a glimpse of them as they are passed around the jury.

There are more photographs of the scene of the crime, my clothing and Rob's, complete with ragged tears, lost buttons and stains; a few more witnesses, and then the prosecution case is closed.

It's a strong one, and as we break for lunch, my confidence has bounced back enough to face Jody and Mira. We eat sandwiches in the little rose garden by the court and I pretend to fall asleep in the sun so as not to have to answer any of Mira's questions.

When we get back it's the accused's turn to give evidence. As he stumps up to the witness box, the material of his suit pulling into wrinkles across his slab of a back, I remember the tackiness of his skin, the taste of salt when I bit him.

He gives his own account of the events of New Year's Eve. It's all pretty unbelievable stuff. The most unbelievable thing about it, of course, is that it's the truth.

His barrister cross-examines him, and then it's the CPS's turn.

*Is the court supposed to believe that I approached him out of the blue and asked him to have sex with me? And that I insisted we have intercourse outside even though the temperature was minus two degrees?*

*Is it correct that his girlfriend was present at the party?*

*How would he explain the fact that I was covered in mud and patches of my hair had been pulled out?*

His answer, that I fell over crossing the pitch, and that my hair must have got pulled out because I'd asked him to be rough with me, draws gasps of disgust from the public gallery.

'What, *this* rough?' says the barrister, holding up the photo that made most of the jurors wince.

During the cross-examination the jury is increasingly restive, and by the end some of the women are glaring him with barely disguised loathing.

But all is not lost for him.

Next they bring in character witnesses who, to a man, insist upon what a great bloke he is. Salt of the earth. Heart of gold. Wouldn't hurt a fly. Etc. We hear about his trek across the Andes for Sports Relief, his commitment to the rugby team, how every Sunday he visits his granny in her nursing home.

And then we're done. It's all over apart from the summing-up by each side. The prosecution evidence was strong, but there's no denying we are left with the impression of a confused drunken fool who *made a terrible mistake*.

As we file out of the court I put on a brave face for Jody and Mira but all my doubts have crept back in.

Rauf is waiting for me outside and I tell Mira and Jody I will see them back at home. His expression makes my heart sink into my shoes. Silently he leads me back to the witness room and closes the door behind him. I collapse onto the sofa, in dire need of whatever caffeine is left in the rat's piss the machine provides.

And then his face splits into a grin.

I stare at him. 'What? How was that not bad for us?'

He laughs then, and I want to hit him. 'Seriously, Rauf. What the hell is so funny?'

'Ah, come on, Miss Mackenzie, you're the laywer!'

I fold my arms and glare at him.

'They've introduced bad character reference for you, trying to make out that you like rough sex. And good character reference for him: all that shit about Granny Elsa. So . . . ?'

'So, *what*?' I still want to slap him.

He grins. 'So we get to introduce *rebuttal* evidence.'

My heart lifts, just for a moment, until I remember that I don't change my gran's nappy every weekend and my friends are not about to hop on a plane to tell the court what a truly saintly corporate lawyer I am.

'Do we have any?'

His infuriating smile becomes sly. 'Leave it with me.

So I do. I leave him to it and go off to enjoy my weekend, which is all the time the seriously pissed-off judge has given us to patch holes in our case. We should have given him warning in the prosecution case statement that we intended to do this, and he's within his rights to refuse to allow it. But Rauf and the CPS barrister somehow work their charms on him, to the disgust of the defence barrister, who's spitting blood as we file out of court.

Jody, Mira and I head straight for the station and by five o'clock we're lying by the pool in a spa hotel in the middle of Kent. Mira, who must have sensed what the trial is taking out of us, has banned all conversation to do with the case, and we simply read, eat good food, drink decent wine, and watch videos of a laughing Flori, smeared in fruit puree.

Arriving back at St Jerome's on Sunday night, my mood has lightened enough to gift me an unbroken night's sleep, but when my alarm goes off on Monday morning the dread descends once more. Aside from whatever rebuttal evidence Rauf has managed to dredge up, we are left with the summing up and my victim impact statement. I must somehow manage to make myself cry. I have to. Or he walks.

On the way to the station I buy a pack of tissues – I can press them to my face to hide any lack of tears.

The courtroom is quieter this morning. The rubberneckers have heard all the titillating stuff and moved on to the child-murderer in the court next door.

The first few minutes are taken up by the CPS barrister's creeping apology to the judge, who laps it up like a fat, cantankerous cat. All the while the defence barrister twitches in irritation, tapping her pen on the desk, and Rob sighs and shifts in his chair.

Finally the CPS barrister is ready to proceed.

He clears his throat, waiting for his audience to give him their full attention, and I remember the thrill of power this part always gave me. I can't wait to get back to work. I hope Jackson has a decent case lined up for m—

'I'd like to call Daniel Stillmans.'

There's a moment's silence, then white noise fills my head, so loud that I don't hear the clip of his footsteps as he walks past me to take the stand. The chair creaks as he sits down, his blond hair catching a bar of light slanting in from the high windows.

No, oh no. He's going to tell them everything I told him in the café. He's been biding his time, waiting for the perfect moment to blow the case apart.

'Would you please tell the jury how you met Miss Mackenzie.'

Wait. Calm down. The *prosecution* has called him, not the defence. And there's no way they could have known about him unless Daniel got in touch with them. Which means he's on my side. Isn't he?

'On the plane from McCarran.' His voice is clipped and professional.

The court is completely silent. All my attention is fixed on his face, willing him to turn and see the desperation in my eyes. Just get up and walk away. Please don't do this to me.

'We hit it off straightaway and over the ensuing weeks became close.'

I blink. He's making it sound like we had a relationship. His handsome face is drawn. The fat girl in the wraparound dress can't take her eyes off him.

'And what happened after the night of the New Year party?'

This is it. I wince. *Please*, I think. *Please don't tell them . . .*

He sighs and runs a hand through his hair. 'I'd planned to go with her, but Mags insisted I spend the night with my children.'

I stare at him.

'They love New Year's Eve and, well, it's been a long time, what with my divorce.'

Rauf glances at me and I can almost feel him thrumming with excitement. *Leave it with me.*

One of the jurors shifts in his seat. Perhaps I'm not such a hard bitch after all.

309

'If I'd gone it would never have happened. She would never have been . . . raped.'

For the first time he looks across at me. His eyes are shining. Christ, he's good. Though I know it's all an act, my heart balloons in my chest.

His head drops in an Oscar-worthy demonstration of shame and when he speaks again his voice is soft. 'After that, things were different. She didn't want me anywhere near her. What happened to her made her afraid to be close to someone again. She doesn't trust anyone any more. She's built a wall, I think, to protect herself.'

I feel the eyes of the court fixed on me, and for the first time since I set foot in the musty-smelling building, the emotion that blurs my vision is genuine. I let my eyes well up and over, before dabbing the tears away with my sleeve.

The defence brief sighs at this cheesy attempt at emotional manipulation and, in one fell swoop, alienates the whole courtroom.

'So you noticed a definite change in Mary's character,' the barrister says, 'before the attack, and after?'

I nod and the transcriber's fingers fly.

'And prior to this, you never saw any evidence of mental health problems or this "hatred of men" my opposing counsel implied?'

'No. Of course not. That's nonsense.'

'The defendant has tried to convince us that Miss Mackenzie liked *rough sex*.' He speaks the words with distaste. 'I'm sorry to have to ask such an intimate question, but did Miss Mackenzie ever ask you to hurt her in any way during your lovemaking? To beat, or scratch, or bite her? Anything that might have caused the injuries you see here.'

He walks across the room and hands Daniel a sheaf of photographs. For a moment I'm glad Rauf didn't tell me, because I'd never have allowed Daniel to see me that way.

He gives a sharp intake of breath.

Now that he knows how far I have gone in this deception, the depths I have stooped to, will he be disgusted? Will he feel he has to speak out?

He isn't looking back at me.

Not the merest rustle of paperwork or murmur of breath disturbs the silence. It's so quiet we all hear the slap of the photographs as he tosses them onto the floor. They fan out, face down with shame.

'That,' he says softly, 'isn't making love. It's torture.'

The barrister walks over, picks them up and tucks them back into the file. Then he turns back to Daniel. 'So that we can all cast these unpleasant aspersions aside, I must ask you to confirm whether Miss Mackenzie ever asked you to . . . hurt her in the ways depicted in the photographs.'

Daniel's lip curls. 'No. She did not.'

'Thank you, and my apologies, but it is, alas, all too common in these cases, even in the twenty-first century, to see the victim branded as a liar, or *mad*, or an indulger in "rape fantasies".' His air speech marks perfectly communicate the contemptibility of this idea. 'My commiserations that what happened that night destroyed this fledgling relationship, a normal, healthy relation- ship based on affection and respect, not sadistic torture fantasies.'

'Thank you. I still hope that . . .' Daniel swallows. 'That one day, after all this is over, maybe we can start again.'

I can't look away, even as I hear the fat girl sniffle. The defence brief is muttering to her client. Jody's knee glances my own. The sun through the thin window is a blade of light bisecting the room between us.

And then tears are spilling down my cheeks. I fumble in my bag for the tissues, but it falls to the floor with a clunk. I am stripped bare in front of all these people. Eventually Jody hands me a hand- kerchief and I press it to my face, letting my hair fall like a curtain.

'Thank you, Mr Stillmans,' the barrister says. 'Your witness.'

'No questions, Your Honour.'

At the end of the day there's a delay as both counsels speak to the judge about something. I have arranged to meet Rauf in the coffee bar around the corner and, to his credit, my thunderous expression when he walks in does not give him pause. He stands by the counter, taking his own sweet time stirring his latte, letting me stew.

'Why the hell,' I hiss as he slides into the booth, 'didn't you tell me?'

He shrugs. 'Worked, though, right? You looked one hundred per cent human, for once.'

'Quite a risk, don't you think? He might have said . . . anything. And how could you have predicted my response?'

He sips his coffee, then licks the froth from his shapely top lip. 'Mr Stillmans and I had a long conversation, from which I gleaned that your feelings for him might be worth exploiting.'

'You're a shit, Chaudhry. Don't ever do that again.'

He inclines his head, smirking.

'I'm glad you find my discomfort amusing.'

Now he grins openly. 'I can make it up to you.'

I place my own cup down on the sticky table and fold my arms. 'Please try.' As he speaks in his quiet, silky voice I realise I was wrong about him. He isn't *going* to be good. He *is* good.

But before I can think of a way to respond in a way that doesn't exacerbate his unbearable smugness, my phone rings. Its position, face up on the table, means that both of us can read the name on the display.

Rauf waggles his ridiculously bushy eyebrows. 'My pleasure,' he says, and gets up and walks out of the café.

I hesitate for the briefest moment, then draw my finger across the name to take Daniel's call.

# 41. Rob

Kathy says it'll be time for the summing up soon and then the jury will retire to try to reach a verdict. She says our chances are fifty-fifty. The bitch doesn't seem to give a shit either way, mind, and she's started taking calls about other cases, as if I don't matter a toss.

I've been making eyes at the fat girl and it was going quite well until that cheesy bastard with the perfect teeth opened his mouth. Kathy said that was a bad moment, that the lying slag's tears looked genuine enough to *convince* the jury. I tell her that maybe she decided to make it up because otherwise he'd have thought she was screwing around on him. Not that I should have to come up with this stuff. That's her job. My parents are paying her enough.

Without looking at me she gives a noncommittal 'hmm' and I know she's not convinced by my version of what happened at New Year. That's probably why she's not giving it 100 per cent. After all this is over I'm going to complain about her to the barrister's association or whatever. Maybe I'll suc her.

Their bloke walks in, bald head shining under the lights, heels clicking against the wooden floor. Smart shoes. Expensive. Another couple of years at the firm and I'd have been able to afford shoes like that. Course that's never going to happen if we lose. I glance at Kathy, but she's looking down into her lap. The bitch had better not be texting someone.

Before we came in this morning she told me to prepare myself for a *worst-case-scenario custodial sentence*. Which means I might go to prison. Apparently they've got a new witness. Kathy tried to stop it but because we'd already called witnesses to my good character, they're allowed.

Across the aisle, in the public gallery, the lying slag sits down. As she tucks her skirt under her arse she catches my eye, just for a moment, and gives me a flicker of a smile. I look at the jury to see if they've clocked it, but they're looking at their papers.

It was this smile, when someone handed her a glass of water on the first day, that made me finally recognise her as the girl from the bleachers. It was a horrible moment and I'm not ashamed to admit that my balls shrank right up into my pelvis. I didn't understand it then and I don't understand it now, but I'm not going to feel sorry for myself. She's a fucking nutcase and Kathy's bit about it being inherited from her nutcase family should work if the jury's got a single brain cell between them.

Baldy stands up. 'I'd like to call my next witness.'

The door opens behind me and footsteps shuffle up the aisle. I'm expecting a geriatric. Some old cow whose car I scratched or whose letterbox I shat through, but it's a skinny guy of about fifty or sixty who takes ages to clamber up to the stand. When he turns around people grimace. He looks like he's got terminal cancer.

I have no idea who he is, but a smell that fills the court makes me gag. I swivel in my seat and give Kathy a look. *Seriously?* But her eyes stay fixed on the cancer guy.

'Felix Goddard, you were a childhood friend of the accused.'

There's a high-pitched gasp behind me, as if someone recognises the name, but for a moment it doesn't register with me. Then it's like being hit by a train.

Felix?

*Felix?*

A *prosecution* witness?

'Yes.' His voice rasps, like it hurts to talk. I guess his vocal chords have been shredded by crack.

314

'We were mates since, like, four or five, right up to . . . I don't think I'm allowed to say, am I?'

'Correct. Please stick to answering the questions I ask you.'

Kathy shifts in her seat. Her jaw's tight. She looks like she's about to jump up and shout 'objection!', but she stays put.

'How old were you when the friendship ended?'

'Seventeen.'

'That's very specific. Clearly you remember the incidents surrounding the break-up very well.'

'Objection! Counsel is encouraging the jury to make negative inferences towards my client.'

'Sustained. Change your line of questioning.'

'Don't worry,' Kathy breathes as she sits down. 'They're not allowed to bring up the other rape trial because you were acquitted.'

'Tell me about the nature of your friendship up to that point, please, Mr Goddard.'

I lean back in my seat, staring at him as he lists all the shit we got up to as kids. It sounds bad when you put it the way he's putting it. He's making out that guy's heart attack was solely caused by us playing our music on his front wall and dropping rubbish onto his lawn. He mentions the caution we got for squeezing the au pair's tits at the bus stop and I whisper to Kathy to see if he's allowed to bring it up. She nods tightly. The fat girl on the jury has stopped looking over at me, and the stocky tattooed bloke's just staring at the ceiling, as if there's something nasty playing on the telly and he doesn't want to watch.

'From what you describe am I to understand that the pair of you had little respect for women, seeing them only as objects for sex?'

Felix nods.

'Is that a yes?'

'Yes.'

'Did you ever feel remorse for these acts, Mr Goddard?'

Felix looks down. 'Yeah. Later on. After we did some . . . worse stuff.'

Kathy huffs and taps her pen on the table.

315

'I felt really bad. I wanted to blot it out and drink seemed to help that, and then drugs did too, and now,' his voice cracks, 'look at me.' He holds his arms out like a broken Jesus on the cross.

'Your witness.'

Kathy stands up. 'Perhaps we could spare the self-pity, Mr Goddard, and stick to the facts.'

Over the next half an hour or so she tries to make out that it was all Felix's fault, leading me astray, using the fact that he became a junkie while I straightened out. But even I can see it's not enough.

It's coming up to lunchtime when Kathy wraps up.

'Thank you, Mr Goddard, no more questions.'

But he doesn't go anywhere. My eyes burn into him, willing him to feel the hatred I'm firing in his direction, the fucking Judas. His hollow eyes are scanning the court. Then his body gives a jolt.

'Jody,' he says, his voice cracking.

I turn around, following his gaze. And whatever bullet just passed through Felix now passes through me, making my heart judder to a halt.

Jody Currie is sitting in the back row of the court.

'I'm so sorry, Jody. So very, very sorry.'

'Strike that from the record,' the judge snaps. 'Leave the stand now, Mr Goddard.'

He walks past me but my vision has fuzzed over like someone's just tackled me too hard.

Finally I get it.

The lying slag with the dead brother. The brother who didn't kill himself, like the papers all said. Who lived next door to Jody. She and Jody, somehow . . . To get back at me . . .

I need to tell Kathy.

But how can I? *Actually, I'm not a rapist, only a murderer.*

I'm trapped.

# 42. Mags

Jody, Mira and I waited for the verdict in the rose garden. The plants were still just dry-looking stalks, but at the end of each twig was a tiny, tight bud, as hard as wood but already snaked with the tiny fault lines from which the blooms would detonate. By June the place would be glorious.

Mira called home while Jody and I shared a packet of crisps, too nervous for anything more substantial, though I kept insisting it would all be fine.

The finger-whistle made us all jump.

Rauf stood on the steps of the court, his white grin glittering in the sunshine. He gave me a thumbs up. The jury was back already, which could only mean one thing.

As we approached the gate my eye was caught by a brass plaque on the wall. The garden was a memorial for twenty-nine people killed by a direct hit from a German V-2 bomb in 1944. Beside the list of names an angel hung his head in sorrow. I thought of another angel, drifting down through jewelled light, never landing.

Nine years.

It was never going to seem enough. Not for murder, or for rape. But it will well and truly screw his life chances when he gets out. The three of us stood up as he was taken down, for the three lives he had torn apart: Jody's, Abe's and Loran's.

We cremated Abe on a spring morning before Mira went back home.

It'll be time for me to go back soon, too. Daniel's there already. Not exactly waiting for me – just waiting-and-seeing.

But before I go there's one more thing I need to do.

Something I should have done years ago, when I'd finally found the life I wanted to lead. I should have shuffled off my bitterness about my past back then, not let it become the baggage I always criticised other women for displaying with such martyred zeal.

Because however misguided they were, our parents thought they were doing what was best for us. And though I may dismiss it as a childish nursery tale, they considered their faith as a truth to live by.

So, this last loose end, I must tie up.

I must go home to tell my parents that their son is dead.

Father Archibald is long gone, but the church secretary promises me that Father Chinelo will call me back. When he does he tells me, in a booming Nigerian voice, that both my parents are alive and well and still worshipping at the same church.

'I didn't know they had a daughter,' he says, but I just thank him and say goodbye. I wonder how my father feels about an African priest leading him in worship.

On the long train journey from King's Cross I have plenty of time to think. I believe that after the initial shock and grief they will be satisfied with the manner of Abe's death. He died a hero. Protecting the weak.

I will tell them that the man who killed him is in prison and will be there for many years.

I will tell them Abe was loved, and if they ask the name of his partner, I will give them Jody's name.

I will not tell them he was homosexual. They're too old to overcome their prejudices now. Let them imagine the grandchildren they might have had (and perhaps will have one day, after all).

I will tell them that he kept the ring, and let them believe, in the end, that Abe found his way to Jesus, and that given a little more time, he would have found his way home. As I have done.

In the end they will consider it a good way to go.

At Edinburgh I change onto the local train and chunter through endless purple valleys threaded with silver streams and waterfalls, and the odd loch that crisply reflects the landscape around it – a looking glass that Abe has stepped through.

The names of the stations are so familiar: Crianlarich, Tydrum, Loch Awe, Bridge of Orchy.

To get to Eilean Donan I will have to travel further north. I wonder how many will have gone before me when I stand on the parapet and scatter Abe's ashes into Loch Alsh. I wonder how long it will take them to get to the sea.

The train slows, passing my old school, and the bridge that Maisie Ross jumped off for a laugh, into the burn that swept her away, never to be seen again. We pass the road that leads up to the old people's home where my nana died, and the pub where the wake was held, and where my father wouldn't let us join in the ceilidh dancing.

I start to feel sick as we pull into the station and my arms are so weak a man has to help me get my case down. Clutching it before me like a shield, I step off the train into the station I left fourteen years ago, vowing never to return.

The station concourse is bitterly cold, and every time the entrance doors slide open, there's a blast of icy wind. But it brings no litter, just a few fallen leaves.

I walk out of the station and emerge onto a roundabout. Even here, on the busy main road that runs up to Inverness, the air is different. Clean and mineral-tasting, like fresh water. To my right the loch sparkles. Whatever the weather, the surface of the water is always black. It has kept its secrets for ten thousand years.

This is my father's country. My mother was a second-generation Irish immigrant, but this land moulded him. And me, perhaps.

319

We were two stones clashing together. No wonder there were sparks.

Do they regret the way they treated us, or are they still deluding themselves that they did the right thing and it was we who were in the wrong? The lie would have been easier to bear, but if nothing else, my father was a brave man. He brought seven half-dead climbers off that mountain, in weather that would have given the hardiest Sherpa pause. Of anyone, he might have had the balls to face up to his mistakes.

Ach! – I punch the button for the pedestrian crossing – what does it matter any more. Their child is dead. That's punishment enough.

I cross the road and enter my hometown.

The shops have changed: local independents have been replaced by the franchises you see in every other British town. The greasy spoon where I gossiped with the Proddy girls when my father thought I was at netball has become a Starbucks.

I walk past the war memorial, the rumble of my case wincingly loud in the silence. Away from the main road the street is empty of traffic, and the few pedestrians hurry on their way, their heads bent against the wind.

It was always so windy at St Jerome's. Was it Abe trying to tell me something? *Go home, Mags.*

I'm glad to be wearing his parka. The sweet smell of him still lingers in the fur. It's a smell I remember from long evenings of Bible reading on the sofa at home. I would slip a paperback into mine, but Abe never did. I used to sneer at him for his apparent devotion, but his eyes, though they gazed dutifully at the text, were always distant, as if fixed on some other reality. I wonder what you were thinking about then, Abe. Or who. Was it Dougie Kennedy, the cheesy football champ who most of the girls fancied? Or did you have my taste in boys – Pete Goldring, for instance, the dark, clever one who was never afraid to pass sardonic comment on the behaviour of the class morons, and got his face bashed in a few times for it?

How strange that I can picture them all so clearly.

The once grand Royal Highland has become a budget-chain hotel. It was the best I could find, and at least there's a bar. The place has that thick-carpeted hush of all provincial hotels, and the air smells of over-stewed vegetables. KFC for dinner, then.

A boy I went to school with is on reception. He doesn't recognise me and I give a different surname so as not to have to make conversation. Currie. It's the first name that pops into my head.

He gives me my room fob and I go up. The room is huge and bare, with a white-sheeted bed and a cheap-looking armchair. For company I turn on the TV as I run a bath.

Afterwards I feel different. I have been baptised in the waters of home, and it has washed something away. My confidence? My self-esteem? My sense of security?

No, I'm just afraid.

To steel my nerves I order up a gin and tonic and sip it by the window. If I'd raised my head as a child I would have seen that this place is breathtakingly beautiful. No wonder they get religion up here and never lose it. The place looks like it has been moulded by the hand of God.

I'd like a second drink, but I don't want to arrive at dusk so, slipping Jody's silver charm into my pocket, I head out.

The wind has died down and the loch is as still as glass as I walk down the steps.

I could make the short trip up the hill with my eyes closed. The road snakes up past the funeral director, the hairdresser, and the house with all the china dolls on the windowsill – all unchanged.

I take a deep breath and turn the corner.

There is the playground where he broke my arm. The sandpit replaced by a wooden castle surrounded by a blue rubber moat.

And there is my house. White walls, green door, slate roof, roses snaking up next-door's garage wall.

There is my bedroom, the rainbow sticker still in the window, its colours faded, almost transparent.

321

There is my father, digging in the rose bed. My fingers close around the guardian angel in my pocket.

The soles of my trainers are silent on the pavement as I walk the last few yards to the garden gate.

He was a big man, the muscles gone to seed when he stopped the mountain rescue, but always there; now he's leaner, and the coarse grey hair has thinned and become wispy. I never saw my father in jeans before. Jeans, a plain sweatshirt, and grey slip-ons that are caked in mud. His moustache is gone, revealing full lips like his son's. The ice-blue eyes are framed in square bifocals.

Oh, Daddy.

When he sees me he straightens up and frowns for a second, as if trying to remember. Then the trowel goes limp in his hand and the soil tumbles like confetti onto the multi-coloured petals below.

*The high road is busy.*

*It's a mild evening, the Indian summer seems to be going on forever, and people on their way home from work pause to browse the vegetables outside the Lebanese supermarket, or take a tiny paper cup from an aproned young man standing in the doorway of the new coffee bar. His silver tray reflects a pink and yellow sky.*

*The Cosmo waiters are laying out the tables for the evening rush. It got into some London restaurant guide and now the locals can't get a table for love nor money, or so she has heard.*

*She waves at the woman in the pharmacy who gestures a cup tipping at her mouth: coffee? She holds her hand to her ear, finger and thumb extended: I'll call you. After shaky beginnings the two women have become friends. The pharmacist's mother has dementia and sometimes she needs a shoulder to cry on.*

*She crosses at the lights and turns into Gordon Terrace.*

*An explosion of colour halfway down marks out the house of the new family from Syria. They held a street party to celebrate their arrival and have since been filling their little front garden with flowers that would never grow under the harsh Arabian sun. There are roses and hydrangeas, a Californian lilac, hanging baskets of fuchsias, window boxes of lavender, and some pointed red and yellow blossoms that look like flames.*

*For a moment he flashes into her mind. The man she thought she loved. The man who saved her life. In all the lies and confusion she thought she had lost any notion of what was real and what wasn't from that crazy time, but the memory has come back so clear and so strong that she knows it must really have happened. Her grill pan caught fire and he rushed over and put it out with a wet tea towel. That was all.*

*She understands now why it affected her so powerfully. It made her feel cared for. And it felt good. She wanted more of it, but she*

323

was knocking at the wrong door. It took her too long to realise. She is sorry now, but her friend Mags says not to have any regrets, because he saved her life. And that was an act of love even if love wasn't in his heart.

Mags insists on telling her she is loved. Once, when she'd been drinking in a bar with Daniel, she told her, 'I love you.' The thought makes Jody smile.

Then Daniel took the phone and said he loved her too and when was she coming to visit them in Vegas. She promised she would, in the summer, if she had enough money.

They said forget the money, they would pay, but it's important to her to pay her own way. It helps with her self-esteem. Marian says that by next year she will be ready for a management role and there's a charity shop two miles away with a vacancy coming up because the manager's retiring. She's not afraid of the journey. The youths who used to hang around Gordon Terrace have moved on because the police patrol it now, and the face she feared to see on every bus that passed her will be very changed by the time the prison sentence is over.

At the end of Gordon Terrace she steps onto the path that runs up to St Jerome's. The new girl from Flat Three and her toddler are working on the community vegetable garden with Dale and Sara. Tessy the terrier skitters about, snapping at the white butterflies that have been disturbed by the presence of the gardeners. It's time to harvest the beans and she has promised to help, so she tells them she will just go and change out of her work clothes.

As she passes the ground-floor window she murmurs hello to Mrs Lyons. She's in a home now and doesn't recognise Jody, but sometimes she visits and sits on the sofa watching the Carry On films that still make the old lady laugh uproariously.

Dale's wheelchair has left muddy tracks through the foyer. José will be livid.

On the table is a postcard from Mira who is visiting relatives in Budapest with Flori. Jody smiles wistfully. She had hoped to see Flori grow, but of course it was right for Mira to return home to her family. If Jody had family she would have done the same. She will have to save up for those flights too, as the invitation to Albania is an open one.

She passes through the door into the stairwell, aglow with the colours of the stained-glass window. There's a young man sitting on the stairs, drawing with pastels. He is so thin she knows it must be the recovering anorexic who has moved into Flat Ten. He's absorbed in what he's doing and only looks up when her shadow falls across the page. He starts and drops his crayon.

'Sorry,' she says, picking it up.

'Hello,' he says. 'I'm Benno.'

They shake hands. His fingertips leave coloured spots of chalk on her skin.

'I'm Jody. Flat Twelve. We're almost next-door neighbours.'

They talk about the logistics of the flats: the unreliable availability of hot water, the dodgy tumble dryer in the basement that shrinks socks, the ambulance that arrived in the middle of the night to take the woman in Flat Seven to hospital. Benno says he was lucky to get a flat in such a beautiful place and did she know the window was by Thomas Willement? For a moment they gaze at Jesus. His mild brown eyes gaze back at them. Willement was good, Jody thinks; she cannot look away.

'Well, nice to meet you,' she says, finally. 'If you get bored, we'll be outside picking runner beans for the next three hours!'

Benno laughs. 'With these artist's fingers? I'll think about it.'

She goes upstairs and lets herself into the flat, dumping her bag and kicking off her shoes. She's got time for a cup of tea.

She listens for the sounds of the church: the distant gurgle of plumbing, the heartbeat of the organist's foot, the sighing of the wind around the spire, then she puts on the radio.

The kettle boils and she takes her tea to the table by the window. She used to think this view was terrible: looking down over the bins. But you don't have to look down. You can look up.

Above the shabby flats opposite the gulls soar through the sudden afternoon sunlight, their backs ablaze with gold and red. She watches them a moment, wheeling through the blue, never to land, then she goes to get changed.

325

# Abe

It's cold and the wind's whipping my jacket around like mad but I don't go inside. I like the feel of the salt spray on my face and the boom when the ferry bucks through a wave. I'm standing at the front, right up by the chain, as far as they let you go, and I can't help the feeling that if I look back I'll see my da striding over the water to fetch me back.

Mam found me packing. I thought she'd try to stop me, or go and fetch my da from the prayer meeting, but she didn't. She just stood in the doorway watching me stuff a few pairs of pants and socks and some toiletries into my case. She must have seen the mobile Pete gave me when he got his iPhone, sitting on top of the pile, but she didn't say nothing. I didn't take many clothes. When I can afford it I'm going to buy new ones. Tight ones that cling to my body: *like a little tart*. It's not just girls that can be tarts, Daddy.

I met a man online who lives in Dublin. He's older than me and I don't fancy him much but he says he'll put me up, help me find a job, get me on my feet. Like a real dad should. I'll do whatever I need to to pay for it. I think I know what that'll be, because one of the other boys showed me a video online.

'Goodbye, Mam,' I said.

'Goodbye, Abraham.' When she said it her lips hardly moved.

I'd left myself only a couple of minutes to spare before the bus left, but they were the longest moments of my life as I waited in the wind for my da to come striding down the slope.

Even as I got on the bus I didn't believe it. Even as it pulled away and went rocketing down the motorway. Even as it clunked onto the ferry and the metal doors went down and the engines roared.

Still I was looking for him, not quite believing I'd made it.

I've not much to thank you for, Mary. And you've not much to thank me for – we were real bastards to each other, weren't we? But this one thing, I'll be grateful to you for my whole life.

You showed me it was possible to leave.

You laid a trail of white pebbles for me, and here I am following them. Da always said I was weak. Well, you've taught me to be brave, to fight for my dreams.

I know yours will come true. You were always clever and strong; you didn't take any shit from Da even when you were little. I always admired you. Even when you were grassing me up, or whipping my arse with that belt. I hated you, but I admired you. I reckon you'll be something really special. And I reckon that when you don't have to fight to stay alive any more you'll be a decent person.

I'd like to meet you then.

Seagulls have followed us all the way from Liverpool. Sometimes they're high up in the sky like white confetti, other times they fly really low to the water, and you can see the rippled reflections of their bodies. If I came back as an animal I'd like to be a bird. But all that reincarnation guff is heresy, Da, isn't it? When I die I'll be gathered into the bosom of the Lord Jesus, eh? Hope he's as hot as he looks in *Stories for Young Believers*. Big strong arms from carrying that bloody great cross, a decent tan, black wavy hair like Pete Goldring.

The ferry terminal comes in sight and I turn back to see if Da's made it across the Irish sea yet.

A man on the other side of the ferry is watching me. He's probably ten years older than me, short and stocky with a broad nose and a wide mouth. When I catch his eye I smile.

327

And then I laugh.

I am free.

I am free.

As the ferry starts to slow down a gull's white wing skims the surface of the water beside us, throwing up an arc of spray that catches the sunlight, and for a moment I can see a rainbow.

# Acknowledgements

As ever, outpourings of gratitude to my agent Eve White, for her constant support, advice and championing. Without her TATTLETALE would never have been written. Also thanks to her trusty sidekick, Kitty Walker, who answers my pedantic questions with promptness and grace.

The team at Trapeze are a joy to work with. Along with her searing narrative insight, my editor, Sam Eades, seems to possess the energy of a five-year-old mainlining E-numbers. With epic publicist Ben Willis beside her, the world will know my name.

Thanks also to those working so hard on TATTLETALE'S behalf behind the scenes at Trapeze, including Laura Swainbank in marketing, Susan Howe and the rights team, Rachael Hum (who when we last met was sucking her thumb but now is, apparently, rather good at export sales), Ruth Sharvell in production, Loulou Clark in design, Sara Griffin and Katy Nicholl.

On a personal note, thanks to hotshot lawyer Jane MacDougall, who helped me tread the line between accuracy and drama in the trial scene.

Huge gratitude to all the early readers, the bloggers and authors who liked the book enough to get a buzz going on social media. And finally, of course, thanks to my stalwart first reader and biggest fan, my ma, Jill Smith.